T0369537

Behind the Open Door

Seven Stories of Mystery and Intrigue

Christopher M. Hull

iUniverse, Inc.
Bloomington

Behind the Open Door
Seven Stories of Mystery and Intrigue

This is a work of fiction. All of the characters, names, incidents, organizations, and dialogue in this novel are either the products of the author's imagination or are used fictitiously.

iUniverse books may be ordered through booksellers or by contacting:

iUniverse
1663 Liberty Drive
Bloomington, IN 47403
www.iuniverse.com
1-800-Authors (1-800-288-4677)

ISBN: 978-1-4502-7553-8 (sc)
ISBN: 978-1-4502-7555-2 (dj)
ISBN: 978-1-4502-7554-5 (ebk)

Printed in the United States of America

iUniverse rev. date: 1/5/2011

Contents

In the Mind of a Child

Working as a night server at the small town truck stop was not a pleasant job, but it was something Melinda tolerated for the cost of putting herself through school. Forced to live at home with two spoiled younger brothers, a drunken father, and a lazy uncaring drunken mother was just one reason that drove her to do all she could in order to escape. Attending the local community college, she studied away her free nights. Being from the small town of Bangor, Maine, where everybody knows everybody might sound appealing for some, but for her it was nightmare. No rain or ignorant clientele would keep her from her goal of becoming a psychologist.

This night had started as just another typical Wednesday night. Truckers following their nightly travels along Route 95 had sat along the bar stools downing coffee. Some read the paper while others just sat watching the small television that hung from the ceiling. The booths, on the other hand, had housed several of the local teenagers and bar hoppers. Jelly packet towers formed as the kids dined on appetizers, coffee, and pop. Nothing more than slurred speech came from the drunks as they pounded their coffee while wolfing down greasy-spoon eggs. None of this bothered Melinda—not with her friend, Mary, on her side.

Mary, an experienced server, had worked at the truck stop since she was seventeen. Now, at thirty-five, she worked hard to fend for her five kids. She was always there when Melinda needed her. It had been Melinda's night to work the bar, the job she hated the most. At the bar, ignorant comments always came, and she could feel the dirty, overweight men eye her like candy. Not wanting to deal with the leers, she had pleaded with Mary to swap for the night. With her finals coming up, Melinda did not need the distraction. Mary gave in as she always did, giving the floor to her friend.

At the start of the shift, Melinda could never have predicted who was going to come in the door that night.

A family of three had pulled up in their BMW, parking as close to the building as possible. A man in his late thirties emerged from the car, along with his wife of about the same age, and their eight-year-old son. They ran in from the rain and looked as if they had not been hit by a drop. Very well dressed, the family stood there, clearly outside of their element. The mother, with her nose in the air, scoffed at the sight of the customers. Her shy son peeked out from behind her blue dress. His bright green eyes stared at Melinda from behind his shaggy brown hair as the hostess sat them. The father acknowledged nothing around him, silently walking behind his wife. Walking up Melinda could see the angry expression held by the mother, a snide smirk lined her heavily made-up face. Hair perfectly up and wrapped in a purple silk scarf, she looked of a much higher class than Melinda is used to dealing with. Their eight-year-old boy quietly watched, waiting for her to come. Timidly the boy pressed himself against the corner of the booth as Melinda arrived at the table.

"How can I help you folks tonight?" Her piercing smile focused on the boy to help bring him comfort.

"It's about time you showed up," the mother snapped, slamming her menu shut on the table.

"I'll just have coffee and a bagel with cream cheese," his father snidely demanded.

"And for you, ma'am?" Remaining calm and cheerful Melinda did her best to keep them happy.

"I'll have the fruit salad, with an orange juice, and no pulp. If there's pulp don't bother with it, just bring me apple juice or something." The rude tone in her voice told Melinda her place.

"And how about you little guy, what'll you have?" Melinda asked behind soft blue eyes.

"Spaghetti," the timid boy quickly blurted out.

"No! You'll have the chicken strips," Her mother snapped again. "You're not getting spaghetti."

"Chicken strips, I guess." With a sigh of disappointment the boy sunk into his chair. "And milk."

"OK, I'll be right back with your order." Melinda held her tongue as she walked into the kitchen to find peace.

"See, what did I tell ya? Piece of cake," Mary cheerfully stated.

Anger and disappoint covered Melinda's face. "Those people with this kid, man, I feel sorry for him, his parents are mean as hell."

"Really?"

"All he wanted was spaghetti and his mom tore into him and told him he's having chicken strips. She's a definite bitch," Melinda explained as Mary carried the food from the kitchen. As the doors shut, her smile returned.

Grabbing a fresh pot of coffee, Melinda returned to the floor to make her rounds. Cup after cup, she poured to the masses with a smile; in return, all of customers were satisfied. As she filled the cup for the timid boy's father, the mother huffed impatiently.

"Is our order almost ready, we have to get back on the road soon?" she rudely questioned.

"Yes, ma'am. It'll be up shortly." Melinda looked sorrowfully towards the boy, knowing he must have to deal with this everyday.

Reaching into her apron, she pulled out a single blue crayon. The mother rolled her eyes as Melinda reached across the table to hand it to him. Heading back to the kitchen she checked on the order, wanting to get rid of them as fast as she could. Melinda returned with their order in hand to see the boy just staring down at the table.

"Here you go, enjoy your meals," she stated placing them down on the table.

"I just wanted spaghetti," the boy mumbled. Not wanting to hear what was coming next, Melinda quickly walked away but was still within ears reach.

"You are going to eat your chicken. goddamn it, and that will be all of that, young man. Do you understand?" Melinda heard the mother say as she went into the kitchen.

Looking at the clock, Melinda found comfort in knowing her shift was coming to an end. When the customers leave so could she. Mary walked in shortly after to see Melinda with tears in her eyes.

"I know what you mean by working the counter, those men are pigs. You okay, honey?" Mary asked placing a hand on Melinda's back.

"Yeah, I just wish that boy didn't have to deal with his asshole parents like that. He seems so nice and that mother of his is so mean. The dad just sits there not saying a word as she tears into him. I'd love to go tell her off and take him from her," the angry waitress explained with a hate-filled smile.

"That's just what you need, a kid. Take it from me you'd never get out of here. Don't worry, in a little while they'll be gone and you'll be on your way home." Reaching out Mary pulled her in for a hug. "You got class tomorrow, kid?"

"I've got my finals in my psychology class," Melinda sighed. "Thanks, Mary, you always know how to cheer me up."

"No problem, dear, that's what I'm here for. Now go hand out some checks and go home."

Her tears dry, Melinda forced a smiled once more as she went to push out her customers. With food and sauce all over the table, she was thankful she didn't have to clean up behind the teens. After handing them the check, they quickly tossed down a five dollar tip and made for the register. Both of the drunken guys had gone, leaving four dollars in change on the table covering their bill with a bit left over. Approaching the last table she saw that the boy had barely touched his food.

"Do you need a container to go?" Melinda softly asked him.

"No, he had his chance to eat." The mother glared at her son. "He can go hungry for the rest of the trip, little brat. Can we get our check?"

"Here you go. Have a good night," Melinda stated forcing her smile harder than she ever had before.

Pulling out a fat money clip, the father placed a single dollar on the table. As they left the mother jerked her son along by the wrist. He stared sadly at Melinda as he was pulled out of the restaurant. She watched as they climbed into their sleek black BMW with Illinois plates. A heavy down pour fell as they began to pull away. Melinda, fed up with the night, headed into the back to find Mary on the phone.

"I know, dear, calm down, it's just a little rain," Mary explained into the phone. Covering the mouthpiece, she turned to Melinda. "The kids are freaking out, says there are tornado warnings all over the TV." Returning to the phone, she continued to try and calm her kids, "Well if you hear the sirens get your asses down in the basement." With a smile on her face, Mary rolled her eyes. "You be careful going home, girl, okay? I should have never given the kids my number." Mary returned to her phone call as Melinda walked out.

Outside, the storm grew threatening. Huge, heavy raindrops fell, swiftly soaking her as she struggled trying to get the key in the car door. Finally getting inside, she fired the ignition on her tiny, rusted-out Volkswagen. With a puff of smoke from the exhaust, the tiny car rolled out of the lot onto the dark road home.

With the faster Route 95 being under construction, the dark back roads were her quickest option. Heading out on Carmel Road, she started her journey home.

Melinda squinted tightly, concentrating on the road as she made her way through the torrential rain. With the full moon's glow hidden behind heavy black clouds, she relied on her headlights to guide her way. Her long, curly blonde hair now lay saturated and flat, sending shivers down her neck with every freezing drop.

Unable to drive in the flats she had to wear at work, she always kept a pair of tennis shoes in her car. The dry shoes brought her little comfort though as she focused on the night she had left behind.

Thinking back on the scene, Melinda again felt hatred for that woman as she continued her drive home through the storm. A bright gleam of headlights rushed past her, the vehicle's wheels sending a wave of water over her windshield. She kept calm as she hit the wipers up to their fastest speed. Still a long way from home, she tried to think of anything to take her mind off the child and his disgusting mother.

Now fully surrounded by forest, Melinda slowed in advance for the Western Avenue intersection ahead. Soon more headlights were shining in the rearview mirror, gaining at a furious rate. Suddenly, a large black 4x4 passed her, sending another wave across her hood. Losing all sight, Melinda began to swerve. As she fought to keep the tiny rusted-out car out of the ditch, her heart began to race, feeling as though her demise was approaching. She lost control. Spinning relentlessly, her car came to an abrupt halt as it smacked into a massive tree. The car flew straight up, the roof caving in as it met the mighty trunk. Forcefully tossed into the windshield, Melinda's head split open. Her vision went dark.

Melinda awoke with a start to the sound of a hundred exotic birds chirping in the midday sun. She opened her eyes to find herself in a small wooden room. There were no true doors or glass windows, just openings in the walls. Peering from one of the windows, she looked out over a vast forest from high in the treetops. Dim light peeked through the thick blanket of leaves created by the trees. Far below, just at the base of her tree, two large female lions sat waiting for her to come, patiently lingering.

Turning back to the inside of the tree house, Melinda noticed for the first time something that had been there all along. A crayon drawing of a copper-colored dome floating above ocean waves stood out on the dull wooden floor. Beneath the drawing, in white, were the words, "Gurod Orminta Dastura." Glancing around, more pictures came into view—one on every wall. Depictions of a fallen and destroyed city clouded by layers of black smoke covered the back wall. Another wall showed images of a tribe at war with an army of what appeared to be demons. Dark figures slaughtered those around them and burned the village. Lastly she saw, sketched next to the door, a small hut with a symbol of a snake above it.

Confused and sore, Melinda walked over to the doorway. At her feet the words, "Don't fear them; they will guide you," wrote themselves before her eyes out of nothing.

Climbing down, she felt her heart pounding in her throat. The only thought that filled her mind was, *they're going to eat me.* Hesitating, she checked below to see if the lions were watching her. Both remained still, looking out into the distance.

Closing her eyes tightly, her foot finally reached the ground. She felt shock waves of nerves pulse quickly through her body. However, as one of the animals rubbed her hand with its head, all of her fear faded, and she opened her eyes to see two great golden eyes staring back.

"You're a good girl, huh?" she asked, scratching under its chin. Both of the great cats stood, pushing against her body as they circled her. "So, if you two are my guides, then where am I?"

For an answer, the two lions began to walk north. Turning back, they paused to wait for Melinda. "Okay, I'll follow you. I sure hope you know where you're going."

At a casual pace, the lions led Melinda through the opaque wilderness. Melinda stepped quietly, taking in the beautiful songs that the birds cried out from the treetops. Within the oddity of the situation, she accepted that at least she was alive. Hours passed as they made their way through the lush wilderness. The sun began to fade into night, and the birds sang their final notes. Bright glows of red and orange filled the gaps between the leaves, a remarkable sight to Melinda's eyes. As the sun's rays withered, so did the enchanting forest's song; soon, within all of the silence, there was not even a cricket's chirp heard.

A single rush of cold wind embraced Melinda, sending chills rippling up her spine. Both lions halted their stride as the sound of children's laughter filled the air. Facing back from where they came, Melinda's eyes opened wide at the sight of hundreds of translucent children running through the woods. Teeth bared and snarling, the lions poised themselves to strike. Lost in the moment, Melinda froze as the children passed all around and through her. Her amazement fell quickly to fear as a terrifying, deep roar came out of the ever-growing, encroaching darkness. Shrieks replaced the cheerful noise given by the children.

The lions abandoned Melinda's side, charging back into the tangibly malevolent darkness. As panic set into Melinda's mind, she frantically followed the spirits of the running children leaving the lions behind her. Another roar came, echoing through the trees. Melinda could feel its frigid touch on the back of her neck. Dodging trees and cutting through the brush, she pushed her body to its fullest potential. Suddenly she broke from the woods to find herself in a large clearing. With the darkness only seconds behind her, she fell to her knees, wrapping her hands around her head for cover. With a final mighty roar, the darkness charged past her and continued through the woods. As everything grew quiet again, she looked up from the tall grass. Feeling safe once more, she fell into a stress-induced slumber.

Her exhaustion carried her through a peaceful night of sleep. Melinda awoke calm, still feeling the grass bed that had held her softly within the darkness. With a deep stretch and her body revived, she stood, trying to figure out where exactly *here* was. The new day's warm sun gracing her, she desperately searched around for a way out of this place. Behind her lay the woods that she so quickly fled, the lions were nowhere in sight. Ahead of her, sighted along a path leading from the clearing to the outer edge of the woods, Melinda saw a large hill. She could see several small spires reaching toward the sky from its peak, some taller than others. Still in confusion's grip, she continued to walk through the open path of the clearing toward the hill.

As she neared, its massive size made her feel meek. She paused at its base to gather herself. With last night's experience deep in her mind, she dared not go back into the woods. This hill being the only thing that separated her from her fears, the decision came easily. Her mind rested in the thought of what she might be able to see from the top—maybe a way back home.

Starting her climb, she began to remember her day's planned events, remembering what she needed to do. Her job, school, the final that she was missing, and all of what her life consisted of pulsed in her mind. It drove her to get through the hellish task that she was faced with.

A lone tree greeted her on her path quite a ways up the slope, a fine resting place that provided comfort from the sun. Sitting in the tall grass, she leaned against the tree's thin trunk. She closed her eyes to take in the gentle breeze that wrapped around her tired body. In a rush, all of her thoughts caught up to her, and tears started falling down her cheek. Hope became a fading sense in her heart.

From above her head came a rustling in the tree as a small, white finch landed on a nearby branch. It let out a slight chirp, grabbing Melinda's full attention. She looked up, wiping the tears from her eyes. "Hello, little bird," Melinda responded in sadness. "Are you lost?" she asked, taking a closer look at the creature. "I am. But you can't be lost because you can just fly off to anywhere. I wish I had your wings."

Its black eyes focusing on her, the bird chirped, cocking its head back and forth. "Can you show me my way back?" Melinda asked. She extended her hand for the bird to perch. "It's okay," she explained as it chirped back. Just as its feet graced her finger, it flew back off, toward the top of the hill. It was a simple reminder that she too must press on if she were going to make it home.

Continuing on the path, Melinda tried to clear her mind of the haunting thoughts. She focused solely on the immediate now. Every muscle in her legs throbbed as her heart pounded profusely inside her chest. Finally she reached the end of the long, difficult path that led her to the peak. Without so much as a glance at what stood above, she collapsed to her back, huffing to revive her burning lungs. As the moments passed, though, her curiosity grew. Rolling onto her stomach, her eyes focused on the massive stone pillars that stood in a circle before her, extending into the sky. Most of them lay partially crumbled and broken. Only three remained at their fullest height, all of them connecting at the top.

Covered by the long, lush grass in which she'd collapsed, she had failed to see the colossal stone that the pillars encircled. When she stood, all of its intricate detail came into perspective. Its center held a carving of the sun that shone on twelve figures lining the outer rim of the stone. All of them resembled a cross between man and a different animal. A man with the head of goat bowed, offering a vase of water to the sun. To her left a man with the body of a serpent offered a cow. At her right was a man with spider arms coming from his back, he offered a man. All of the figures respectfully bowed in the presence of the sun, each holding a unique offering of appeasement.

Another carving, barely visible, marked the center of the sun. Melinda stepped from the grass to the stone to get a closer look. Every step caused a vibration to course through her. Approaching the sun's outer rim, an immense vibration came, distorting the world around her. Everything moved and bent within waves. Light-headed and dazed, her ears became filled with the sounds

10

of deep, loud chanting. Rumbling thunder echoed through her mind. She kept stumbling forward, but she stopped short as visions of men dressed in dark cloaks surrounded the stone. With shrouded faces, they reached into the night sky, continuing their mantra. Unsure of what do to in this moment, Melinda continued on sluggishly toward the sun. Upon reaching its center, the chants ended as the orators stood with their arms stretched out toward her. They cast out a vibration so intense it brought her to her knees. She too must bow in the presence of the sun.

Now that the center carving was plainly in view, Melinda found the worshippers' God. A man with the head of a cat sat in the center of the sun holding a scepter in the form of a cross. It radiated vast energy. Reaching out, she brushed the etched image. Her hand graced his face, releasing her back to the sun—back to normality.

"This place can be very interesting, can't it?" a man's deep voice asked.

Quickly rising to her feet, Melinda searched for the speaker. Her eyes stared in confusion as she found him sitting atop of the three tallest pillars that reached up two stories. His short, dark hair shifted in the slight wind as he smiled down at her. Wearing the meekest of clothes, he was dressed in black, very plain, pants and a white short-sleeved shirt.

"Who are you?" she timidly asked.

"That is a good question," he replied, dropping down from his perch. Emerald green eyes greeted her from behind his dark hair. His bare feet landed on the stone with a loud smack. "It's been a long time since I've thought about that. I have had many but none of which I have chose," he added.

Amazed by the feat, she stood lost within his answer. "How long have you been here?" Her voice fell in awe of his presence. He stood as the perfect being within her eyes. Everything about him, from his eyes to his manner, spoke to her of love.

"That is another good question," he stated, circling around her. "Well, I guess I could say all of my existence. Who are you?"

"My name is Melinda Elaine Rowley. How did you get up there?" Her nerves grew as she spoke as she slowly became lost within his eyes.

"I always come here. You, on the other hand ... you just appeared from nowhere. Where did you come from?"

"The tree house," Melinda explained "At least that's where I woke up. What is this place? Do you live close by? And can I use your phone?" Her excitement grew with the thought of figuring out where she was.

"I don't really live anywhere," he explained. "I travel everywhere my feet take me. I don't have a ... phone."

The man's answer left her dumbfounded and without answers. He walked past her toward the hillside from which she climbed. "The tree house, huh? That's where I was going when I stopped to rest and found you just now." His calm demeanor spoke of a fearless adventurer.

"You can't, there's something in those the woods!" Fear rose in Melinda's voice as she ran up to the strange man's side. "I don't know what it is, but I don't ever want to see it again!"

"This place contains a lot of strange creatures. I know the darkness of which you speak; it covers the land and is not bound by the forest," he calmly explained.

"What is it?" More fear came as he assured her of the darkness being a reality.

"I'm not sure, but I've seen it all over the lands here."

The man looked up at the sky, prompting Melinda to do so as well. With day passing the sun began to quickly fade. "Night is coming. I have to get moving. You can come with if you'd like," he kindly offered with an outstretched hand.

Tears welled in Melinda's eyes. "I'm not going back there. Why don't you come with me and help me find my way home?" she requested.

"I can't; I have to follow the path I am on, as you must follow yours. There is an old woman who lives in a nearby cave. Just keep walking that way and you'll find a stream." He pointed out, aiming toward the three pillars. "Walk against the stream's flow and there you'll find her, behind the forest's drapes." Turning, the man continued to walk away. Melinda watched until he disappeared down the slope.

Alone again, Melinda turned to face her path once more. With the way down being a far easier feat, she reached the hill's base to face the still-setting sun. Gorgeous orange and red beams gave the forest that lay ahead a peaceful aura. Sounds of a flowing stream off in the distance rang in her ears. Melinda felt comfort set in at knowing that someone who could help awaited her.

Soon she was weaving between skinny, young trees on the outskirts of the woods. As she drew near, the sound of the roaring stream filled the air. She reached the edge of the crystal-blue water. Kneeling down to get a drink, she felt happy to see something she understood. Palm full after palm full of the cold, crisp liquid graced her lips until her thirst was satisfied.

Dusk turned into full night as she drank, leaving her to the guidance of the moonlight. Full and bright, it gave the forest a soft glow. The stream reached out of view in both directions, leaving Melinda to choose her way. Within confusion's grip once more, she stood, contemplating the option. Both ways appeared the same, and with no cave in sight, she sat in despair.

"Is everything all right?" asked a soft, proper, female voice from behind. Melinda turned to see a tiny bright-green light floating in the air. "Sitting here is not going to get you there. And just where is the *there* where you want to go?"

"What are you?" Melinda asked curiously.

"What do you want me to be, a fairy, a sprite? Perhaps I am just a wisp. Either way you are lost and I am not. So do you need my help or what?"

"Yes. I'm trying to find an old woman who lives in these woods. The man on the hill told me which way to go, but I can't remember," Melinda explained.

"Well, you have some nerve for calling her old!" the green-light creature responded. "She is only ten thousand, seven hundred and fifty-two years old. Passing throughout the ages gives her great knowledge, so you mustn't be so crude when you meet her." Whipping around, the green light circled Melinda from head to toe. "My name is Wind—for there is nothing faster than, stronger than, or as unstoppable as I."

Wind dashed off upstream in a flash. Pausing after a moment, she shouted back to Melinda, "Well, do come on! She doesn't have all night."

Melinda ran toward Wind as the flash of color darted off again. At full speed, Melinda tried her best to keep up. After a distance, stopping at a vine-covered rock wall, Wind waited for Melinda to arrive. Finally reaching the cave, the girl fell to her knees, gasping for breath.

"It's about time you caught up," Wind boasted with a better then thou attitude.

"How much do you weigh?" Melinda asked between breaths.

"I … um … I don't know how much I weigh. I'll have to ask Mother." Wind's voice was filled with confusion as she pondered the question.

"Who is your mother?" Melinda asked, still huffing, as she rose to her feet.

"You are about to see." Passing between the vines, Wind disappeared into a dark opening in the thick rock.

Spreading the vine curtain with her hand, Melinda peeked inside. A dark, narrow tunnel greeted her with a hollow but warm feeling. The orange glow of fire danced off the distant curve of the stone wall. She crept down the tunnel toward the aura. Reaching the corner, she paused, anticipating what she may face.

"Don't be shy, dear," a scratchy, old woman's voice called out. "No one here is going to hurt you."

Stepping inside, Melinda found something the likes of which she used to only read about as a child. The tunnel opened up to a dome-shaped room. Several rows of aged, wooden shelves lined the walls. Each harbored hundreds of bottles of all shapes and sizes. A large, steel caldron bubbled and boiled over a fire in the center of the room. An ancient-looking woman that resembled every aspect of a witch was stirring the pot. Long, scraggily, platinum-colored hair draped past her pale, wrinkled face and long, pointed nose all the way down to a dingy old brown robe. Her tiny frame still held its strength as she drew the ladle steadily to her lips.

"You must be hungry after such long travels. Come eat, yes?"

Ladle in hand, the witch waved for Melinda to come closer. A small wooden bowl floated from a shelf over to the witch, passing right before Melinda's eyes. Wind appeared from underneath it as the witch's long, bony fingers grasped it. "She is far more timid than the others, my sweet Wind," the witch humbly remarked. Pouring some of the caldron's contents into the bowl, she smiled greatly, revealing long, pointy teeth.

Frozen in the moment by her disbelief, Melinda could only stand there staring. Wind swiftly flew to her side. "You are being very rude! Mother has spent all day preparing this especially for you," Wind snapped in her ear.

"You knew I was coming?" Melinda asked, still locked in a daze.

"Of course I did, but enough questioning. Come eat; yes, eat," the witch replied. "Melinda, your name was spoken in the forest's breeze," she continued as the girl walked up, dumbfounded and confused, to retrieve the bowl.

Melinda stood, holding the bowl, lost within the surreal setting around her. Looking down into the thick soup filled her with a sense of reality, she had to eat. With a slow stir of the spoon she made her decision. "This is really good, thank you. I'm sorry if it was a lot of trouble to make. I didn't know you were expecting me." Her plight was a means of digging for answers.

"Of course you didn't, and how could you? Don't pay too much attention to Wind; she can be a little cold at times," she said with a laugh, as another bowl floated over to her hand. Wind had remained next to Melinda's side. "Come and sit at the table with me," the witch beckoned.

Along an empty wall rested a small, wooden table with three uneven stools. Choosing the smallest of the three, Melinda placed her bowl down and then sat.

"Now, why did you pick that chair? Like being close to the ground?" the witch asked, sitting in the middle-height chair across from Melinda.

"No, sorry, should I not have sat here?" Melinda replied in a panic at being wrong or somehow impolite.

"That's not what I asked. Now, why did you choose that chair?" Melinda's host questioned again, sipping from her soup with a smile.

Melinda hesitated before saying uncertainly, "So … we could be at the same level when we talk."

"Do you hear that Wind, at the same level." She let out a cackle that echoed off the walls. "Those words I have never heard before, always have they been so senseless. Do you think we are the same, little girl, you and I?" Another laugh filled the air.

"No, I didn't mean for it to sound that way," Melinda blurted out.

With a deep-cut smile the witch continued with a calm soft manner. "To sound what way—the way it did or the way it was intended?" Pausing for a moment, the witch looked deep into Melinda's eyes. The girl could only stare back feeling the intimidation of her questioner. The witch continued, "Remember, there are no wrong answers, only truth and lies. You still haven't eaten much yet." Looking down into her bowl, Melinda became more nervous, nervous with the fear of insulting her host.

Returning her full attention to the witch, Melinda could not lift her eyes as they both ate. Upon finishing her soup, the witch continued to speak. "It has been a long time since anyone has graced this old woman with their presence. Do you know why I named her Wind?" Floating over to them, Wind danced about above the table.

"Because of her grace, I think?" Melinda answered in question.

"Good guess, but no. I was walking in the fields beneath the floating cities of Malcara, when I was young." The witch stood up and began pacing around the room as she spoke. Looking over the bookshelves, she continued, "Their shadows were like small moons, covering everything as they passed. Cool and strong, I could feel it whipping around me. In the forest it danced around the trees, passing without being stopped." The witch stopped and quickly scuffled over to a specific shelf, retrieving a couple of bottles. "Even within its fury as it gathered and intertwined, ripping across the land destructively, it is perfection. That is when I decided to birth her. Gathering all of the element's kinship took hundreds of years as I explored every corner of this world." Two ceramic cups rose from another shelf and came to her, hovering in the air as she continued. "I became familiar with everyone and everything. It wasn't until the darkness came that I was able to finish my spell. When Malcara fell, it created something new in the land—fire and ash within death. Not one creature of Malcara survived. It was their deaths that gave Wind life." The witch began to mix the floating contents into the cups.

"What caused Malcara to fall?" Melinda asked, fully caught in the story.

"Some say they did it to themselves, that power and greed created war among them. Others claim it was a great force of evil that infected the people."

"What do you think it was?"

"Then, it didn't really matter to me. I was clear on the other side of the world when I first felt it. Every soul passed through me as they peacefully went into the stream. As time drifted on, the earth swallowed the city's remains, and it became a story of folklore and legend. There is an evil in the land, most of which it has consumed." The witch returned to the table with the cups. Steam poured out over their rims as she set them down on the table. "Hundreds of civilizations have risen and fallen over my time."

"Have you ever seen this evil?" On the edge of her seat now, Melinda sought to know if it was the shadow darkness that she herself had seen.

"Only in a mist form; it scours the world looking to end all that is here." Outside, a wicked crash of thunder rippled through the air and into the cave. Melinda jumped with a start, but the witch sat unmoved. "It's just a storm, my dear."

"I saw it, I saw the mist. It was chasing children through the forest," Melinda explained in a panic.

"That is the last of the people here, those of Korithian. They never grow beyond eight and remain hidden deep within the world. Not even I have seen them."

"Then how do you know they exist?"

"I have seen them," Wind replied. "One followed me through a forest once."

The witch added, "They are bound to the confines of their land. If they leave, they will turn to stone."

Sadness filled Wind's voice. "That is what happened to the girl who chased me. Slowly, as she reached out to touch me, her whole body turned to stone. She was smiling." Wind flew off as she finished.

"She doesn't like to remember that. It has been hundreds of years and it still upsets her. But she will be all right," the witch assured Melinda. "Do you know where you are?"

"No," she replied, as the reality of this new world seeped into her. "I woke up here in a tree house," she added trying to rationalize the situation. "The man told me—"

"Man? What man, what did he look like?" the witch asked frantically.

"He … I can't remember." In deep concentration, Melinda could only bring one thing to light. "Green eyes … he had emerald eyes. That's all I can remember. He was the one who told me how to find you, but I got lost. That's when Wind found me."

Looking deep into Melinda's eyes, the witch grew angry. "What did he say to you?"

"Nothing, really," Melinda stated defensively, "just that he was on his way to the tree house. He didn't like traveling at night, I think, because he said he had to get there before nightfall."

"Strange, I have never seen a man with green eyes except for ... but he's ... hmm ..." The witch appeared to focus deeply on Melinda's mind. "What else do you remember?"

"There was a drawing in the tree house with something written beneath. Guro Omina Dastra, I think."

With Melinda's words, the witch's eyes grew wide, full of excitement. "Gurod Orminta Dastura!" Jumping up, the witch nearly knocked over the now-forgotten cups. "We mustn't let it find you! Tonight you are safe within this cave, but in the morning you will start on your path." The witch's excited tone with a word of there being existing danger, had Melinda afraid to hear more.

"Where, where is it I am supposed to go?" muddled words came as Melinda now sat in a full state of confusion.

"The fallen kingdom shall arise." Picking up one of the cups, the witch sucked down its contents in one gulp then slammed it back down on the table. "I have to prepare; I didn't think it would come so soon—and with the others ... I never would have thought."

Eagerly the witch snatched one of the empty bowls from the table. Tossing it into the air, it floated to the center of the room. Still amazed by her surroundings the lost girl sipped some of her bubbling smoky brew. The concoction tasted of sweet nectar that she found pleasant and soothing to the body. Melinda watched as bottles drifted off the shelves. They moved about, back and forth, leaving a drop or two of their contents in the bowl then returning to their respective places. Melinda's head began to grow dizzy as the display continued.

The witch walked over to a blank wall. Passing through it, she disappeared into another room. Melinda, her chin resting in her palm to spell the dizziness, looked into her cup as she groggily drank. On the verge of passing out, she jumped with a start as the witch returned to her.

"I knew I'd find it!" the witch shouted with excitement. Moving in between the floating bottles, she carried a small, wooden box to the table. "This is for you," she stated, placing it in front of Melinda.

Melinda's eyes opened wide as she gazed at the tiny, intricate carvings that lined the box's crest. An inlay of gold held the same image she saw in the tree house of the domed city, Gurod Orminta Dastura. With one finger she flicked open the small, gold latch that kept the box shut.

"Open it; it will keep you safe from the darkness—protect you from it," the witch reassured her. As Melinda slowly cracked the box open, a blinding white light filled her eyes. Engulfing her, as well as the room around her, everything vanished from her sight.

When her vision returned, Melinda found herself standing in the center of a large, marble walkway. Behind her stood a crystal pyramid that towered over her, reaching up into the night sky. Several smaller pyramids lined the walkway, which led to the massive pyramid. Unsure what else to do, Melinda wandered down the path. She passed several people, but they did not take notice of her.

Finally she found herself standing at the edge of a great floating city, feeling the winds whipping past her. The ground lay far below, etched out with farms and towns. Off in the distance she could see three more floating cities trailing behind. Her mind desperately tried to grasp her situation as the earth slowly moved by below. With nothing connecting the cities, she could not see of any way this one or down to the ground.

Suddenly Melinda glanced up to see a man walking across the sky toward her. Each footstep caused ripples in the air as he continued across the nothing that somehow supported him. As he drew near, one of the trailing cities sent out a shock wave caused by several explosions. Burning brightly in the darkness, it fell from the sky. Both of the other cities followed closely behind, as they too burned and fell.

Stepping from the sky onto the marble path, the figure came fully into Melinda's view. Consisting of a translucent smoke, it held no features. It moved past her as if she weren't there, instead traveling on toward the people of the city. The figure touched everyone that it passed, causing them instant insanity. Some of the people attacked each other maliciously, while others stormed toward the pyramids. Melinda, fearing the outcome, ran back toward the great pyramid, even as several small blasts blew portions of its walls away. Feeling the city tilt beneath her, she fell to her back. The last thing she saw was the ground rushing toward her.

Waking in a saturating sweat, Melinda found herself lying on a bed of leaves and brush inside the witch's cave. Only a small light from the fire's remains gave her sight. Bottles still moved about the room, but Wind and the witch were nowhere to be seen.

Moving carefully through the room, Melinda made her way outside. There she discovered the rising sun hanging on the horizon. Still dizzy from the dream, she knelt down along the stream. Sparkling water trickled from her hands as she scooped it to her face. It cooled her burning head, but it could not hold back her sickness.

Wind flew out from the cave's entrance and rushed over to Melinda's side. "You must not be out here right now. Mother is almost finished with … Are you all right?" Wind paused as Melinda sat up, holding her head. "It's too soon for you to come out. You have to come back inside; Mother will help you."

Melinda staggered to her feet. Wind flew around her with a great diligence that tangibly engulfed her body. As Melinda fell limp, Wind caught her with her great force, which carried her back inside. Slightly conscious, Melinda heard all though saw nothing.

"Put her back on the leaves, Wind," the witch requested as Wind brought Melinda inside.

Christopher M. Hull

"Yes, Mother. Will she be all right?" Wind asked, placing Melinda down on the thick bed. Slumping down, Melinda sat with her head hanging limp. Still floating in the center of the room, the concoction creation in the bowl was finally complete. All of the bottles returned to their original places as the bowl floated to the witch's hand.

"She will be fine, but she has to drink this—all of it," she explained, placing her right hand under the bowl. As she moved toward Melinda, the bowl floated just inches above the witch's hand. "Hold her head up so I can pour it down her throat."

Without question, Wind flew beneath Melinda's chin and started to lift. Melinda's mouth opened wide as her head fell back. Circling around, Wind pushed the lolling head slightly forward. On her knees, the witch carefully lined the bowl up with her charge's mouth. "That's perfect, just hold her there." Bowl in hand, she poured the brew into Melinda's mouth.

Once Melinda tasted the sweet, chalky liquid, her eyes opened fully as she became instantly alert. Looking around, wide-eyed and amazed, she took the bowl for herself. Her body tingled and pulsed with unspeakable energies.

"Not too fast, dear. You don't want it to hit you all at once," the witch explained with a smile as Melinda gulped it down. "You are at the beginning of something great. This is where your true journey begins."

"Where am I going?" Melinda asked, eager and ready for anything. Whipping the overflowing drops from her bottom lip, she got up with determination.

"Gurod Orminta Dastura—that is where this path will end. But it shall not be simple." Walking toward the cave's entrance, the witch waved for Melinda to follow. "This land is a dying entity's dream. You must wake him," she added, stepping out into the sun. Melinda's eyes adjusted instantaneously as she entered the bright rays.

"Do you know how to get there?" Melinda asked confidently.

"No. No one really knows where it is—no one except for the Korithian, and no one really knows where *they* are. You have to find them. The drink I gave you will help get you in tune with the land. You will know, and you will find them."

Thoughts began to dance about in her head, memories of home and duties that now held no meaning. This place had consumed Melinda on every level. Even thoughts of the man she met on the hill began to pulse deeply within her heart. "How can I thank you for your guidance?" she genuinely asked, eager to start her journey.

"Free those from the darkness and all will be worth the while of this creation. Wind, my faithful daughter, will help you on your way. Wind, come, I have something for you to do," the witch called out.

"Yes, Mother," Wind called back, dashing out to join them. "What do you need?"

"You must aid this girl on her quest, keep her from harm. Take her to Mathia," she explained with a smile.

"Mathia? I don't know how to get through the desert," Wind's voice intoned, filled with concern. "Mother, I—"

"Find the moles; they will help you," the witch stated simply, touching Wind with her fingertip.

"Yes, Mother ... I will do my best." Wind floated over to Melinda's shoulder in silence.

"Thank you again. I promise I won't let anything happen to her. You have my word," Melinda reassured the witch. Turning to Wind with a smile, Melinda found that she was desperate to begin. "Which way, Wind, you lead and I'll follow. Just try to remember that I can't fly like you can."

"Yes, I will remember." Wind replied with a chuckle. "We have to continue on through the woods that way until we reach the stone valley. Come, this way!"

Wind darted off into the forest as the witch smiled into Melinda's eyes one more time. "Go, child, and find your destiny," the witch encouraged. Melinda didn't respond, simply smiling as she turned and dashed off after Wind.

Wind had quickly rushed ahead, but now Melinda found herself able to catch her using little effort. Weaving around the trees, she moved as though she and the woods were one. Wind stopped as Melinda passed her with a smart smile. In a swift dash, Wind shot forward to catch her. Bobbing over and under branches, the sprite was amazed that Melinda was nowhere in sight. Fearing the worst, she hit full speed, tearing through the branches. With a puff of dust and in a swirl of leaves, Wind burst from the forest to see Melinda standing at the mouth of a mountainous stone valley, her eyes wide in amazement as she stood gawking at its enormous size.

"You shouldn't rush off like that; there is more than the darkness to fear here," Wind explained with a huff in her breath.

"Look at it ... wow, I've never seen anything like this." Melinda stared at the wide furrow, so wide that it could hold four city blocks. Its walls towered beyond the tallest skyscraper. Crystals of all shapes and colors protruded from the higher peaks of stone within the valley, giving the sunlight a chance to create spectrums of rainbow light. "This is so wonderful. How could a place so beautiful be dying?"

"Even if all life here fell, this place would still remain," Wind stated.

"But with no one to enjoy it, what's the point?" Melinda felt another surge of intention, another reason to free the land. "Are we going there?" she asked, pointing to the mountain at the end of the valley.

"Not exactly, there is a cave that will take us through it."

"Is that where the moles are?"

"Yes, the moles there are the experts of the desert. And though they all seem friendly enough, they still give me the willies," Wind admitted.

"Then let's move." Determination in her heart, Melinda began to walk, taking in all of the rainbow light show.

"I'm not sure where the cave is. I try to avoid the moles as often as I can," Wind added, moving up to Melinda's side.

Both traveled lightly in silence, fully aware of everything around them. Reaching deeper into the ravine, Melinda's nose picked up a sweet smell that turned out to be of rotting flesh. They drew closer to the remains of what appeared to be a deer. Bones protruded through torn skin, and the creature's eyes bulged from shattered sockets. Lying just a few feet ahead was another, then another. As far as Melinda's eyes could see, the path lay littered with death.

"What could have done this?" Melinda calmly asked, stopping at the remains. Ready for anything, she began to set up her mind for a fight.

"They came when the darkness appeared in the land, infesting the land like parasites. Mother cast them out of the forests," Wind explained in a hushed tone.

"What came? She cast what from the forests?"

"There is no name to describe them." Fear grew in Wind's voice. "I just hope none of them are here. We should get moving now."

Melinda walked past the first rotting animal, looking over its wounds to see if she could gain an idea of what she might have to face. Jagged teeth marks scarred the bones with deep grooves along with wide, penetrating rips clawed into the carcass's skin.

"Are there a lot of these things here?" Melinda asked, trying to pry some information out of Wind.

"At times, yes, at other times there is just one, which is one more than you want to see. We have to be quiet if they hear us—"

Wind's speech halted when several small rocks swiftly rolled down the wall to the path in front of them. Both stopped cold in their tracks to see what caused the commotion. Two small black balls tumbled downward, following the path of the rocks. They moved over to a distant corpse, rolling around it, stopping by its spilled organs. With a slight shake, tiny, skinny legs emerged from the ball creatures, which began to walk quickly around the bloody mess. The legs carried the baseball-sized bodies as they quickly moved about. Reaching down with matchstick arms, they began to tear into the carcass with three clawed hands each. Mouths that covered half of their heads opened wide, exposing sharp, rigid teeth as they devoured chunks of flesh. Snakelike scales of deep blue and purple gleamed in the sunlight from their backs as they dove into their meal.

"Don't move," Wind whispered. "If they don't see us, hopefully they won't want to eat us."

"But there are only two of them, and they're so small," Melinda whispered back, with a plan already in her head.

"Yes, two—two of the most vicious creatures in the land, and you want to challenge them?" Wind stated in pure disbelief.

"How long do you plan on waiting?" Melinda asked, impatiently. "Just fly up in their faces as a distraction, and I'll try climbing up the hill. If I hide behind the crystals they won't be able to see me. It'll take us a bit longer but I think I can make it around them, and then we'll be back on the trail to the moles."

"What, are you crazy?" Wind exclaimed.

"Nothing can catch the wind, right? Isn't that why your mother made you?" Melinda expressed. "You can do this!"

As she tried to cool down her fear, Wind slowly moved toward the creatures. Melinda readied her escape plan. High above them, Wind traveled along over their heads as their faces dug deep into the carcass. She floated down, making sure both remained in her sight, hovering inches from their grasp. Creeping ever so slowly, Melinda made a tiptoe attempt to reach one of the steep walls nearby.

"H-h-hello, boys," Wind mumbled as her glow pulsed rapidly with fear.

Both of the dark creatures instantly pulled their faces from the rotting meat. Their single large, black, egg-shaped eye stared directly at Wind. One of the creatures lunged forward with the clear intention of devouring her. Wind swiftly evaded even as the second one tried to catch her with its hands. Both chased after her as she led them farther along the trail. Weaving about, she dodged them easily each time they struck out to hit her.

Melinda got closer and closer to the canyon edge, her heart racing as adrenaline pulsed through her veins. Being at a ninety-degree incline, she struggled to maintain her footing. Using the bases of the crystal growth as stepping stones, however, she clung to the steep wall.

Still eluding the creatures, Wind danced about, causing them to slam into each other. To Wind's surprise, the two small creatures became one that was double their original size. Without a thought, the new, single entity took the opportunity to smack Wind to the ground.

Just as the creature readied to pounce, Melinda lost her hold on the wall. Grabbing onto one of the large crystals, she held herself. But slowly the crystal began to shift, pulling away from the wall. With an echoing thud, both she and the crystal landed on the hard, tilted ground. Turning around, the creature searched for the disturbance.

Melinda remained motionless, hiding behind the fallen crystal. Her heart raced in her chest. Closing its eye, the creature sniffed around in the air, finally picking up Melinda's scent. Wind recovered and swiftly moved in around the creature's face to create another distraction. But Wind's efforts went unnoticed, and it slowly stepped toward Melinda's hiding spot. Little by little, the creature drew near. Wind continued to buzz around like a mosquito in the hope that it would become annoyed, but to no avail.

Stopping on the opposite side of the crystal from Melinda, the vile creature opened its horrid mouth, trying to catch a taste. Saliva dripped down its teeth as it opened its blackened eye. Melinda scurried along the ground just as the thing leapt over the crystal. In a cloud of dust, she rushed to her feet. Stepping through, the menace finally caught sight of its target. Melinda ran back toward the forest, feeling retreat might save her skin. To her utter surprise, when she glanced back, Melinda saw the creature stop and watch her go. It opened its mouth and let out an odd, high-pitched scream that echoed through the ravine. Piercing through Melinda's eardrums, she dropped to her knees covering her ears. After a few moments, all went silent.

Moments later, Melinda stood again to see the creature standing next to the remains of the fallen crystal. Turning back toward the woods, she spotted hundreds of the baseball-sized black balls rolling down from the walls. Each piled on top of its neighbors, forming into one giant creature, the top of its head even with the mountainous walls.

Wind quickly joined Melinda's side. "Now what are we going to do, oh, fearless adventurer?" The sarcasm didn't hide the panic that filled Wind's voice.

"I don't know! I was hoping you had a plan," Melinda stated. Looking back and forth, she weighed her options heavily. "If we can get to the top of the wall, we can probably outrun them. Where is the cave entrance?"

"It's hidden from view, behind a crystal that we have to find," Wind explained, as the giant creature took its first step.

"Great, which crystal?" Panic took over Melinda's mind as well as she started to run toward the small, much less intimidating creature. "There are thousands of crystals, Wind." Both dashed past the smaller creature. It did not follow, instead choosing to roll into a ball to join with the massive one.

"Just keep running!" Wind shouted as the creature's pace grew.

With thunderous footsteps, it charged toward them, ready to devour. Melinda pushed her limits in order to stay ahead. As they ran deeper into the ravine, the walls begin to lose their steepness. Melinda instantly began to climb the sloping walls, hoping the crystals scattered about would help slow down the beast's pursuit. One of its clawed hands reached out for her, swiping at the ground. Missing its target, the hand grazed a crystal. Pieces of creature flew from its hand, re-forming back into smaller ones.

In a single leap, two of the small creatures covered the distance between them and Melinda and grabbed onto her clothes. As one climbed up her shirt, she sent it flying with a swift punch. The other clung to her pants. She grabbed it by the arm and flung it at a third one, by her feet. Both rolled back, merging into the giant again.

Melinda soon came to halt, as the path grew steeper once more. Being unable to advance to the top, Melinda started cutting her way across the large crystals embedded in the slope. The shadow of a massive hand descended as the creature smacked at her again. More pieces broke off as the hand became impaled on crystals. Each tiny piece struggled to climb as they rolled back down to the main one's feet.

"Keep going! We have to be close!" Wind shouted out.

"I sure hope so. If not, we are in serious trouble!" Melinda shouted back, moving among the widespread crystals.

The creature swiped again, this time hitting right next to Melinda's head. As she leapt to shelter behind another crystal, the one beneath her fell, hitting the creature's eye. The beast covered its wound with its hand, yelling out with a deafening squelch. Melinda's eyes opened wide as the creature used its remaining hand to blindly strike about.

Just as she felt her life was at an end, the wall behind her opened up. Falling inside the opening, Melinda and Wind found themselves inside a dark tunnel. The creature took one final swipe at them as the door closed. With a deep sigh, Melinda laid on the cold stone floor to catch her breath.

In moments, two tiny hands grabbed her shoulders in the dark and began to drag her deeper into the cave.

"Wind, *help me*," Melinda screamed out. "Wind!"

Startled, Wind swiftly tried to follow, but a tiny wooden box closed around her, quickly ending her effort. Slamming into the walls of her cell, Wind struggled to escape.

Shortly Melinda's captors released her in the absolute darkness. Remaining motionless, she listened to quiet high-pitched murmurs that surrounded her. Little footsteps scuffled against the ground as the creatures moved around her.

"You will help us, yes?" a squeaky voice said behind her. "You will help us as we have helped you, or your sprite will remain our prisoner."

"What have you done with her?" Melinda demanded, rising to her feet.

"She is safe for now, but unless you retrieve the Spirit Stone from the heart of darkness, she will become lost in the depths of the abyss," the unseen voice explained.

"Let us go you … whatever you are! Show yourselves! Or are you afraid of what I might do to you?" Melinda's anger rose as she lashed out with extreme force.

A bright-orange light burst from the darkness, blinding her unprepared eyes. Adjusting to the light, she could soon see her captors. Standing no more than three-feet tall, a strange-looking people surrounded her. The interrogator held a brilliant crystal in its glove-covered hand. Large, bulging eyes stared at Melinda from a perfectly round face. Its egg-like body, covered with leather, twitched about as it pulled large, dark goggles over its sensitive eyes. Others hid behind rock formations and crystals within the large hollow.

"Are you the moles?" Melinda asked.

"Yes. I am Gaton, leader of the mole people. You were sent here to help us, yes?"

"You do know that the sprite you have captured is Wind, right? If her mother knew you—"

"Mother, Wind, none of this matters to us—only the stone matters," Gaton interrupted. "You will bring it back to us."

Melinda's voice grew stern as she tried to calm her anger, saying simply, "Where is this stone?"

"It is in the center of the fallen city of Mathia. That is where you will find it. I will take you there," Gaton explained, with a childish grin on his face.

"If you know where it is, why don't you get it yourselves?" Melinda snidely questioned.

"Darkness surrounds the ruins of what once was a powerful city. We have been trying to retrieve the stone for centuries. None who have traveled to the temples have ever returned," Gaton stated, as the crowd broke out in quiet murmurs.

"What makes you think I will?"

"Because you are not one of us, see?" Gaton grabbed Melinda by the hand and began to pull her toward another tunnel. "Come. Soon it will be night; we can only travel outside then."

"All right, I'll help you, just let go of me!" Melinda demanded, pulling her hand away from the mole man's soiled glove.

She followed behind as Gaton continued down the tunnel. Several of the other moles crept behind them, trying to listen in. Looking back, Melinda watched as they disappeared into darkness. The tunnel grew gradually smaller, forcing Melinda to crawl on her knees. Gaton casually walked ahead, giggling at her struggles.

"Watch your step, now," Gaton stated, passing through a small hole ahead of him.

Forcing herself into it, Melinda barely fit as she wiggled her way through. On the other side, she froze. They were at the edge of a thin, stone bridge. Nothing except for open space leading nowhere lay below. Cold winds rushed past her face as she stared into the eternal darkness. Gaton paused as she stood, nerves pulsing through her legs. Looking above, Melinda found an equal amount of nothing. With the bridge's destination out of sight, she looked to Gaton. "How far does this go?" she asked shakily.

"This will take us to the crystal cave. It is far brighter there than here. The abyss below extends beyond even our sight," he clarified, as he moved on. Taking a few small steps, Melinda tested the way. "Do not be afraid," Gaton said. "Thousands of moles have trekked over this pit." He began to laugh as he jumped up and down.

"Stop that!" Melinda demanded, reaching out to stop him.

"It's simple. Just look ahead—never up, never down, just ahead." He chuckled, landing hard from his final jump.

With full concentration, Melinda stared straight ahead, fully focused on the path. Drowning out thoughts of what lay below; her path and Gaton were all she could see by the crystal's light. Ease settled in, making the trial of her path simple. Soon her pace caught up to Gaton's.

"We didn't always live this way, under the dirt," Gaton began to explain as they crossed.

"What do you mean?" Melinda's fascination about this place—this world, not just the mole's cavern—had fully taken over. Her home world was only a glimmer in the back of her mind.

"Legend tells that we used to live under the desert sun. We are descendants of the Mathia people ... Surprised?" He lightly laughed, and Melinda remained silent, waiting for him to continue. "Before the darkness ripped through this land we were a race of strength and intelligence. We created the floating cities of Malcara. After they fell, *it* came straight for Mathia. Even with all of our weapons of light, it could not be stopped." Covering his crystal's light, Gaton pointed ahead to a small light, now visible, that shimmered from a distant wall. "There were several energies in the land that fed everything." Exposing the crystal so its light could guide once more, they continued toward the opening in the wall.

Melinda asked, "Why do you need the Spirit Stone so badly?"

"I was coming to that. It has been said that the Spirit Stone is the source of those energies. With it we can finish our weapon to destroy the darkness and come back to the surface." Taking her hand in his, Gaton led Melinda forward.

Gradually, bright white replaced the pitch of darkness. Drawing close to the opening, Melinda blindly stepped into the shimmering glow, at the mercy of her guide. Swallowed by its intense radiance, both vanished within its glow.

As her eyes adjusted to the change, a vast room of glowing crystal appeared before Melinda. Shimmering blues created purples as they intertwined with radiating reds. All colors displayed a spectrum of grace in Melinda's eyes. Gaton turned with a smile as he tossed his crystal to the ground.

"They're so beautiful." Melinda stepped forward, placing her hand on a bright-blue crystal. Mesmerized by it, she reached up to its towering peak.

Energies filled with comfort rushed into her body. Every ounce of her being vibrated, overflowing with the ecstasies of love and understanding. Visions of her childhood danced within her mind, reminding her of the days before her family fell apart, before her father was a drunk. As she slowly pulled away, the feelings dissipated, leaving her invigorated.

"There is great power within the crystals; one should be careful when touching them. Some are happy, others are sad. Come this way." Gaton continued onward through the crystal-lined path.

"How do you plan on using them as a weapon?" Staring at the crystals as she walked, Melinda felt their power pulse through her.

"It's actually quite simple," Gaton explained, pulling a small stone mallet from a satchel Melinda just now noticed in the fuller light of this area. "Even within the vibration there is energy." He lightly tapped a nearby crystal, which created a slight humming vibration that rippled throughout the cave. The vibration's rebounding off the other crystals caused them all to hum ever so slightly. "See, just the smallest amount of disturbance can cause great things to happen." As the vibrations grew, Melinda could feel them moving through her body. Dizziness set in as she wilted down to the ground. "Don't worry, it will pass in time," Gaton reassured her. Slowly the vibrations ended, along with her debilitation. "This way," Gaton continued, as she caught up to him. "With the Spirit Stone we can power all of the energies within the crystals and send a beam of light into the darkness's heart, if it has one."

"Are you sure this will work?" Melinda questioned, still with little understanding.

"We're not sure of the weapon's stability ... or if it will fire at all. But bring us back the stone and we will see. Here, we've reached the desert."

Pointing to a small, dark opening in the wall, Gaton pulled off his glasses and stepped through it and out of the crystal chamber. His large eyes could see perfectly in the darkness, but Melinda's could not. "Just a little farther now," the mole man urged.

Her eyes adjusting, Melinda could see that a large boulder rested against the wall, blocking their path. Gaton used all of his tiny might to roll the boulder aside.

Both stepped out into the night and were greeted by a clear, star-filled sky. As Melinda's eyes slowly adjusted further, she found herself standing on the side of a rocky mountain, overlooking a vast desert. Cold winds rushed past her, sending a chill up her spine. However, that chill seemed minute compared to the sight of a grand temple, as it stood monumentally in the center of the barren desert. Her heart frozen in her chest, Melinda could not fathom what awaited her there.

"Is that Mathia?" she asked in awe.

"Yes," Baton stated, pointing to the pyramid. "And that, the city's great temple, is where you will find the stone. I will help you down the mountain, but you must travel alone from there." His tiny legs carried him along in a slow descent. "I will wait for you here until morning. If you haven't returned by then, you won't return at all."

"I will bring you your precious stone," Melinda snapped, passing him on the way down. "But if I don't, you promise me you'll let Wind go."

"If you do not return, it won't matter, because the darkness will kill us all." Gaton stopped as she continued on down to the base of the hill. "One more thing!" he shouted. "Be wary of the living sand."

Melinda took in his words but did not hesitate on her way. Reaching the desert floor, she looked toward Mathia, filled with the same determination as when she'd set out from the witch's cave. As she took her first step onto the hard sand, she contemplated Gaton's words of life. With a slight beat of fear in her heart, she started on her way. Nothing stood between her and Mathia except for the cracks in the barren wasteland. With a third of the night passing, she finally reached the end of her desolate path, arriving at the broken gates of Mathia.

A great wall of stone surrounded the city. It lay broken and worn from the years of desertion and erosion. Large iron gates that once sealed the city littered the ground, half-buried in the remains of their supports.

Stepping past the fallen entrance, Melinda slowly headed toward the great temple. Several small houses of sand and wood still remained in blocks lining the way to the pyramidal temple. Their darkened doorways and windows haunted her as she passed.

"You again," a familiar voice came from behind. Turning, Melinda found the man from the hilltop standing in the doorway of a nearby house. "You get around quickly."

"What are you doing here?" she asked, standing in the center of the street.

"I've been coming here for a long time now," he explained, as he started walking toward her. "I've been trying to figure out what happened to all of the people here. Why are you here … are you following me?"

"What?" Melinda instantly became lost in his emerald eyes. "No, I was sent here by the mole people to find their stone."

"Stone? I haven't seen a stone here, just lots of sand." He glanced around at the empty city. "I've never seen anything here, not even any form of writing. Are you sure it's here?"

"They said it was in there," she explained, pointing to the temple. "Have you ever been inside?"

"No, that place scares me; there's something about it. Are you really going in there?"

"I have to. They're holding my friend hostage until I return with the stone, which they think will get rid of the darkness. And they also said that they used to live here … I don't know if it's true or not, but I have to save Wind," Melinda explained, as she turned and continued toward the temple.

"Then I'll help you find it," the man said. "Besides, you can't go in there alone. I've heard of creatures made out of sand that roam the inside," he explained, catching up to her.

"Thank you. I hope that whatever it is they are trying to do works. I have to get to Gurod Orminta Dastura so I can go home again." Melinda's determination grew as she reminded herself of her goal.

"I've heard of that place, but I was told it was just a myth."

"The old woman you sent me to sure believes it's real and thinks I can find it. She told me to find the moles—that they would take me there—but all that did was get me into this."

"So you found her, good. I knew she would help you. I have never seen her, nor have I seen the mole people, but I've heard all about them through legend from those who used to live in the great city of glass before it fell to the darkness. It was the last to fall, and since then things stay hidden. They fear the plague that has ravaged their land." Both he and Melinda stopped just outside of the temple's entrance. "Are you sure you want to go in there?" he asked, seeking her reassurance.

"I have no choice; I have to save her." Fortitude filled Melinda's mind as they stepped into the temple's dark hall.

Both clung to each other as they cautiously moved along the narrow, stone path inside. In the distance, a slight, soft-blue glow glimmered off the wall. Slowly they crept toward it, like it was a guiding star, expecting anything that might come at them. But none did. They reached the hall's end and the blue light's source.

Two staffs stuck out from the side walls, their ends covered with several small, blue crystals, creating the perfect radiance for lighting the way. Melinda pulled one staff from its ancient resting place, watching as the dust coating it fell to the floor. As the disturbance settled, she spotted several figures and writings carved into the wall. Looking them over, the pair searched for an answer to what might have happened here.

"Well, what do you think?" the unnamed man asked.

"I don't know, I can't read this." Melinda brushed her hand along a carved figure that resembled a woman with the head of a feline. "Though I think these people really had a thing for cats." Melinda paused for a moment to give her companion a discreet glance. "I've come up with a name for you, been thinking about it since I first saw you."

"Really?" the man queried. "And what name have you surmised?" he asked, turning to face her.

"Christian," she replied as her temperature rose with her blush. Quickly she turned back to the hieroglyphs, trying not to panic. "I don't know, I was just thinking—I mean, how you helped me before—"

"Christian, I like that. It has a nice ring to it. Christian."

With his smile and words of approval, Melinda felt relieved. "Well, where are we going from here?" she asked, quickly changing the subject.

"We don't have many choices, so …" He paused at the faint sound of something walking on the path behind them. "Did you hear that?"

Melinda paused. "What, what is it?" She quickly rushed to Christian's side as her heart began to race. Both listened quietly as the sounds of large footsteps approached. "Shit, what are we going to do?"

"Shh, don't move." Seemingly with a plan, Christian pulled the second staff from the wall and threw it like a spear toward the source of the noise. It hit its mark at the end of the hall, dimly lighting the far corner. The noise halted, and then something rushed toward the glow. It was a large panther made of sand, revealed as it came into the light. Its nose sniffed along the staff then into the air. Instantly it picked up Melinda and Christian's scent. "Remember what I said about not moving?" he asked, grabbing Melinda by the arm. "I've changed my mind. Run!"

In a full-out sprint they darted further down the path. The sand cat turned, spotting their trail of dust. Letting out an echoing growl, it took up the chase at full speed. They reached the path's end and quickly turned the corner, only to end up in another hall.

"Keep moving!" Melinda shouted, pulling her friend by the arm.

They kept at full stride, staying ahead of the creature. Coming to this hall's end too, they were left with only one option: another turn.

"Wait!" he shouted, pulling away from Melinda. "We can't run forever. Here, give me the light. Be ready; if this doesn't work, you better run."

Melinda handed him the staff and fearfully watched as he stood directly in the creature's path. Inches away from the wall behind him, Christian stood his ground, awaiting the moment to strike. Melinda just stood there trying to anticipate his next move. The sand cat charged at him in full stride, letting out a vicious growl. With a massive leap, the cat dove right for Christian's head. But just as the cat's claws were about to graze his face, Christian dove and rolled toward Melinda. The growls silenced as the cat met the solid, unforgiving wall and disintegrated, leaving only a cloud of sand.

"I can't believe you did that!" Melinda exclaimed, pulling him to his feet.

"It worked, and that's all that matters." Brushing the dust from his clothes, he handed her back the staff. "I just hope there aren't any more of those things in here."

"We should keep moving. Are you ready?" Melinda asked softly, as she fell deeper into his eyes than before.

"Yeah, we might as well just keep going this way," he replied, calming his nerves. "It's not like we have any choice."

As they continued down the hall they came to a doorway cut out of the sand wall on their right. Inside the next room they found a staircase that spiraled up. Both listened intently, searching for any sign of trouble. Only the sounds of a hollow space echoed down from above.

"I'll go first." Christian stepped onto the stairs with his eyes cast above. "Keep the light close. We might be coming down in a hurry."

"I hope not," Melinda remarked, following him up the dusty steps.

Quietly and calmly, they moved up the spiral stairs. More carved depictions like those they'd seen at the end of the main hall covered the staircase's center column, etching out a story. Floating cities and flying machines resembling insects that were evidently powered from a single source surrounded a vast, golden city.

"This must be what the moles told me about," She commented, "I wonder if this is the Spirit Stone, their power source."

Within its center stood a colossal pyramid, the temple in which they stood. Another carving of the cat woman showed several people bowing to her.

"And this must be Mathia, before the darkness came, it was much bigger then." A slight smile formed on his face as he ran his finger around the outline of a cat woman. "These have to mean something; there are carvings of them everywhere."

Melinda and Christian slowly continued along the glyphs, trying to decipher the story being told.

"Here, it's like she's offering them power," hypothesizing, Melinda continued to tell the tale. "Is that the Spirit Stone she's holding?" She looked to Christian for an answer, who only shrugged his shoulders. "And this must be the floating cities of Malcara Wind's mother told me about, before they fell from the sky."

Christian, looking on ahead, pointed out his discovery. "I wonder what this means?" he asked, looking over the markings. Here that story had changed, telling of a great city's hunger for power.

"It seems like they're using the stone to control the weather," Melinda thought, as she saw something resembling a tornado. "They're using it against other cities? I thought they were peaceful people."

"I guess not. Look, here is where their darkness comes from," Christian explained, touching the carving of a dark figure.

"Malcara falls," the story unfolded before her, "everyone died there, I saw it in a dream." Christian, confused, waited to hear her story. "I was there when the dark figure appeared. All of the people in the city began to go completely insane, killing each other. There was an explosion and the city plummeted down. It was so real."

"Strange, how did you know it was Malcara you were dreaming about?"

"Wind's mother told me about it before I fell asleep, it doesn't matter, it was just a dream. Oh, look here." Melinda's excitement grew when she saw a picture of a dark serpent wrapped around the Mathia temple. "This must have been when Mathia fell. They must have just abandoned this place before the darkness came," Melinda figured, as she wiped her hand on the barren wall.

"That's it, there has to be more pictures here somewhere," she thought out loud as she searched around with the staff. The pictures ended, though the hall continued on.

"Seeing the fall of Malcara must have scared them off," Christian added. "So, the mole people said they were from here? They must hate knowing that they had to leave all of this."

"That's why they are so set on destroying the darkness. I hope they can succeed," Melinda exclaimed in anger, as she pushed onward.

"I think you need to worry about what *you* are about to do right now." Christian stopped as the stairs ended, leaving them at another doorway.

Taking the light from Melinda, he peered around the corner to see if it was safe. He noticed first off that straight in front of them stood a small doorway. The faint glow of the staff dimly reflected back from inside. Two more staircases that could take them higher into the temple were on either side of the narrow hall. Finally there were choices to be made.

"There's another room here, and more stairs. I think we should just go inside the room first and not rush on, just in case there are any more surprises," Christian reported.

Stepping out into the hall, he pulled Melinda into the small room behind him, stopping a few feet inside. A faint glow of dust-covered gold cast the staff's light around the room. Dusty swords and shields hung from the walls behind six small pillars that displayed miniature figures. Each figure was made of gold intricately detailed in the fashion of different flying insects with crystal wings.

"Christian, come look at these," Melinda stated. "They look just like the things the people were flying in the hieroglyphs."

"Interesting, but I'm more interested in these statues," Christian pointed out.

In all four corners stood ten-foot tall statues of female figures, each with a dark-black head of a cat adorned their perfect-figured bodies. Small, golden robes barely hid their anatomy, leaving little to the imagination.

Without hesitation, Christian handed Melinda the light then removed one of the swords from the wall. After looking it over, he drove it forcibly into one of the statues' stomachs. As he pulled the sword out, the statue fell to dust, spreading throughout the room.

"I just wanted to be sure," he assured Melinda, gagging and coughing on the cloud he'd created.

"You'd better hold on to that," Melinda stated, closing her eyes as the cloud filled the room. "We might need it."

As the dust settled and their vision returned, he once again checked the hall, hoping nothing else had heard the disturbance. Seeing only the last remains of dust floating through the air, he felt relief. Melinda crept up behind him to see for herself. Once the dust had fully settled, it was time for them to move on.

"I think we should go this way," Christian remarked, pointing with his sword to a set of stairs leading up to the right.

"Why, what's that way?"

"I don't know, but either way, we're going up," he stated, shining the light at the opposite end of the hall. "This way is as good as any."

"Okay, I'll follow you," Melinda replied with a smile. Her heart raced for him as he took control. She stared into his eyes, as he passed her the staff. No matter how hard she tried to shake her feelings they dug their way deeper inside. This man, this stranger, had stricken her heart. Love pulsed through her nerves with a tingle as their fingers touched. Even though she wanted the moment to last she knew they had to continue.

He led the way with the tip of his sword ready to strike at anything that blocked his blade. Melinda's breath on his back, she lit their way up the steps. After just a single bend and a few more steps, they reached yet another doorway. Slowly they stepped through, entering a vast room with a dark so deep it nearly drowned their light. A large pillar at their left extended up to an unseen ceiling.

"Are you ready for this?" Christian asked, as they faced their dark surroundings.

With a gulp, Melinda looked to him for assurance in their safety. "As ready as you are."

Bravely, they traveled out into the darkness, seeking to reach the center of the room. After a few steps they found several long, wooden benches lined up in a row.

"This must be some sort of church hall," Melinda whispered in her companion's ear. "I wonder what's over there," she questioned, pointing the lighted staff down the path into the darkness.

"I guess we'll find out," Christian replied with a half-smile of doubt.

Inch by inch they moved past the rows and up the dark path. Melinda, clinging to his shirt, stared straight ahead into the unknown. A slight quiver ran up the staff to the crystal as fear filled her heart. The rows of benches ended, leaving them alone in the darkness.

Melinda stepped forward to find a groove cut into the rock floor. She crouched down with the light to investigate and found that the groove was part of a large line cut into the floor in a half-circle. Beyond that was another groove, and another, each progressively smaller than the previous, all leading to a small hole in the floor. Christian, looking over the hole, reached back and took the staff from Melinda's trembling fingers. He placed the staff inside, finding that it was a perfect fit.

In pure amazement, they watched as the dim light now reflected around the room, faintly lighting every inch. They could now see the massive pillars lining the walls, with doorways between them. On the opposite side of the circular pattern and directly in the center of the room, two colossal statues of the cat-headed females towered over them. Each held a large, jagged spear, the tips of which pointing directly at a softball-sized rock resting upon a perfectly polished, black marble altar. Its dull form stood out from its surroundings.

"Is that the Spirit Stone?" Melinda asked with pure disbelief.

"I don't know," Christian replied. "You sound disappointed."

"Oh, I just thought it would be flashier."

"Well, just remember that it's only a legend. The mole people might believe all this, but it doesn't mean it's—"

"Don't you remember the sand cat that almost ripped your head off back there?" Melinda remarked sarcastically. "That was real, so I think the rest of the legends might be too."

Melinda's eyes focused on the two large, jagged spearheads that pointed to the stone. She started to walk up to the stone, but pausing, she realized that she had no idea of what, exactly, to do.

"Here, just pick it up," Christian stated, setting his sword on the ground. Gripping the stone with both hands, he pulled with all of his might. "It's not moving." Huffing with disgust and fatigue, he stumbled back. Melinda, thinking he was joking, went to give it try.

No luck. "You're right … it's not going anywhere," she said. Stepping back, Melinda glared at the stone while thoughts of Wind's captors filled her mind. "We have to get it out of here. And the moles said I needed to be back before sunrise. There has to be a way." Her mind desperately raced for a solution as she stared at the immovable object.

Unknown to her, Christian had developed a plan of his own. With a firm grip on his sword, he struck the stone with a massive blow. Its blade gave off a deafening ping as it hit its mark. Melinda covered her ears and gave him a dirty look. Quickly dissipating into an echo, the vibration faded.

"Well, if no one knew we were here, they do now," Melinda stated, with a roll of her eyes, as she snatched the sword away from him.

"It was worth a try," he remarked, shrugging his shoulders. "You try. At least it's a way to release some frustration."

She contemplated his suggestion while staring at the reflection of her eyes in the shiny blade. Wind, the stone, and the possible dangers flowed through her thoughts. With her decision made, she looked up at the stone. In a blink she attacked the stone with a single strike. A dull ping reverberated off of the steel.

Christian began to chuckle as she pulled the blade back from her attempt. His laughter was quickly silenced, however, when the stone split down the center. Both halves fell to the altar, revealing a hidden core. A bright, white light filled the room, emanating from the sphere the size of a large marble. It floated freely above its resting place.

"That's it! That has to be the Spirit Stone." Melinda's eyes grew wide as the artifact's glow engulfed the room.

She dropped the sword to her feet in her amazement and reached out with both hands as she approached the orb's blinding light. Immense power passed through her body as she grabbed the orb, enfolding it in her hands and drowning out the light. The pulsing thoughts of a billion minds invaded her being. They flowed into her and then back to the orb, leaving her in a daze.

Calmly, she slowly blinked as the tips of the massive spears from the nearby, towering statues silently stabbed into the altar. She gave no reaction as pieces of stone flew past her head. Turning back, she watched in slow motion as Christian grabbed the sword and pulled her back. Another spear struck the floor, but not before it cut deeply into her left leg. She saw only Christian's wordless mouth yelling at her to move, seemingly without sound. Her mind finally returned to the moment, and her ears became filled with the sounds of crumbling stone.

"What are you doing? We have to get out of here now!" Christian's voice returned, filled with command. "Come on!"

Suddenly the pain of her previously unfelt wound came as the warmth of flowing blood covered her calf. Dropping to one knee, Melinda turned back to see the two large statues walking toward them. Small quakes rippled across the floor with every footstep. A massive thrust with a spear decimated the wooden benches lining the path. Through the flying debris, Melinda rose to her feet again in a mad dash for the way they'd come in. At full speed, both tried to stay ahead of their pursuers. Focusing on the door, they stopped as two smaller female cat-headed statues emerged, both fortified with swords and shields.

"Shit!" Melinda shouted, pulling at Christian's arm. They urgently searched around for a possible escape route, but now from every door stepped a sand cat. "What the hell are we going to do?"

"There has to be a way," the man mumbled to himself. "There!" he yelled out, spotting a clear doorway. "We can go this way!"

Releasing her from his grip, they dashed for the door. No sooner did they begin to run did the sand cats engage in the chase. With a gigantic statue looming just over their heads, they both froze and assessed the situation, finding they were surrounded. Two cats charged at full speed, targeting them from both sides, while four others stormed in from behind. A third of the smaller-sized statues joined in, following the first two. This one waited back, allowing the cats to do their work.

Gripping his sword tightly, Christian prepared for battle. Melinda watched as the mammoth-sized spearhead, wielded by the large statue, rose straight above them. Meanwhile, Christian focused on two of the cats closing in from behind. In deep concentration, he plotted his next move. As they leapt toward him, Melinda pulled him out of the path of the plummeting spear, additionally causing the cats caught in mid-pounce to collide, reducing them to dust.

"Thanks, *watch out*," Christian stated in a hurry.

Her eyes wide in horror, Melinda quickly glanced left and right to see two more cats closing in. The unobstructed doorway was only a few feet away; there was no option of failure. Focusing once again, Christian studied every aspect of the scenario. Just a foot from the door, the cats lunged on their mark. Thinking quickly, Christian shoved Melinda through the doorway and then turned back just as the rear cat arrived. Rolling with the cat's momentum, he threw it into the trailing two. Melinda ran back toward the darkened room only to be blinded in a cloud of dust. She attempted to reenter the fray but was quickly stopped as the massive statue's immense spearhead closed off her path. Pushing against it, she frantically struggled to get back to Christian.

"Damn it!" she screamed, as she pounded against the blade.

"Just go!" the man's faint voice called out through echoing sounds of clashing steel. "I'll catch up to you ... get out of here." She opened her mouth to reply, but he cut her off. "You can leave me ... it will all be worth it if I can stop whatever is doing this. Go!"

Melinda slowly backed away from the blocked door, listening as the battle continued on the other side. Fear rushed through her body as she dug in her pocket for the Spirit Stone. Cupping it in her hands, she tried to contain some of its radiance while allowing enough out to light her way. With full view of her surroundings, she found herself caught at a dead-end in a long, narrow room. Six large, metal statues of insects lined the outer wall. They were exactly the same as the figures in the sword room.

Gleaming with gold and crystal wings, beyond centuries of dust, they rested in perfect condition. Overcome with awe, she investigated the full-sized versions. As she grew near them their wings began to radiate with a soft, green glow. A faint, soothing hum filled the room as the flying machines gained power. Melinda approached one that resembled a dragonfly and nervously reached out to touch it. Vibrations traveled through her body as her fingertips brushed the metal. Placing her palm on its golden body, the wall in front of her began to glow brightly, and then it disappeared, opening to the clear, star-filled sky. Off in the distance she could see the mountains of the mole people.

Stripped away from her thoughts by the rumbling of stone, Melinda saw the spear that was blocking the doorway shift. Escape became her only focus as she climbed on top of the dragonfly. Sitting behind the wings, two handles popped up out of its back. Melinda pushed the Spirit Stone back into her pocket, frantically trying to figure out the controls.

"Christian!" she yelled out, as tears filled her eyes. "Christian?" In every sob her heart plummeted deeper.

Suddenly the spear rose up from the doorway and pointed at her, a vulnerable target. Pushing the left lever forward experimentally, she found it caused the dragonfly to hover. Melinda struggled to hang on as a sand cat entered the room, startling her. It sniffed the air as a small statue followed from behind.

Accidentally hitting the right control with her arm sent her rocketing forward and out from the temple on board the dragonfly. She ripped across the sky as she frantically pulled back on the handle, managing to slow her pace. It wasn't long before she learned how to control the aerial vehicle. She crossed over the wasteland, heading straight for the mountain. All she could do was hope that Christian made it out okay, as the temple grew distant behind her.

Not being able to judge her speed well in the darkness, the mountain came on her unexpectedly. In a desperate attempt to pull up, she tugged viciously on the left handle. The nose began to rise, but she started to slide up the rocky mountainside. Gravel spewed as the contraption dug into the mountainside. The dragonfly came to a sudden stop. Every muscle in her body gripped it as she trembled in terror.

"You made it!"

Though his voice was familiar, Melinda still jumped when Gaton greeted her. "I know you have retrieved the stone. There is little time; we must hurry," he explained, helping her off the dragonfly. "You're hurt, but no worry. We'll get you fixed up and out of here before it's time."

"How do you know I have the stone?" Melinda questioned with a groan.

"Look there." Gaton pointed toward the temple. Turning to see, Melinda shuddered at the sight of a giant serpent of black mist coiled around the temple—a clear presence of pure evil. Its head stretched out high above the temple's peak and overlooked the city. "Come," Gaton commanded. "We have to get the stone inside."

Gaton pushed a boulder aside, leading back into the cave system. Melinda's pace was slowed by her torn leg muscle as they made their way back to the rest of Gaton's people. Eagerly awaiting their arrival, the moles gathered in the main hall of the cave.

Quiet murmurs filled the air as they spoke among themselves. Gaton cut through the center of the crowd.

"My people, listen to me!" he announced over their chatter. "She has returned with the stone. We shall finally avenge those who have fallen to the evil in this land. Bring what is rightfully hers." In an instant one of the moles cut through the crowd, carrying Wind's prison. She was once again set free to fly.

"Thank you!" Wind exclaimed as she dashed over to Melinda. "Are you all right?"

"I'm okay, I'll explain later," Melinda remarked, caught up in the moment.

"Now, for the stone," Gaton demanded. "We will have revenge."

Melinda pulled the stone from her pocket, allowing its glow to fill the massive chasm. Hundreds of mole people shrieked out, covering their eyes with their dark glasses as they gazed upon it in wonderment. Melinda set it in Gaton's hand as the crowd packed together to get a better view. Placing the stone inside the box that formerly held Wind, he softly sealed it away.

"We must arm the weapon quickly and fire before the sun rises," he announced to his people. "The darkness has covered the temple, and that is where we must strike." Gaton passed the box back to the mole that brought it. "We must prepare to awaken the stone. Everyone knows their place. Now go."

Quietly the people dispersed, leaving Melinda, Wind, Gaton, and the mole with the box behind. "We will go to the weapon first," Gaton explained. "I want you to see what we're about to accomplish. I will have your wounds dressed, and then you have to leave ... in case we fail." Gaton took Melinda gently by the hand and led her toward another tunnel filled with brilliant, dancing light.

"What do you mean, fail? I thought you said you were going to destroy it," Melinda questioned.

"There is a chance that the stone will not awaken. If that happens then we are doomed. But no matter what, once the stone is in place, Dylan here will lead you to the path of the Korithian.

There you will find solace from everything. Stay there, and the darkness can never find you," Gaton finished, with assurance in his voice.

They passed through the bright tunnel into a perfectly round room cut from the mountain. Its massive size claimed half of the mountain's peak. This room housed a colossal cannon made of wood and stone. It filled most the room as it stretched out to the distant wall. "This is what we hope will stop the darkness. Our ancestors began its construction after they fled from Mathia." Gaton continued to walk Melinda to the rear of the cannon. "They knew this day would come."

Gaton opened a small panel on the back of the weapon as his helper readied the box with the Spirit Stone. The faint glow coming from the open box was nothing compared to the crystals. "With the power of the stone pulsing through the crystals we can fire a beam of pure light into the destroyer." Taking the stone from the box, he gently placed it within the panel, and then closed it inside. "Dylan, take them to Muna, then lead her to the tree," Gaton requested. Looking back up at Melinda, Gaton continued, as she was led away, "Keep your heart and mind on the downfall of darkness; it will feed the stone. Thank you and be safe." Those were the final words Melinda heard from Gaton as she was led into another tunnel. Knowing she needed to press on, she willingly followed along, though she kept Gaton's words in her mind.

"Come, this way," Dylan stated in a deep, raspy voice. "We have to hurry; the prayer will begin shortly."

After a slight hike, the tunnel ended at a small opening. Inside, Melinda was amazed by the small laboratory powered by crystals that lay before her eyes. A female mole was scurrying about, documenting different liquids that boiled above dark-red crystals. Dylan nudged Melinda toward a small table.

"Muna, quit playing with your toys and get over here," Dylan called out, as he urged Melinda to sit.

Muna turned around to see Melinda as she sat on the table. Her jaw dropped in awe. "Is she the one?" she eagerly asked in a speedy squeak. She rushed over to see into Melinda's eyes. "Then it's true; you brought back the stone!" Her voice trembled with excitement as she spoke. "It's a good thing you've done, yes, yes, good."

"There's no time for this!" Dylan exclaimed, throwing his hands in the air. "They are going to start the prayer soon. Fix her leg; I've got to take her to the tree." His tone sharpened with every word.

"Going to the Korithian village?" Muna questioned, as she started looking over the wound.

"Yes, I—" Melinda began to say.

"Good, you'll be safe there." Walking back with a handful of supplies, Muna began to work on Melinda's leg. "Wonderful people are the Korithian. They will take care of you from here."

Finishing the wrap on her leg, Muna was fulfilled to see Melinda's smile. "Well, it was nice meeting you." Muna turned toward Dylan and continued, "I'll see you in the circle. Be swift, we'll need you." With that the flighty Muna headed off down the tunnel, leaving Dylan to continue his task.

"It's not far now," Dylan stated, as he helped Melinda to her feet. "We'll come out on a distant peak far from the weapon, you should be safe there."

Standing with her weight upon it, she noticed the pain of her leg fading. The mole man's hand in hers, he led her into a narrow tunnel across the room. Wind's glow was the only thing lighting their way as they scampered along the winding path. Dylan huffed, moving at full speed, while Melinda tried to keep up. Before long they reached a large stone, which Dylan struggled to move aside. Shifting, it rolled aside to create an opening to the outside.

"On the other side of the ridge, you'll see a forest. Seek out the large, dead tree in its center. The firestorm will lead you. That's where you will find it," Dylan explained hurriedly. As soon as

Melinda and Wind had passed through, he quickly started to move the stone back into place. "Now hurry, and don't let the darkness find you."

"Thank—" The stone was back in place before Melinda could finish, "you." With a deep sigh, she looked around to see the temple off in the distant desert, the serpent still coiled around it.

"What happened to you? What did they make you do?" Wind frantically asked now that there was time.

"I went there." Melinda pointed toward the temple.

"What is that?" A tremor in her voice, Wind felt the fear of darkness. With no reply from Melinda, Wind continued. "We better do what he said. Let's get around this little ledge and get to the Korithian's forest." She started flying along the mountain.

"Wait, I want to see what they're going to do." Melinda sat down on the rocky mountainside, wondering if Christian had made it out, if he was alive.

Suddenly a massive vibration of sliding stone erupted from the peak of the moles' mountain. Melinda stood to see a bright ball of energy form from the mountain's face, pointing directly at the temple. Growing larger as seconds passed, it quickly drowned out the dim light of the now-rising sun. Suddenly, in an instant the ball formed into a beam of pure energy that collided with the temple, briefly connecting it to the source. As the light dissipated moments later, the temple exploded from the massive heat it had just endured.

"No!" Melinda's eyes filled with tears as she collapsed to the ground. The dust from the explosion slowly settled, exposing the intact head of the serpent. But the once-great temple had become nothing more than rubble remains.

Another ball of energy formed from the mountaintop, a second attempt to wipe away the darkness. As the light rushed toward the serpent, the dark creature coiled around the beam and accelerated toward its source. Reaching the mountainside, the serpent disappeared, and the beam faded off in the distance. All became silent. Melinda awaited a sign, a signal to say everything was all right.

Wind's fear-filled voice broke the silence. "Melinda … Melinda! We better move before that thing comes back. Come, the Korithian are so close, and the moles said we would be safe there."

"He was in there," Melinda mumbled to herself.

"What?"

"Christian was in there when it exploded." Tears welled in Melinda's eyes as her words became stifled. "He saved me and now, now he's gone. It's not fair! It wanted me; I had the stone!" A free flow of tears poured down her cheeks as she stared off at the temple's remains.

"Who is he, a mole?" Wind slowly flew back to Melinda's side.

"No, he's the one who told me about your mother, who I met before you found me. He was exploring around the homes when I got there." Gathering herself some, Melinda stood to face her path. "When everything started attacking us he pushed me through the door. He was trapped on the other side with them. I don't know if he made it out. If he didn't …" Cold, saddened, and worn out, Melinda wanted to fall, as well.

"Is there a chance he could have escaped?" Wind hovered just in front of Melinda as she sluggishly started to walk along the ridge.

"I don't know. If he did, I hope to see him again … I'd like to thank him." As they reached the other side, the sunrise emerged over a vast forest that waited below. "That … is beautiful," Melinda muttered in awe. All of her pain was wiped away with the scene's inspiring beauty. "How could anything want to destroy this?" Her eyes sparkled with the sunbeams as her tears turned to ones of joy.

Carefully they made their way down the rocky mountainside toward the lush, green forest ahead. Off in the distance Melinda could see a lofty dead tree standing out from the rest of the forest. Its size greatly out-measured the trees that surrounded it. Songbirds softly filled their ears with song as they looked down to the treetops below. As they traveled, hard stone beneath their feet became replaced by soft, comforting dirt. Exhausted from her deeds, Melinda continued to press on. Once they reached the Korithian there would be time to rest, or at least she hoped.

"We have to go to that big tree, right? And didn't he say something about fire?" Wind asked, still confused by everything that had happened.

"Yeah, a firestorm, I wonder what it means."

Upon reaching the edge of the forest, Melinda was filled with a warm, inviting sensation. "Once we find the Korithian, I'm going to sleep for a week," she stated. Pushing on doggedly, she stepped into the lush foliage.

"At least we don't have to worry about anything here. Only those with the knowledge of the Korithian can find their way through. Otherwise you will travel in circles forever," Wind expressed, floating above Melinda's shoulder. "Mother told me that when I was . . . wait do you feel that?" Wind's glow became bright, giving off a sense of happiness.

"Yeah, it's tingly." A slight energy pulsed through Melinda, beating within her heart. It wiped away every thought beyond that of the dead tree from her mind. "I know where it is; we have to go this way." Melinda closed her eyes and pointed toward a large cluster of trees. Her eyes remained shut as she cut her way forward with a smile. "It's not far now." She passed between the trees with perfection. "A few more steps ... there." Coming to a large clearing, the massive dead tree stood towering over all.

"Well, I think you have successfully found it. Now what?" Wind asked with a smart tone.

"The firestorm—we have to find the firestorm. I don't know what that means." With a sense of confusion, Melinda turned to Wind. "What do you think?" she asked, before turning to investigate the base of the tree.

"I'm not sure. Um, do you think we should start a fire?" Wind replied with her own question.

"No, but maybe …" Making her way around the tree's base, Melinda discovered a small opening that led inside. "I found something!" Shimmying inside, she pushed her way into the tree's hollow interior.

Shreds of light poured down from a small hole near the treetop. Right next to the beam, just out of reach, grew a large, budding plant rooted in the dead wood of the tree. It was large enough to swallow Melinda, if it had had an opening. Its hand-sized green leaves lay curled and sickly, pointing down to the dirt below.

"You shouldn't disappear like that!" Wind yelled out, discovering Melinda's whereabouts. "What are you doing?" Flying up behind her, Wind watched as Melinda knelt at the light's edge. Remaining quiet, Melinda studied the light as it slowly crept toward the sickly looking plant.

Confused and impatient, Wind started to grow angry. "What are you doing?" she demanded.

"Shh, just wait. It's coming," Melinda whispered, not once breaking her gaze.

Still confused by the situation, Wind landed on Melinda's shoulder, trying to figure it out. Inch by inch the light slowly rose. As the rays barely started to touch upon the leaves, they began to uncurl into the light. With every drop of sun that graced it, the more alive it became. Now fully engulfed by the sunbeam, the plant's massive buds shot up, unraveling with a drapery of fiery orange petals that spread across the ground.

"Firestorm," Melinda stated in awe, as a yellow cloud of pollen filled the dead tree's trunk. A sweet smell covered her senses, followed by euphoria. "Wind, do you feel what I feel? I feel all liquid, like I'm melting into the dirt."

"You don't look like you're melting. Are you all right? Melinda?" Wind frantically dashed around Melinda as she slumped over into herself. "What is this thing?"

As Wind flew over to investigate the bloom more closely, the floor beneath them shifted and then dropped away. Melinda lay in the fetal position, falling like a stone into a grooved section that had appeared in the dirt below. Wind quickly lost sight of her as she slid away. The sprite followed Melinda down just as the floor swung back shut. In the blink of an eye, she spiraled along the descending path in an attempt to catch up.

Moments later, upon reaching the end of the path, Wind found Melinda lying on her side inside of a small dome-shaped cave. Not high above the floor, Wind found the hole that led them there. The dark, cold slide that carried Melinda stretched back up to the tree. Embraced by the sun's mighty rays, Wind drifted towards the source, a small archway that served as the cave's exit. From outside the sun beamed in, leading to the unknown.

"Are you all right?" In a panic, Wind flew over to Melinda's face. The human girl's eyes were completely rolled back and white as she lay unconscious. "Oh, come on." Wind fluttered in front of Melinda, fanning her face with fresh air. "Snap out of it; you're not water."

Suddenly Wind heard several high-pitched voices coming from outside of the exit. They spoke in whispers that kept her from making out their words. Moving along the wall, Wind inched her way toward the opening. Though the whispers had grown louder, she still couldn't understand them.

"Where the hell are we?" Melinda's unexpected voice gave Wind a start. "What are you doing?"

"Shh, there are people out there," Wind quietly demanded as she returned to Melinda, who amazingly stood with no problem.

"What? What people? How did we get down here ... did I really turn into water?" Melinda's excitement grew with the possibility.

"Water, no. The floor dropped away and you slid down here. The problem is, I don't know where *here* is or what's out there, so would you please keep your voice down?" Wind fluttered toward Melinda, causing her to step back.

"Well, we were going to go see the Korithian, right?" Melinda snidely asked.

"Yes ... but—"

"Then they are the Korithian, I would guess. Come on." Melinda stepped around Wind's attempt to block her and headed toward the opening. Wind pulled at Melinda's shirt but soon let go as Melinda continued on. "Would you relax, Wind? Besides, what do you think they'll do?"

Stepping out into the sunlight, Melinda's eyes slowly adjusted to the brightness. Now completely focused, she found herself standing before fourteen small children. Within a glance she figured their ages, a possible range of about eight to eleven. With their animal-skin clothing and wooden spears, she understood that they truly lived off of the land. She noticed that oddly, they all had snow-white hair and skin, and each had gleaming, emerald eyes.

"Hello, are you—" Melinda began to ask.

"We are the Korithian. My name is Tara," one of the female children replied, as she stepped up before the others. "No one has come here for a long time."

"Not even the moles come here anymore," a male child from the crowd added.

"Are you alone?" Tara asked as the other children began to back away.

"No. Well, yes, but there's ... hang on a minute." Melinda turned back toward the small cave where she and Wind entered this land. "Wind ... Wind? Come on, Wind, where are you?" She walked over to the dark tunnel that had led her here. "There's nothing to worry about. They're just kids," she explained.

"I know," Wind quietly stated as she drifted toward her from down the dark tunnel. "I don't want to go out there. They know I ... I'm just going to stay here."

"All right, have it your way. I'm going to find some food and a place to sleep. If this is where we'll be safe, I'm taking a break from this nightmare." Returning outside, Melinda saw that out of all the children only Tara remained. "Where did everybody go?"

"There's work to be done, and we all have our place. Come, I will take you to see Gavin." Looking over Melinda's leg wrapping, Tara grew visibly concerned. "You're hurt. Are you okay to walk?"

"Yeah, the moles took care of it. As soon as she wrapped it, the pain went away," Melinda explained, unmoved by the wound.

"Let me look." Tara bent down and undressed the wound. Under the cloth wrap she pulled off several large pieces of moist moss, sniffing a small piece. "Hmm, smells like Runga tree sap. Whoever did this used their best medicines. There isn't even a mark on you."

Melinda looked down to see that the deep gash was completely gone. Tara discarded the dressing onto the ground, where the moss would simply wilt away.

Taking her hand, Tara wordlessly led Melinda along a well-kept path cut through the forest. All of the surrounding grass was perfectly cut, with every tree trimmed and encircled by radiant, blooming flowers. Several of the children were busy as they pruned the fields around them. Each one stopped and stared as Melinda passed.

"You're Tara, right?" Melinda nonchalantly asked, embarrassed by not being able to tell the Korithian apart. Off in the distance, Melinda could see a small village.

"Yes, and we understand that you are confused by our appearance. We all have grown so much alike." Tara's voice was polite, but Melinda detected a bit of agitation in her about these facts. "It wasn't always like that, though. So many years spent in this forest has made us this way."

As they drew closer to the village, a smooth dirt path replaced the forest grass. Both sides of the path were lined with gardens that stretched out over the land. Many of the children were at

58

work gathering fresh fruits and vegetables, while others weeded and removed dead plants from the growth. Melinda's eyes gazed over the wide variety of plant life. At the same time, a grumbling deep within her reminded her of how long it had been since she'd had a meal of any sort. Salivating, her taste buds yearned for a bite of a fresh strawberry growing in the patch.

"How did you get here?" Melinda inquired, as she tried to block out her hunger.

"All of your questions will be answered in time. Let us walk in peace. Take in everything around you," Tara said in a peaceful tone, describing the oneness between the people and the land.

Continuing on into the village, Melinda's astonishment was heightened by the sight of how the children lived. Five massive, hollowed-out stumps stood scattered throughout the circle of the village, each providing residence. Log-built homes filled in the gaps between them, enough homes to house hundreds. Nearby was a small stream, and next to it were several long, windowed buildings, each lined with chimneys that bellowed out thin, white smoke. More and more questions battered Melinda's mind as they passed these dwellings. How long had they been here in the forest, why does everyone know that it's safe here but yet they stay outside, is Christian still alive?

The children of the village all remained busy repairing roofs and tending to the grass, though each of them lost concentration at the sight of the stranger that passed.

Walking beyond the village, Tara and Melinda traveled toward a thick forest that met with and followed along the stream. Growing wildly without care, the foliage soon became thick, making their passage through the trees difficult. With the snapping of twigs and the rustling of grass, they eventually came to a small pond. Resting along its shore and overshadowing it was a huge, moss-covered stump. A soft, blue aura poured out from several oval windows cut into the wood. Next to the stump Melinda found a small wooden boat floating alongside a dock that reached out into the water. Tied to the dock with a thick vine, the boat swayed in the water, knocking into the pier. For the first time since she'd come to this land, Melinda was reminded of home.

Tara simply smiled as they approached the illuminated stump. Light spewed from in between the slats. Above a child-sized door hung a plaque with the words "The Great Gavin" carved in it. Without hesitation, Tara opened the door, blinding Melinda. Grabbing her softly by the hand, Tara guided her inside. The door closed with a slight bang as the light vanished, then returned as a dim green glow. Vision still blurred, Melinda followed Tara to a small set of stools encircling a large, rectangular, wooden table. Sitting, her sight slowly returned to see a male child standing there, staring at her in pure disbelief.

"I-I didn't think it would ever be true, but here you are, sitting at my table. Tar,a thanks for bringing her here," he stated, fumbling his words in excitement.

"You're not being very polite; she's come a long way. Now try again. This time tell her what you're supposed to," Tara chided in a harsh tone.

"Yes, I'm sorry. My name is Gavin, and I'm the seer of the Korithian." He slowly moved toward Melinda, never shifting his gaze from her eyes. "Forgive me, I still cannot believe it's true. They said that one day you would come, but I never fathomed it would happen."

"Who said I would come?" Melinda quickly asked.

"The mole people," Tara blurted out, giving Gavin the evil eye. "Just tell her what you're supposed to."

"Right, um, let's see, uh …" Gavin paced around as though he had forgotten his lines in a play. Laughing at their antics, Melinda eagerly anticipated his story. Finally, the boy said, "We are the Korithian, so named by those who brought us here thousands of years ago. All most of us can remember of that time is a dark plague infecting the land. That's how the elders put it."

"Who are the elders?" Melinda prodded, as she grew comfortable in her chair.

"They are the ones who brought us here," Tara explained. "They are the ones responsible for our sanctuary."

"Yes," Gavin added. "They put us here to keep us safe, to keep us hidden from the darkness. They stayed with us for a short time to teach us how to live."

"We all looked different then," Tara chimed in. "Some of us had dark hair, even red hair. Our eyes were blue, brown, soft green, and some of us even had darker skin." Her voice became colored by tones of envy as she continued reminiscing.

"Ahem," Gavin cleared his throat, cutting Tara off. "After they got us living on our own, they went away. Fifty years passed, and then they returned."

"In that time we had already begun to change," Tara cut back in. "Our skin began to lose its color, as did our hair."

Gavin glared into Tara's eyes as he picked back up. "When they returned, only a few of them came. Some of them didn't even talk to us. They just walked around writing things into books. Not even one night passed before they left again. Every fifty years thereafter they would return, each time in fewer numbers."

"By the last time they came, we had completely changed," Tara added. "They just told us the cycle was complete, and we never saw them again."

"Two hundred years passed before we saw another again," Gavin stated, breaking back into the conversation. "A woman came. She told us she was to become the new mother of the land. What was she looking for?" Gavin looked to Tara for an answer.

"A mushroom," Tara contemplated for a moment. "No, it was next to the mushroom, growing from one of the stone markers. A flower, she said it was the only one of its kind. It wasn't even very pretty. Dark purple and black, it looked like it was dead."

"She would come to visit in times to come," Gavin stated with a smile of remembrance. "She would dance with us, and she even taught us music. Tonight we are going to throw a festival in your honor."

"My honor?" She inquired, in full denial of her purpose. "Why am I important?" The simple girl couldn't understand how she could be so vital to these people.

"I'm coming to that," Gavin continued. "One day, Mother told us she couldn't come back to see us anymore, that she had to watch over everything. She never told us of the darkness."

"The moles told us about that," Tara snapped. "Out of nowhere and with no warning, the hole where you came from opened up. Inside were seven oddly shaped men. That was the first time the moles had come. Without a word they walked around our village, along the stone markers. Then they brought us the crystals. Now we can light up the night without fire."

Gavin's eyes grew wide, as did his smile. "Over time they taught us many different uses for them. We can even see outside of our boundaries." Gavin pulled Melinda up from the table and rushed her over to a small cauldron of water. Beneath the water lay a small blue crystal. With a quiet whisper, Gavin waved his hands over the water, chanting. The crystal's dim glow brightened to give off a dancing aura of light that illuminated the entire room. "Look there." Gavin pointed into the water in the pot. "Here is the forest outside of our valley, and that is the tree you came through."

"What was the flower inside the dead tree, and why did it make me feel like I was water?" Melinda questioned.

"The firestorm?" Tara asked back, walking up behind Melinda. "After the moles had made that entrance, it started to grow. It is also the only one of its kind. They left it there, I think, because they liked it. They would always be smiling a lot when they'd first arrive. It made you feel like water?"

"Yeah, like I was seeping into the ground. I couldn't feel my body," Melinda stated, stumbling to explain.

"Here!" Gavin let out with a shout. "Look here; this is what you need to see."

Melinda gazed into the water, staring deeply into the rippled image. "What is that? It's a city! Is this my world?"

"Your world—is that what it looks like?" Tara's voice grew with mounting excitement.

"In my world there are cities that look just like this, but what happened here? Everything is destroyed." Melinda forced herself to further displace thoughts of her own home world as she focused on the water. "Is this the city of glass?"

"Yes, how did you know?" Gavin questioned, confused.

"Christian told me about it. He said it was the last to fall into the darkness. I have to go there?" Melinda exclaimed. "Gurod Orminta Dastura is there, isn't it?" Melinda's heart began to race as she could see her final destination. "How do I get there?" As Melinda looked up at Gavin, he began to grow visibly nervous.

"I will show you the way, but first you must rest." Gavin ended the energies in the water, shutting off the image. "Come, Tara. Take her to your home. There she can rest until the festival."

"No!" Melinda demanded. "I have to go now."

"Please, I know this has been hard for you," Tara expressed. "But you must rest and eat. The most difficult journey is still to come."

Calming down with the realization that what they said was true, Melinda agreed. Together Tara and Gavin walked her from the stump and back to the village. As they approached the homes, fatigue clenched Melinda tightly.

Passing between the cabins, Tara led them toward the largest stump. "It's that one, right?" Melinda asked, pointing to the large stump.

"Yes, how did you know?" A smile crossed Tara's face as they drew closer.

"From all of the different flowers around it, you seem to have a thing for beauty," Melinda remarked.

Opening the door to her home, Tara took Melinda inside, leaving Gavin to wait outside. The cozy, two-room home felt inviting to Melinda with several kid-sized, fur-covered chairs, a stone fireplace, and a small table. Melinda felt she could find comfort here. Everything in the tidy home stood in its proper place. In the second room waited a small, fur-covered bed. Tara sank down into the fluffy, fur mattress as she sat.

"You can sleep here," Tara said. "It's stuffed with the finest feathers and lined with the softest pelts the forest provides. If you have trouble sleeping you can start a fire and relax out there."

"Thank you, Tara. I could use some sleep. It has been a long couple of days," Melinda said with a grin. Sitting down, Melinda found the soft, inviting comfort embracing her. "Oh yeah," she said as she lay down and grabbed the equally soft fur pillow. "This will do just fine."

"Good. Well, get some sleep; I have to help ready the feast for tonight." Tara stood, giving Melinda all the room she needed. "If you need anything, just ask and we'll get it for you."

"Thanks again," Melinda stated, as Tara walked out of the room.

Hearing the door softly close, Melinda moved about on the bed searching for a position of contentment. Nodding off, her mind began to wander. Thoughts of Gavin's story, the history of the Korithian people, and the visits by Wind's mother all danced within. Why had the witch said she'd never met these children? What had she been hiding?

Racing thoughts pulled her exhausted mind quickly into a dreamland. Visions of the witch's cave flashed in her mind to the point where they seemed to be reality. Seeing clearly, she watched as vials and bowls danced about in the air, all mixing and pouring into each other endlessly. Wind's mother danced about, moving between the vials. But the entertaining mood swiftly fell as a dark mist rolled in, bearing the shape of a serpent.

"I knew you would come," Mother stated, completely unmoved by the darkness's evil presence. "She has come, and not even you can stop her." With those words the serpent coiled itself around the witch, consuming her soul. All of the floating potions crashed down, spilling to the ground as her lifeless body plummeted to the cave floor.

Tossing in the bed, Melinda's mind took her to another place: back to the temple of Mathia. There she watched as Christian fought against the living sand. He cut through a cat with his sword as it tried to pin him down. Her heart frantically raced as she watched him use his sword to climb up the leg of the large cat woman statue. He hung tight to its body, hacking at its neck. With the loss of its head, the statue crumbled as it took its final step.

Melinda's sight then followed Christian as he ran into a dark hallway. With her vision completely cut off, she searched in the darkness for him. Sweat poured out as she glanced back toward the dimly lit doorway. Suddenly a sand cat lunged straight for her.

Several hours passed in her dream state, suddenly Melinda awoke to the pounding of her heart. Sitting up, she held her dizzy head, trying to piece it all together. Her mind became overwhelmed with all of the conflicting stories she'd heard. As she walked from the bedroom, bright daylight poured in from the openings cut into the stump's walls. She covered her eyes to block out the blinding rays. Outside, a soft, warm breeze greeted her as she stepped out to face her relatively new surroundings.

She glanced around quickly to see if anyone had noticed her. Without further hesitation, she snuck off to find Wind. Now with new concepts given to her by her dream, maybe the two of them could put the puzzle together, to figure out why this was happening.

With the thick foliage as cover, she found her way back toward the small tunnel that had delivered them there. Just as she reached the opening, two of the Korithian children emerged from the nearby brush carrying large, round baskets. Both chatted away about Melinda's coming. Being so caught up in their conversation, they did not even notice her as she dashed inside the cave.

"Wind," Melinda whispered into the air. "Wind, oh, where are you, Wind?" Stepping farther into the pitch black, she searched up the immense slide that had brought her there. "Damn it, Wind, I know you can hear me." Continuing to whisper, she tried to hold back the desperation in her tone. "I need to talk to you! It's about your mother."

Finally, Melinda spotted Wind's faint glow approaching from above.

"What about Mother? What did they tell you?" As Wind's concern grew, so did her glow, soon fully lighting Melinda's face.

"Nothing, I had a dream," Melinda explained. In a sad tone, she continued. "I saw your mother; she was dancing while mixing some potions. The darkness came. It came and it ..." Tears sparkled within Wind's light as they began to pour down Melinda's cheeks. "I watched it take her."

"No ... she can't be. Oh, Mother!" Wind slowly drifted to the ground, her glow fading into darkness. "I felt it. I felt it when she passed. It was when I was in that box. She touched me."

"The Korithian did tell me something; they said she had been here before," Melinda added. "That she came here a lot."

"But she told me she'd never seen the Korithian, that everyone believed they were a myth. Why would she lie?" As Wind pondered the explanation, her fury rose. "They lied to you! Mother wouldn't do that. She loved everything in this world; that's why she was our mother. She took care of everyone!" Flying up in Melinda's face, Wind wickedly wisped about. "She, she—"

"Calm down. I don't think she lied to you on purpose, but that she was just protecting them. Why did you come here all those years ago?"

"Mother told me to seek out my origins, to touch the individual sources of my creation." Thoughts of the past calmed Wind as she floated down to Melinda's knee. "I am constructed of several elements of this world, each of which is unique and only exists in their separate regions. I am tuned to them, being of them. With that connection, I went to see where I came from."

"The flower," Melinda stated, interrupting. "It's on the stone marker."

"Yes, that's right." Hearing this, Wind began to believe what Melinda had said. "I saw the girl. She was carrying a large basket in her arms. Putting it down, she had started to pick berries off of a vine near the stone. When she noticed me, her eyes lit up brightly. I didn't know that she'd …" Sadness in its purest form came onto Wind. "I started to fly around her. She danced about, laughing and smiling. I felt every bit of her joy. As we spun around each other, we began to move farther away from the stone into the woods. She followed me, blinded by the moment. Reaching out to me, she just kept smiling. I landed on her finger and it was no longer skin; it had become stone. I rushed home and told Mother what had happened, and she told me why. I've never come back to this place since, nor have I left my mother's side until now. And doing so has brought me back here." Wind's glow returned as a flicker as Melinda held her.

"It's all right, Wind. I'm here now. I'm not going to let anything bad happen to anyone. This isn't over; the Korithian know what I need to do next, and they said I can stop the darkness. I will find out as much as I can. I'm leaving in the morning to finish this, and I want you to come with me." Melinda slowly pulled her hand away, leaving Wind to float. "Now I have to get back before they notice in order to keep you a secret."

"I'll be waiting for you here. I'm sorry, Melinda," Wind expressed.

"I understand." Melinda smiled, as she peeked outside the stone passageway. With no one in sight, she made her way back to Tara's home.

Going fully undetected, Melinda crept back into Tara's cozy house. Her mind was still trying to piece together the puzzle of her predicament, but she once more found comfort in the soft bed. Her gaze focused on the ceiling as she concentrated on what had been said. A puzzle that spanned thousands of years lay broken before her. If Wind's mother had never been here, then how had Wind been led here? Who are the elders the Korithian spoke of? Were they of … Mathia? If so, how long had they known about the coming of the darkness? And the moles—why hadn't they told Melinda about their past, or at least told the Korithian the truth about who they really were? Melinda's thoughts were still scattered when Tara quietly came in the front door. Melinda's gaze set on the ceiling, she listened as the quiet footsteps drew near.

"Oh, you're awake. Did you sleep well?" Tara softly asked.

"Yes, thank you," Melinda answered, flashing a fake smile to save face. Sitting up, she stretched with a deep groan.

"There's still time before the festival, so feel welcome to look around. I will find you when we're ready," Tara explained as she walked from the room.

"Okay, I'd like to see more of the village. I'm sure it's quite beautiful." Walking behind Tara, Melinda followed the girl out of the house.

"Well, I've still got work to do, so go ahead and explore. No one will bother you, and there's nothing here to fear," Tara added, parting from Melinda's side.

Melinda watched as she walked toward the center of the village and went into one of the long, chimney-lined buildings. Smoke wafted out from within, no doubt created by dancing fires. Curiosity getting the best of her, Melinda walked over to one of the long-house's windows for a peek inside. Looking in, she saw several kids moving about in a giant kitchen, each working on his or her contribution to the night's dining. Tara walked down the middle, checking dish after dish, giving her approval. Five children walked past her, each carrying baskets filled with fresh fruit and vegetables. As the scent of roasted bird and succulent pies filled her nostrils, a deep growl came from within Melinda's stomach.

"We'll eat soon enough," she said to herself, placing her hand over her belly.

Forcing herself away, she headed back toward the rough wilderness. Children passed her and worked in the fields around her, each greeting her with bright eyes and eager smiles. Continuing along the path, Melinda sought out the stone markers she had heard about. She pushed her way through the lush outer rim of the village, still trying to conceive an answer to all of it. How does it all work? These children have really never aged in thousands of years? What do the markers hold that's so important?

Stepping forward, Melinda's foot got entangled in some vines growing along the ground. She unexpectedly fell forward and disappeared into a thicket of long weeds. Her hands pushed through the tangled vines looking for the ground beneath her. Feeling around, she discovered a large, stone spire buried within the tall grass and vines. Anticipation ripped through her being. Quickly she tore at the vines to free her leg. On hands and knees, she parted the weeds, uncovering her find. A three-foot spire appeared, resembling a stalagmite growing from the dirt, straight into the sky. Rubbing her hands at its base, she could feel an immense vibration that dissipated farther up the spire.

Now Melinda noticed that nothing grew along the ground in a large strip extending away from the stone in two directions, like a border. Closing her eyes, she crawled along the barren strip in the center of the path, her body consumed by the pulsating from below. Melinda, curious to see what was causing it, gripped the ground beneath her, burying her hands in the soft soil. Slowly she dug deeper into the ground. With a hole formed from her efforts, the vibrations intensified, rippling up her arms. Several shock waves rushed through her as her fingers hit something solid underneath the siftings—an energy so great it tossed her from the hole back into the soft cushion of the nearby weeds. Shaken, though not hurt, Melinda stood and saw a shiny crystal emanating bright, white light from the hole she'd made.

"This whole place must be surrounded by these," she stated to herself as she got up and walked along the barren path.

Turning back, Melinda found that she could no longer see the stone from where she started. Continuing on around a bend in the bare path, she found another stone. It was of exact width, height, and diameter as the first.

"So, knowing that the darkness was on its way, the people of Mathia built this to protect their children. But why so long before the darkness's coming?" As Melinda pondered her theory, she continued along the path.

"It goes around the entire village," Tara's familiar voice broke in from the thick vine patch. "Nothing has ever grown there."

"What's on the other side?" Melinda asked.

"We aren't allowed to go beyond the path. If we do, we become stone. Only one of us has ever willingly gone beyond the borders. She is a constant reminder to us," Tara explained, not stepping even an inch closer.

"She didn't believe it would happen?" Melinda questioned, climbing back through the thick brush and vines.

"No, she was chasing a little green glowing bug. Dancing around, she went right through without noticing. Those who saw were too late to stop her. They just watched as she changed into a lifeless, gray figure that now forever stands reaching out to the sky." Tara moved back to the short grass of the village, giggling as Melinda struggled to get through the tangle. "It's time; the feast is prepared, and now all we need is our guest of honor."

"You never told me—" falling once again, Melinda landed in the soft, trim grass, "—what it is I'm being honored for."

"You are going to free us from this prison. The moles told us that one would come—one who is not of this land, one who asked to see the fallen kingdom." Helping Melinda up, Tara led her back toward the village. "Then they told us that when this stranger—you—passed through the barrier, that we would be confined to the forest no longer," she added. "That's why you are being honored. You are all we've been waiting for."

Tara stopped and pointed toward the center of the village. There Melinda could see several long, wooden tables—both sides of which being fully occupied by all three hundred forty-eight children of the village. Everyone remained quiet as Melinda and Tara approached. Walking along, they passed everyone at the table until they arrived at the only two available chairs. Offering

Melinda a place next to Gavin, Tara sat to Melinda's right. With everyone present, Gavin stood to greet the gathering.

"Thank you, everyone, for being here. As you know we have a guest, a very important guest. For thousands of years we have been trapped here, not knowing of the outside world. Soon that is going to change. So, tonight we dine on our finest foods, drink our finest drinks, and celebrate our freedom." Gavin raised his crystal glass high into the air, and the others followed in perfect sync. "Here is to the key who shall unlock our cell!" Putting the glass to his lips, he quickly downed its contents, as did all the others. As he sat, the food began to be passed around. The plates danced about in perfect rhythm as they passed hands.

Melinda's eyes grew wide with delight as they feasted upon the cornucopia that lay before her—from roast pig, lamb, and chicken to salads of greens and fruits. Squash, eggplant, pumpkin pie, and fresh bread all tempted her. Lining her plate with a little of everything, her mouth began to water. Everyone waited in silence as she took her first bite. A deep-cut smile lined her face as she slowly chewed a piece of the roasted pig. With her satisfaction given by a deep *mmm*, the others dove into their plates. Sipping from her glass, Melinda was surprised to find a sweet-tasting red wine.

Some of the children, finishing their meals quickly, started to clean off the unneeded, empty dishes. As the tables slowly emptied, several children grabbed them to put them away, teetering as they carried them off. Upon finishing his meal, Gavin remained seated as the others cleaned around him. Once Tara was finished, she got up to help the others. Having been so long since she had eaten, Melinda savored every bite, finishing last. With her plate finally clean, the children came to pick up her dishes.

"Now it's time for the real celebration to begin," Gavin stated to Melinda, as he rose from his seat. "Come." Extending his hand, he led Melinda away from the village and toward a thick patch of forest. "Tonight we shall light up the sky so bright it will swallow the darkness."

They came to a narrow path that divided the thick woods in two. As the sun slowly set behind the surrounding mountains, the night unfolded in the valley. Gavin walked ahead, leading Melinda along the winding trail. Slowing her pace, she marveled at the trees towering over her. Gavin escaped from her view due to her lack of attention. As the night took over the sky, Melinda was left blind and alone to find her way.

Off in the distance she heard a fierce rustle, as if a kite were fighting against violent winds. Moving toward it, a dim glow of orange and yellow flickered through the holes in the foliage. A turn in the path led her to a massive lake surrounded by a field, where a fire in the lake's center reached up over the trees. "Is that an island?" she asked in amazement.

"This is the actual center point of the village," Gavin stated, walking up beside her. "Everything flows to this place from the forest through the underground streams."

Ripples of flame cracked loudly in the night as they furiously whipped about. All of the town's children spun about ritualistically, as if hypnotized. Their tiny figures appeared as dark marionettes performing in front of a burning backdrop. Melinda watched the children dance as she walked along the outer edge of the circle. Alongside the encircling forest were several poles sticking from the ground. Each bore a different colored crystal at its tip.

"It's amazing," Melinda replied. Moving toward the fire, she stopped at the edge of the great lake.

"Yes, this lake is a perfect bowl, and the island is at its exact center, as the lake is to the field, and the field to our land." Gavin blushed, apparently embarrassed at his own knowledge. "I've studied everything in this village; there is nothing here I don't know," he explained when Melinda gave him a questioning look.

"With all of the time you've spent here, I can imagine," Melinda expressed, with an understanding smile. "What do you know about the city of Mathia?"

"Mathia ... I have never heard of that place. Is it in our world?" Gavin questioned curiously.

"It's just over the mountains, in the desert. That is where I came from on my way here," she explained, as they walked along the water's edge. "It was a city made of stone and sand. The moles sent me there to retrieve the Spirit Stone so they could attack the darkness with it. As I was on my way here, they destroyed the city with a beam of light."

"Interesting, did they do it—did they destroy the darkness?" he quickly asked.

"Unfortunately no, they fired at it a second time, but the darkness followed the beam back to the mountain. From there I don't know what happened." Stopping at a long, wooden bridge, Melinda looked down its length toward the fire as the dancers continued their ritual. "Are you sure I am who you think I am?" she asked seriously.

"Yes. Nothing Mother has ever told us has been wrong." He paused for a short moment to gather his thoughts. "Not even the curse of stone." Gavin grew quiet and started across the bridge.

Melinda stepped onto the large, log-built structure, following quietly behind him. She strolled toward the side to look at the water. Being wide enough to handle four lanes of traffic, the bridge made her feel small. With her hand locked onto the wooden rail, she peered over into the crystal-clear water. Several small fish swam around along the smooth rock bottom of the lake. Even in the distant depths she could see clearly to the bottom.

Gavin was now a small, dark figure within the fire's light far ahead of her. She quickly ran to catch up to him. "Sorry, it's just this place is so different. I can't believe you built all of this," Melinda explained, as she slowed at Gavin's side.

"We didn't build it alone. When the elders brought us here, they helped us build this bridge system. The small bridges are used to drop nets for fishing." He smiled as they finally reached the island. "When they originally built this, there was a statue where the fire now burns. It stood as high as the flames and was made of solid stone. They told us it watched us and knew what we were doing."

As they drew closer to the fire, the sounds of ritualistic drumming faintly graced Melinda's ears. Gavin continued, "If we did bad things to each other, the statue would send those who did the bad things out to become stone. The night would come, and by the morning they stood as stone outside of the circle. Then they would disappear. Being good would bring us rewards, like healthy crops and bounties of food. We learned quickly to do what we were supposed to do. We offered food every seven days, enough food to feed us all. By the morning all of it was gone. Once the elders stopped coming, though, the offerings went untouched." Gavin strolled along the water's edge, coming to several small stumps that stuck out from the grass. Sitting down, he continued his story. "Like good children, we did as we were told, and they made sure we still believed. Then *she* came, the one to be mother, the one who told us of God."

"What do you mean?" Melinda asked, her curiosity piqued.

"When she came here, you could see the statue from anywhere in the village. When she asked about it, we told her why it was there and about all of the things that had happened. As she looked it over, all she did was laugh. She said that this was no God; it was a figure of what someone wanted us to believe was God." Gavin took a breath, watching as the others moved about in their ceremonial dance.

"They move so gracefully," Melinda commented, watching as the figures swirled, flailing their arms in the air.

"That is how God dances, with all of the freedom in the world," Gavin stated with a smile. "All that we do is of God; that's what she taught us. God is within us all, as well as the trees, the animals, the lake, and even the ground we walk on. They dance as part of God's joy, to be happy within the moment of being. Come." Standing up, Gavin extended his hand to Melinda. "Let's join them."

Reaching out, Melinda was pulled into the ritual. She fumbled in an attempt to mock the others' movements. Gavin led her as they repeated their steps, turning, stomping, and clapping their hands high in the sky as they circled the mass of raging fire. A smile cut deep into Melinda's face as she synced up with the others. Then, after one complete pass around the fire, all of the dancers broke away. Dumbfounded, Melinda watched as several of the children returned carrying large chopped tree trunks. Working together, they moved them with ease as they stood them up and fed them into the fire. Melinda moved back to stay out of their way as she searched around for Gavin.

"I'm so glad you're here." Tara's familiar voice had come from behind. "I want to show you this next dance; the one called Mother taught it to me."

"Okay, sure," Melinda agreed, with a giggle. The feelings of being a child once more filled her heart.

"All right, follow what I do. Step one, two, back, three, four, now twirl left, right, hands here, yeah, make them float through the air. Move with the wind." As Tara repeated the steps over, Melinda was taken back to her dream of Wind's mother. Tara swayed, and Melinda joined her. "Good, that's right. Have you done this before?"

"No, but I think I'm getting the hang of it." Melinda began to dance with perfect rhythm, and it was as though they were one.

After a few minutes of learning the pattern, Tara said, "You did that great." With a smile on her face, she pulled Melinda out by the fire to face the crowd that now sat focusing solely on them. "Okay, we start here and end here. One time around, that's all. Can you do it?"

"I'll try my best," Melinda affirmed, feeling all the confidence of a pro.

With the start of a heavy drum beat, Tara began her enchanting routine. Melinda followed right beside her with absolute precision, every step perfectly placed, every twirl met with accuracy. Falling into the moment, Melinda felt as though she were possessed, taken over by the entity of Wind's mother. The flickering of the flames went silent to her, as did the beating drums, which guided her steps. All she felt was total peace as they enchanted all who watched. Closing her eyes, she allowed herself freedom within her steps. She heard not a single sound as they twirled in slow motion, completing the circle. Nothing except for the whisper, "Thank you," entered her thoughts. Passing over her, the vibrations of the crowd's clapping finally released her back to them.

"That was amazing!" Tara panted, trying to catch her breath. "You were perfect," she added, as they walked back toward the crowd.

"Thanks, it was fun!" Melinda replied, gasping as well.

As they headed toward the stump seats, the others got up and ran toward the fire. Gavin remained sitting there with a deep-cut smile. Not even making it to the stumps, Tara and Melinda collapsed on the ground, falling to their backs. Both gasped for air, taking deep breaths as the cold ground soothed their worked-up bodies.

"That was the best performance I have ever seen," Gavin said, chuckling as they lay there giggling. "It was like you two were one."

"Thanks, that's what we were hoping for," Tara stated, turning her head toward Melinda. "She made it perfect."

As they caught their breath, the others started preparing for the next dance. Rolling over to her stomach, Melinda waited with anticipation. The drum's beat started them off into a melodious, enchanting, and joyous romp.

"We really should be going," Gavin remarked, breaking in on Melinda's mood. "There's much to discuss about your final journey."

"Gurod Orminta Dastura," Melinda replied in a hushed tone.

"Yes, but first you must pass through the city of glass," he explained. "You have to be ready for that."

Melinda's eyes grew, as did her eagerness. "What's in that place?"

"That is where the darkness has made its home," Tara quietly explained. "It circles the temple of Gurod, though the darkness doesn't know the temple is there."

"We should go. You can explain it on our way," Gavin reminded. Turning to Melinda, he continued, "You will need your rest tonight." He stood up and reached out to help the girls stand. "Let's go to my place. There are some things I need to show you."

"Gurod was the first to come to this world, in the days before the world held any true form," Tara explained, as they started on their way. "Resting above Terisan Lake, the center of our world's surface, Gurod began to create life. At first these life forms were only simple forms, they could only survive with no concept of reason. Within its creations pulsed a vibrant energy—energy not unlike its own. Drawing the energies in, Gurod began to grow. Life continued to change until it created something similar to itself. Man stepped into the sun to see the glimmer of their creator's temple. It was the early humans that were the only ones to ever see him. He taught them how to live, taught them about the land and what it provided. The first cities were built around the Terisan Lake, but Gurod never returned to the land and never again allowed passage to his temple. He left it up to the humans to just be, just exist."

"So no one has ever seen this temple except for the first people who existed?" Melinda questioned.

"No, the temple remained there throughout our history," Gavin answered. "There are caves even in this village that have drawings of it floating high above the water."

"But over time, the temple disappeared as well," Tara chimed in. "Over time, people began to forget why it was there. Their way of living also changed. All of the teachings of the world fell away as value started being placed on everything around them. Life became about self-indulgence and the desire for control. The temple of Gurod vanished completely. Some say it floated away to find another world, while others think it sank into the bottomless lake. Only a small amount of the people remembered the truth, and they carried on the teachings out of faith that one day Gurod would return.

"Man grew more and more intelligent, creating massive structures where one man would rule over many. Those of the Gurod belief grew smaller and smaller in number as they were wiped out by those who demanded their own ideals. Civilizations grew and fell continually throughout time.

"Finally there was one that grew far past the others. Slowly these people began to reach out over the world. With their technology, they forced their ways upon everyone; those who did not follow were destroyed. It was they who released the darkness into the world. On their quest for power, they learned how to manipulate nature. Food, shelter, clothing, tools—all could be made in masses. They used their technology to enslave the people by creating false limitations. Starvation and poverty spread through the world. Only those in control would ever see the spoils of life.

"In this time, Malcara watched over the land, floating above it to make sure everything was in order. That was the first place the darkness came to. When it fell, those who created it grew scared. One by one the cities began to fall as the darkness began to grow. The city of glass was once a place of great power. It was built to house hundreds of thousands of people. All types of people lived there—from the rich, to those who served them, to the poor ones who lived off the remains of the rich.

"In time the slaves began to outnumber their rulers, and a fight for survival turned into a fight of freedom. But even those who fought were misled by their own selfish rights. Feeling all of the world's hatred there, the darkness made Malcara its home."

"How do you know all of this?" Melinda asked, as Tara opened the door to Gavin's home.

"Mother taught us," Gavin said, "when she taught us about God. Finish up the history, Tara; I have to show her the city." Running to the cauldron, Gavin prepared the crystal in order to show Melinda.

"Okay. The darkness has been looking for Gurod since it came here," Tara explained. "Legend has it that if it destroys the temple, then everything in the world will be reborn by its design." Finishing her story, Tara walked behind Melinda to see if Gavin had found the images he was looking for.

He had, and he beckoned Melinda over to the cauldron. "Here is Terisan Lake," Gavin pointed out. "It's in the center of the city."

Melinda stared at the image with uncertainty. "What am I supposed to do once I get there?"

"If you are not of this world, then Gurod will come," Gavin explained. "Mother told us that, as did the moles."

"So, I'm supposed to walk through the city of evil to a lake where a floating city no one has ever seen is going to appear?" Doubt filled Melinda's voice.

"I know this is a lot for you to understand," Gavin added, trying to spark her confidence. "We don't understand it ourselves. But you must get some rest now; tomorrow we will guide you on your way. There's a bed you can sleep on in the back corner of the room."

"Thank you." Melinda's politeness was far from her expression of the situation. "But where will you sleep?"

"He can stay with me," Tara quickly stated. "We will come get you in the morning. Sleep well."

Both left Melinda inside Gavin's stump, walking off toward the village. Melinda listened as their murmured conversation trailed away. Finally alone with her thoughts, Melinda found the bed and lay down to rest her weary mind. Though it didn't hold the comfort of Tara's bed, it was still better than what she was accustomed to. Her head swirled with everything she had learned.

As before, her mind raced to piece it all together. Slumber came, filled with complex concepts.

Visions tossed about in her head, feeding her the image of a massive lake that swallowed the horizon. Standing barefoot on the soft, white, sandy shore, she gazed at the full moon as it reflected off of the water's motionless surface. She walked peacefully along the lake's edge, careful not to disturb the tranquil setting. A gentle breeze lifted her hair, caressing her neck as the strands danced freely about.

Off on the distant shore of the lake, several large, black stones protruded from the beach. With a long path of tracks behind her, she reached the tallest of the rocks and climbed to its top. She stood high above the shore, seeing nothing except the water and the shoreline below. Within the peace, she felt a warmth unlike anything she had ever felt. She just sat on the ledge of the rock, relaxed, looking out over the perfectly smooth lake.

After a short while a monstrous gurgle came bubbling up from deep within the waters below. Lying on her stomach, she leaned over the stone's edge. Large, white bubbles rippled and exploded from the surface. The bubbles began to flow faster and faster. Suddenly, with a great wave blasting from the water, a dark demon of smoke shot up and towered over her. Its bony, dragon-like body filled the clear sky, drowning out the bright moon's light. Large, red eyes focused on Melinda, studying her. Then, without warning, the skeletal dragon quickly opened its mouth to devour her.

In a deep sweat and heart-pounding panic, Melinda woke inside Gavin's dark home. She sat up in the bed and tried to shake off the images of the demon that now haunted her mind. She could hear outside the melodic sound of frogs chirping around the pond. She got up and went to the door.

A gentle breeze greeted her as she stepped out into the night. Though she didn't understand why, she felt comfort at the sight of the small pier. She removed her shoes and socks and walked to its end, then she dangled her feet into the cool water. Several bats glided down over the surface, plucking insects that hovered above. Her dangling feet broke the calm of the crystal clear water's surface, sending couples of sleepy fish scurrying away. They tickled her feet as they passed beneath them. Swaying her legs in the water, she watched as the ripples reached out and then disappeared toward the pond's center. Her only thought was why.

"Couldn't sleep?" Tara's voice rang out, startling Melinda. She turned to see Tara standing on the shore at the edge of the dock.

"No, I had a dream," Melinda replied, as Tara walked to her.

"What did you see?" Tara, also shoeless, sat down beside Melinda, her toes just breaking the surface of the pond.

"It was a lake. It extended out farther than I could see. There was a sandy beach with three black rocks that reached out over the water. I climbed up one to look at the moon's reflection, and the demon came. It was shaped like a dragon made out of mist. Just as it tried to eat me, I woke up."

"It must have been Terisan Lake. The demon doesn't want you to find Gurod; it's trying to scare you." Tara grew excited with her analysis. "It's afraid. It's afraid you'll find it and stop it."

"Yeah," Melinda sighed as she stood, letting the water drip off her feet. "*If* I can stop it, I just hope I am what you believe I am."

"Why else would you be here?" Tara demanded while Melinda slowly walked away.

"I don't know. Hell, I don't even know where I am!" Putting her socks and shoes back on, Melinda felt the pressure of her role. "Do you even know what happened to Mathia?"

"We know it was destroyed." Tara's voice was filled with sorrow as she walked toward the shore. "Just before you arrived there was a terrible noise from outside. Gavin was the one who heard it; the rest of us were still asleep. He looked in the cauldron water to see what had caused it. When he saw that the temple was gone, he woke up everyone in the village. He said it was a sign that the time of your coming was here. As he scanned the forest, he saw you walking into the hollow tree. That's how we knew you were there." With Tara's explanation complete, Melinda became angry. She couldn't accept Tara's simple answer.

"So what does that prove? Mathia was destroyed by the moles because they thought they could stop the darkness! But the darkness is still out there, and there's no way that me—little ol' me—is going to be able to stop it!" All grew silent after her outburst. Even the frog's chirps quieted to stillness.

Without another word, Melinda stormed off toward the ceremonial fire pit in the center of the village. Tara softly followed behind her. With the moonlight to guide her, Melinda broke from the wooded path to come upon the massive bowl lake. Fully focused on her destination, she went straight for one of the large bridges. Tara lingered in the distance, watching Melinda go through her motions, feeling her determination to prove the predictions wrong.

Without a second's pause, Melinda proceeded to the fire pit. Her eyes searched over the smoldering remains of the night's festivities. Unsatisfied with her findings, she continued along the edge, searching for something to dig with.

Finding a comfortable place to sit, Tara watched as Melinda frantically ran about. Off in the deep brush, Melinda spotted a branch sticking out above the grass. She marched over to it only to find that the branch was connected to large tree limb. Tara let out a giggle as she watched Melinda's struggle. Finally breaking the branch free, the outsider marched back over to the ashes. Melinda poked around in the ashes to the point of pure frustration. Feeling her defeat, she threw the branch into the fire pit and then headed over to where Tara sat.

"What were you looking for?" Tara asked quietly, fully aware of the situation.

"The statue Gavin told me about. I wanted to remind you of what belief can bring," Melinda huffed, as she sat on the ground

Behind the Open Door

beside the child. "How can your people believe anything without knowing the truth?"

"Truth? Truth about what?" Tara let out a deep sigh as she drew back to mind times she'd tried to bury. "We remember those days when we obeyed that statue. Its eyes still watch us from the bottom of the lake, staring up at us every time we pass. Once we found out the truth, we burned it. As the stone burned immensely the whole statue exploded. The head fell into the lake and has sat there ever since."

"And you believe that what you know is the truth?" Melinda asked in a lightened tone.

"The truth," Tara let out a tiny laugh. "No one knows the truth."

"What about those who brought you here, and where you come from?" Melinda blurted out. "Doesn't any of that matter? The people from Mathia are—"

"Of no importance," Tara interrupted. "All that matters is what is happening right now."

"And what's that?" Melinda snapped, frustrated. "Me sitting here in a crazy nightmare talking to a two-thousand-year-old child who is trying to convince me I'm—I'm some kind of chosen one!" Covering her face with her hair, tears began to flow down Melinda's cheeks. "I just want to go home."

"What is home to you, exactly?" Coldly, Tara stood and walked toward the smoldering fire pit. "For us it has been a tomb that we were sent to by people we never knew." Her voice grew heated as she explained the pain of her people. "They gave us belief, a God to believe in. With that faith we had to be good, we had to follow their rules. Our people died so they could rule us with fear. When we found out the truth, we were outraged. All of us worked as hard as we could to destroy it. This area was covered with the tallest trees then. We cut them down, this entire forest, to burn out our enslaver's eyes because we believed its destruction would save us. We danced around the fire as it engulfed the statue, celebrating our release. When it exploded, more lives were lost—more lives at the expense of our beliefs!"

"So then what do you believe now?" Melinda asked, peering out from behind her hair.

"I don't know what to believe." Tara's tone grew more somber. "I can only go by what I have seen, experienced, and been taught. In reality, I can only have faith in what I see by my experiences. I believe you are what they say you are because of what has led us to this point."

"Which is what?"

Looking up, Melinda saw Tara staring her directly in the eyes, never once blinking as she spoke. "A course of actions that was set in motion the second you arrived. Our celebration last night was not entirely for you. You came here on the day of our yearly festival celebrating the destruction of that abomination God and the lives that were lost because of it. Gavin did see you, that is true; that is why he believes the possible coincidence of your presence is the sign we've been waiting for. I have thought about you constantly since I learned of your coming. And even within your self-doubt, I still envy you. You are going to do something wonderful." Her voice was filled with confidence now. "You are going to set us free."

With those words, everything became still. Both looked to the sky to be greeted by the rising sun. From within the surrounding forest, the chatter of woodland birds lulled them with song.

"They have faith in the sun," Tara added. "Faith that it will rise every morning and set every night. It keeps them safe; it gives them comfort. Never once do they question why they're here or where they came from. All they hold dear is that they *are*."

"What does that even mean?" Not being able to conceive the thought, Melinda stormed off toward the village. "I have to get out of here!" Her heavy footsteps met the bridge, where she saw Gavin approaching.

"Wow, you're really ready to go." Gavin's excitement fell short when he saw her angry face. "Did I miss something?"

As Melinda continued by, he looked to Tara for an answer. "She doubts herself," Tara explained, joining his side. "Maybe you can talk some sense into her."

Gavin chased after Melinda along the long bridge, trying to think of what might pacify her anger. Pausing for a moment, he watched to see where she was heading. Furious and frustrated, Melinda paid no attention as she scuttled along a random path leading into the woods.

With her eyes focused on the path and her mind racing with the doubt of her own being, she lost her way in a thick maze of thorny brush and trees. Turning down every corner, backtracking, even tracing her own footsteps in the soft dirt led her in a dizzying circle. Finally she dropped to her knees and drove her fist into the ground; rage and hysteria had taken over.

"Giving up so soon?" Gavin's voice broke into her mind. "You're not lost. You only believe that you are."

"What?" Melinda's face poked out from behind her hair as she looked into Gavin's soft, comforting eyes.

"You woke up to find yourself in a different world." Reaching out, Gavin helped her to her feet. "I know this all must be strange to you. It's a lot to take in, but you have to understand or at least accept it … you are here for a reason."

"Yeah, and what's that reason? To destroy some kind of demon that's destroying everything?" she stated sarcastically, looking through tear-filled eyes. "I can't handle that kind of responsibility. I'm a waitress at a shitty restaurant, who lives on Falvey Street in Bangor, Maine, going to a community college next to an *airport!*" Melinda's anger turned to madness. "I dumped my boyfriend four months ago because he'd become a drug dealer. Now I'm stuck in this forest in a place that … that …" Dizziness came over Melinda's mind as she lost her train of thought.

"It's okay, just relax and breathe," Gavin softly spoke, trying to calm her. "Are you breathing? Good."

Regaining her composure, Melinda slowly walked back along the path in front of her. Gavin, quiet so as to not disturb her thoughts, followed alongside. Slowing her pace, Melinda's mind tried to grasp her new reality.

Understanding her plight, Gavin continued. "Everything around you—what you see, feel, hear, and experience—is real, is it not?" he asked, pinching her arm.

"Ouch, I know it's just me. How can I be what you say I am?" Melinda's mind twisted at the concept and what she felt. She was rejecting the responsibility through the disbelief in herself.

"Life is not about possessions or about the things you have done. The possibilities are there for a waking moment when you can hold no fear and do everything you can for what is right at that moment of happening so a future can be born. This is your part. And this is my part—living in this prison and waiting for freedom. Different roles intertwine, and fates cross hundreds of paths. These are the keys to the existence of one through all within every variation and form of being. Just as without focus or fear, you found my home."

Fully caught up in Gavin's speech, Melinda came to find the large stump next to the pond. Inside, Tara waited for their arrival. She perched above the cauldron, staring at images within, her eyes wide and unblinking. Gavin and Melinda, curious what she was gazing at, walked over to join her. From over her shoulder they watched as visions of the decimated temple of Mathia flashed over the water. Crosswinds ripped over the desert, blowing clouds of dust over the crumbling remains.

"You must be very powerful to destroy that temple," Gavin remarked with a smile.

"I didn't do it, the moles did. All I did was go in there to fetch their Spirit Stone," Melinda explained in disgust. "None of that matters now." Leaning over toward Tara, she angrily made a request. "Show me where I need to go. I want to get this over with."

With a nod of agreement, Tara used her mind to draw in the cauldron the image of the city of glass. Reaching into the cauldron, she produced a ripple in the water with her finger. As the tiny wave settled, the image became clear.

Melinda's eyes froze and her heart sank at the nightmarish sight of the rotting city. Towering buildings stood cracked and leaning over the vacant cars that littered the streets. A thick, dark haze enshrouded everything as it swirled around light posts and the buildings' shattered windows.

"Is this the only place you can see here?" Melinda asked, her voice hardened like a soldier's.

"No, there's another place, but the darkness is strong there," Tara replied, as she once again touched the water. "Here, this is outside of the desert. Like the forest, it has begun to swallow the remains."

A new image developed with the calming of the water as the ripples subsided. Here only partial remnants of the buildings poked out from beneath the dunes. Only tiny pieces of the road could be seen under the blowing sand. The headlights of buried cars barely stuck out from under piled sand. Clouds of darkness floated stagnant in the sky, shrouding the sun. Off in the distance, the viewers noticed something moving in the mist. Tara concentrated, focusing all of her thoughts on the motion, bringing it into perfect view.

The thing's body resembled a bean. It shuffled along, hunched over its long, narrow legs and tentacle-like arms waving about. Suddenly it stopped in the center of the road as if it were searching for something. Turning, it faced directly at them with burning red eyes. Seeing them, it hobbled closer, its translucent, formless face filling their watery screen. Fear filled the room as Gavin, Melinda, and Tara froze in panic. Breaking the image, Tara dizzily stepped away from the cauldron in a deep sweat.

Melinda felt Tara's fear as she went to comfort her. "What was that thing?"

"That is one of the darkness's minions," Tara explained with a tremor in her voice. "They are what devoured the life from the land. They eat the souls of the living, leaving them as part of the darkness."

"All of those that remained in the city after its downfall were hunted down by the minions," Gavin added. "Now, nothing remains except for clouds of darkness."

"Do you think it actually saw us?" Tara asked in a panic.

"No. At least I don't think so. Even if it did, the darkness can never enter this place," he replied with confidence.

"Why is that?" Melinda asked, questioning his certainty.

"The vibrations make us invisible to any eye in the forest except for those who know where to look. For thousands of years we have held this land in safety. I don't think we will lose it now. And your being here proves that this can all be stopped." Gavin's tone held its confidence as he continued. "We have watched as civilizations have risen and fallen to the plague of darkness. Never once has an outsider of a world far beyond our own touched this soil. You are the one to stop this."

"I hope you're right about that," Melinda stated, though she was still filled with doubt. "How do I get there?"

"I will take you to the edge of the village, to a path that will lead you there," Gavin assured her, as he walked Tara to his bed to lie down. "You just rest here, Tara. I'll take care of it from here."

"Thank you, Gavin." Tara's hand rested on his cheek. "I know you will, just as I know she will." Tara's eyes sparkled as she looked softly into Melinda's.

"Come, Melinda. It is time." Gavin took her hand and led her toward the door. Outside, he continued to explain. "Continue straight through the woods. Once you see where the forest swallows the city, you will have found the entrance. Pass through the city to the desert. Terisan Lake waits in the desert's center. Gurod will rise for you."

Reaching the end of their journey along the path, Gavin made a final statement. "The deeper you go inside the city, the stronger the darkness becomes. Stay true to the path you walk on, for it will save you from the darkness." He held up a shining object, taken from a pouch at his side. "Take this crystal. It will help light your way. Go—free the world from its shroud."

With those last words, Gavin turned and headed back to his home, leaving Melinda in the lush forest on her quest for Gurod.

As the village began to disappear from her view, Melinda slowed her pace, waiting for Wind. Songbirds continued their tunes as she waded through the thick brush. Little time passed before Wind made herself known.

"Were you just going to leave me back there?" the sprite furiously asked, dashing past Melinda's face.

"I knew you were following me the whole time back there. You saw everything," Melinda stated, with a deep smirk. "Did you like the dance I did?"

"How did you—? Yes, it reminded me of Mother." Wind's tone was one of sadness. "You moved the exact same way she did when she was putting things together in the cave."

"I'm sorry, Wind. I shouldn't have mentioned it." Reaching out to the creature, Melinda tried to comfort her. "Well, this is it, our final path to Gurod."

"Yes, I know. Is it all right if I … go see the girl?" Wind timidly requested. "I want to see her again, to tell her I'm sorry for what happened."

"Sure, I understand. Take all the time you need," Melinda said softly. "I'll keep going, and you can catch up to me when you're done."

"Thanks. I will be back soon." Wind flew off, leaving Melinda to travel on through the woods alone.

Reeds snapped beneath Melinda's feet as she pushed on through the thick brush toward the city. Birds chirped out, warning the other animals of her presence. Soon the brush thinned as the ground became covered in the shadows of gigantic trees. Small patches of light broke through the gaps in the leaves like spotlights illuminating the dirt below. Closing her eyes, Melinda entered the largest patch.

The warmth of the sun's radiance consumed her. Slowly opening her eyes, she saw that the forest had vanished. Her mind eased as she let go of what stood before her. A great nothingness washed over her, piercing her forehead. Visions flashed then faded beneath the blanket of light. The light was all she acknowledged beyond the presence of herself.

Within the millisecond's bliss, she was instantly drawn back by the sound of approaching footsteps. Focusing on the sound, she pinpointed the direction and distance, both of which were just footsteps away. She held no fear as she stepped from the light. With her eyes still focusing, she saw nothing except for a dark blur.

"Melinda? You're alive!" Christian called. "Where have you been?"

Her eyes focused to see that he was covered in bloodstained clothes.

"What happened to you?" Running up to him with a smile, she embraced him with delight. "Are you all right?"

"Yeah, I got out of there just before the place exploded. After that, everything went black. I woke up in the forest and have been wandering around trying to figure out how to get out of here!" he explained, as she looked over his wounds.

"Let me help," she stated, grabbing a piece of moss from a nearby tree. "Put this on your head and it will heal it faster." Handing Christian the moss, she embraced him tightly. "Thank you for helping me back there." This was the moment she was waiting for, a chance to feel him around her.

"It's no problem," he replied, with a painful whimper. Melinda quickly loosened her grip. "And where are we off to now?" he asked with a smirk.

"I'm going to the city of glass." Looking toward her path, her voice grew soft. "I have to find Gurod."

"Well, I'm going with you."

As he joined her side, her eyes fell to the ground. "I have to go alone. Besides, you're all beaten up; you'll just slow me down.

Go to the Korithian, they'll take care of you. I want someone to come back for when it's over." She rubbed her hand lightly over his bloodstained cheek as she smiled deeply into his eyes. "I don't want anything to happen to you." Moving in, she closed her eyes as her lips locked onto his. Her heart raced within the deep embrace of her love. After several moments, they pulled apart. Melinda breathed, "I promise I will be back for you."

"But I—"

She cut him off, giving instructions. "With the deepest part of your mind, picture a massive, hollow tree. Inside there is a plant called the *firestorm* that is what will take you to the Korithian." She pointed Christian in the direction of the hidden village in hopes he'd actually go without a fight.

"I've been walking around these woods since I woke up here. I haven't seen anything like that. Just let me come with you," he begged.

"No, you have to think about it," Melinda explained. "Envision it with your thoughts. Just go; there isn't much time." Growing frustrated with his plight, she pushed him toward the village. "Don't be stubborn. Everything will be fine; they'll take care of you. Go."

Her eyes softened to see his acceptance. "Fine, but you better be all right." He walked toward the deeper area of the woods as she forced him off. "No giant statues or sand cats this time," he called, teasing.

"I hope not!" she yelled out toward his retreating form. "I hope not."

Melinda watched him walk until he vanished from her sight. A genuine smile formed at her knowing that he was alive and safe. Looking on ahead, she envisioned concepts of her own, concepts of what awaited her in the city of glass. Swallowing her fear, she took the first step ahead on her path to Gurod.

Sweat beaded on her skin as the humidity around her rose to tropical heights. Bright greens littered the path ahead as the foliage flourished between the trees. Brushing the giant leaves aside, her hands seemed small, being a third of their size. She went up a small incline, and coming out into the bright sun, she emerged from the forest's edge to the top of a large cliff. Very little plant life sprouted from the hard, cracked ground beneath her feet here.

Walking to the center of the overlook, she stopped at a patch of what appeared to be asphalt sticking out from the center of an ivy blanket. She dug into the earth with both hands, uncovering a small amount of road. Now she could see that several of them made a path straight for the cliff's edge. Running with anticipation, she headed straight for the precipice.

"Melinda!" Wind shouted from behind. "Oh, where are you? Melinda! There you are, I didn't think I would ever find you." She huffed from a lack of breath as she glided over to her companion.

"We're here," Melinda pointed out. "The city is just down there."

"What, already?" Wind followed behind as they reached the cliff's edge.

"See?" With a smile, Melinda sat down on the edge and began searching over the ruins from on high.

The sun graced the ruins with its warming rays, revealing its splendor. Foundations of buildings stood covered in the very ivy that helped cause the collapse of the once-towering metropolis. Trees had broken through the shattered sidewalks, towering over the rusted heaps of abandoned cars. Off on the distant horizon, some of the skyscrapers still towered over the streets as the forest that had engulfed the city thinned.

"We're going *there*?" Wind gawked frightfully at the wreckage below.

"Don't worry, we're just passing through. We're actually going to Terisan Lake in the center of the desert beyond." Melinda tried to come to terms with the situation as she searched for a way down the steep wall.

"Wait, Terisan Lake? No, I can't go there!" Wind exclaimed in a panic. "Mother said—"

"The Korithian told me that's where Gurod is. They think it's sleeping at the bottom of the lake. They told me that if I could awaken it, the darkness would be destroyed."

Spotting a broken tower near the side of the cliff, Melinda saw a possible way down. A large tree root protruded out of the rocky cliff wall, allowing her a safe climb into the cracked-open building.

"Terisan Lake is surrounded by the darkness. How do you expect to get past that?" Wind questioned, joining Melinda as she climbed inside the office wreckage.

"I'll figure that out when we get there," she replied, caught up in what she was seeing. "This is so weird," Melinda stated, as she passed the standing cubicles. Chairs, desks, and even computers rested under a thick layer of dust. "It's just like home."

Investigating one of the desks, she spotted several dust-coated papers lying in a neat pile next to a computer. With a swift breath she blew away the dust so she could read her findings. Nothing on the outside page was clear, so she picked up the document to open it. Its dry pages crumbled in her fingertips, leaving a small portion in her hand. The text was written in a language she had never seen.

"I wonder how it happened, how they were wiped out." Letting the paper fall to the floor, Melinda hunted around for a staircase. "This will take us down," she said, opening a heavy steel door that led them to a dark stairwell.

"Good, this place is scaring the hell out of me," Wind uttered, keeping close to Melinda's side.

Using her gift from Gavin as a light source, Melinda climbed down the forty stories of steps to the ground floor. Wind drifted down, glowing as brightly as she could. Inside the lobby, they found nothing more than overgrown, dead planters and the same vacant sense of the lifeless city as they'd felt looking out over the desolation from the cliff.

Outside, fallen pieces of the building littered the decimated street. Only a partial wall leaned against a bent light pole. Several cars lay crushed under rubble in the street. Off on the distant horizon, the edge of the dark cloud slowly swirled overhead.

"We should be safe here," Melinda stated. "Once we get deeper into the city …" Hesitating, she tried to develop a quick plan.

"What are we going to do? I don't like this one bit. Can't we just go back and stay with the Korithian?" Wind flew up to Melinda's shoulder as they both stared off at the cloud.

"Look, Wind, I don't really have a plan, I mean I haven't planned for any of this." Melinda felt the weight of her task pressing down on her. "I don't know what we're going to do once we get there, but we better get moving if we want to get there by sunset." Melinda started, striding along the broken sidewalk, trying not to show any of her fear.

Flowers, reeds, and trees blossomed through the cracks in the concrete. Most of this urban jungle lay in ruins devoured by nature. Where beings once lived and played had become home to the wild. Traversing mounds of destruction, Melinda walked down the patchy streets and deeper into the city—past fallen restaurants, bars, even places that served fast food—they moved through the ivy-covered city. Thick dust clouded over the windows, keeping their insides hidden from view.

"Have you come up with anything on what you are going to do here?" Wind quietly asked, trying not to disturb Melinda's thoughts.

"No. I'm still trying to figure out what happened here."

Melinda tried to peer into one fast food restaurant's window. Even with both hands by her face pressed to the glass, she could barely see the table on the other side. "Damn it. I need something to …" Frantically she searched around the broken sidewalk. "Got it."

Grabbing hold of a large chunk of concrete with both hands, she stumbled toward the window. Heaving it through gave her instant access to the building. "Look, there are still trays on the tables. It's like they just vanished. Not even a single bone, nothing."

"Well, if they just vanished, maybe you could have just used the door," Wind remarked, passing through the disturbance of dust Melinda had created. "It definitely would have been cleaner."

"I'm serious, Wind. Think about it—they all just vanished. Why?" Melinda's mind began to reel around the possibilities. "Maybe there was a plague … but there are no bodies. Maybe they—"

"Maybe they grew smart and got out of here while they could, which is what I suggest we do … now!" Wind's tone grew with fear as the eerie atmosphere consumed her. She pulled anxiously at Melinda's shirt.

"All right, I agree; it's much creepier in here than out there." Heading for the door, Melinda decided to test Wind's theory. With a slight push, the door opened freely.

"See?" Wind smartly replied.

Just as Melinda opened her mouth to respond, she was cut off by a loud roar. "Is that the lions from the tree house?" Melinda asked herself, making a dash down the street straight for the sound.

"Wait for me!" Wind yelled, doing all she could to keep up. Coming to a cross street, she discovered Melinda waiting in the intersection's center. She was frantically pacing back and forth. "What are you doing?"

Hearing another roar, Melinda took off without a word. "You're not supposed to run *toward* the loud, scary sound!" Wind expressed, following behind her.

Melinda continued to run as one roar after another filled the air. Zigzagging her way through the forest-overrun city, she came to where the trees no longer held the streets. At the same time as a final roar, she turned the corner to find the horrific source. One of the female lions that had protected her when she first arrived lay slain in the center of the road. Seven swords stuck out of its cold, lifeless body, one for every roar they'd heard.

"It is, oh my ... why?" Tears rolled down Melinda's face. She rushed to the fallen creature's side, searching for any indication of life. "Who did this? Who ... who did this?" she screamed. Her tears turned to all-out sobs as she wrapped her arms around the lion's bloodied neck.

"Oh no," Wind spouted out, finally catching up to her friend. "What happened?" Flying to her side, Wind felt Melinda's sadness.

"Why would anyone do this?" Melinda asked from under her tears. "It's not fair; it didn't do anything."

"The darkness is powerful. It makes things happen ... horrible things." Looking up into the sky, Wind came to see that they had come to the outer rim of the cloud. "Speaking of which, I don't think we are too far off." The fear in her voice gained Melinda's attention.

"What is it?" she muttered, regaining her composure.

"Have a look for yourself."

Drying her blurred eyes, Melinda realized that there were little remains of the forest, and the buildings now stood strong. Finally noticing the dark cloud above, she felt Wind's fright. But Melinda's fear dissolved and was suddenly replaced by anger at what had been done.

"I've had enough of this!" Her nostrils flared as she turned to walk deeper into the city.

"Wait a minute!" Dashing in front of her face, Wind stopped Melinda's irrational move. "This place is really dangerous, and you need to think about what you're doing." Wind pushed her back to the sidewalk.

"All right, calm down!" Giving in, Melinda sat on the curb, biting her lower lip in impatience. "What do you have in mind?"

"I'll fly in and see if I can find any hiding spots. We'll go there, and you'll wait as I go find another. Those shadow monsters definitely won't be able to catch me; I'm far too quick," Wind explained, drifting back and forth as though pacing. "Teamwork, right?" she added, trying to convince Melinda of her plan.

"Okay," Melinda agreed, "but be careful out there, and don't be gone for more than fifteen minutes. If you see anything strange, get back here, all right?"

"Wish me luck," Wind said simply, as she headed off for the deep city. "I can't believe I'm doing this," she muttered to herself.

Melinda kept her full attention on Wind as she disappeared around a building. As time slowly ticked away, she tried to focus on her next move. Her mind racing with the responsibility that had been forced upon her, Melinda's self-induced pressure grew. Trapped within her thoughts of facing the darkness she paced back and forth, chewing her nails.

A loud snapping of steel broke into her thoughts. The sound echoed through the empty streets. Off down a distant alleyway, a massive dust cloud formed as one of the gargantuan towers crumbled and fell to the street below. The enormous cloud reached up to the sky and then blanketed down, covering everything around it.

Not much time had passed, but after this scary event Melinda fought her urge to search for Wind. Standing, completely uncertain what to do, her mind created a distraction—something to keep her from falling apart. Glancing over at the slain lioness, her sympathy returned. She sat down beside it, slowly rubbing its wounds, wishing she could heal them. All she could do was hope that Wind would safely return to her.

"What happened here?" Christian's voice came unexpectedly from down the street. Melinda turned to see him coming up the sidewalk.

"Why are you here?" she snapped, stomping toward him. "I told you to stay with the Korithian. It's too dangerous!"

"There's a problem with the Korithian," he stated simply.

"What, you couldn't find the tree?" Melinda asked, cutting him off.

"No, I found the tree and that weird plant. But there were no Korithian people. I saw the village and the lake with the head in it, but no people. It was like they had just vanished," he explained, as Melinda reexamined his wounds. "I lost the moss on my way here. Climbing down that cliff was tough."

"I found a busted up building I could get into, took the stairs," she replied with a smart smirk. "Well, you're here now, so all we have to do is wait for Wind to come back and we can keep moving." Melinda walked back over to the dead lioness then sat down beside her.

"Wind? Oh, that's right, she's the one the moles had captive. Where is she?" Watching Melinda pet the dead animal, he questioned her sanity, but said nothing on the subject.

"She went on ahead to find us safe places to hide. It's been a while and she's not back yet." As if in a trance, Melinda just stared off into the city.

"What happened to the lion?" Christian asked, coming up for a closer look. "These look just like the swords from inside the temple."

"Are you sure?" Melinda asked, snapping out of her reverie. Inspecting them to the fullest, she realized he was right. "How could they have gotten here?" Standing suddenly in a panic, her eyes began to well up. "Wind, Wind! Come on, Wind!" Tears in full flow ran down her face.

"Calm down," Christian said levelly. "Haven't you seen the massive, dark cloud swirling in the sky? The last thing we need is for it to know where we are. She probably just got turned around in that concrete maze. We'll find her, you'll see." Trying his best to reassure her, he began to walk her toward the city of darkness. "I'm with you all the way."

"Thanks, I'm glad someone's here. I don't want to be alone." Side by side, they entered the city beneath the swirling cloud together.

Staying close to the buildings, they quietly crept down the sidewalk. The stillness of the streets allowed fear to fully embrace

Melinda. As they approached an alley, she pressed her back against the building, peeking around the corner. Her eyes opened with terror as she spotted a creature made of black smoke shuffling down the alley away from her. She pulled her head back, gripping the wall and breathing heavily.

"What?" Christian whispered. "What is it?" Moving in front of her, he looked for himself. "There's nothing there. What are you doing?"

"It was there," she whispered back, glancing back around. "I saw it; it looked like a person made out of dark cloud." She moved back away from the alley, closing her eyes, trying to figure out what was real. She was at least thankful that the smoke creature had vanished.

"Well, it's gone now, so let's keep moving before it comes back." Christian took her by the hand and they continued along the sidewalk. The cloud grew thicker the deeper they went, swallowing the sky.

"Why are you doing this, anyway?"

Melinda was fully confused by the question. "What are you going to get out of all of this?" Christian followed up.

"I get to go home," she replied. "Besides, they told me I'm the only one who can do this. This entire world was destroyed by this thing. I think it's time for it to die." An evil grin grew on her face as she spoke of death.

"So you think you're going to kill this … thing?" he questioned, doubting her rationality. "And what *is* this thing that you're trying to kill, anyway?"

"I don't know. All I know is that everyone has told me that's why I'm here and that they believe I'm the only one who can stop the evil here. And if I find this so-called Gurod, I might be able to get home," she explained. "Once we find Wind, she'll tell you. Oh, believe me. I know this whole thing is nuts."

"Sounds like it. Well, I'll do what I can to help." But Christian's condescending tone told of his faith in this. He continued, "Have you ever seen this thing?"

"No. I had a dream about it, though. It came up out of the water. It was huge. Looking down at me, it tried to eat me, but I woke up as its mouth snapped shut." More fear came through her voice as she told her tale. "There was something in that alley. The Korithian showed me a place, and I saw one there too. It walked straight at us as though it could see us looking at it through the divining water. It was horrifying—I don't ever want to see one again!"

"I wish I could have seen it. So, what are we going to do if we see more?"

"Run, I don't know. We'll have to wait and see if that happens." Growing uneasy with his questions, she tried to focus elsewhere. "Wind has to be lost. Let's just keep looking for Wind; she can't be too far off."

"Wait, so you're telling me that you're following what others have told you to do on faith that it might be true? And that you have no plan on what you are going to do?" Christian quietly laughed.

Melinda's anger rose. "Would you just shut up?" she shouted as he rolled his eyes. "Okay, you know what? First, we have to find Wind, all right? There's the plan!"

"No plan, no Wind sprite, and no understanding of what's going on." His tone grew smarter, pushing her to her limit. "I'm really starting to feel safe in this."

"Why are you doing this? I thought you were here to help me, not chastise me on what I'm doing." Melinda stormed over to him in rage, pushing him against a wall. "You say you've been here since the dawn of time and what have you done? Nothing! You just sat back and watched as everything around you fell apart. You never lifted a hand to help anyone!"

"That's not true; I helped you," he calmly replied. "You never would have gotten the stone without me. Which was impressive, I must say. I didn't think moving that thing was possible." Backing off of him, Melinda stopped to regain her thoughts. He continued,

"Yes, I watched this world die, because they brought it upon themselves."

"How can you say that? I mean what could they have done that was so wrong that everyone, including their children, had to die?" Melinda demanded.

"Everything dies eventually. Besides that, these people—these are creatures that make themselves righteous by doing what's right for them in the name of a god that doesn't exist. The stories are told and passed on through generations who blindly follow something no matter how out of place it might seem." His voice had turned into almost a pleading tone, begging release from society.

"So, you're saying there's no God? If that's true, then what the hell is that?" she snapped back, pointing to the sky.

"Wait, I never said there was no God. I said they create false Gods for their gain. Truly there is evil in the world—an evil that has scattered across the land and infected everything. It is those people who you feel sorry for," he explained. "With their unnecessary advancements beyond their needs, they poisoned the skies and lakes. And as they seek the power to rule over all, they kill and enslave one another. Games are played, but there are no true victors. The world becomes entangled in a web of absolute lies. From the food they eat to the clothing they wear, they are told how to live. Now, if there is anything more evil than destroying hundreds of families for one's own personal gain, then there is no evil at all. This death is what they brought here through themselves."

Melinda remained speechless as they continued toward the cloud's center. The darkness above had grown thick and hazy, further dimming the streets. Coming to a large park, they peered around a building's edge to see if the open area was safe. Melinda glanced around to see, through the park's dried-up foliage, several mist creatures lurking about.

"There, look, there's a whole bunch of them," she quickly pointed out.

"Oh my ..." Christian muttered, seeing the mist creatures. "There are even a couple sitting on the benches too. Great, now what are we going to do, fearless leader?"

"We'll have to go around. It's weird they're at the park," she stated, heading back to a nearby side street.

"Why is that weird?" he asked with a chuckle.

"I don't know. I just never thought that the darkness would like a park. Here, we can go this way." She pointed down an open alley that ran parallel to the park. "If we keep going, we'll get past the park. Hopefully there won't be as many here as on some other streets."

Some moments of silence passed. "So, what did they tell you about Gurod?" Christian finally prodded, as they headed down the alley.

"Several things, Wind's mother told me the darkness came and destroyed Malcara then slowly took over the world in search of the Korithian. The moles told me that they were the Mathians and needed the Spirit Stone to take back their land. And the Korithian were told so many things that they themselves hadn't developed any real truths of their own, but believed in whatever the people who'd helped them believed in. Though as far as a real truth, I have no idea. All I could gather was that Gurod created everything here, then what he'd created forgot about him, so he went away. As these people grew dominant, the darkness came and wiped them out. There are too many stories to try to piece together."

"That's the problem with all of their stories. Even within all of their similarities, there are so many things that don't line up. This here, the darkness—it doesn't lie or make up stories. It is pure in what it does." Christian smiled deeply, as though with admiration.

"What, destroying and death? The Korithian were hidden from it so they could have a chance to start over."

Coming to the end of the alley, they found themselves standing on a direct path to the center of the swirling cloud. "There's a lake on the other side of the cloud, and that's where Gurod is supposed to be," Melinda explained.

Keeping a sharp lookout for any mist creatures, they continued their debate. Christian said, "No, that's not true. The Mathians had grown too large to sustain themselves. They took their own children and put them in that forest to grow and gather food for them. Once they figured out how to control nature, they slowly began to conquer the lands around them. Their creation of Malcara was to watch over their new territories, making sure none spoke of revolution. Those that did try to get out from under their grip were slaughtered by the powers of great wind or flood. They awakened what had been sleeping since Gurod was born. This darkness had been here; they just gave it the power to consume." Stopping at one of the cross streets, he waited for a reply.

"What do you want me to say, that killing everyone is justified because those who were in charge decided to be greedy and power hungry? No, there is good in people," she expressed with anger in her eyes. "The Korithian were very kind. They fed me, let me sleep in their homes—they even let me dance in one of their rituals with them."

"Only because they didn't know the truth about their lives, which is what evil is—knowing the truth of how you're a slave under the power of someone who controls you and doesn't care about you." A smile cut across Christian's face as Melinda stood frustrated and speechless. "And you, being so naïve that you believe them when they tell you that you are the one, making you a slave to their beliefs." He burst out in wicked laughter. "You are a slave on a mission to destroy that which cannot be destroyed."

"I will destroy it!" Melinda yelled out, storming off toward the cloud center and the lake beyond.

"Wait, aren't you forgetting something?" Reaching into his shirt, Christian revealed a small leather pouch that he carried around his neck. He just stared at her as he pulled the drawstring, opening it. With an evil grin, he dumped part of its contents into his hand.

"And what's that?" Melinda smartly asked, not knowing his next move.

"Your precious Wind sprite, my dear." With a smile he tossed her one of the objects he'd taken from his satchel—a smaller pouch. It spiraled through the air. Astounded, Melinda dove to catch it.

With a sense of deepening confusion, she slowly opened the tiny leather pouch. She spread it apart with her fingers and received a clear view inside. Eyes wide with horror, sadness, rage, hatred, and heartbreak, Melinda trembled at the sight of what it contained. Tears unlike anything she had ever felt gushed down her face in full flow. Her heart was crushed at the sight of her fallen friend, the dead remains of Wind.

"Why?" she pleaded, falling to her knees. "Why did you ... I—"

"What, why would I kill everyone, as you so put it?" Gloating, he could feel his power over her as he smiled.

"How could you kill Wind?" Melinda held herself up with her hands, feeling a sickness coming over her.

"That's my job, remember? To kill, everything I see must die, and now is Gurod's time. Take me to him!" he demanded in a deep tone, storming over to her.

"No," Melinda muttered from behind her tears as she backed away. "I won't let you kill anymore because of me. I can't believe I told you ..." Her sobs continued to grow, but she was able to yell, "You killed them, didn't you, the Korithian? Didn't you?" Scooting away, she managed to get to her feet. "The moles, Wind's mother—they're gone, aren't they?"

Christian just stood with a smile. "This is funny?" Melinda asked as her sorrow became replaced by anger. "Answer me, damn it. Answer me!" Rage filled her being as she advanced on him, backing away. "I know you killed them! Even the lioness ... it was you ... you bastard! Why, why did you kill her?"

"You had become distracted, and I was growing bored. Do you know what this is?" he calmly asked, holding out a closed hand. Opening it slowly, he exposed the other object he had removed from his pouch. There, glowing in its entire splendor rested the Spirit Stone.

"You *bastard*, no wonder those creatures couldn't hurt you; you controlled them," she replied at the revelation. Looking into his eyes, she couldn't believe how cold the man she had once loved had become.

"This stone encases the souls of those who have died, but only good souls are allowed. That is why the stone is so tiny. Only half of all good souls are worthy. Even among the Korithian there were only twelve. Twelve—don't you think that's a little pathetic for children? Anyway, the good souls come here and gather. That is what gives it its power," he explained, as the stone's glow pulsated.

"It's pure blasphemy that you are allowed to touch it!" Melinda said, her tone now harsh and strong, her anger turned to hatred.

"The Mathians used this power to control everything. This was their source, the enslavement of the righteous. And do you know what types of people are inside—kings, warriors, noble men of the cloth, maybe gurus and teachers of the faith?" He began to chuckle then burst into deep gut laughter. "No, it is those who did not follow or fear any driven belief, those whose faiths were a definition of themselves, those who saw through God's eyes directly. Gurod is a figure to behold, created within the mind—a mind that needs to end."

"You can't justify the death of creation on something like that," Melinda snapped back through angry lips. "So how many then, how many souls have *you* enslaved?"

"As many as are swirling around above you now, and those who walk among us." A deep smile penetrated Christian's cheeks as they became surrounded by several mist creatures. "Anyway, I don't really care about that. I'm going to free them from their prison and send them back into the stream. This is my step, and soon you better make yours." His smile faded as he clenched hold of the Spirit Stone in his full fist.

Melinda heard the violent crunch from within his grip. Moving his fingers back and forth, his hand chewed the crystal stone into sand. Christian released his hold, allowing the gentle breeze to clear away the remains. Suddenly a small, glowing orb appeared, floating above his palm. Slowly it began to pulsate and grow, reaching the same size as its now-shattered shell. Instantaneously its light washed out everything around, leaving only outlines of Melinda and Christian. Even the dark mist creatures became reverse silhouettes.

Pulsing with the power of all that was pure, the ball continued to grow. Both humans stepped back as it reached past their heights. A deafening shriek echoed throughout the city as the energy erupted, spilling out the individual souls. As they fanned out to begin their ascension, the mist pulled them from the sky, devouring all that it could.

Those souls that made it beyond the ground dwellers found a threat Melinda had never seen. From out of the swirling cloud, hundreds of winged demons formed, their bone-like bodies carried fast within the sky. She watched as every pure soul was vanquished, extinguishing the light.

"Now that they are free, only he and I remain." Christian's smile faded as he looked upon Melinda to make his demand. "Now, take me to him!"

"Never, you're a monster, an abomination! I was in love with you with every meaning of the word," she cried out as the mist creatures encircled them. "There's no way I'm letting you kill him."

"Then I will kill you. Either way, I win this game." He slowly closed in on her while his minions watched, clapping quietly above their heads. Backing away from him, Melinda felt her fear returning. "You better run, Melinda, time is running out." His voice was distorted and evil; his face resembled that of a demon.

"What are you?" Backing away through the crowd of creatures, Melinda tried to escape.

"Anything I need to be," he explained, transforming himself into an exact duplicate of the female cat-headed statues. "For the Mathians I chose this form." His voice had also changed, to the sensual and inviting melody of a female. "I took it from their shaman's deepest inner thoughts, like a sick sexual fantasy. I became a God to them, by their naming. I pulsed within their deepest desire and their selfish lives, uncovering what life was truly about, what they held dear."

Returning to his normal form, Christian continued his story of truth. "I am whatever it is the seeker wants to see." His voice became calm and warm, like when Melinda and he first met. "This is what comforted you, what you wanted to see—essentially, what you created. Not my best look, but I can't complain." Backing her into a wall, he pinned her in with his hands. "Now, little mouse, what are you going to do?"

In complete silence, her eyes, glazed over by tears, locked onto his. With the speed of a striking serpent, she smashed his throat with her fist, causing him to collapse to the ground. Melinda used her opportunity to dash like the wind. Twisting and turning through the maze of streets, she ran deeper into the city. Dashing past several large windows, she noticed several naked mannequins beneath the layers of dust. She had not a second thought beyond that of finding the perfect hiding place. Following the advice of her fallen friend, she went for the front doors.

Creating a cloud of dust as they pushed in, the doors allowed her entry. Quietly she crept into the abandoned store. Not a single piece of clothing remained. Empty hangers littered the racks while once-used figures of fashion stood fully exposed. Moving steadily down the main aisle, she hunted for a way to get to the second floor.

Reaching the store's center, she came to an enclosure of glass counter display cases. She peeked inside the glass to see what had been left behind. Her eyes grew at the sight of sparkling jewels, golden trinkets, even crystal figurines that lay locked away, forgotten and valueless. Though enticed by the shiny treasure,

Melinda knew there was no time for spoils. She quickly continued looking for a way up.

Moving past a wall, she stopped at what appeared to be the shoe department. She turned the corner. There sat a wide set of stairs that led upward, disappearing into darkness. Using the crystal Gavin had given her, she lit her way into the unknown.

But halfway up her crystal's bright light faded, smothered by the dense cloud of darkness that poured down from above. Realizing there was no way up, Melinda returned to the bottom of the steps. Glancing back, she noticed two glowing, red eyes staring at her from the engulfed stairs. Forming from the mist, Christian's creature slowly hobbled toward her. She stared, frozen in fright, as its mouth opened down to its legs. Letting out a high-pitched squeal, it called out for reinforcements.

More eyes appeared within the mist, advancing down the stairs toward her. In a wicked dash, Melinda darted toward the store exit. Coming around the corner, she ran straight into a mannequin, taking the whole display down as she tumbled to the floor. She quickly got back on her feet and looked around, only to see more mist creatures coming toward the doors from outside.

Off in the distance, a dressing room in a nearby wall came into view. Melinda kept low and out of sight as she quietly made her way to an empty stall in the back. She crawled from one to the next, closing every door and locking it. Hiding in the dark, she perched on the small changing bench inside one of the booths. She jumped as she met her own dim reflection in the mirror.

Silence fell. With no sign of anyone near, Melinda held her breath. The thin beam of light peering in from the opening to the changing rooms faded, leaving her in absolute darkness. Melinda gripped the crystal in her hands, holding it tight against her chest.

Suddenly a door from one of the other rooms was ripped from its hinges and thrown against the wall. Seconds passed, and another followed, then another. Waiting for it, Melinda anticipated what was to come. But to her surprise, two dim red eyes appeared right in front of her—then disappeared. A clicking noise came from her door, and then it slowly opened with a long, drawn-out squeal. Pouring in, the mist engulfed the room. Multiple soft hands caressed her skin as the mist wrapped around her body. They moved their way to her mouth, rubbing her lips with a single finger. Then the sensation abruptly ended as the mist pulled away, leaving Christian standing before her.

"Do you really think you can hide from me in my own den?" he coldly asked, leaning against the doorway. "My eyes are everywhere, and my reach is boundless. I could hunt you down for all of eternity, but there's no thrill in that. I'll kill you now."

As he reached out for her throat, Melinda exposed the crystal's intense light. Using it as a weapon, she slashed at his arm. The sharp crystal grazed his skin like a razor, spilling black blood onto the floor. His eyes cowered before the light. She held the crystal out with a firm grip, parting the mist like with a hot knife. Cutting her way through, she managed to dash back outside the mist-shrouded store.

A thick cloud awaited her. It quickly parted at the light of the crystal. Melinda turned down another street, the mist disappearing before her light. High above her, the cloud had grown thicker, with several small funnel clouds forming. She pocketed the crystal and ran.

Twisting through the streets, she tried to keep her heading pointed toward the desert. Passing several dust-covered cars, she felt the dryness of the air. She stopped to lean on one vehicle to catch her breath. Rubbing her hand across the car, she noticed that the dust was really sand. She scanned the area ahead and saw that the buildings were becoming scarce. Only small portions of a few floors remained standing, as if the remainder of each building had been eaten away by harsh winds.

Slowly continuing now, Melinda moved up the center of the road toward the remains. Small patches of sand littered the street and covered the cars in small dunes. Buildings lessened and the sand grew, soon completely covering most of the street. Ahead of her stood two towers that once rose into the sky, now their great mass stuck out from a mountain of sand like a tomb. With no options left, she was forced to make the climb.

Beneath her the soft sand gave way, burying her feet as she stepped. Hand over foot, she dug in, using everything she had to pass the tenth floor of the building next to her. She made it. Exhausted and sweaty, she collapsed at the dune's peak, gasping for breath. She tilted her head to glance back and see if she had been followed. With nothing in sight, she looked above to the dark cloud. Melinda saw patches of the setting sun passing through. She grasped a small glimmer of hope.

After catching her breath, she sat up to see what waited ahead. Sand covered most of the landscape, with only small portions of the once-powerful city poking through the dunes. Off on the distant horizon she could see a small crack of blue—Terisan Lake. Keeping it in view, she crawled across the top of the massive dune to the edge. A smile arose on her face as she peered down the gradual slope, knowing the way down would be so much easier.

Her ankles sank deep into the sand. Descending slowly and cautiously, she safely reached the bottom. Thunder-like rumbles filled her ears from the swirl of darkness above. But now with nothing in her way, she pushed on straight into the barren region, heading for the lake. Passing small protrusions of the last remaining buildings, she approached a patchy street, looking on as the city faded behind her.

Covered in sticky sweat and dirt, Melinda came to a circle of partially standing towers, the last she'd see. She climbed over mounds of stone and debris before stopping at the remains of a small statue in the circle's center. Around the statue was a light dusting of sand, as it stood high upon its marble monument. Only the figure's bare feet and ankles remained. The stone ledge surrounding the statue seemed like the perfect place to rest. She sat in preparation for the rest of her journey.

"Are you enjoying the game?" Christian whispered in her ear as he instantaneously appeared sitting next to her. Melinda jumped up, falling back into the sand. "I told you this is my den and that you cannot hide." Laughing at her position, he reached out to help her up but was disappointed as she backed away.

"Stay away from me!" Getting to her feet, she stared him down, smiling at the mark she had given him with the crystal. "I know your secret. I know what you're afraid of, and you can't hurt me." Her mood did not change as hundreds of mist creatures arrived to surround them.

"Really?" he sarcastically asked. "I will kill you, don't hold any doubt about that." Moving toward her, she held her stance. "Just take me to him and everything will be fine. You can go home, and this world will be nothing more than a memory."

"No," Melinda calmly stated. "I will get home, but not at the price of giving anything to you."

"But you have given me so much already. Those disgusting moles—they scampered about in their caves not knowing who was real and what was being fed to them. They ripped each other to pieces."

"Stop," Melinda demanded, as tears welled in her eyes.

"And the slaves—I mean the children. Did you know I have spent hundreds of years trying to figure out that forest? You made it simple, as did they. When I got there, they were all gathered around the lake, praying and dancing in celebration of their freedom." Snickering under his breath, Christian continued toward her. "Freedom ... I guess it's all in how you look at it, right? After all, I did free them. They're not in the forest anymore."

"Shut up, you *bastard,* your path ends here."

Pulling out the crystal, Melinda lunged toward him. All of the mist creatures backed away from the shard's intense radiance. Covering his eyes, Christian slowly backed away. Melinda said, "I understand that everything dies, but you have no right to take that upon yourself. And you, even you can die. That is why I am here—to end this, to end you." Only a few feet from him now, Melinda drove him to his knees with the light. "I will avenge all that you have taken."

Raising the crystal above her head, she aimed at his heart with a malicious attack. But just as the crystal was about to meet its mark, he disappeared, reappearing behind her. Pivoting, she turned, striking at his face. Inches away, he ducked back, grabbing her wrist in the process. He tightened his grip then plucked the crystal from her hands with two fingers.

"Did you honestly believe that something so simple would destroy me?" Tossing the crystal over his shoulder into the sand, he tightened his grip, severely bruising her wrist. "The chosen one—this is some kind of sick joke."

Releasing her to her knees, tears ran down her face as defeat and pain sheared through her body. "The chosen one," Christian yelled out to the mist creatures, as he busted into laughter. They advanced, silently clapping as they shuffled along.

Not giving in, Melinda used her legs to scoot to the ledge of the statue. Christian advanced on her. "I will show you what I showed the Korithian." He pulled the mist creatures into himself, and his form began to change and distort. "I will show you all of my power."

A tornado violently ripped down from the cloud of darkness above, snaking its way through the sky toward them. The mist swirled around as the tornado hit Christian directly in the back, filling him with its energy. Fully engulfed within the swirling mist, Christian's delay was Melinda's moment. Using her good hand to push herself up, she moved to the far side of the statue. She watched as the darkness grew. From out of the cloud, two large, bony wings appeared, blocking out the sky as they spread. The creature's head and neck became substance, stretching out above her. As it peered down with massive red eyes, Melinda remembered exactly what she feared. Fully formed, the bony dragon towered over her, just as it had in her dream.

Letting out a deafening roar, the dragon tilted his head to the sky and called for several of the smaller demons to join him. All focused on Melinda as they awaited the order to attack.

With a swift, crushing snap of its jaws, the dragon destroyed the monument, exposing Melinda from her shelter.

Desperately seeking a way to buy some time, Melinda inched her way toward one of the buildings in the outer circle. Her pace quickened as the smaller demons dove from the sky. Her racing heart, fed by fear-based adrenalin, pounded as she scaled a small dune. Finding an opening in a half-standing building she quickly ducked inside.

Everything inside lay in shambles; even small portions of the ceiling were crushed and broken on the floor, revealing her location through the cracks above. Melinda watched as the demons swirled about above her, searching. Catching her breath, she cautiously passed through the decimated office, looking for a way out and away from this nightmare. She spotted a doorway at the top of a slight incline on the far side of the room.

A demon screeched above her, calling for others, as it spotted her through the cracks. It swooped down swiftly, clawing and reaching through the broken ceiling in an effort to grab her. Inching along the wall, she narrowly escaped its reach even as more descended. Reaching the door, Melinda twisted the knob and slammed her body against it. The door gave, dumping her into a small conference room. Another door waited on the other side of a large table surrounded by torn leather chairs. She sprinted for it just as the entire ceiling was ripped away by the sharp claws of the dragon. Melinda fell through the door at the same moment it wedged its head in the room, trying to eat her. Standing up, she heard the crumbling of stone from behind the doorway and was suddenly left blind in the dark. With her hands guiding her, she moved along the wall, seeking a way out. Thoughts of Gurod were her driving force.

An unseen smile crossed her face as she discovered another door. She opened it and felt her way around to make sure all was safe. Her good hand out in front; she stopped at a large pile of broken concrete in her path. The way was blocked.

As she turned back, a small piece of rubble caught her foot, sending her down concrete stairs. Bashing her left knee into the wall, she landed after a few steps. "Great, just what I needed, a new injury," she thought to herself. Defeat not being on her agenda, she moved on nonetheless, keeping only light pressure on her leg. After hobbling down several flights of stairs, she came to another dead end. Nothing but cold concrete walls stood before her.

She frantically searched about, feeling along every nook. Stone turned to steel beneath her fingertips as she stretched up toward the ceiling. Several small pipes ran along the wall's edge. Cold and wet with condensation, they led her through this tomb. She followed it with both arms stretched out and soon felt the walls closing in to a small hallway. At its end she was met by a solid, steel door. She struggled to open the heavy door, her anticipation growing.

Finally she forced it open a crack. Barely squeezing past, Melinda shimmied her way into the next room. The door closed behind her with a loud, echoing clank, sending shivers up her spine—for fear of being forever trapped in this grave. With her hands out ahead of her, she hunted in the darkness for anything that might give her a clue as to her location.

Dust showered her head as a rumble from above sent shock waves through the building. Another more powerful blast caused her to lose her balance, falling onto her good knee. Scooting along the cold ground, she bumped into a large, concrete pillar. She wrapped her arms around it for balance until the quaking stopped. She used the pillar to get back to her feet. Her injuries throbbed, reminding her of their presence as she shifted around the pillar. Leaving it behind, she dared to venture off into the unknown darkness.

Blind and sore, Melinda hobbled along until she found a small concrete ledge. She cautiously peeked over the side, ready for anything, but with hopes of some good news for once. Amazement, glee, and the purest hope came to her eyes as she saw several tiny threads of light coming in from way down below. Now with light coming in, she could make out what she realized was a parking garage. Never losing sight of the light, she hobbled as quickly as she could along the wall, doing her best to ignore the pain.

Reaching a corner, another staircase led her farther down. She hopped her way along, keeping a strong grip on the center rail. Another tremor shook through the building, forcing Melinda to tighten her hold on the railing. Echoing sounds of cracking concrete rippled throughout the building as it settled. Melinda continued to race toward the bottom. Limping down the last steps, she saw the source of her freedom: a four-lane tunnel that led to light.

More dust fell from above, followed by broken chunks of concrete. One after another, the building was bombarded by quakes. Feeling there was little time left, Melinda swiftly limped toward the exit. She noticed two other roads leading off of the tunnel in opposite directions, but her focus on the light stood strong as the tremors worsened. Crackles turned to louder sounds of the structure's collapsing, the noise and destruction gaining on her.

Fifteen feet from the exit, she stopped, covering her head as debris fell down around her. Everything went silent as the disruption settled. Melinda stood again, surrounded by a cloud of thick dust. Turning in circles, she lost her sense of direction. She covered her face with her shirt, waiting for the dust to settle. She looked back through the dissipating cloud to see the wall of wreckage several feet away. Roars from the dragon echoed in from outside, reminding Melinda of its presence. Snapping her head toward the exit, her fury for the beast intensified.

Finally outside, far from her pursuers, she faced the setting sun. Melinda closed her eyes to soak in what little light remained. With nothing except for determination in her mind, she opened them to see the lake only a short distance away. She abandoned her cover to cross the open wasteland. Now her racing heart slowed as she faced the final steps of her path.

Quietly she hobbled through the soft sand, keeping her mind calm in the hope that Christian wouldn't find her. From behind, another loud crash, followed by another roar, inundated her ears. Turning back, she saw the dragon clawing into the building's remains, digging through the pieces in a desperate search for any sign of her. Using the distraction to her advantage, Melinda moved with haste through the open desert. She held back the pain of her knee as she sank into the sand with every step.

Before long, a change appeared in the sandy floor beneath her feet. The gold over which she had once tracked now had become the purest white. Drawing near the lake's waters, she glanced back to see that her pursuers, off in the distance, were still ravaging through the wreckage. Her mind was eased by the sight of the still waters of Terisan Lake, and her battered body demanded a rest.

Investigating her surroundings revealed nothing beyond the lake and a never-ending, white-sand beach. Melinda strolled along the shoreline in hopes of finding anything that might lead her to Gurod. This place was a reminder of her dream, in which she'd first seen the demon's true form, remembering the three black rocks.

The sun shined its last light upon her as it disappeared into the horizon. Now with only a tiny shred of the moon's light to guide her, continued on rounding the lake. Her fear of the dragon faded as it became a distant speck on the horizon. Tired and frustrated, she stopped to clear her mind. Using the soft sand as a cushion, she sat facing the lake's flawless, smooth water. She stared at her own reflection, wiping away everything else around her. A comforting breeze drifted over her, filling her being with peace, driving out all of her pain and sorrow. Above, the swirling cloud opened, allowing the full moon to light up the sky.

A ripple formed over her reflection, waking her from her peaceful trance. As she blinked, the ripple vanished, leaving her dizzy and euphoric. Toppling over in the sand, she lay motionless, feeling absolutely nothing. Moments passed, but she knew she had to continue.

As she dug her hands into the sand to push herself up, three small, jagged objects poked into her right palm. Still in a state of confused bliss, she grabbed them, along with a handful of sand. The sand ran out from between her fingers, leaving only three tiny black stones in her palm. She became more lost than ever as she stood to face the water, urgently seeking an answer.

"This is it? This is what you give me? What the hell am I supposed to do with these?" Melinda yelled out over the water, feeling defeat once more. "I've come so far," she mumbled to herself as she sadly looked over the stones. "Please just do something, anything." Her pleading went unheard as the motionless water blankly stared back at her. "Damn you!" she shouted at the water, as she weakly pitched a stone to create a disturbance.

Upon impact, the stone sent out a splash as if it had been a hundred times its size. Confused, Melinda lightly threw another. Again it smashed into the water, sending out a powerful wave. Her mind grew keen as she bounced the last stone up and down in her palm. "That's it, that's it!" Melinda stepped back, throwing the final stone as hard and as far as she could. It soared through the air before plummeting into the water, launching a tidal wave that rippled the entire lake's surface.

Waiting in anticipation, Melinda watched as the entire lake exploded with a dance of massive bubbles. She witnessed an intense glow beginning to radiate into the night sky from beneath the water, matching the moon's light. Slowly a massive dark spot rose from the lake's center, blacking out the light. Staring in awe, Melinda froze as four golden spires penetrated the surface, gleaming in the luminosity of the temple as they ascended. Waves rushed out then back as a small dome appeared between the spires, growing as it climbed.

Thousands of year's worth of sea growth covered the golden palace, allowing only small glimmers of its once-glorious splendor to shine. Sending out a wave that washed over her legs, the palace finally stood at its fullest, covering most of the lake's surface. From beneath two large doors, a mass of thin, golden, rectangular plates unfolded to form a bridge that ended at her feet.

From behind Melinda heard the roar of the dragon, making her feel like a caught mouse. She looked back, her eyes widening in terror as the dragon advanced through the sky with excessive speed. Adrenalin pulsed through her body, giving her the strength to run for the doors. Gaining on her at a tremendous rate, the dragon swooped down to line up with her and the bridge. Halfway to her goal, Melinda glanced back; the beast's mouth was moments from striking. Thinking quickly, she hit the bridge, rolling to avoid its attack. Instantly coming to her feet, she lost little speed. The dragon circled around for another attempt.

Melinda focused on the doors. They opened inward for her as she quickly advanced toward them. Diving through the small crack, she narrowly escaped the dragon's snapping jaws for the second attempt to take her life. Swiftly she pushed the heavy doors shut as the dragon circled back over the shore.

The doors closed with a dull boom. Melinda fell back against them and slid to the floor, feeling relief at being safely inside. Fully spent, she fell in and out of awareness for a brief moment. Finally she gained a grip on her mind and shook free of her daze.

Melinda had trouble grasping the new reality that lay before her. Within this hellish world she now found herself in a long, golden hall lined with large, majestic statues of women. Her image reflected back off of the golden floor as she headed down the hall. Bowls of fire rested on pedestals between the statues, lighting her way through the vast hall. Each statue was of a unique figure, though the statues were only displayed in two different postures. Figures holding shields at their breasts with swords raised high into the air lined the right side of the hall. Figures groveling in fear and hopelessness lined the left.

At the end of the hall, a great light shined down from nowhere over a small, golden bed. A small, childlike figure lay silhouetted behind the enshrouding drapes. Pulling back the curtain, all of her feelings collided into themselves as the bed's occupant came into full view. She could not fathom how she now faced the child from the truck stop, the child with the evil mother. He lay motionless as she ran her fingertips across his face.

"How did *you* get here?" Melinda whispered. "Are you okay? Can you hear me?" Lightly shaking him gave no response. She quickly turned around when a loud crash vibrated from off the doors. "You have to wake up now; he's here."

Pushing in, then closing again, the doors rumbled as the dragon worked to break them down. Rage filled Melinda's being once more as she stormed toward one of the statues. Ignoring the pain in her wrist Melinda climbed up the monument, pulling down a sword and shield, to ready her for war. Nothing would stop her from destroying the darkness.

She stormed toward the doors just as they blasted open. Its head barely fitting inside, the beast let out a hellish roar. Melinda stood unmoved by it. Filling the hall with its vile breath, the dragon snuffed the burning fires. With a heavy snort it pulled its head free and then leapt back into the sky. With only the light emanating from the child's bed to guide her, Melinda walked slowly toward the doors, watching as it flew off. Circling back in the sky, it rocketed straight along the bridge at full force. It pushed with its wings, sending it on a crash course for the entrance. Melinda held her ground halfway between the door and the child.

Slamming into the opening, the dragon took on its human form once more. Christian flipped through the air in a trail of mist, latching onto a shielded statue. Removing a sword, he jumped down, striking at his enemy's shield. The blow sent Melinda tumbling to the floor.

"You really are naïve," he stated with a deep growl. "You led me right to him."

Drawing back his sword, he struck again. Melinda blocked the blow with her sword, but she lost hold and her weapon was knocked away. "Do you think you can win?" Christian's evil eyes focused on hers deeply as he began to laugh. "I will kill him. Do you hear me? I will kill you!" Christian shouted toward the bed.

"You will not," Melinda coldly stated, pushing him back with her shield. Standing up, she held her defense as she glanced around for her blade. "I'm not going to let that happen."

Upon an instant, Christian stood right before her. "You don't have a choice." Slamming the butt of his sword into her forehead, he smirked with wild eyes. Her scalp tore, and the blood flowed down her face. "I've wanted to do this since the day we met."

Melinda stumbled back, falling to the floor as blood filled her eyes. The shield hit the floor and rolled away from her. Her fingers brushed against her fallen sword as she struggled to grab it, inches away.

"Do it, pick it up." Christian watched as she fumbled like a drunk to do so. "Come on, you can do it. Pick it up!" Failing with several attempts, she finally grasped it and rose to her feet. Her knees trembled as they tried to maintain her balance. Christian grinned. "This is where you die."

In an instant, he dashed directly for her with his sword high in the air. With both hands, Melinda gripped her sword tightly out in front of her as she dropped to her knees. In his bull rush attack, Christian failed to notice as her sword pierced through his chest and ripped from his back. Letting out a deep groan, he accompanied her on the floor, huffing in deep pain as he gripped her trembling hands.

Melinda let go of the sword, leaving him there motionless. Using his shoulders for balance, she slowly stood, stumbling as she straightened her head. A pain-filled sense of victory came over her as she stumbled toward the child.

But not five paces away, Melinda felt an unexpected grip on her shoulder. With one quick pull she was turned to see Christian standing before her, the sword still sticking out from his chest.

"We're not finished here," he said, seething. He delivered a swift kick to her ribs, sending her flying back down to the floor. Loud, vicious laughter filled the hall as he pulled the sword from himself. "You are pathetic and weak. Here is another dark truth for you. I win this time."

Heading straight for the bed with Melinda's bloodied sword in his hand, Christian's intention was perfectly clear. His eyes grew with delight as he drew closer to the bed. The bloodied blade cut through the air to strike. Melinda, seemingly appearing out of nowhere, blocked his attack with her shield, sending Christian bouncing back. He stood in disbelief as she stared him down with pure hatred. She hid her face behind the shield, though keeping her gaze locked upon him, ready for the next attempt. Letting out a scream, he lunged at her with a thrust. Again she knocked his attempt away. The force of his attack pushed her to the floor as his sword flew out of his hand. Melinda again stood up before her foe, tired and beaten. Filled with rage, he charged her, grabbing her by the throat.

"That is quite enough," a soft child's voice called out from the bed. "Let her go!"

With this demand, Christian released his grip. "She has proven herself well," the boy said. Sitting up, the child faced them both. Christian stood over Melinda as she lay there, bloody and weak. Dropping out of the bed onto bare feet with a light thump, the child slowly walked over to them. "I knew you would find me, Melinda. Your time here is almost over. I will alleviate your pain for that time here."

Melinda's arm began to glow in radiant blue as the child touched it. Instantly her pain faded, freeing her of debilitation.

"Rise, child." Melinda slowly stood, glancing between the child and Christian behind him. "Allow me to explain everything."

Taking her by the hand, the boy walked with her along the hall toward the doors. Christian followed quietly behind them. Reigniting as they passed, the bowls burst with fire once more. "Many have come before you," the boy commented, pointing to the statues. "Some held the strength to make it here, while others fell to selfishness and fear. Do you understand?" Seeing the confusion drift in Melinda's eyes, he continued. "I chose you as

I chose them, within the decency of a sincere heart. Each of the strong faced their own trial, though theirs weren't far from your own. Through all of their struggles and pain, some forgot and didn't believe, taking everything they'd learned for granted. They became left behind, but their remains here stand victorious."

"So all of this was a game? You're not, and he's—?" With all of the boy's words, Melinda confusion over the situation grew.

"No," the child replied with a smile. "You saved me. You saved me from the darkest evil in existence ... myself."

Christian walked up beside the child. Turning into mist, he engulfed the child. With one deep breath, the boy blew the smoke away. "If you can do that, to the point of your own life, then you can do anything. You have a great strength within you, within your heart, and that is what *mother* means." With those words he placed his hand upon her stomach.

The doors to Gurod opened to the outside, which radiated with a great, white light. Shining brighter than the sun itself, it engulfed them completely. "Don't forget me." With his final spoken words, the light became darkness. "It's time for you to go home."

Pain washed over Melinda within the darkness as sounds of shattering glass faintly echoed inside her mind. Feeling a firm grip around her body, she floated along, surrounded by muffled voices. Drifting in and out, her eyes fluttered about as she focused on the paramedics lifting her into an ambulance. Before the doors closed, she saw the twisted wreckage of her car as it lay mangled against the tree. Beginning their drive, they readied her with an IV. Everything in her mind went black, leaving only the sounds of sirens. She realized she had come home.

Awakening to dead silence, Melinda felt a chill from the dark hospital room. Noticing she was wearing a gown instead of clothes, a smile slowly formed across her face. Pain from the tight wrap around her chest shot through her body as she attempted movement. In one arm was an IV; the other was in a cast from the elbow down.

Fighting off the pain, she struggled to get up, but the pain quickly took over. She dropped back into the bed. Searching around with her good arm, she hit the call button. Just as her thumb released the tiny red button, a small, brunette nurse rushed in.

"Oh good, you're finally fully awake." A grin covered the nurse's tiny face. "You've been in and out for a few hours now. How are you feeling?"

"Okay, I guess. What time is it?" Melinda asked, feeling the stitching in her scalp as she tried to run her hand through her hair.

"It's 3:15 in the morning, dear. It's lucky they found you when they did, or you might not be here," the nurse explained, watching as Melinda moved her fingers along the stitching.

"What happened?" Melinda's concern grew as she felt the bald skin around the wound. Finding the stitches' end at the top of her head, she began to weep.

"It's all right, honey," the nurse said sympathetically, as she rushed to her side. "It should grow back. Look, you were in a terrible accident and are lucky to be alive. When they got there they had to cut you out. But you're alive, so don't let a temporary hair loss get you down. Is there anything I can get for you?"

"Yeah," Melinda smiled from beneath her tears. "I need help getting to the bathroom."

"Sure thing, come on." Moving her IV, the nurse aided her as she struggled in pain. "Just a little farther now, do you need me to help you in there?"

"No," Melinda groaned in pain, "I'll be all right, thank you." Exhaling her words, Melinda pulled her IV in and closed the door.

"I'll wait for you, so take your time." The nurse waited patiently just outside the door. After a few minutes Melinda emerged, needing the nurse to help return her to her bed. "Feeling better?" she asked, taking the patient by the hand. "Any dizziness?"

"No dizziness, but my ribs are killing me," Melinda stated, slowly lying back down and flinching as the pain darted through her.

"I'll bring you something for that." Stepping out for a short moment, the nurse quickly returned holding a small paper cup. "Take these. They'll help with the pain." The nurse handed Melinda the cup and poured her a cup of water.

"Thanks again." Melinda tipped the pills into her mouth and washed them down with the cool, soothing water.

"It's okay. Now try to get some rest. The doctor will be in to see you in the morning." The nurse walked to the door but turned back to Melinda. "If there's anything else you need, just hit the buzzer."

With a smile, she closed the door, leaving Melinda in the dull light from the lamp above her bed. Staring at the ceiling, her eyes faded out everything around her. Slowly her pain subsided, allowing her to fully rest. Her quiet mind slept in peace, giving her a well-deserved and overdue break.

Sleeping through early morning, Melinda woke to the sun peering in from behind the faded yellow blinds that covered the windows. With the medication wearing off, the dull pain of her wounds returned as she tried to sit up. Even with all of the pain, Melinda felt relief in knowing she was far from that wonderland. Giving in to the pain, she lay back down, drifting off into memories of what she'd been through.

Her thoughts were quickly broken by the click of the room's door. Opening to its fullest, a medium-sized, elderly man wobbled in, reading her chart.

"Ah, Melinda, you're awake, that's good. I'm Doctor Daniels. And how are we feeling today?" he asked in a calm, soothing voice.

"Fine, other than the pain." Holding her ribs, Melinda tried to sit up. "Can I get something?"

"Sure, I'll get the nurse to bring you some medication when I'm finished, okay? Now, it says here you were in a car accident, suffering from a fractured wrist, two bruised ribs, a hundred stitches on your scalp, and a minor concussion," he explained, pulling a small light from his shirt. "Open your eyes really wide ... thanks. Have you felt any dizziness?"

"No, my head feels fine. It's my ribs that hurt," Melinda replied.

"You're lucky to be alive," Doctor Daniels stated, looking over her scalp. "And don't you worry; this should heal nicely."

"Thanks." She let loose some laughter, though it caused pain to rush through her body.

"Do you remember anything from the crash?" the doctor asked, writing down his assessments.

"It was raining, and I was on my way home from work. Something happened, causing me to lose control. I was headed for the grass, and that's all I can remember," she answered, holding back her story of the palace and the child.

Leaning in closer the doctor whispered softly, "There's a policeman here who wants to ask you a few questions about the accident. It's alright, you're not in trouble or anything." After he finished clueing her in, the friendly doctor continued his speech. "Well, don't you worry about a thing; you'll be up and out of here before lunch." Moving back toward the door with a smile, the doctor placed her chart under his arm. "Oh, we have also contacted your family, so they know you're okay. You might want to call them yourself."

"Thanks again," Melinda remarked, as he walked from the room. Her nerves began to rise, not in fear of talking to the police but in fear of her family knowing.

Only seconds passed before a nurse appeared carrying a paper cup. "Here you go, sweetie." Setting the cup next to her, the nurse gave Melinda a big smile. "The doctor says you're healing nicely, so if there's anything you need, just hit the call button. Breakfast will be brought up for you in a minute." Picking up the paper cup, Melinda took her medication. Lying back, the pain stricken girl eagerly anticipated its effects.

The nurse walked out, giving passage to the policeman that was patiently waiting in the hall. Closing the door behind him, the officer pulled over a small chair for visitors and calmly sat beside her bed. He smiled as he took off his hat, hoping it would lighten the mood for the injured girl.

"Hello, Melinda," his calm, soft spoken voice came as a soothing deep vibration. "I'm officer Garth Turner." Melinda just stared blankly, not knowing what to expect. "Now, I'm not here to arrest you or anything like that so you can be calm and relax, I just want to ask you a few questions, that's all."

Melinda felt at ease by his smile, "What would you like to know?" she timidly asked.

"Was there another car involved with your accident, did anyone hit you or you hit them?" With a small notepad and a pen ready, he was prepared to take her statement.

"No, I didn't see another car, other then the two that passed me. I don't remember anybody hitting me, just spinning out of control and when I woke up I was in the …" pausing for a moment Melinda realized what she was about to say. "Car, the paramedics, or someone, cut me out. Why?"

Thinking about her story, even though he saw her hesitation, Garth could see the truth in her eyes. "There was another car about a hundred feet or so from yours. It was completely smashed, there's no way in telling what happened," he explained. "There was an emblem left on the ground next to the wreckage, it was a BMW. It had an out-of-state plate too; at least that's what it looked like. If there is anything you know it would help us greatly." The officer waited, in hope that she could tell him something.

"I'm sorry," she stated, thinking back to the car the child had been in. Could it have been them? Putting her questions aside she continued. "I wish I knew, everything is just a blur, the way it happened, I don't know."

Feeling defeat but not giving up, Garth handed her one of his cards. "If you do remember something, don't hesitate to give me call. Thank you for your time, Melinda." Standing with a smile he placed the chair back over by the window and headed for the door. "I hope you feel better soon."

"Thanks," she smiled, showing her appreciation. With the questions done, Garth left Melinda to rest.

Time passed slowly as she began to feel the release from her pain. A short time later, breakfast was delivered: stale, dry eggs, apple sauce, orange juice, coffee, and gelatin. Nibbling at the cornucopia of food, Melinda watched the door, hoping that her mother would come. She only ate small portions of everything, leaving the rest to be taken away with her tray after a while.

Being left alone with her thoughts, Melinda stared at the phone. A debate broke out within her mind, should she call or avoid it for as long as she could? Her mind began to wander back to the dream world she narrowly escaped from. The insanity—was it all just a dream? The presence of Christian washed over her mind as she visualized his very touch, feeling his lips pressed to hers.

Her fanciful vision abruptly ended at the sound of her door opening. To her disappointment, only the doctor walked in.

"Well, good news, Melinda! We are able to let you go home. Here are a few things. First, a prescription for an antibiotic; we don't want you to develop an infection or anything," with a smile he handed her the slip, "and here's one for a high-milligram ibuprofen for the pain. I want you to come back and see me in five weeks; until then, try to stay off your feet and relax, alright?"

"I'll try," Melinda replied, with a half-smile, thinking about what she was in for at home.

Smiling back, the doctor continued. "If you feel any dizziness or nausea, I want you to come straight here, alright; accidents like these can sometimes have delayed effects." Reaching over he re-inspected his handy work on her head. "And the stitches in your head will dissolve, so they'll just go away on their own. "Well," he sighed in relief, "I'll see you in five weeks, until then try to get plenty of rest."

"Thanks, doc," she responded with a smile, relieved by his reactions. "I'll come back if I need to."

With his explanation completed, the doctor headed out just as a nurse brought in a wheelchair with some scrubs resting on the seat. Taking out Melinda's IV, the nurse helped her into the scrubs. They quickly headed down the hall straight for the elevators.

Melinda's mother waited outside the hospital, frantically smoking as she sat inside of a beat-up 1985 Buick Regal. Its faded blue paint was dotted with patches of rust. As the nurse walked Melinda out to the curb, her mother jumped out of the car to help her inside.

"Oh my God, you're a mess!" Melinda's mother exclaimed as she opened the passenger door to the car. "By lookin' at you I know that the car can't be pretty. Your father is gonna be livin' when we get home."

Melinda struggled under her mother's arm, trying to avoid the smoke. "Livid, Mom, not livin'," she cracked back, struggling to get into the car.

"Don't be a smart ass." Slamming the door, her mother quickly scurried over to the driver's seat. "How many prescriptions you got?"

"Just two, but I only need to get the one so it'll be cheaper for you," Melinda mumbled. "Mom, I—" Stopping herself from apologizing, Melinda kept quiet as her mother proceeded to continually chastise her.

Arriving in their driveway, Melinda's heart sank, fearing what waited inside. Dropping her off, her mother went out to get the prescriptions filled. Melinda stumbled up the weed-covered walkway to the front door. She opened it to reveal the same cluttered house. Melinda began to wish she wasn't there. Blaring video game noises came from behind her brothers' door, traveling throughout the house. Moving past the mess of empty beer bottles and leftover food, she went straight for her room.

Pounding on the door with her good hand, Melinda stopped at her brothers' door. "Can you guys keep it down?" she shouted over the game noise. She continued down the hall. After a few steps, the game went quiet as the door opened.

"What happened? Mom said you wrecked your damn car," said Brian, her twelve-year-old brother, as he ran up to her.

"Yeah, what the hell's wrong with you?" added Tim, the ten-year-old brother, as he poked out from around the door.

"First of all, you two watch your mouths. And secondly, shouldn't you be in school?" Melinda turned to face them showing them her marks.

"You look like shit, sis. It's one of those teachers' meeting days," Brian remarked with a smirk. "Now how are you going to impress the boys?"

"Are you all right?" Tim asked, more concerned than his brother. He dashed from behind the door to Melinda's side. "Look at your face. And what happened to your arm?"

"Thanks, Tim. Glad at least someone cares about me. My wrist is broken, and I bruised some of my ribs. I'm just going to go lie down until Mom gets home with my pills. How's Dad about this?" Concern and dread filled her voice, fearing the worst.

"Dad's at work; he won't find out till he gets home later," Tim replied, comforting her.

"You're lucky it's Thursday," Brian added with a smirk.

"Well, I'm going to go lie down. Just do me a favor and keep the games down. And Tim, could you bring me the phone? I need to call the school about my tests."

Tim agreed and left Melinda to her room. As she opened her door, disappointment set in. All was as she remembered it—from the pile of clothes on her floor to the scattered schoolwork on her desk.

"Here, sis." Tim popped up from behind with the phone.

"Thanks. Can you shut my door on your way out, please?" Melinda politely asked, with a plea for sympathy in her eyes.

Closing her door, Tim went back to his room. No sooner had the door closed than she could hear the faint sounds of their game.

Once Melinda had covered herself regarding school and her job, she could rest with ease—at least until her father came home. She drifted off into her thoughts as the faint sound of game music danced within her ears, slowly silencing everything else around her. Within a vision, she returned to that place, her concept dream. It was a short-lived reality that now had her debating her own. She thought to herself: the child from the restaurant—was it his parent's car they had found at the other accident scene? Was he dead? Her brain throbbed as she tried to piece it all together, determining what was real.

Melinda heard her mother return with her prescription. Even with the medication from the hospital wearing off, Melinda felt very little discomfort. Not being able to face her mother, she rolled over, turning to face the wall as her doorknob shifted. With a deep huff, her mother, less than sympathetic, entered.

"Here you go. I had to get the generic 'cause they was cheaper. What do you plan on tellin' your father?" she asked harshly.

"I don't know, maybe by saying I was in an accident," Melinda quietly replied, as anger began to build up.

"I just know he's gonna be pissed. We can't afford no hospital bills," her mother snapped back, the same way she had always done.

"I'm still covered on his insurance, so it'll be fine. When I go back to work I'll pay for it," Melinda replied in her soft but direct manner, holding back her anger.

"Well, he'll be happy to hear that, but your car—shit, it's already 2:15," she stated, looking at Melinda's alarm clock. "I'm missin' Jerry."

Walking straight out of Melinda's room, her mother darted straight to the television in the living room. Turning it up to drown out the game noises, she sat back with a smile, oblivious to the world around her. Forced to listen, Melinda closed her door in hopes of finding a tiny shred of peace. Drifting off within the minor throb of her wounds, she separated herself away from the noise and fell into a dream.

Fast asleep, Melinda appeared moving through a crowded carnival on the beach. Everyone she had ever known walked about, smiling and speaking in words she could not understand. She frantically pushed her way through the mass of people as though searching for an unknown object. In a less crowded space, she noticed that she was the only one not enjoying the moment.

But the pressure rose as she continued to search as though time itself depended on it. Pushing her way past the people, she arrived at a large cement pier. Fire danced about in the sky, flickering out from an overturned luxury liner's smashed hull. To her amazement, no one around her seemed to care, as if they couldn't see what was happening.

Moving toward the wreck, Melinda was instantly inside. Fire rained from above as bits of the floor, now the ceiling, fell down around her. The boat had little time left afloat. Moving down the hall, she came upon a pool of water in the center of a dual stairwell. There, in the pool surrounded by burn debris sat someone on their hands and knees crying like a child. Panic set in as more fire rained down around her. With tears in her eyes, she took to the ankle deep water to see if she could help. As the figure turned to face her, there were no features to be seen—nothing except a blur. A sense of knowing washed over Melinda, telling her she knew this person. As he began to speak, nothing clear rolled off his tongue. Both became completely surrounded in fire as the floor/ceiling above gave out.

Sitting up with a start back in her room, sweat poured down Melinda's face as she gasped for breath. She calmed her nerves with slow, rhythmic breaths. Reading 9:45 on her clock, Melinda couldn't believe she'd slept that long. Feeling some hunger pangs, she ventured out of her room. She heard the same game noises going on as she passed by her brothers' room.

Melinda wished she were back in the forest of Korithia; at least it was peaceful there. Her mother, out cold on the couch, lay next to the same mess that had been there for years. With a deep snore, she rolled over as Melinda passed into the kitchen.

Opening the refrigerator, she searched around for any scraps she might find. Digging under her father's beer, she discovered two-day-old pizza still in the box. She closed the door and almost dropped her pizza as she saw that her drunken father stood on the other side.

"You're here, but where's the fuckin' car? Hmm?" he asked, slurring his words, as he held himself up with the wall.

"I was …" Melinda hesitated as she felt the hatred for what she'd returned home to.

"You was what, you dumb ass? Stupid-ass female." His voice grew louder, as did his anger. "You all goin' to school 'cause you're so damn smart, but you sure ain't smart enough to keep your damn car on the road." Melinda closed her eyes as she listened to the same repeated messages she had always had to endure. "That's right, I heard all about it from Paul. He said they towed it away early this morning, and there ain't no fixin' it. Do you think we can afford to get you a new one? And look at ya. There's gotta be twenty-two thousand in hospital bills standin' there. I can't afford all that, and it's all because—"

With those words, something inside Melinda snapped. "I'm a girl, right, a dumb ass, worthless girl that can't do shit!" Her eyes gained back the glare they had held for Christian. Moving toward him, she backed him into a corner. "That's all I've heard from you my whole life! I don't know what did this to you, but these bullshit days of you treating me like shit are over. You're nothing more than a pitiful, tired old man who'd rather live in a drunken haze than look at his own life. Well, look at it, Dad. It's nothing more than these empty bottles that you and Mother leave throughout the house. It's hollow and broken." Using her good arm, she whipped an empty beer bottle against the wall. It shattered, its remnants dripping down the faded blue paint.

Her father trembled as Melinda left him cowering in the corner of the kitchen. Her mother pretended to still be asleep, silent and listening, as Melinda calmly walked back to her room. Deep within, Melinda felt the awe of her emotional release, and all of her rage became replaced by joy.

Closing her bedroom door, she separated herself from the world she had always just accepted before now. Turning her light off, she allowed complete darkness to engulf her. As she sat on the edge of her bed, a smile crossed her face. She lay back in pure satisfaction with what she had done.

Staring into the darkness, Melinda was amazed at how fast her pain had faded. Now with her mind free of her father's wrath, she opened her mind back up to her dreams. Deeply comparing what she had just dreamed and the experiences she had had, she debated back and forth with her own concept of possibilities within the so called bounds of reality. Was it all just a metaphoric dream, a form of symbolism that had now taken over her being? This newly found strength, was it driven by the same force that drove her through the fallen city?

Nothing came that led her any further than she had been when she was in that other world. An exhaustion set in that pulled her back into slumber.

Morning came, and Melinda awoke to a silent house. With her father at work and her brothers in school, she was left to face only her mother. Putting it off for the moment, she went straight to the bathroom. Not yet seeing how she now looked with her injuries, she anticipated how bad they had left her. Never really having believed in her beauty in the first place, now Melinda just smiled at the caked-on blood around her eyes and the stitching going up her head. Pulling off the wrap from around her body, she uncovered the bruise on her left side. She pushed on it with the tip of her fingers from beneath her wrist cast, but she felt nothing. Even her knee hadn't bothered her since she'd left the hospital.

Keeping her right arm out of the water, Melinda carefully showered, washing away what felt like days' worth of sweat, dirt, and blood. Finally clean and back in her clothes, an overwhelming feeling rushed over her, as though she owned the world. Fear being far from her mind, she walked out into the living room. Her mother sat there, puffing away on a cigarette as she watched a game show.

"Mom, I need the car," Melinda sternly stated, looking directly in her mother's eyes.

"Okay," the woman nervously replied as she looked up at Melinda then quickly turned away. "Just be back by four or so. I have to pick up your father."

"Fine." Melinda snatched the keys off the hook in the kitchen.

Firing up the car, Melinda sped off for the college to see if she could take her tests. Everyone on campus just stared as she walked past. She had forgotten the way she looked since the accident. Once inside the administrative offices, she requested to take her finals. They provided her with a private room and the best of luck. She breezed through the tests with a newfound intelligence that came as natural to her as breathing. With little time passed, she headed back out on the road.

Growing bored with the sights around her, Melinda began to zone out. A horn blast from behind snapped her back into reality as the stoplight turned green. Giving the Buick some gas, she headed for the local mall's parking lot. With the kids in school, finding a space wasn't a problem.

Everything around her seemed different now—stale and dull. Bored and feeling out of place, she itched to leave. But her mind halted at the sight of the corner jewelry store on her way back to her car. She went in.

Confusion set in as visions flashed over her eyes. In an instant, she once more stood in the decimated, darkness-filled city, looking at the same vacant counters she'd seen there.

"Can I help you?" A female attendant politely asked, calling her back to reality.

"No, sorry." Walking off in a hurry, Melinda felt like a freak as she dashed through the mall to the book store.

Quietly, she weaved through the maze of shelves, heading straight for the New Age section. Melinda grabbed any titles that looked as though they might hold an answer to her dreams. Coming up with several books on dreams and out of body experiences, her desire to learn forced her to buy them all. She headed straight home and was back by 1:30. Her mother still sat on the couch, puffing away, as she watched Melinda carry in the bag of books with her arm cast.

"You all right?" her mother asked, stopping her as she walked down the hall to her room.

"Actually, Mom, I feel better now than I have ever felt in my life. I went to the school and took my finals, and I don't have to go back to work until my cast comes off, so I picked up some books," Melinda stated, lifting the bag. "I'm going to get in some reading since I've got nothing else to do." With a smirk on her face, she walked off to her room, leaving her mother speechless.

Dumping the bag out onto, her bed Melinda shuffled through the books, trying to decide where to start. Unsure, she ripped into her backpack looking for a notebook. Tearing out the used portions, she began to write down everything she had experienced. Writing on only the back sides, she left the opposite pages open for later notes.

Researching the weeks away kept Melinda's mind busy as she stayed locked in her room. Only stepping out to use the bathroom and occasionally to visit the kitchen to dig for food, no one spoke a word to her—not even her younger brother, Tim. Mumbling under her breath as she walked about the house, she dove from one theory to the next.

Four weeks passed, but she'd gained nothing more than a newfound sense of madness and a growing itch under her cast. She tried and tried to scratch, and she tore through her notes again and again, making sure everything lined up. All at once it came tumbling down around her, the itch and her unsettled mental state driving her over the edge. With no one home except for her mother, Melinda stormed off to the garage.

Everything in the garage was completely covered in a thick layer of dust. With the inside being undisturbed for the last seven years, many spiders had made their homes there. Melinda turned on the light, though it barely shined through the dust-covered bulb. Covering her mouth with her shirt, she dug around for anything that might help her remove her cast. Her father, never being a fixer-upper person, had very little use for tools. Coming across a hacksaw sent a large smile across her face.

Calmly and carefully, she slowly cut into the cast. Placing the blade between her middle and ring fingers, Melinda knew of the consequences of cutting too deep. Keeping safe, she only penetrated halfway in. Her mind raced, trying to think of a way to break through the rest.

Inside a small toolbox, she found a flat-head screwdriver. It became the perfect wedge for prying at the weakened cast. Puncturing through it, she accidentally pushed the corner of the screwdriver into her wrist. Ignoring the pain, she continued to whittle away until she finally broke free. Finally with a chance to scratch, she satisfied her urge with a smile. She walked back into the house, seeing, to her amazement, that the puncture wound from the screwdriver had just disappeared.

Back inside the house, Melinda washed her arm, washing away the built-up sweat, dirt, and the newly released stench in order to clear away the itch. With a pure sense of accomplishment, she sought to carry on her research.

Two more days swiftly passed, and her mind was still plagued by the dream about the carnival and the sinking ship as it reoccurred in her slumber. Sitting up in her bed in the morning, she felt puzzled and extremely nauseous. She made a mad dash for the bathroom and started her day by throwing up. Afterward, a dizzy sensation came over her, dropping her to her butt. Taking slow, deep breaths, her equilibrium steadied. The few steps back toward her room brought the dizziness back. Slowly she lay down in the doorway then crawled her way into her bed. As the wooziness wore away, she drifted off to sleep, catching a few more hours of rest.

When she woke, the dizziness had gone, along with her sickness. In a small state of panic, she remembered her doctor's words about experiencing these symptoms. Calling the hospital, she talked to a nurse explaining the situation. With her doctor already at the hospital, the nurse advised she be driven in.

Not wanting her mother involved, Melinda got dressed and rushed out to the kitchen. Feeling as though she couldn't rely on anyone for help, she snatched up the keys and sped off straight for the hospital   all the while hoping the dizziness wouldn't return while she drove.

The emergency room was quiet that afternoon, with only a few people waiting to be seen. Melinda explained her situation about the car accident to the nurse. Overhearing everything, another nurse opened the door from the back, pushing in a wheelchair. Quickly moving Melinda into the back, the second nurse took her to a small, private room. She told Melinda to lie back on the paper-covered table. Melinda did so and stared up at the ceiling, contemplating all of the possibilities that could be causing this. Only moments passed before Doctor Daniels entered her room, holding her records.

"Ah, Melinda, you weren't supposed to come back in for another week. How are we feeling?" Before she could reply, he glanced up from the chart. "You took your cast off?" Rushing over to her exposed wrist, he examined her arm.

"Well," she nervously replied, "I used a hacksaw for most of it, but I had to use a screwdriver to get the rest. The crazy itch was driving me nuts." She smiled faintly, giving a giggle.

"Does it still hurt?" he asked, flexing her wrist gently back and forth.

"No, and I didn't even need the prescription pain medication after the first day," she proudly explained. "My ribs even stopped hurting."

"Then what brings you in?" Sitting down, he awaited her answer.

"When I got up this morning, I got really dizzy as I stepped out of bed. I even got sick. I don't know if I felt sick before, or if I became sick from the dizziness. I just got nervous with my head injury and all, so I came in." Concern filled her voice. She waited, hoping for a simple answer.

"Well, if it wasn't something you ate, then maybe you have an infection. Or maybe ..." Examining her scalp, he went over the faded stitches. "Perhaps there is something that we didn't see in the X-rays. Either way, I'd like to take some blood and run a few tests. It will only take a few hours to get some results, so if you want to wait out there, we'll let you know shortly." His calm voice soothed Melinda's fearful mind. "I'll have a nurse come in and get what we need, and I will see you in a little while."

For the first time in her life Melinda felt anxious to see a needle. Drawing two vials of blood, the nurse explained how many different types of tests there were. Concentrating on the few possibilities within her mind, Melinda discarded the rest. The blood taken, the nurse dismissed Melinda to the waiting room.

Seeing the sun shining brightly outside, Melinda stepped out to enjoy the warm rays. Across the road, she spotted a small patch of long, cushy grass. She thought it would make the perfect spot for her to relax for a while. Its soft touch was so inviting that she lay back and started imagining shapes in the clouds, like a child. One cloud drifted by, blocking out the sun. Shadowing over her, its structure slowly changed, forming the head of the dragon. Melinda's wide eyes focused on it as it grew and then broke apart. Within the comfort of the grass, she drifts off into a peaceful sleep.

Waking within the grass her heart raced in hope and fear that she had returned to the other world. As she sat up to see she was outside of the hospital, her mind returned to the task at hand. Not knowing how long she'd been out for, Melinda headed back inside to see if anything had been discovered.

The nurse smiled as Melinda stepped through the automatic doors. "Just who I was looking for," she said, and she escorted Melinda back to the same room as before, where she was left to wait. Melinda's mind burned with anticipation that made every passing minute feel like hours. Finally, to her relief, the doctor entered.

"Well, I think we might have found the cause of the problem," he explained with a partial smile. "It seems that you're pregnant, Ms. Rowley. Congratulations."

"What, no that's not possible, there has to be *something* else!" Melinda demanded, knowing it had been months since she had been with her ex-boyfriend.

"No, that's all that we found. Blood tests are usually accurate for these things. If it's unexpected, I can understand," he intoned in a comforting voice, sitting down beside her. "But I think once you start noticing it, you'll grow to be okay with it." Suddenly the doctor's beeper rang out, interrupting the conversation. Looking at the message, he quickly started to head out of the room. "Just relax and let time take its course," he advised as he ran off, leaving Melinda to see herself out.

Angry with the outcome, Melinda stormed out of the hospital. Squealing her tires, she sped down the street in a cloud of smoke, all the way home contemplating how this could be possible. She jammed on the brakes as she pulled into the driveway, stirring up a cloud of gravel dust. A swift gust of wind slammed the front door shut behind her as she entered, startling her mother.

"Where have you been?" her mother demanded.

"I had to go to the hospital, Mom," Melinda explained. "You know my car accident? I felt dizzy this morning, so I went to see if they could figure it out."

"And?" Curiosity grabbed a hold of the older woman, pulling her to the edge of the couch.

"And nothing, it came back that I'm pregnant," Melinda stated with a roll of her eyes and shaking her head. "Which is—"

"I knew this was gonna happen! How many times did I tell you to stay away from that there Kyle Hammond kid? No good drug dealin' piece of shit." Furious with the news, Melinda's mother began to cry. "I wanted better for you, ya know, for you to have a chance. Why did ya have to get pregnant by him?"

"Mom," Melinda yelled out in anger, "I'm trying to tell you there is no way that it can be possible! I haven't seen Kyle in three months, let alone slept with him. They're wrong, the test is wrong. I can't be pregnant, so don't go telling Dad anything!" Angry that her mother would accuse her of being with her creep of an ex, Melinda stormed off and locked herself in her room.

That night Melinda kept to herself, denying her problem. More than anything else, she was trapped within the conundrum of her reality. What was real? She questioned everything, even in this world; nothing made any sense. One thing she did know is that it was time for her to return to work. Calling her boss she let him know her state. With the restaurant being in desperate need of help, he scheduled her for the next night. With that out of the way, she could finally relax.

She stepped out to the bathroom. Checking on her hair growth in the mirror she was amazed the hair had already started to return. Dumbfounded and lost, she just added to the riddle of her reality with more concepts. Is this world real? What makes it any more real within the limitless accounts of impossibilities, like her pregnancy, and how fast she had healed? More dizziness came as her mind raced through the spiral of her thoughts.

She drew a warm bath, hoping it would help block out her thoughts as she floated peacefully in the dark. Seeking silence for her mind, she pushed out the echoing noise of her brothers' television and dropped into a deep meditation.

Her external form appeared before her as a spark of energy, radiating with bluish-white light, fully consuming her body. She floated alone within the cosmos of the spectral stream. Her luminosity drowned out the darkness around her. Within, she felt a true form of peace, becoming one with all that existed. As her energy expanded, she felt another spark coming from inside her. Twisting and bending around themselves, the sparks formed another life. The sensation of her heartbeat rising caused her to pull back from her blissful state.

Sitting up in her bath, she slowly came down from blissful ecstasy, her mind quiet and calm. She pulled the plug out and felt her weight return as the water gradually swirled down the drain. She rinsed herself off in a cool shower while she thought over the images she'd seen. Wrapped in a towel, she headed back to her room to add her experience to her map of reality. After all was scribed, she closed the binder to allow this night to end in peace.

Her mind being clear brought her sleep without interruption or vision. Waking the next morning with a stretch, Melinda planted her feet on the floor with a sense of defeat. In the hall she began to experience the effects of cabin fever. Thankfully, in her mind, today she had to return to work. At least that might help relieve her with a harsh dose of reality. Seeking to get out of the house sooner, she decided to visit the one spot that brought her comfort. With a snatch of the keys and tossing her uniform in the back seat, she drove off.

While picking up some fast-food breakfast on the way, her mind longed for the quiet seclusion of the local forest preserve. Melinda pounded down the fake food as she passed through town. She slowly pulled into the preserve lot and parked the car to continue on foot along the gravel path that led into the woods. She tried to push out her thoughts. Lush with green and purple wildflowers, the forest offered her an uplifting sensation.

Still finding its grace to be impressive, her thoughts were drawn back into the forest of the Korithian. Gavin, Tara, the ritual dance of Wind's mother—all of it remained fresh in her mind. Glancing around to see if she was alone, the trance of memory took over, causing her to dance down the trail. Once more she closed her eyes with a smile, gracefully twirling about.

Finishing her steps with a bow, she stood at the side trail that she was searching for.

With a transition from stone to dirt, she continued on the narrow path through the thick woods. The treetops shadowed her, providing her with perfect comfort from the warm, beaming sun. Around one bend, then another, her journey came to an end as she broke from the thick timber. A deep, wide river stood before her. Only a few steps from the forest canopy took her to its muddy edge. Moving along the bank, a small cove appeared in the distance. Out over the calm, shallow water stood a small wooden dock. Its weathered and aged timber curled and cracked as she walked to its edge. This was her place of security—a place secluded from everything. Here there were only the fish and her thoughts. Taking off her shoes and socks, she dangled her feet into the cool water. Though aloneness had brought her comfort in the past, now she desperately wished for someone to come. Tears ran down her face as she looked to the sky, mourning for Wind and the others. A breeze danced through the trees, blowing through her hair as it passed. Her eyes, unable to cry any longer, simply closed, allowing her to take it all in. No matter how she tried to abandon her thoughts, she couldn't shake the desire to be back in Korithia.

After the passing of some time, she had to return to the waiting world. Back on the road, she headed straight for work in the hope that it would keep her mind occupied. Growing closer to the spot where her car had met the trees all those weeks ago, a tingling ran up her spine. She approached the sight, taking a long pause to see the tire marks in the grass. Thinking back, she tried to remember how it happened.

A blast from an impatient driver's horn shook her back to reality. Slowly moving on, Melinda was quickly passed. Her nerves began to pulse when she spotted several broken trees off to her right. Hitting her four-way flashers, she pulled over and stopped to get a better view. An urgency to investigate the destruction overwhelmed her. She got out of the car and cautiously slid down the embankment into the tall grass of the ditch. Losing her step, she fell into a deep, muddy rut. An image flashed in her mind of a car speeding through the mud as it smashed into unforgiving timber.

Peering between the wide blades of grass, something blue caught her eye. Its tip barely poked out from the thick brush, lying among cubed broken glass remains. Sitting on her knees, Melinda reached out and plucked it from its nest. To her amazement, it was a blue crayon—the same blue crayon she'd given to the child that night. Chills raced through her heart as she frantically scanned the area for any further remains of the family's car. There was nothing beyond the shattered remains of glass and plastic

She returned to her car, keeping a tight grip on the crayon. With her shift starting soon, she only had time to creep by the site of where she was pulled from her own car's wreckage. Spotting the massive tree she'd hit, she noticed only a mere scratch across its trunk caused by her car.

Arriving at work, she tucked the crayon into her apron as she grabbed the bundle of clothes and went inside. Quietly she sped straight into the back to change out of her muddy jeans. After cleaning herself up, she went to the kitchen. As she had hoped, Mary was there waiting.

"Girl, how have you been? Come here and give ol' Mary a hug." Rushing over to her, Mary wrapped her arms around Melinda. "Oh!" She quickly set her down. "I didn't hurt ya, did I?"

"No, I'm fine now, but you should have seen me. I had a bruise up this whole side," Melinda explained, pointing out her injuries. "I had stitches going all the way up my scalp. I can't believe my hair started growing back so quickly."

"Well, you're still just as pretty as a rose. You do seem different, though." Mary looked her over with a puzzled face, trying to figure it out.

"What?" Melinda asked with curiosity and a smirk.

"I can't put a finger on it, but there's definitely something goin' on with you. But now we better get out there; it's about time for the dinner rush, then it'll be the drunken rush. You sure you're up to this?" Mary asked, giving her a wink.

"I'm here," Melinda replied, raising an eyebrow.

Mary smiled, and both headed out to take on the heavy load of diners. They went through their motions of another typical night at the truck stop. Mary watched as Melinda covered the counter, but she was no longer putting up with customers' ignorance and harsh comments. Without being rude, Melinda fought back, gaining control over the truckers. Mary grinned proudly.

Neither woman missed a beat as they reached the end of their shift. As they were leaving, Mary rushed out to catch Melinda in the parking lot. "Hey, girl, wait up," she shouted. "You did real good tonight at makin' them assholes behave. I'm proud of ya."

"Thanks, I just—"

"Hon, there ain't nothin' to explain. You go home and get some sleep. You deserve it." Hugging her again, Mary walked off to her car.

Melinda watched as Mary drove off into the darkness. Not even thinking of her accident, she climbed into her parents' car and headed home. Feeling the effects of the first night back to work, Melinda dragged herself into her house, looking forward to the comfort of her bed.

For the next three months, Melinda went through her normal motions, keeping her random sickness a secret from everyone. Through that time she began to sense a change within herself, something she had never felt before. Trying to ignore it, she pushed on through her days at work and home. Fatigue consumed her more and more with each passing night. At this point, she felt that school would be out of the question.

Drawing close to the end of the fourth month after that trip to the doctor, she noticed that her once-flat stomach was starting to protrude over her pants. In desperate need, she ran out to get some new clothes. Doing everything she could to keep a low profile, she watched out for anyone she might know.

Riffling through the racks, she rummaged up a few pairs of jeans with waists two sizes bigger than her normal ones. A pop of the restricting button on her pants brought her relief, as her stomach was freed. She sat on the tiny bench inside the small dressing room, holding her overhanging belly. The truth slowly seeped into her. She finally came to acceptance.

Acceptance released a mix of all of her emotions. At first she wept silently behind the closed door. With a sniffle she squeezed into her old jeans and walked to the maternity section. Ripping angrily through the rack, she dug for something acceptable. Little choice presented itself, with all of the options screaming "I'm pregnant." Trying some maternity pants on, they were a perfect fit—more proof of her state. Within the impossibility of her pregnancy, Melinda knew it had to have happened there, in that other world. It was an impossibility she did not want to face nor accept.

Pushing the snap together, she breathed easy in the larger size. She sucked her belly in and changed back into her old pants, but the tight grip around her waist dug into her. There was no choice. Making her purchase, she returned home.

When Melinda opened the front door, she was completely caught off guard to find the living room was spotless. Blown away, she slowly closed the door to investigate the house. Melinda stopped at her parents' room, where her mother stood knee-deep in clutter.

"Mom, what are you doing?" Melinda asked, leaning against the doorway.

"What?" the older woman replied, jumping with a start. "Oh, I'm sick of lookin' at this mess. Besides, if I'm gonna be a grandma I better have a clean house for my grandbaby."

"Mom, I told you I'm not—" Melinda tried to explain.

"Look at you, there ain't no hidin' it. So, who ya gonna name as the father?"

"No one," Melinda quietly replied.

"What?" Her mother's voice rose. "Why?"

"Well, I'd rather have no daddy for it other than Kyle." Though knowing it was a lie, that was all Melinda could think of to say.

"*It*—that's not an *it* inside there; it's a baby, so you better watch what you're doin' out there. No more accidents. But you're right. Havin' no father is better than havin' him." Her mother smiled in agreement.

"Hang on a minute. I'll give you a hand."

Changing into a pair of sweat pants, Melinda returned to her mother's side. Together they cleaned out the entire house, tackling everything, including the dish-filled kitchen. As four o'clock arrived, Melinda's brothers returned home from school. Before they could even comment, both Melinda and her mother jumped all over them. Standing over the kids, they both stated the severity of the consequences if they trashed the house again. Both Tim and Brian, fearing their sister and mother's harsh tone, took their words seriously. They helped carry the garbage out to the cans while Melinda and her mother finished wiping down the kitchen.

Later that evening, Melinda's father returned home. Not being out as late as usual, he was only slightly inebriated. He was so confused by the sight after coming in that he walked back out again to make sure that he was at the right house. Reassured, he came back inside to find everyone sitting in the living room watching television. Stumbling, he just stood there staring at them, unsure of what to do.

"You're early," Melinda's mother commented as he looked around in disbelief. "There's pizza in the fridge; Melinda treated."

In a daze, he stumbled into the kitchen. Melinda's mother turned to the kids. "You guys head off to your rooms. I need to talk to Dad alone," she said.

Melinda, Brian, and Tim all headed off to their rooms before their father returned. Closing their door, the boys turned on their game to occupy them. Melinda sat with her back to her closed door, listening as her mother explained the situation to her father. First there came the yelling, something Melinda had anticipated. But to her amazement, the tension was short-lived. Her father lowered his voice as the discussion continued. Melinda quickly moved to her bed moments later when she heard her father's footsteps approaching.

Her door crept open, and her father entered. "Hey, girl, your mama told me what's goin' on." He calmly sat down on the bed beside her, staring at the floor. "Now, I'm not mad … it's … it's just unexpected, that's all. I know your workin' now, but your ma and I decided we're gonna help ya out."

"Thanks, Dad," Melinda softly replied, though she was waiting for the hell to break loose. "I've been saving some money so you won't have to worry about—"

"You keep that money for your schooling," he demanded, cutting her off. "You're still covered on my insurance, so that's all you need to be thinkin' about."

"I don't know what to say," she replied, as tears began to drip down her cheek. Sitting up, she hugged him tightly for the first time since she was seven.

"Oh, not so hard girl, you got to be careful with that young'in in that belly," he remarked with a smile, wrapping his arms gently around her. "All right now, you get some sleep." Getting up, he walked out into the hall. "A grandpa already … I'm not ready for that." Laughing under his breath, he closed her door.

The following morning, Melinda woke up to the scent of cooking bacon. Still not believing the phenomenon of the spotless living room, she walked through to the kitchen. Her mother, preparing breakfast, asked her to sit and listen. She went on to explain what she had gone through when she was pregnant the first time—how she was young and not truly ready for the responsibility. Recalling her memories, she began to cry as she served Melinda a dish of scrambled eggs with three strips of bacon. Continuing, she explained what Melinda would need to do as an expecting mother, including the side effects. As they finished their meal, Melinda's mother informed her of a doctor's appointment in an hour. Gobbling down every bite, Melinda ran to her room to get dressed.

They arrived at the doctor's office, and Melinda's mother followed her inside. She sat patiently in the waiting room as Melinda saw the doctor. Coming out, Melinda reported that everything was normal. She had the receptionist set up an appointment for her first ultrasound. With a three-day wait, both Melinda and her mother tried to settle their eager minds.

After the appointment, Melinda's mother treated her to lunch. They joked around, discussing different names and guessing the sex, though Melinda knew for sure that it would be a boy. As the conversation continued, Melinda realized that this was the first time she and her mother had ever had a moment like this. Not taking it for granted, she kept her mouth shut rather than pointing it out.

That evening, while getting ready for work, Melinda tried her best to hide her growing belly. Standing in front of her mother, she forced her to judge every angle. Once she felt comfortable with her mother's reassurance, she left for work. Out on the road, she passed her father as his friend drove him home. He waved to her, a deep smile on his face. Caught off guard, Melinda looked back in confusion as they continued down the road.

At work, Melinda's secret was instantly uncovered by Mary's intuition. She admitted her state, and her friend asked a million questions. Melinda told her the same story she told her mother, keeping back the truth.

More changes came to the world around Melinda. Through her entire shift of working the counter, not one person made a rude or ignorant comment. Even the truckers, who usually stared and made disgusting gestures, treated her with pure respect. Being the busiest night of the week, her shift flew smoothly by.

Over the next few days, time was not so kind. Melinda grew anxious for the ultrasound. The days trickled away slowly.

With Mary off those nights, and being light on customers, time seemingly stood still. She watched the clock through every second. Finally, with her shift over, she would rush home to force herself to sleep.

Her nerves pulsed as her heart raced, keeping the luxury of sleep from her grasp. Drifting off only in spurts, she danced in between states of consciousness. Seven o'clock on the day of the ultrasound rolled around, and her alarm echoed through her mind. Still in a haze, she readied for her nine o'clock appointment. Her mother, full of excitement, burst into her room and began chatting at a hundred miles a minute. Melinda's mind was still resting in a thick fog, slowing everything down and allowing only partial fragments of her mother's words to process.

Melinda's mind drifted off in the car, losing the trip to the hospital in a blank space of her mind. With the lack of rest, she felt herself floating as her mother helped her inside.

The checked in and were instantly taken back with no waiting. As the brisk cold of the hospital hall met her skin, Melinda became more focused. Reaching the room, she changed into a gown. Both Melinda and her mother grew restless as the nurse readied the machine. A shiver rippled through Melinda's body as the nurse squeezed out a tube of gel onto her stomach.

Hitting buttons and moving the scope across her, she focused on the image of the baby. The nurse turned the monitor for Melinda and her mother to see, pointing out the details of the healthy child. With a tear in her eye, Melinda was hit with the true sense of being a mother. Scheduling another appointment, the nurse explained that the next time the baby would be developed enough so she could find out the sex. Finishing up, Melinda changed back into her clothes while the nurse printed her off a picture of the baby. Melinda's eyes never left it as they walked out of the hospital.

At the next ultrasound, Melinda's certainty was proven with the new photo—there was no doubt that it was a boy. Over the next few months, Melinda's life began to drastically change, and far beyond the pregnancy. At home, her brothers had taken charge of keeping the house clean, as their mother worked part-time to help bring in some money. Her father's drinking had dwindled away to the point where he had become sober.

Starting another semester of school, every subject came as simple as though she had always known them. Even her job seemed to come easier, with the customers now calm and friendly. Everything in her life flowed perfectly and fluently.

Her school finals came and went, and Melinda cleared her second year with her GPA the highest it had ever been. She gained an internship at the local hospital, and almost instantly she gave Mary a proper good-bye as she stepped out of the restaurant for the last time. With only a short time of her pregnancy remaining, the whole family prepared for the boy's coming. Unfortunately for Melinda, having all this time, she still hadn't decided on a name.

On the exact day of the nine-month anniversary of her accident, Melinda was rushed to the hospital to give birth. Pushing, with only minor labor pains, she brought into this world a healthy baby boy. Her eyes locked onto his as the nurse laid him in her arms. His name came to her as he spoke it through his soft, blue eyes: Christian Marcus Rowley. Becoming the mother she needed to be, the happy family was released the next day.

At home with Christian, an inner peace washed over Melinda that she had never felt before. Christian fell in line with a schedule that gave her the peace she needed through the night, and her family was quick to help her out in any way they could.

Furthering her education in psychology, Melinda returned to the community college. Quickly learning what it meant to be a mother, a student, and a teacher to her child, Melinda herself began to change over the next few years. Time ran together as she graduated top of her class. Receiving a large grant she headed off to the highest regarded university in Maine to earn her master's degree. Being so close to home she could leave Christian in the care of her mother while attending. Christian, also learning at a dramatic rate, excelled past the children around him at the preschool he went to on the days his grandmother worked. With his intelligence booming, Melinda took full advantage by teaching him more every day as they played.

Melinda continued to further her education at the university, earning her PhD with ease. Again she finished at the top of her class, opportunity quickly knocked. This finally gave her the prospect of her dreams: an escape from her small town prison. Though with the changes that had come in her life, Melinda found she had trouble letting go, even as her family wished her well.

Christian, starting kindergarten, fit right in with the kids around him. He excelled academically above them all. Everything came as Melinda wished, though she never expected how easily time could get lost or forgotten.

Returning from work one day, Melinda stepped into her luxurious home to find the nanny relaxing in the living room, with Christian nowhere to be seen.

"Hello, Ms. Rowley. You're early today," the nanny stated as she nervously stood up.

"It's all right, Olivia," Melinda replied with a smile. "I'll surprise him. Is he in his room?"

"Yes, he said he was going to draw with his crayons and didn't want to be disturbed," Olivia informed Melinda, imitating him shaking his finger.

"We'll see about that!" Melinda walked off, heading up the stairs. Slowly making her way down the hall, she paused at his closed door to listen. Reaching out for the knob, she jumped as it opened on its own. "Christian?" she quietly called out.

"Come in, Mother. I have something to show you," he explained in a calm tone as he sat with his back to the door. "I've been drawing all day; it was a dream that I had. See?"

Slowly pushing the door open, Melinda's eyes opened wide at his work. There, hanging around the room, were pictures of every step she had taken in the other world. From the lionesses at the base of the tree house, to the fallen city, every place she'd visited was there, all placed in order, ending with the same picture of Gurod that had laid at her feet in the tree house.

"This is my world."

Dark Sphere

"Captain's log 8043: Four thousand years have passed since our home world, Earth, was destroyed. Mankind was the cause, though how has been lost over time. Approximately two hundred thirty-seven million humans escaped in thirty separate vessels. Over the ages, they all began to realize what was most important: finding a new home. Divisive differences became irrelevant. Banding together, they united their ships, building what is now called the *Nexees*. Our world's top scientists built the *Nexees* to be a solar-powered, self-sustaining, floating metropolis that would carry us to salvation.

"Time has not been so kind to their plan. As we have progressed, we have lost our differences. All hair has become black, and our skin is white. Even our eyes have lost their color and grown slightly larger. Thanks to plagues and planets with hostile life forms, we are now down to only three remaining humans. We have found nothing. All alien life is hostile or seemingly of no intelligence, nor has a single trace of sustainability been found. As far as the *Nexees* is concerned, it is now a clunker, falling apart. We are truly at our end."

"Aaron, are you talking into that damn recorder again?"

Alice, a fit soldier in her late twenties, stepped aboard the bridge. Only patches of her pale skin showed through layers of dirt. Angered by Aaron, a scientist and captain of the *Nexees*, she stormed over to him. "You need to stop with all of this crazy 'we're going to die' crap."

"I can't help it. Do you know how many times I've weighed the odds? Do you?" Aaron quickly spun in his chair to face her. "There's no chance that we can find—"

"Look, we've still got enough food to last us another twenty years." Alice ran up beside him to his computer, pressing a few buttons. "Even our water supply is fine. We just have to use it sparingly. I really don't see what you're so worried about." Pushing her filthy nose up to his, she smeared dirt all over it. Alice had fallen deeply in love with Aaron after he saved her life from a hostile bug on a foreign world. Aaron on the other hand kept more focused on their overall survival instead.

"I don't know if you've noticed, but there's a huge shortage of people here!" Aaron shouted. His tiny yet fit frame shook as he grew heated.

"Well," Alice stated, putting her arms around him, "we could always start the repopulation process ourselves." Her heart raced as her desire swelled.

"Could you be serious for five minutes?" Aaron whispered, her lips inches away from his. "I've been charting our way through this entire system, and there's nothing. We are going to die."

"Who's going to die?"

Mark, a pilot, soldier, and mechanic in his early twenties, walked in behind them. Covered in grease, he flexed his muscles. Being larger than Aaron, he was the daring one. "He's not on that damn kick again? It never fails; once a month, we're all going to die. Get over it."

"Is the *Scavenger* ready?" Aaron asked, as Alice climbed off him, glaring at Mark for his interruption. Aaron walked over to a small panel on the wall. The lights dimmed as a shrunken down holographic image of the universe filled the center of the bridge.

"I've found two more planets we can explore." With a pointed finger, Aaron touched a spot on the universal map causing it to instantly zoom to their location. This tiny solar system consisted of only five planets, all circled around a small red flaring planet. With a moon three times its own size, the light emanating from the red planet was short lived. Being on the outer rim of the system they could see the *Nexees* passing a massive purple sphere. Swirling storms danced in its atmosphere, most being large enough to swallow their seemingly small ship.

"What about this one?" Alice asked, pointing to the small red planet.

"Too hot, there were several thermal spikes sent back by the probe. I've been thinking about … this one." Aaron pointed to a large black planet orbiting hundreds of miles from the red one. "Other than several mountainous areas, I have found no apparent dangers. Then there's this one," he pointed out to another. A massive white planet slowly passed ahead of their path. "If we go here we are definitely going to need our snow gear. With an average temperature of minus fifty degrees centigrade, I'm thinking it's a no go."

"A lot of good that does us, brain boy," Mark spouted off.

"I'm hoping that there'll be some cave systems down on the black planet. If any moisture exists down there, that's where it would gather."

"What did the life scan report?" Alice asked. She had seen a lot of action from alien life forms in her years as a soldier, from giant insect types to acid slugs.

"Both reported back nothing, but that doesn't mean that there is nothing." Aaron gave Mark a strong look. "Ready the *Scavenger*; we'll be in orbit by tomorrow morning."

Mark walked off as Alice stomped over to Aaron. "You already set this up, didn't you?" Her temper was what made her a great soldier. "You couldn't discuss this expedition with us first? Damn it, Aaron, I thought we were together on everything. You told me—"

"I've got a feeling about this one. I don't know what, but there's something about this place." His eyes gleamed with the planet's image as he stared into the hologram.

Aaron watched from the diminutive, domed bridge at the head of the ship as the flying metropolis known as the *Nexees* slowly progressed toward the planet. The ship's two solar panels, like wings, extended out from both sides at the rear of the ship. They gathered all the energy they could from the tiny sun in the galaxy's center. A multi-ringed, blue planet's rainbow-colored rings reflected off the shiny windows of the abandoned living quarters as the ship drifted by.

The massive dome stood high above the solar panels. At one time it had housed hundreds of thousands, but now it sat vacant. For the last twelve years, after the last of the crew were lost on a hostile planet, no one had set foot inside. The remaining three had made their rooms closer to the self-maintained but rapidly decaying biosphere in the center of the ship. From there they had easier access to the sick bay, bridge, and launch bay.

Inside of the ship's belly, Mark worked on the *Scavenger*. This small, twelve-man pod had carried the trio on all of their explorations throughout the years. Mark held faith in the vessel for how many jams it had gotten them out of. Pounding away on its hull, he welded a small steel panel on its underbelly. With all the *Scavenger* had seen, it was now held together by patchwork.

Alice, in her small quarters, gathered some of her favorite weapons from off her wall. Crew going out had rarely been so lucky as to avoid casualties, so she wanted to be ready for anything. Gathering an armful of her favorite firearms, she headed down to the *Scavenger*.

"Here's a good start," she stated to herself, placing the guns inside. "I'll get more, just in case." Hearing Mark pound away on the ship always made her a bit nervous. "Do me a favor and make sure you fix it right," she called to him.

"I will!" he shouted out from below.

"Damn screw up." She walked off, leaving Mark to his work.

Grabbing a small piece of plate steel, Mark held it up to the hole. With his welder in hand, he set several small tacks to hold it in place. Searching blindly for a hammer, Mark felt around on the floor, only to find Aaron's boot.

"As long as you're there, could you hand me the hammer?" Mark calmly asked.

"I don't think I like the idea of you beating on the hull with a mallet," the other man expressed, handing it to him.

"Look, you just fly this rotting hunk of junk you call a ship. This … this is my baby, and she loves me. Don't you? Yes, you do." Mark rubbed the ship's belly, patting the warm metal.

"You know, there are times I worry about you," Aaron said as Alice stumbled in, carrying more guns than she could easily lift. "Don't you think that's a little much?" he asked.

Alice stopped, dropping a few on the floor. "What? After that trip to Quantis Seven, I'm not taking any chances." She loaded the remaining guns into the ship. "I'm ready … sir," she properly stated, kicking one of the guns on the floor under a seat.

"Well, we're not going anywhere until I patch this hole," Mark interjected as he continued making his repairs.

"I'm going to go get some sleep," Alice stated with an outrageous yawn, giving Aaron a dirty look.

"You really pissed her off this time, Aaron," Mark joked as he pulled himself out from under the ship.

"Yeah, it won't be the first time. Well, I'm going to go get some sleep. Think you'll have it finished by morning?"

"No problem." Mark crawled back under, continuing to beat on the steel as Aaron walked off to his chambers.

Aaron woke early on his small cot hours before the *Nexees* reached the planet's orbit. Sitting on the bridge, he watched as they slowly passed by the small red planet. Several flares erupted off its surface, reaching out just passed its moon. With no large suns gleaming here and being light years from any massive stars, this was the first non-ship produced light they had seen in over a year. As Aaron grew comfortable in his seat, Mark walked up from behind.

"There's one thing about all of this I still can't get over. It's all so beautiful," Mark stated, basking in the view.

"Yeah, beauty with death and danger around every corner. I just hope there's enough light coming off of that planet so we'll be able to see down there, on the dark one." Aaron walked over to the hologram map, turning it on. He watched as it showed all of the planet's motions. "For a short time, this planet is eclipsed by the red one, but it shouldn't last long. We should be able to take off again a couple of hours after we land."

"We've got time—plenty of it—so if we have to wait, it's no big deal, you know?" Mark said, keeping his voice calm for Aaron's sake, despite his own jitters.

"No, we have to get back off the planet as soon as we can." Aaron walked over to the window and gazed at the massive, dark sphere. "There's something down there. I don't know why, but I've got this gut feeling."

"It's probably something you ate last night," Alice sarcastically interjected, as she stepped into the cabin behind them. "If I had a drop of water for every time you had a gut feeling, I could make it rain in here for a hundred years."

"We're getting closer. Why don't you two go finish packing up the *Scavenger*?" Aaron suggested. "Make sure you put in several light sticks. We have no idea what could happen down there."

"Yes sir!" Mark yelled with a salute, as he walked off the bridge.

"I've got enough weapons to kill off a small army. We'll be fine," Alice assured, as she followed Mark. Aaron just stared at the planet, contemplating the possibilities.

Down at the *Scavenger*, Mark crawled under the ship and gave it a final going-over on the repairs. Alice loaded up more supplies—food, water, light sticks, and medical supplies. Ever since they'd lost the last group of people to a plague, each of the remaining three had taken on several roles. Alice was a fighter, but she was also the team's medic. Aaron arrived, carrying his helmet, with the suit tucked under his arm.

"Mark, is that thing going to hold together?" Aaron asked, kicking the hull.

"I hope so. If not … boom, we're a fireball!" he yelled out with a laugh.

"Did you have to say it like that?" Alice rolled her eyes then walked off to retrieve her suit.

"Shit! Hey, Aaron, hand me the welder. Thanks. I've got one little spot here." As Mark struck an arc, Alice returned to see sparks flying.

"What the hell is he doing?" she exclaimed, tossing her suit inside the ship. "Mark, I swear—"

"Would you relax?" Mark cut her off. "We're going to be just … fine … Done." Mark crawled out from under the ship with a large grin. "Okay, let's go."

"Got your suit?" Aaron asked.

"Loaded it last night." Still holding a smirk, he jumped aboard the *Scavenger*.

Alice and Aaron boarded the tiny ship and were at the mercy of Mark's piloting skills. Every door connecting to the bay closed, sealing off the rest of the ship from the vacuum of space. As the ship hovered above the floor of the *Nexees*, Alice gave Aaron a concerned gaze. Flashing orange lights filled the room as it depressurized, then the bay doors opened before them. With a great burst of speed, Mark launched out, casually guiding them to their destination. All was quiet aboard the vessel as the three crew members anticipated what they might be facing.

"Hold on, boys and girls, here we go." Mark pushed forward on the stick, rocketing them into the planet's atmosphere.

Alice closed her eyes and established a death-lock grip onto Aaron's hand. Her heart raced with fear. With a massive hit, the small ship broke into the atmosphere. Shaking vigorously, they broke away from the fire of entry. All they could see was the dull surface of the black planet. Everything lacked a form of color, from the flatlands to the mountains.

"I'm going to pass over a bit of the surface," Mark informed them, going low. The jagged, mountainous landscape left little room for him to fly. "It's like a giant trench. There, that looks like a good spot." Mark guided the ship to a large patch of open land. With a teetering effort, he put the *Scavenger* down safely.

"All right, I'm going to go check out the surface. Be ready for anything." Aaron stood up as Mark tapped a button to open the door. Just as he stepped out, the light from the red planet faded away. With a quiet crack, Aaron snapped a light stick, giving him a ten-foot radiance of soft light. "Okay, by my calculations this should only last for about three hours. Don't use the lights; we don't want to exhaust any of the ship's energy—just in case we have to take off in a hurry."

Aaron slowly placed his foot onto the ground below. "Soft, stable, it feels like sand." Dropping down, he quickly fell to the ground. "There seems to be a bit more gravity than I estimated from the report. It's stronger then the ships electro mercury drive systems too," he stated, getting back to his feet. "And it's so dark."

"Enough of the small talk, is there any life?" Alice's voice rang out over his head set.

"My scanner isn't showing anything." Aaron made his way toward the back end of the ship. "Wait, I'm getting a signal, it's—"

"Rah!" Mark yelled out as he jumped from the shadows, freaking out Aaron.

"Damn it, Mark! Can't you be serious for one moment?"

Alice sighed. "I'm coming out." She grabbed a few weapons and tucked them into her suit belts on the way to the hatch. "This sand looks so weird," she exclaimed, walking toward the moving light stick. Getting close enough to see, she found the two fighting. "Would you two knock it off? I don't think we need attract too much attention."

"He started it!" Aaron yelled, pointing at Mark.

"I don't care whose fault it is; we need to move. This place is creeping me out," Alice explained, staring out into the darkness.

"Okay, Alice, you take a light stick and head east. I'll tell you when to stop," Aaron ordered.

"Got it." Alice headed off, still glaring at Mark.

"Mark, you—" Aaron went to say, but he was cut short.

"Yeah, I got it, head west, and stay in view ... whatever." Mark cracked his light stick and started off.

"Stop, Alice. I can barely see you," Aaron called out over the head set.

"All right," she quickly called back.

"Am I far enough yet?" Mark sarcastically asked.

"There is no such distance," Alice spouted back.

"Yes, Mark, you're good—and you two knock it off. I'm not going to listen to you argue this whole trip. Anything on your scanners?"

"No!" Both Mark and Alice answered back simultaneously.

From out of nowhere, a bright flash of green lightning ripped through the sky, followed by a ground-shaking rumble. All three just stopped, stunned by the marvel.

"Did you see that?" Aaron asked in awe.

"Yeah, beautiful," Alice replied.

"See it? I *felt* it. Amazing," Mark added, as it began to rain. Several purple drops landed on his visor. "Guys, it's raining purple?" he said quizzically. More lightning flashed throughout the sky.

"It's funny—even with the lightning, I still can't see a thing," Aaron pointed out.

"Yeah, you're right," Alice chimed back.

"Hey, there's something on my scanner," Mark blurted out. "It's moving really fast. Oh shi—" Mark's transmission went silent.

"Mark, you better not be screwing around. Alice, head toward me." Aaron ran off toward Mark's last-known location. Only his light stick lay there across drag marks in the sand. "Alice, do you see anything?"

"No ... wait, it's coming up from behind me. Aaron!" she yelled out in terror. Gun in hand she spun about, searching for it.

"Run!" Aaron dashed toward her as the storm worsened. He found her, catching up from behind. "Got you, now where is it?"

"I don't know. Where's Mark?" she asked, wrapping her arm around Aaron while still pointing her pistol out into the darkness.

"Gone, all I found was his light stick and some tracks," he explained.

"We have to get out of here. We have to get back to the ship!" Alice demanded, pulling him along.

"Okay, we'll stick together and follow our tracks back."

Gripping tightly onto each other, they started their way back. The drizzling rain became a fierce, heavy downpour as they struggled to find their way back. With their vision skewed, they stumbled along what they believed was their path.

Off in the distance, Alice spotted the gleam of something shiny. "A ship," she pointed out, running ahead. "I don't remember seeing this before."

Aaron advanced the final few feet toward it. "There's a symbol of some kind on the side. Wait—it can't be! I think this is one of Professor Helix's ships!" Aaron exclaimed in confusion while fidgeting with the door.

"Who?" Alice asked.

With Aaron's struggle, the door slowly slid aside. "I can't believe it's open." Excitement filled his voice. Pushing it enough to get them through, Aaron pulled Alice in.

It was a tight fit for both of them. Aaron desperately tried to close the hatch. Struggling, it finally gave. Aaron silently searched about the ransacked quarters.

"So, who is this professor?" Alice asked, pulling on the door to make sure it had latched.

"Professor Benjamin Helix," he explained, looking through the wreckage. "Two thousand years before the Earth was destroyed, he sent up twelve separate vessels. Each one was transporting a different species of Earth animals' DNA. He had hoped they would make it to unknown worlds and begin new life. Each ship was fitted with a tracking device so that they could be found and their progress documented. Up until now, no one had ever found one." Excitement filled his being, knowing he had been the first to make such an astounding discovery. "I thought it was a myth, one of the stories we passed down for fun. I can't believe it's here, this far out."

"What was aboard this ship?" Alice asked, fearing the worst.

"I don't know. It doesn't matter. As soon as it stops raining, we're getting out of here, but we have to search for Mark," he stated, reassuring her.

"How much longer until the next light?" Alice asked, full of hope.

"After studying the cycles on the *Nexees,* I figure we have a couple of hours." At that moment both of their light sticks began to fade. "Then we'll get out of here, find Mark, and get off of this tomb of a planet."

"At least if I die … it'll be in your arms." Alice smiled as darkness flooded the room.

Sitting in silence, they waited out the storm. Outside, the thunder continued to rage on.

Alice jumped as something landed on the roof. "Oh my God, did you hear that?" she said, shaken inside but doing her best to hide it. She stood as the sound of footsteps and the scraping of metal came from above. "I don't want to die, I don't want to die, I don't want to die." Alice repeated over and over, curling up.

"Don't worry, we're—"

With a crash, the hatch opened suddenly, and the two were pulled out by unseen hands. With one hard smack each, they fell unconscious, to be dragged off by their assailants.

Aaron woke up to the sound of water dripping into pools echoing around him. Football-sized glowworms dimly lit their dark cave surroundings. Alice still lay unconscious while Aaron investigated through the thick, bamboo-like bars of their man-made prison. The bars were tightly tied together with strong vines, making any form of escape impossible. High above, they were locked in by an unreachable door. From behind he could hear a slight noise coming from an unlit part of the cage.

"Aaron, help me … they're too … strong … can't fight," Alice cried out in her sleep.

Aaron lightly shook her, trying to wake her from the dream. "Alice. Wake up, Alice."

"Aaron! Oh, we're alive!" she yelled excitedly, her voice echoing through the chasm. Jumping on him, she shook off her grogginess. "Water, is that water? What happened?"

"I'm not sure, but stay quiet while I figure a way out of here. We don't want whatever it is to come back."

"There is no way out," a familiar voice spoke from the shadows. "They'll bring you some food, some sort of fruit, I think." Mark crawled into the dim light.

"Did you see it?" Aaron questioned.

"Them. There's more than one; and no, I couldn't see until they left," he explained, rubbing his head.

"What do you mean? There's all these glowworms," Alice remarked.

"Watch." Mark clapped his hands, all of the glowworms stopped glowing. "See?" With another clap, the light returned.

"Why didn't you turn them on while they were giving you food?" she asked.

"Are you serious?" Mark replied, with concern for her sanity. "There is no way I'm going to single handedly—"

From out of nowhere a loud clacking sound echoed through the cave. All of the glowworms went dark, leaving the humans blind. Alice listened as the footsteps drew closer and closer.

Desperately seeking to face her captors, she clapped just as the steps halted. "Face me, you!" she shouted, instantly stopping at what she saw.

To her surprise, she was greeted by the face of a humanoid cat creature. Standing six feet tall, it towered over her. Its human-like body was rippled with muscle and scars. Wearing the garb of a tribesman, it was dressed in homemade clothing. Emerald-green eyes stared softly at Alice.

Several sharp-looking fangs protruded from under its curled lips as it spoke in a deep, raspy voice. "She was right; you *do* look like the creator!" Its eyes focused on Aaron. "Have you come to guide us with your wisdom?"

"Who is your creator?" Mark asked, lost in confusion.

"The one who sent us here, the one who gave us life," the cat creature replied.

"Professor Helix? But how do you know what he looks like?" As Aaron stood dumbfounded, Mark slowly moved up behind him.

"Shut up and go with this; it's our only way out of here!" Mark whispered into his ear.

"Let us out of here. We don't mean you any harm," Alice said, fearful. She just wanted out of this nightmare. "We'll just leave. I promise."

"What do you think, Saphron? Should we let them out?" Addressing the shadows, the creature revealed that it was not alone.

"Yes, they are so puny. What harm could they do?" a female's voice responded, calm and soothing, yet direct. Stepping out of the shadows, the female joined the other, a male. Her golden eyes, encircled with green, gleamed in the worms' glow. Fully clad in jewelry, she appeared to be of nobility. Though more slender than the other, she was just as muscular.

"Zenda, my father is going to be pleased with our find." She glanced over at Mark. "This one put up a fight; it must be their warrior. If he's their strongest I think we'll be able to handle the rest," she snidely stated.

"Thanks a lot, lady," Mark quietly snapped back.

With one great leap, Zenda jumped onto the top of the cage. Opening the door, he dropped down inside. He walked over to Mark, glaring at the human all the way. Grabbing him, Zenda leapt out and back to the other side. He released Mark to Saphron and went back into the cage to retrieve the others.

"Thanks," Mark uttered, brushing himself off.

"If you try to deceive us, you will not survive," Saphron reassured him, peering into his eyes. Zenda returned with the others in one leap. "We will take you outside of the sphere and feed you to the Great Machool," she added.

"Come," Zenda softly requested, giving Saphron a harsh look. "We want you to see what we've accomplished in our time here."

Grabbing Aaron gently by the arm, he led the humans deeper into the cave. The echoing sounds of the dripping water grew strident as they made their descent. Saphron headed the rear, watching Mark with a close eye.

"So, what is this Great Machool again?" Mark asked as she passed behind him.

"She," she loudly stated, "is the one who gives birth to the Valkata. If we hadn't taken you into the sphere, the Valkata would have feasted on all of you."

"Sounds pleasant, are they big?" he replied with a gulp.

"You will see soon enough."

Saphron's assurance sent chills up Mark's spine. "Remind me not to ask you anything, ever." Mark became silent, watching Saphron as she watched him. Sounds of a distant waterfall filled the catacombs.

"Is that water?" Alice moved up next to Aaron, leaving Mark to Saphron.

"Oh, yes, there is lots of water within the sphere." Zenda put his arm around her and continued with a grin. "It flows through the rock into great pools. You will see, all in due time."

Turning to Zenda, Aaron's mind filled with endless questions. "What do you mean, inside of the sphere? How many of there are you?" Aaron fumbled through his questions while trying to grasp everything around them.

"All in time," Zenda stated with a mischievous cat-style grin.

As Zenda finished his statement, they arrived at a large opening. There, a waterfall made of purple liquid fed a small pond. Alice stared in awe as she slowly walked over to it.

"This is so beautiful. Can you drink it?" Her thirst had taken over; water had been scarce on the *Nexees* in recent months. Zenda nodded in approval.

Kneeling down before the pool, Alice drank the mysterious water. "You've got to try this; it's amazing! It tastes sweet and it's so good."

With confusion and curiosity, Mark went to join her in drinking. "She's right. It's strange; it feels cold but doesn't make my hands cold." He put his arm in up to the elbow. "Weird."

"Drink and relax. All you will ever need is here," Zenda expressed as Saphron held a look of disgust.

Alice, taking off her shoes, socks, and pants, dipped one foot into the water, testing it out. Aaron tried to stop her, but Zenda held him back. Stepping out, Alice waded up to her waist. Saphron cringed, closing her big, golden eyes.

"It's warm; I don't believe it, but it's warm." A smile covered Alice's face as she dove under.

"Really?" Mark stripped down to his underwear and rushed in behind her. "Oh, this feels so good." He splashed Alice, who in turn splashed him back.

"Strange creatures, aren't they?" Saphron stated, putting her paw on Zenda's arm.

"Yeah, I haven't seen them get along like this for more than five minutes in years," Aaron commented.

Walking over to the pool, he reached down to take a drink. When he glanced up, he noticed that both Alice and Mark were a light shade of purple. Swiftly pulling his hand up, he checked it over. Seeing no effect on him, he came to a conclusion. "Guys, I think you might want to get out of the water. You're turning purple."

Alice and Mark looked over each other and then themselves. Filled with shock, they quickly swam out of the water.

"How long do you think it will last?" Alice asked in a sad tone tinged with desperation.

"I don't think it's a stain; I think it's from drinking it." Aaron replied.

"We should be on our way," Saphron stated. "My father is awaiting your arrival," she added, trying not to laugh as she looked at Mark.

Aaron returned to Zenda's side as they began to walk. Alice and Mark gathered their clothes and ran to join them. Shaking her head, Saphron followed behind, watching as they struggled to walk and dress.

Around the next corner, the glow worms vanished. For a brief moment they were consumed by darkness. Then a blinding light flooded the tunnel from an opening ahead.

Stepping into the light, this tunnel led them to a lush field of flowing, blue grass. Once their eyes come into focus, the human trio could see thriving land all around them, vast and forested with strange growth. Trees with black bark towered over them, blanketing them from an unknown light source with their deep-blue leaves. Some bore large fruits that looked like yellow and green melons.

As a leaf fell from above, they watched it slowly drift to the ground. Aaron quickly reached down to examine it. Being larger than his head, he could clearly see the veins bulging through the deep-blue skin. A silent awe filled the humans as Zenda granted them passage into the forest. Birds unlike any they had ever seen, even within the ship's archives, flew about and rested in the trees. Calls rang throughout the treetops as the creatures landed to stretch their massive, green-feathered wings. Off in the distance, a huge lake of purple resting in the center of a tiny village came into view. Mark and Alice looked at each other with embarrassment at their pigment.

Passing through the woods, they entered the small village. Homes made of the bamboo-looking material, along with wooden carts on dirt paths, set the visitors' memories back to the primitive years of man. Making their way through the village, several other cat people saw them on their travels. Each one dropped what they were doing to stare at the peculiar sight. Some even began to follow, though keeping their distance from them. Soon an open dirt path paved their way into another thick patch of forest, where a grand, black temple awaited them in its center.

"This looks like something out of the ancient times recorded in the ship's archives. Like Aztec or Mayan cultures of our past," Aaron pointed out. Mark and Alice were far too lost in the moment to respond.

Walking up the steps that led into the temple, Aaron glanced over his shoulder to see hundreds of the cat people standing and staring. Zenda lightly pulled him inside. Torches lined the hall, lighting their way down the long, black-walled tunnel.

Zenda paused just at the hall's end. "Wait here. I will tell him of your coming."

Zenda walked into the main chamber. "Great Noma," his voice echoed throughout the temple, "we have brought you the creatures that we found."

"Bring them before me." The deep, growling voice vibrated through the chamber, sending chills up the humans' spines.

"Okay, let's go," Saphron stated, as she pushed them into the room, where they saw Zenda on one knee. "Kneel before Noma."

All three dropped to one knee, staring at the massive figure before them. A great humanoid tiger sat in a throne made of what looked like black, insect exoskeletons. His right eye was closed over, sealed shut by a gaping scar. His other stared, stern and powerful, with a golden gleam. This massive beast could single-handedly tear down a hundred humans. Thousands, if they were unarmed.

"What have you brought me, my daughter?" He rose from his throne and slowly walked down to Aaron, his hands gripped behind his back. "Yes, he is the one, he understands. Stand and speak with me." Aaron stood, feeling how puny he was next to Noma. "You must have many questions of your own?" the great tiger asked.

"Yes. How is there light here? How long have you been here? What—"

"One question at a time." Noma lifted his paw and lightly laughed. "Come with me; I will show you everything."

He led Aaron by the hand, and they emerged from where the group had entered the temple moments before. Hundreds of the cat-kind stood, waiting for their great leader to speak.

"For generations we have been told he would come to our world," Noma addressed to his people, "that he would guide us on our path." Noma lifted Aaron's hand into the air, almost lifting him completely off the ground. "He has come!" All of the inhabitants began to cheer, standing in visible awe of his presence. "Now that he is here, we must respect him, let him be in peace. There will be plenty of time for our ponderings. Go back to your homes, and tonight there will be a festival in his honor."

The crowd slowly dispersed, though many lingered and watched as Noma and Aaron walked off into the woods. Noma, like an excited child, swiftly pulled Aaron along. Mark and Alice both stood in awe watching as Zenda helped disperse the crowd. Saphron grabbed them both by the arm, dragging them along to join her king.

Noma and Aaron, far ahead of the others, broke from the forest to a large clearing that led to a cliff overlooking an ocean of purple. Noma pointed up at a small, glowing sphere in the sky, no larger than a medicine ball. "This is what gives us light."

Caught in a daze, Aaron stood there trying to come to terms with the existence of a hollow planet. Its tiny internal sun gave birth to all within. This place held more life than he had ever physically seen.

Saphron and the others had finally caught up to find Aaron still gaping as he stared off into the reverse horizon. The other humans quickly joined in his moment of amazement.

"What are these creatures?" Saphron asked her father.

"I'm not sure, but I feel as though they hold a great importance for us," Noma whispered.

Saphron and Zenda walked back toward the temple, leaving the humans to bask in the awe-inspiring light. Aaron sat down at the cliff's edge, looking down at the massive ocean below. His mind raced with all of the possibilities of this planet's existence. Lost, as a flock of birds flew by high overhead, Alice and Mark were likewise speechless.

"Come, it will be dark soon," Noma explained.

"Dark?" Aaron asked, baffled by the statement. "How does it become dark?"

"There is a smaller, nested partial sphere that floats around the sun. As it turns, it engulfs the light," Noma explained. "Now, there is food being prepared, followed by entertainment. There will be plenty of time for questions."

Noma turned and began to walk back to the temple. Aaron remained close by his side. Mark and Alice quickly joined, as they disappeared into the woods.

Making their way through the forest, darkness slowly set in. Aaron and the others remained in silence as they arrived back at the temple. Two stone bowls raged with fire outside of the entrance. As they approached, a large cat stepped out of the dark entrance, carrying a large spear.

"Noma, all is ready," he stated, bowing to one knee.

"Thank you, my child." Placing his hand on the soldier's arm, Noma released him to continue his duties.

The hall inside the temple was lined with kneeling soldiers. As Noma passed, they rose, following him into the main chamber. Pleasant aromas filled the air as they entered to see three massive banquet tables set up with enough food to feed hundreds.

"You will dine by my side," Noma stated, as he made his way to the center table. Sitting at its middle, Noma waved for Aaron to sit on his right. Alice quickly plopped down next to Aaron. Mark went to sit on Noma's left as Saphron entered the room. Followed by several other females, she was dressed in her finest robes and jewelry, looking as a true princess. All of Mark's attention focused on her as she slowly glided to the table. Without haste, Mark pulled out a chair for her to sit next to her father.

"You sit next to me. I want to keep an eye on you," she stated as she sat. Mark followed her command, sitting down next to her without removing his eyes from hers. "Why do you keep staring at me?" she calmly asked.

"Sorry," Mark nervously stated. He quickly glanced around the room and down at his empty plate in embarrassment.

The main hall quickly filled up with many of the kingdom's people. Men, women, and even the children were allowed to dine with their king. They all lined up behind their chairs and awaited Noma's blessing. He arose, and the people sat.

"Tonight is a very special time for us. Many of our warriors have approached their Humana—" the surrounding crowd roared out, "but we have new friends and honored guests." Aaron and the others, uncertain of what to do, quickly stood and sat back down. Looking over toward her, Mark could feel Saphron's stare.

Noma continued, "This shall be a celebration unlike any other." With his head high in the air, Noma released a deafening roar.

Suddenly, from behind, several females entered and began to load the king's plate with food. With his first bite, the females quickly served everyone else. Mark looked at what was laid on his plate with skepticism, absolutely uncertain of what he saw.

"That's the finest part of Valkata," Saphron explained.

"What were those again?" Mark asked, repulsed at the sight.

"First eat." A smirk lined her face while she took a huge bite of her food.

Aaron, trying to be polite, picked up a small portion with his finger. As he doubtingly swooshed it around in his mouth, he discovered it to have a very appealing taste. Turning to tell Alice the food was okay, he saw that she had already dug in. Her lips were lined with the slimy coating of the Valkata meat.

She stopped with a startled expression. "What?" she asked with a grin.

Everyone continued to eat until every plate was clean. Noma, picking his teeth with his claw, grinned deeply. Aaron, Alice, and Mark were completely content with their bellies full.

Noma got up from the table and turned to Aaron. "It is time." With another mighty roar, everyone rose and began to leave the temple in silence. "Come, you will enjoy this." Taking Aaron under his arm, Noma led him and the other guests out.

Outside, many warriors knelt on both sides of the path. Each held a torch to guide them through the thick forest. Small fireflies danced about in the night sky, blinking in and out of the thick grass. In the distance, they could hear faint sounds of a deep, entrancing drum beat. As they drew closer, the drum beats became louder, reaching their maximum volume as they entered a clearing just at the rim of a giant crater.

Inside the crater was a natural maze of rock formations and stalagmites. Its inner rim was lined with millions of long, jagged rocks, making any form of escape from the indentation impossible. Everything looked just as the surface of the planet above.

On the opposite side of the crater, two large, wooden drums hung down from wooden frames. They created an entrancing tune as they were rhythmically beat by a single cat. His lightning precision drove the crowd as they gathered. Other warriors lined

173

the crater's outer edge, spinning the torches they held as they danced about to the beat. A massive throne and seating for hundreds, all made from the exoskeletons of what the humans now recognized as the Valkata, awaited the crowd.

"This is the only place inside the sphere that is as the surface," Noma explained as he led the visitors to their seats. "Since our dawning we have used this place to prove that we are warriors—that we can survive."

Upon reaching their seats, Noma addressed his people once more. "Many have come here!" The seats quickly filled up. Noma continued. "Many have died to prove their skills as warriors, as survivors, as destroyers of Valkata. Those who wish to prove themselves, step forward."

There was a peaceful silence as young warriors lined up at a large opening to the crater. Both males and females of all sizes waited patiently for their chance. "This year looks more promising than the last." With his hand, he waved the fighters his graces and permission to step inside.

Noma sat and watched as each warrior grabbed a long-handled club and entered the crater-arena. Positioning themselves in different locations throughout the maze, they readied for battle. As the last one entered, a massive wooden gate closed behind him. Standing straight up, they rested their club heads on the ground.

"Call forth the Great Machool!" Noma demanded.

Suddenly, and in perfect sync, the warriors began to bang their clubs heavily on the ground. The colossal steel-knobbed heads dug deep into the ground as they quickened their pace. Harder and harder they pounded, until the dirt below began to violently quake. Clubs in hand, they kept their focus on the ground below. Dirt flew into the air as something large ripped through the crater. High-pitched squelches echoed out as the thing broke the surface and burrowed under again. Only its dark back could be seen as it traveled to the darkest point in the crater. A cloud burst shot into the sky as the ground exploded again from the shadows. With an eruption, a giant insect spiraled out of the darkness. Hundreds of legs flailed about as it squealed from behind razor-sharp pinchers. Turning from the light, it quickly burrowed back underground.

All went silent; only several little chirps came from the arena. His arms shooting up into the air, one of the warriors was pulled under the ground. Then, bursting out of the ground, a much smaller insect jumped out, wrapping its four long legs around another warrior. Drooling pinchers spread wide as it lunged for the warrior's chest. Just before it ripped into his skin, the fighter tore the insect's legs from its body and smashed it with his club. More and more Valkata popped up from the ground; a true battle of insect versus beast ensued.

As the action continued, Mark jumped to his feet. Within all of the excitement, he started to grow thirsty for some action of his own. Without a second thought, he darted from his seat toward the crater. Leaping in, he barely cleared the jagged rocks.

Noma stood with a gleam of excitement in his eyes as Mark landed safely inside. Roaring cheers echoed throughout the crater from the audience as Aaron and Alice, both dumbfounded by Mark's irrational act, could only watch in confusion as Mark made his move.

A Valkata instantly made a mad dash for Mark as he ran around the corner towards a fallen warrior. Thinking on his feet, he ducked as the creature lunged at him. It smashed into a pillar of rock, sending the stone crashing down and splattering the Valkata all over Mark.

Wiping the goo from his face in disgust, Mark noticed another was watching him. In a relentless stride, he sped toward one of the fallen warriors' clubs. His sticky hands gripped the handle. Trying his best to lift it, he was pulled to the ground by its intense weight. With nowhere to turn, Mark stood at the mercy of the giant bug. It leapt up to fly but was quickly grounded when its eyes hit the light coming from above the crater's edge. Squealing, it crashed down just in front of the human.

But the Valkata regained its footing quickly and scurried after Mark again. It managed to pin him against the wall but not come in for the deathblow. Mark struggled to hold back its head.

Pinchers just out of reach, the Valkata suddenly exploded as its body flew from off him and smashed into a large column of rock. Mark opened his eyes to see Saphron standing there, holding a club. Her beautiful outfit dripped with the remains of the Valkata. Tossing Mark over her shoulder, she leapt out of the crater, leaving the remaining warriors to fight.

Everyone around them was spattered with guts as she landed in the audience. Smiling deeply, she set Mark back down to his feet.

"You ruined your dress," Mark stated, receiving a smart grin from Saphron. "I owe you one."

"Next time be more prepared," she remarked back. "Let's go get cleaned up."

"You should see what our weapons do. I could have taken out the Machool thing with … Wait, do you guys like clean yourselves by …?"

"What do you mean?" the cat woman questioned, as Mark trailed off.

"Never mind," he laughed. Saphron led Mark back toward the temple.

Several warriors continued to fight. One by one the Valkata fell, but not without claiming some of the warriors as well. Out of the thirty that went in, only eleven emerged. Many ran up to aid their wounded family and friends. Noma stood with pride.

"We have given birth to a new clan of warriors. They are the fighters of tomorrow," Noma gracefully stated. Roars poured out from the crowd, and they began to disperse.

"Here you are safe from these creatures," Noma assured Aaron and Alice. "You can explore freely as long as you like. When you need to sleep, just come to the temple. At tomorrows light I want to show you something of great importance." Noma walked off, leaving Aaron and Alice at the crater. Looking down, they watched as the Valkata's remains were gathered.

"Let's just not stay here," Alice stated, tugging at Aaron's arm. In full agreement, he led her into the woods. "Do they really think you are this professor guy?" she asked.

"I think so. I've never seen a picture of him, so I have no idea what he looks like," Aaron explained. "I have to tell them the truth."

"Why? What if they get mad and try to kill us?"

"Well, if we lie and they find out it may be worse, like feeding us to those things. I'll look at whatever it is they have and tell them what it is, if I can, and—"

"What … and what?" she asked, doubting his thought process.

"I don't know. Maybe this is home." Aaron pulled Alice toward him for a kiss. "Let's go get some sleep. I want to look at that sun of theirs later." He led her by the hand into the temple.

Morning came, calling out for every bird to speak. Hundreds of different calls and cackles rippled throughout the forest. Aaron, trying to fully wake up, walked into the main hall to find Noma meditating in the center. He sat down on the floor patiently, not wanting to disturb the king.

Alice silently crept in behind him. Unaware of her presence, Aaron had to hold back his surprise as she scared the hell out of him. Mark also stepped in as the two tried to contain themselves. Shirtless, he bore a long, deep scratch down the length of his arm. The couples' horseplay ended as they noticed the mark.

"Did that thing get you last night?" Alice quietly asked, examining the wound. "It's a clean cut. Those things must have razor-sharp skin."

"Yeah, those giant bugs are nuts," he whispered in a contrived manner. "Right before Saphron jumped in and—"

"Saved your ass," Aaron cut him off, whispering angrily. "What were you thinking? Look at you; you're half the size—"

"Saphron's going to give me some of our artillery back and arrange me a personal run. I can't wait," Mark explained with a grin, obviously eager for his second chance.

"You two seem to be getting along well," Alice barged in.

"What is that supposed to mean?" Mark asked, showing dim red embarrassment through his fading purple skin.

Aaron walked off as Alice continued to throw playful accusations at Mark. Traipsing through the lush forest, Aaron's ears were graced by the birds' filling the air with song. Only small spots of light shined through the thick leaves, but it was enough to guide him on his path. Arriving back at the cliff from yesterday brought him back to the moment when he first saw it all. Purple waves crashed against the cliff wall below. He sat watching the sun as it flickered sporadically with rainbow colors. Within the spectacular display Aaron knew there was something not right. Thinking back to the *Nexees'* archives of solar activity it dawned on him. This sun, this tiny little sun, was going to supernova.

As Aaron tried to wrap his mind around what lay before him, Noma silently stepped out of the woods. Walking up from behind, he paid the human the same silent, peaceful respect Aaron had given him minutes ago. Without alerting Aaron, he placed himself down beside the man.

"I knew you'd be here; this place calls many of us to it," he stated with a grin. "This all seems so strange to you, doesn't it?" Placing his paw around Aaron, he pulled him close. "I want to show you something. What you left for us to remember you by." Noma rose to his feet and began to walk along the cliff's edge. "Come."

Aaron scampered to catch up to him. "Noma, I have to tell you something." Aaron's head faced the ground in shame. "I'm not who you think I am. The man who sent you here died thousands of years ago. I just—" Choked off, he looked to Noma, seeking forgiveness.

"Well, if you *are* not him, you are *of* him. You will see."

Noma's reassurance of Aaron's importance somehow only furthered Aaron's doubt. In all of their travels, Aaron couldn't even help himself yet help those who have it better.

Noma turned, walking into the woods. He led Aaron down a short dirt trail. Towering trees with leaves that blocked out all of the sun's light lined their path. Ahead, two large, flaming bowls lit up their destination: a large, dark cave. Arriving at the entrance, Noma retrieved a small torch lying beside one of the bowls.

"This is a sacred place where we come when we are lost within life's questions," he explained, lighting the torch. "Here is the only cave that doesn't lead to the surface."

Inside the torch had little effect against the black cave walls. A slight decline took them on a downward spiral deeper into the planet.

"I had a vision," Noma began, "I saw a man who looked just like what you are about to see. This man, different from us, would save us from a danger we do not understand." Damp, cold air rushed past them as they descended further. "We're almost there," Noma assured him as he continued. "I saw great light filled with hundreds of fallen warrior's souls screaming out. I did not understand it myself, that was until you arrived. When I saw you, it all became very real. We have arrived."

Suddenly the narrow path opened up into grand dome. Noma walked the circumference, lighting torches all around the room. In the center of the room, the people had erected a massive altar made from the shells of Valkata. A small, steel sphere rested atop, a soft hum emanating from it. Book upon book lay stacked next to the altar, each holding each other's weight. "Here is our wisdom, our understanding of life," the cat king said.

Inspecting the books, Aaron was amazed at the collection. Science, history, math, religion—and each tome's pages were fragile from time. Careful not to damage it, he opened a science book, looking for its date. He turned a few pages but feared their brittleness, so he slowly closed the book and placed it back on the pile.

"These books are older than I am, possibly older than this planet." Excitement filled Aaron's veins. "He really believed it would work. Where did you see what he looked like?"

"There." Noma pointed to the metal sphere. "We cannot make anything close to that material," he explained. "All of what you see here is from where you were found." Reaching to the sphere, Noma extended one of his claws. "Here, see for yourself."

Pushing a tiny dot on its side, the sphere's insides began to glow. Bright blues, then reds shot out all over the room as a humming noise grew. Suddenly from atop of the sphere, a holographic image of Professor Helix's head appeared.

"Welcome, travelers," his voice said, broken and muffled. "If you are listening to this, you have survived your journey and are living on a new planet. Hopefully the crossing of the DNA strands was successful in creating something pleasant, something kind. Live in peace, and I shall come for you to see how my creation is growing. Namaste; be one with each other." The message ended, and the image disappeared.

"You see, he said he would come, and you are here," Noma stated with a cat's grin.

"I'm not him," Aaron stated mournfully shaking his head. "He died a long time ago. I just can't believe he did it. Where I come from this was all considered a hoax, something to keep our minds open. I never would have imagined this. Noma, I'd like to take this back to my ship to analyze it," Aaron concluded, a plea showing his eagerness to discover more.

"Analyze? I do not understand. Do you mean that thing that you travel in the sky with?"

"Yes, the computer on my ship can read it and get more information off of this," Aaron clarified.

"If you think it will help you, then yes."

With Noma's permission, Aaron moved to pick up the sphere. To his surprise, the grapefruit-sized sphere weighed more than fifty pounds. It took both hands for him to remove the sphere from its resting place.

Noma led the way as they traveled across the landscape back to the temple. Alice, Mark, and Saphron awaited their arrival. Seeing Aaron toil along the trail, Alice ran up to help. His face red with exhaustion, he stumbled along, dropping the sphere at their feet.

"Father, you let him take the sphere? Why?" Anger filled Saphron's voice.

"Calm down, Saphron; they are here to help us. If he needs the sphere, then he must have it," Noma explained, calming her.

"Alice, we've got to get this back to the ship. This place, and their sun ..." he started to explain, catching his breath.

"Calm down. We don't even know if there's light out there," Alice replied.

"There is light now, but it will not last for more than six hours. If you want to go, you must do it soon," Noma informed them. "Saphron, make sure they get there safely."

"Yes, Father, but I think this one should remain behind, just to ensure their return." Saphron pointed to Mark, who looked quite embarrassed.

Noma agreed. Catching his breath, Aaron tried once more to lift the sphere. Saphron laughed deeply as he dropped it again. With one mighty paw, she picked up the sphere as though it was nothing.

"Let's go." Saphron led Alice and Aaron out of the temple to a nearby cave. "It'll only take a few minutes to get there."

"How do you know how long the outer light lasts?" Aaron asked, his curiosity getting the better of him.

"Our people know everything there is to know about their surroundings, if not then the Valkata will feast on their bones," she replied with a grin. Aaron, completely satisfied with her answers, allowed her to lead the way.

With the soft, blue glow of the worms lighting their path, they traveled quickly through the catacombs. Saphron knew every path instinctively as she rushed along.

"Here." Saphron pointed to a lit opening in the distance. "There is your ship."

"Thanks, Saphron. We will return," Aaron said.

"And not for Mark; you can keep him," Alice added with a smirk.

Saphron smiled deeply then let out a burst of laughter as she handed Aaron the sphere. Almost dropping it, he managed to brace himself and maintain its weight. Stepping out into the light, the humans raced back to the ship waiting nearby, clearly visible in the red light from above. Once aboard, Alice quickly fired up the engines, and the two rocketed off. Ripping through the atmosphere, they headed straight to the *Nexees*.

"What's this about, Aaron?" Alice harshly asked.

"Well, I was watching their sun and how it kept changing color. I think something bad is going to happen," he explained, fidgeting with the sphere.

"Like what? This place is perfect, and here you go acting like a maniac! What is wrong with you?" Alice gave him a slight glare before looking off into space.

"Just wait until we get back to the *Nexees*; I'm not going to explain it and then have to show you too."

Alice landed inside the *Nexees* docking bay, where Aaron quickly jumped out. Almost tripping over Mark's tools, he grabbed a small cart. Sluggishly, he loaded the sphere onto it before making a frantic dash for the bridge. Alice, not so enthused, trailed behind.

As the elevator doors opened to the bridge, Alice saw that Aaron had already begun to pull data from the ship's computer. "Get over here," he demanded. "Look, see their sun?"

"Yeah, it looks just like it ... How is it in—"

"Watch," he cut her off. Her eyes widened as the image of the sun folded into itself, creating a black hole. Everything around it dissolved as it was sucked into the vortex. "We have to get everyone off of that planet!" he exclaimed.

"How did you know? I mean you're not *him*, are you?" She stared deep into his eyes. "Maybe reincarnation?"

"Stop it." Repelled, Aaron pushed her away. "This is serious; and besides, we've been out here a long time. I've read everything there is in those archives." Embarrassed by his knowledge, he quickly changed the subject. "You take the clunker down; I'll take the *Scavenger*. Once we land, you and Mark bring down the other pods. We're going to teach cats to fly." Turning off the computer, he ran back toward the elevator. "Well, come on!" he exclaimed.

Alice stood up with a strident sigh. "Does there always have to be some kind of adventure with you?"

On the planet's surface, many of Noma's warriors kept watch for the humans' return. From out of the dimming red planet the two ships were spotted. Four large cats scurried out to help them back as they landed. In haste, they marched toward the temple. Stepping inside, Alice and Aaron were taken aback by the sight of Mark and Saphron carrying rifles. Laughing, they both appeared to be completely saturated with Valkata guts.

"What the hell have you two been doing?" Aaron asked, completely confused.

"Oh, you're back. She wanted to see what these could do," Mark explained.

"After I saw the first Valkata explode like that, I had to join in," Saphron added, smiling at Mark. "We really should go clean up."

"Wait, Saphron, I need you to get as many of your people here as possible. I've got something you need to hear," Aaron frantically requested.

"My father is inside. Go to him; I will get the others." She pointed to Mark. "You go with them. You guards come with me." Saphron and the soldiers went off to gather the people.

As Aaron jogged down the main hall, he quickly stopped, seeing Noma meditating in the center of the room. "I knew you would come back, and I know that what you have to say is not going to be good," Noma quietly whispered, his eyes remaining shut.

"Yes," Aaron panted, gasping for breath. "I've told your daughter to gather the others. Everyone needs to know."

"Then we shall await their arrival." Noma stood, walking over to him. "I knew you were here to help us." Putting his arm around Aaron, he led him to the throne. "Here, sit and relax. There is always time for worry."

Aaron sat, then closed his eyes, trying to block out the imagery of what might happen. Shortly, some townsfolk arrived, quietly murmuring among themselves. More and more came into the hall, and with each one the whispers became louder. All spoke of confusion.

"Silence!" Noma shouted out. "He has brought us news of our world; we need to listen."

The whispering stopped as all focus turned to Aaron. Standing up, he opened his eyes to see the people. Hundreds stood before him, jamming up the hallways and surrounding the temple.

"Your world is in danger, as are all of you," Aaron stated, looking over the crowd as his nerves began to rise.

"Real subtle," Alice remarked.

"Your sun is going to destroy this planet. Our ship is large enough to carry everyone away before it happens," he added.

"What do you need of us?" Noma calmly asked, as the murmurs returned even louder than before.

"I need …" Aaron paused, waiting for the chatter to stop. "I need!" They became silent once more at his shout. "I need people to gather water and food, all that they can carry." Turning to Mark and Alice, he continued, "You two will fly me up with them; we'll bring back three ships."

"What about the light outside?" Mark reminded him.

"By the outside's light—we have to do it in the light," Aaron addressed the people.

"Hurry, everyone; there will not be light for long. By our nightfall, many of you will have to be ready to leave," Noma commanded.

Everyone rushed from the temple to retrieve what they needed. "And for me?" Noma humbly asked, turning to Aaron.

"Noma, we will take you right away. There is a place on our ship that resembles your forest. There, I believe your people can find comfort. They will come to you," Aaron respectfully stated.

"I understand," the cat king responded, dropping to one knee. "You shall lead us to salvation."

"I don't know what I'll lead you to, but it will be better than ending up inside out." Aaron pulled Noma to his feet. "Let's hurry, my friend."

In a furious dash, they raced toward the surface. With only six hours of light left, they loaded up both ships to their capacity.

They launched and arrived at the main ship in a matter of less than an hour. Aaron led Noma and his guards to the neglected and dying biosphere aboard the *Nexees*. "With your knowledge and care, Noma, I believe you and your people can bring this place back to life," Aaron explained.

Back inside the main hangar, Alice and Mark, in their separate ships, traveled back to the planet. Aaron, grabbing a third ship, joined them. On the planet's surface, as Aaron landed, he watched his cohorts already shuffling people onto their ships. One by one the cat people climbed aboard; many carried food, others water, some even brought what Aaron guessed must be pets—birds and other small creatures. The *Nexees* was to be their ark.

Aaron jumped out of his ship, quickly running over to Mark. "We're going to need a hell of a lot more ships," Aaron expressed loudly over the ship's engines.

"No shit!" Mark yelled back. "We're only going to be able to make a couple of trips before dark."

"Do you think you can teach them how to fly this thing?"

"Are you serious?" But by the look on Aaron's face, Mark quickly realized that this was no joke. "I can try."

"Use my ship. Fill it up, and show as many as you can how to pilot. We've got fifteen ships up there—"

"Thirteen," Mark cut him off, looking to the ground.

"What do you mean thirteen? What happened to the other two?" Mark just continued to look down as Aaron waited for an answer. "Fine, it doesn't matter. Just train them."

Mark darted off to recruit some of the cat people for a crash course in flying space ships. Luckily they were so marveled by the sight of the ships that they did not understand the danger. They quickly signed up for the sake of their race. With a full crew, he slowly took to the air, making his way through the mountainous trench. Giving the crew a quick course in flight controls, he headed up toward space.

Alice launched slowly then shot off into the sky. Aaron, shutting his bay door, followed closely behind. Dropping off his passengers, Aaron realized that this was the last trip for now. Only enough daylight remained to get back to the surface.

Upon landing, Aaron and Alice noticed that the area was vacant, not one person to be seen. Off in the distance they saw Mark blast off into the atmosphere. Saphron ran out from a nearby cave, greeting them a bit frantically as they hurried out of their vessels.

"Come on, there isn't much time, the Valkata are coming," she stated, pushing them toward the cave. "Your friend knows not to return—not for at least ten hours."

Walking back through the caves and toward the village, they passed those who were ready to go. They waited with possessions under their arms. Some slept, while others maintained their children, keeping the panic quiet. All smiled and held hope within as Aaron passed.

"They believe in you, you know. You are their savior," Saphron pointed out. "Come, you must rest in the temple."

Reaching the main hall, Aaron collapsed with the thoughts of all of the people that will be lost. He is the only one with the realization of the situation, a burden that was his alone. The great leader became overwhelmed and fell to the ground. Alice, quick to his side, caught him before his head met the floor. His eyelids weighed heavy on his face, pulling him into unconsciousness. Resting on the cool floor beside him, Alice curled up next to him.

"You love him, don't you?" Saphron inquired.

"Yes, very much," Alice answered, caressing his head. "He means a lot to me."

"I know how you feel," Saphron testified. "I will await his return."

Alice was dumbfounded, but before she could respond, Saphron ran from the temple. Lying beside Aaron, she herself began drifting away to sleep. Movements in their sleep caused them to become intertwined as their bodies searched for heat.

Waking up, they opened their eyes to find themselves nose to nose. Alice's eyes grew soft as she touched Aaron's cheek. Without a sound, she pulled him in, kissing him gently. Light love turned to passionate fire as she rolled on top of him.

"Ahem." Mark's voice came from behind, ruining the moment. "Sorry to interrupt you two, but I thought you might like to know," he announced with remorse, "that there are only ten ships left. A few of them became fireballs on entry."

"How much time do we have until it becomes dark again?" Aaron asked, as Alice climbed off of him.

"It should be about four hours," Saphron answered. "The outside cycle can be erratic, though, so maybe less."

"With ten ships, we can make this process a hell of a lot faster, at least." Aaron sat up, rubbing his hand through his hair. "Have the people already started?"

"Yeah, they've probably already dropped off the first run and are on their way back," Mark explained.

"How much time until *it* happens?" Saphron asked.

"I'm not sure, it could happen at any moment, or in days," Aaron answered, avoiding the true answer. "We have to hurry."

Aaron bolted out of the temple back toward the ships. Saphron followed swiftly behind.

Mark just stood there, gloating over Alice. "You couldn't have waited a half hour longer, asshole," she remarked, walking past him.

"Now, how could I let you two have a moment?" he smarted back, walking up behind her. "Besides, there will be plenty of time for that later, when we get the hell out of here."

They joined up with Aaron and Saphron to see transports frantically landing and leaving. Aaron was helping people board, while Saphron tried to keep the people organized and patient as they ran about in semi-chaos. A ship landed nearby, hard, exploding. Debris flew past Aaron, and one of Saphron's people was hit with a chunk. He was instantly killed, as was the newly trained pilot of the ship.

Chaos became panic, causing the people to run amuck. Several jumped on as a ship started to lift off. Rocking from the weight, it too came down, becoming a fiery ball and taking all the lives around it.

"Aaron!" Alice screamed out, running to him. "How much time do we have?"

"Realistically, only a couple of hours—that's leaving enough time to get away on the *Nexees*." Hearing those words, Alice quickly joined Saphron in getting people calm and organized. Things proceeded more or less smoothly, for a time.

"Aaron!" Saphron yelled out. "We only have a few minutes of light left out here; we have to hurry!" As more people climbed aboard the ships, the light slowly trickled away.

"We can't stop; just keep loading everyone in!" Aaron exclaimed.

"With all of this noise, the Valkata are sure to come!" Saphron shouted.

"Mark, it's time to get hot!" Alice cried out.

Mark ran up to their ship, gathering as many guns as he could carry. Passing them out to the others, they prepared for the inevitable attack. Within minutes, several clicking noises filled the air, drowning out the sounds of the ships flying about. Suddenly one of the ships was attacked by a swarm of Valkata. It crashed down, lighting up the area. Aaron looked across the plain; Valkata stretched out as far as the eye could see, completely surrounding them. Alice opened fire, quickly taking down several as they flew in. Mark aided, helping to thin the ground forces. They were backed by the cat warriors, who engaged with claws, ripping apart the insects. Yet wave after wave flooded the grounds, killing and dragging off the people.

Aaron rushed up behind Alice, blasting a Valkata that splattered all over her back.

"Thanks," she stated half sarcastically, flicking guts from her fingers. Together they blasted their way to a ship. "It's time to go, everyone. This is the last trip," he shouted. With hundreds of Noma's people remaining and only eight ships to evacuate them, escape for all was an impossible target.

Mark and Saphron quickly banded together and made their way toward their only escape route. All of the other surviving ships lifted off on their final trip to the *Nexees*.

Bullets flying, Saphron got caught up as Mark slowly left her behind. From below, the ground began to massively shake.

"The Great Machool comes!" Saphron screamed out.

The remaining people ran to the ship as Machool passed beneath them. Rippling the ground, it slithered past Saphron, feeling her weight above. Finally the creature burst from the ground, sending out a massive cloud of dust as it towered over the ship. Saphron instantly opened fire on it, turning its attention. With her in its sights, Machool pulled its long body from the ground, with hundreds of legs in motion. Whipping over the surface, it twisted its way toward Saphron.

Still holding back the attacking Valkata, Mark spotted Saphron's trouble. Not missing a beat, he hurried to help her. Mark shot unending barrels of fire, which did nothing as the bullets bounced off the creature's exterior. From behind his back, he drew his grenade launcher. Closer and closer the beast came. Mark ran viciously toward it as the mother creature headed straight for him.

Saphron, though running away at full speed, was quickly losing ground as Machool gained. Just as she and Mark passed, he got a clear shot at Machool's head. He fired with a vengeance. In one large blast, the head exploded, covering Mark, Saphron, and the nearby ship in its juices. Even Alice and Aaron, who were standing at the ship's door, were covered as well. As Machool fell the Valkata became furious and swarmed towards its slayers.

Mark and Saphron quickly climbed aboard. Covered in two layers of slime, Mark jumped to the controls. He blasted the ship off the ground headed for space, they being the last to leave. The ship crashed through several flying Valkata, smearing the glass with guts, as they left the planet behind.

"Clear," Mark stated as they broke through the atmosphere.

"We're not clear yet; we have one hour to get out of this planet's orbit or we'll be sucked into the black hole," Aaron exclaimed.

Mark landed the ship aboard the *Nexees*. All of Noma's people had gathered and had even already started to tend to the great garden. Saphron joined Aaron and the others ran to the ship's bridge.

"We've got to move fast!" Aaron shouted, taking the controls. "Alice, go see if anyone down there needs any medical attention."

"Not a chance," she stated as she strapped herself down in the copilot's seat. "I'm not going to miss this for anything. Saphron, can you take care of that for me?" Nodding her head yes, Saphron ran off to the garden.

"Mark?" Aaron called out.

"No, I'm not sleeping with Saphron!" he shouted back in the heat of the moment.

"What? No, pull up the holograph of this galaxy. I wouldn't want to run into a planet on the way out."

"Got it; now get us the hell out of here!" Mark yelled.

As the *Nexees* sped past the tiny red planet a shock wave blasted past it, causing the ship to spiral out of control. Alice's wide-eyed stare focused on Aaron, fighting the controls. Holding on for dear life, Mark gripped his chair. Aaron wrestled the ship back under control as they got a view of the dark planet folding into itself. The bending of space at its core in two separate sections created a frictional force between the rolling negative polarities. Another wave pushed toward them, this one visible as an expanding sphere of fire. The wave spread outward through the system rapidly, engulfing the ship and the nearby planets. Everyone held tight while the ship rattled violently. Sweat poured down their faces as the temperature inside the ship quickly rose. But slowly the wave passed and dissipated, releasing everything from its intense heat. From the center of the dark planet, a new sun was born.

With the chaos at an end, Aaron put the ship in orbit around a small orange planet, both it and the *Nexees* shaken but left intact by the violent wave front.

Aaron sighed with relief. "It's over." Reaching to a call box on the console, he addressed the people in the ship's compartments below. "If anyone down there is still alive, the danger is over. We have survived."

"It's amazing," Alice stated, looking out toward the new sun. "I thought you said it was going to cause a black hole."

"It would have. I think the other mass around their sun must have had similar properties, causing—"

"Who cares, we're alive!" Mark added, cutting off Aaron. Just then, the elevator door opened. Saphron, Noma, and Zenda joined them on the bridge.

"See, I told you that you would help us find our way," Noma said with a grin.

"Thanks for protecting me back there," Saphron said to Mark, "but I'm still covered in guts. Is there somewhere we can clean up?" Mark led her by the hand to the elevator.

"So, now what will we do?" Zenda asked.

"Well, we can float here for a little while until we get the garden running smoothly. Then we'll do what we've been doing for the last few thousand years: look for another planet," Aaron explained with a shrug of his shoulders.

Zenda and Noma, unsure of what to think, made to leave the bridge. "Thank you," Zenda kindly stated, bowing his head.

The elevator door closed, leaving Alice and Aaron all alone. Alice seized the opportunity to her advantage. Getting out of her seat, she backed Aaron into a corner. "You truly are a hero." As Alice kissed him, the two intertwined within each other's passion.

With Aaron's advice, everyone worked hard on the old, dying garden. As the months passed, the grass became green and lush. Trees that were once dying started to fill with leaves, bearing fruits of every kind. Even the house pets the cat people had brought instantly took residence and began to flourish. After six month's time, the ecosystem was running perfectly. A purple-water lake replaced the dried-up hole in the biosphere's center. Everyone was at peace with their surroundings.

Aaron endlessly scanned their maps of the universe, searching for the next possible stop. While scrolling through the different galaxies one particular day, he came to one he had never seen before—one with a large sun and planets that had never been explored. Trying to pinpoint its location, he began to feel the power of frustration. All coordinates continually came back unknown. Exhausted, he sat back in his chair to stew. Alice, who had been working in the garden, took a break to check on him. Staring out at the dark planet's new sun, Aaron didn't even turn as the elevator opened.

"Any luck yet?" Covered in dirt, Alice made herself comfortable in the chair next to him. Aaron continued to stare at the sun, holding back his frustration. "Come on, Aaron, forget this crap and come help us down there for a while. It might help you forget. What's wrong?"

"I found a new galaxy," he stated sluggishly.

"Really, when do we leave?" Alice excitedly asked, spinning in her chair.

"We can't get there; the ship's computer cannot find a point of location." Aaron's dull statement of the truth stomped on her excitement. "The worst part is there might actually be something there. Why does it always have to happen like this?"

"Can't we just find a galaxy next to it and try from there?" she suggested. She looked out the window. "Wow, the new sun is so beautiful," she stated, leaning closer to the super-strong glass.

"What did you say?"

"That new sun is beautiful," she repeated with a hint of questioning in her voice, wondering why he'd asked.

"Why didn't I think of that? I'm so damn stupid!"

Aaron jetted up out of his chair over to the universal map. Pulling up the unknown galaxy, he compared it to the maps from before the creation of the sun. Several differences became apparent. "I should have seen this! Why didn't I see this?"

"What is it?" Alice asked, joining his side.

"The reason why the computer couldn't pinpoint the location is because we are already in it. That shock wave must have changed all of the planets' compositions. That one there, that's the one, I think it might be okay." He pointed to a blue planet that, upon his survey before the adventure on the dark planet, he had found to be covered in ice. "It must have instantaneously created an atmosphere when it melted. Let's get moving!" Aaron jumped back to the controls, plugging in the data he needed to get there.

As the ship started to move, Mark, who had been working on the transports, dropped what he was doing and darted for the bridge. Stepping from the elevator, he ran over to see Aaron and Alice with a spark of hope in their eyes. "What's going on, Aaron? Why are we moving?" Mark fearfully questioned.

"He's found a planet," Alice explained. "Are any of the ships ready?"

"Yeah, the *Scavenger* should be fine. I'll go make sure." Mark ran off, back down to the ship's docking bay.

"We need to tell the others," Aaron told Alice.

They headed off the bridge. As the elevator was going down, Alice smothered him in kisses, smearing dirt all over his face. In the hangar, Saphron was looking over the *Scavenger* for possible problems while Mark lay underneath welding.

"Hand me that hammer, please?" Mark asked Saphron.

"She must be special; I never get a please," Aaron remarked from behind them.

"She'll be ready to fly in a few minutes, Captain," Mark replied.

"Finally, some respect. Saphron, will you go and tell your father we've found something?" Aaron requested. Saphron quickly left for the garden.

"That should do it," Mark said, pounding on the ship's underbelly. After a few whacks with the hammer, he crawled out from under the ship. "Okay, she's flight-worthy."

"Why is it every time you work on this thing, you have to hit it with that thing? I feel *so* safe," Alice stated sarcastically. Saphron returned with Zenda by her side.

"We are going with you on the scouting missions," Zenda demanded, placing a paw on Aaron's shoulder. "If there is any danger whatsoever, we will protect you. We owe you that."

"Besides, I couldn't let anything happen to you." Looking at Mark, Saphron gave him a massive smile. "I owe you one."

Reaching its destination, the *Nexees*'s computer called out, "Planetary orbit achieved." Its female voice rang over the intercom. "All travel windows are open," it added.

"Is everybody ready?" Mark asked, boarding the *Scavenger*.

"I hope this isn't a waste of our time," Aaron stated.

"Don't worry, we'll find something. We have to," Alice assured him.

With everyone aboard, Mark flew the ship out of the bay and into the planet's orbit. From the windows they could see green patches of land surrounded by vast, blue oceans. Pushing at the controls, Mark entered the atmosphere. The ship burned from the intense heat of entry. Flames engulfed the small ship as it sped through. Shaking profusely, the ship gained massive speed as it spiraled toward the planet's surface. Mark struggled to gain back control. Fighting the stick, Mark looked back to Saphron. Leaning over him, she grabbed the controls. With her mighty strength, she slowly pulled back on the stick, leveling out the ship. Mark kissed her cheek as he returned to flying the craft.

Finding a soft beach next to an ocean to touch down on, Mark landed the ship. As the bay door opened, Aaron poked his head out to check the surroundings. Waves from the ocean washed up onto the shore, delivering a cool breeze that crossed over the land. Stepping out onto the beach, he reveled in the sight of the vast forest behind them. The others slowly emerged from the ship, standing in awe of this marvel.

"Where did this all come from?" Alice asked, slowly taking it all in.

"It must have been frozen under all of the ice," Aaron pondered. Suddenly, a large fish broke from the water, creating a huge splash as it landed. "This is so amazing. No one has ever seen anything like this. I need to run some tests on this water, Alice," he shouted out kneeling on the shore.

Alice was amazed by the sights around her. "Yeah, whatta ya need?" she asked, half paying attention.

"Quit daydreaming," Aaron barked out, "get a few of the leaves off of the tree over there. I want to compare their properties to the ones on the ship."

"What, who cares, look at this place, come on, you can do it. Look at it and take it for what it is, *please*," Alice begged.

"We can call this home," Zenda happily stated.

"Yes, I think we can survive here," Saphron added.

"Let's go back and get the others," Mark proposed.

"Fine," Aaron erupted with frustration, "I'm still going to take these samples back with me."

Climbing back aboard, they left the peaceful, warm planet to return to the *Nexees*. As soon as the ship landed, they headed for the garden. This place that once moved them seemed dull in comparison to their new finding. Walking past the working people, the human and cat crew sought out Noma. They found him at peace, posed under a tree in meditation.

"What did you find?" he asked softly. Aaron stepped forward, kneeling down in front of him. Noma opened his eye. "There is no need for you to bow to me, great one. It is we who are in debt. Now, tell me what you have found."

"We have found a planet that will hold us. It's full of life and seems peaceful. I think your people will be safe there," Aaron explained.

"We shall go there, then, and see this place." Noma rose, letting out a deafening roar. All of his people stopped their work and gathered before him. "My people, our saviors have yet again come to our aid. They have found a permanent place for us, a home on the planet below," he explained, as murmurs began to fill the air. "We shall go at once."

Loading up the few remaining travel-worthy ships, Noma, Mark, and a handful of the cat people followed Aaron and Alice in the *Scavenger* to the surface. Everyone became blinded as they stepped out into the bright sunlight. Squinting, they tried to take in the sights before them. Happiness covered their faces as they turned to see the verdant forest.

"You have brought us pure salvation," Noma told Aaron. "My people, we have found a home."

"We will bring all of the others to you," Aaron disclosed.

Leaving Noma and his people behind, Aaron, Alice, and Mark returned to pick up the others. Their task ran them into the night. Noma's people built fires on the beach to give them light for landing. In the morning, the last of the people arrived on the planet. Working throughout the day, they began to rebuild their civilization. Aaron and the others slept through the day, leaving the work for the cat people. When they awoke, they came out to see an entire village standing before them.

"They sure are ambitious, aren't they?" Alice stated.

"Yes, they are," Aaron confirmed.

"This place is great," Mark added.

Saphron emerged from one of the huts to see them standing there. "We have built you all your own homes," she explained, walking up to them. "Come, Noma wants to see you." She led them into the forest to a large clearing. Noma sat back, watching as his people built a great temple of wood and stone. "Father, they're awake."

"Wonderful. Look, we are building this in your honor. It shall be your temple," he revealed.

"We're not staying," Aaron stated, looking over to Alice, who was utterly confused.

"What?" she and Mark both asked at the same time.

"With the sphere from Professor Helix, I think we might be able to locate the other ships," he explained. "We found you, so I think we might be able to find others."

"If you think there are others out there, then you must fulfill your destiny," Noma replied with understanding.

"I will go with you," Saphron demanded, stepping forward. "I want to keep an eye on this one," she added, putting an arm around Mark.

"Are you sure? I mean, we've finally found a place and you want to leave it?" Alice questioned Aaron, frantically hoping he would change his mind.

"I think we found these people for a reason, like we're supposed to do this," Aaron explained to her. "One day we shall return, Noma. This is our home, too." Aaron put his arm around Noma, as a deep smile cut into his face.

"I understand," Noma said with a smile. "We will await your return."

Aaron, Alice, Mark, Saphron, and several families of the cat tribe returned to the beach.

Saphron paused, looking back at Noma. "We want to help them, Father," she explained, "to explore with them and protect them."

"I understand, my daughter," Noma yelled out to those who chose to go. "Be well, my people; help them as they have helped us." All said their goodbyes to friends and families that they were leaving behind.

With the tears, hugs, and roars out of the way, Noma watched as they climbed aboard the ships and took off for the *Nexees*.

After arriving at the large ship, Aaron went to the bridge, while the other tribe members returned to their homes in the garden. Aaron connected the sphere to the main computer system, which sent out a signal into all space. Desperately he waited for any sign of a returning beacon, as Mark and Alice joined him on the bridge. Suddenly the universal computer turned on, pinpointing a weak signal coming from a distant galaxy.

"There, that is where we'll start," Aaron stated to the others. He took the controls and led them on to a new adventure.

Operation Miranda

Mac awoke especially early that morning; his new orders haunting him, sleep had become out of the question. Several hours remained between him and the zero hour. He paced, combing through his own mind, gazing at the ceiling. This was the first time he had felt fear since his first day at the academy. It was a long time past those days now. He had grown to be in the top two out of twenty within the organization. They were the ones to go into the unknown, unnoticed, to fix whatever problem may arise. However, this mission had him sweating in doubt.

Next to his bed on a small end table sat his briefing. Minutes passed slowly as it beckoned to him. Sitting up on the bed, he sipped from a small glass of water he had left there from the night before. As he looked toward the letter, he sprinkled tiny droplets from the glass onto his sweat-beaded, hairless head. This message taunted him like a demon. Pulled in by his fear, he read the paper once more.

Operation Miranda: Location: 40.434096 latitude; 115.475052 longitude. Elevation: 9,770 feet. Nearest city: Spring Creek, Nevada (9.7 miles). Miranda is a large research facility specializing in quantum theory and biological, chemical, and genetic engineering. We have lost all communications with Miranda. No reports to date have shown any signs of quandary. At this time we have many investors who are concerned. You, along with one other agent, will be taken by plane to Spring Creek. From there you will pose as scientists recording tectonic vibrations for study. You will then infiltrate Miranda. *Use force only if extremely necessary.* Report back immediately on anything you find. *This is strictly classified.* You leave at 0500. Your partner will meet you at Sky View Lodge, room 246. You will be briefed further from there.

If there was anything Mac hated about the organization it was that he never knew who he'd be working with. No background or way of determining if they were reliable. Those were important factors in Mac's eyes.

Now only one hour remained until he had to leave. He packed up his things to prepare for the job. Mac always kept himself ready for anything; he made damn sure nothing was missing.

One white tank top for easy mobility; one pair of military-issue black khakis; one pair of ankle-high black socks; one pair of steel-toed, military boots; two Colt .45 1911 pistols with six fifteen-round clips; one 9-millimeter submachine gun with four thirty-two-round clips; one small medical kit containing thread, disinfectant, and a small shot of morphine; and finally, one heavy combat blade. With all of his belongings packed, he headed out to the airstrip.

Outside, the sun had just begun to peek over the horizon. The dawn gleamed blindingly off of the black private jet waiting on the airstrip. Mac, not always at ease with flying, only trusted one man in the air. He had known his pilot, Charlie, for most of his career. Placing his bags into the cargo bin, he climbed aboard.

"There's a suitcase for ya, Mac," Charlie explained with a smirk as he peered from behind his tan beach bum hat.

"What's in it?" Mac asked, picking it up briefly and dropping it heavily in spite of his muscle mass.

"How the hell should I know; I'm just the pilot. We've got a four-hour flight with two stops, so sit back, relax, and we'll be there before you know it." Charlie slipped on his mirrored flight glasses and buckled himself in.

Mac sluggishly pulled the luggage behind him as he made his way to his seat. Charlie, behind the controls, fired up the engines. With a gradual whine, the jet started its way down the runway.

"Take it easy on the takeoff, will ya? Last time I damn near lost my breakfast."

Leaving the heavy bag in the aisle, Mac strapped himself in. Grabbing onto the armrests apprehensively as the jet roared down the runway, he closed his eyes tight. Doing so eased his mind as he was forced back into the seat. "I hate this shit!"

"Almost there, you big baby; wow, you are such a wimp." With a satisfied grin, Charlie took the plane up with a slow climb.

Once the plane stabilized, Mac's grip lessened, leaving imprints in the leather. His mind focused on the next task at hand as he unzipped the bag. In a deep search for anything that might make this mission a little more clear, he rummaged around inside. He found nothing of any important detail. Frustrated, he nearly ripped the zipper off as he closed it again. In pure dissatisfaction, he headed for the cockpit.

Charlie, hearing him approach, hit the throttle, giving the plane a slight burst of speed. Mac stumbled back from the force and fell into one of the seats.

"Thanks a lot, asshole."

"Oh, sit down and cool it. So, what was in the suitcase?" Charlie asked.

"Just some science gear for checking seismic waves and a badge. I'm now John Malcolm; can you believe it?" Mac placed his new name badge on his chest with a childish smirk.

"So, what's this all about?"

"I'm not sure. All I've been told is that we've lost communications with one of our laboratories. Some kind of biological engineering center. I'm supposed to meet up with another guy in town. I'll be briefed more then," Mac explained.

"Nice. Well, you know more than I do. All they tell me is to show up here and take this person there, not so exciting. Except for that one time in Pakistan; they damn near shot the belly of this plane right out from beneath me! But we haven't gone down yet, have we, baby?" Patting the instrument panel, Charlie smiled with pride. "You look worried, Mac. Why don't you get some shut-eye in the back? I'll let you know before get there."

"Cool. Thanks, Charlie."

As Mac walked back to his seat, Charlie pushed the speed again. Suspecting he'd try that, Mac threw his arms forward to grab the seat in front of him. "Real funny."

Mac settled into his seat, closing his eyes, hoping to go to a place of comfort—somewhere other than there. Never truly reaching sleep, he was held in the in-between state of consciousness, a translucent state of being. His mind dashed in and out of past moments. Like thinking of people he had killed in the name of a high-paying investor. Were such things done for the right reasons? This was a question that had plagued him since he'd joined the organization. His mind then began to drift off into the darkness.

"Wake up, Mac; we're at Elko Regional Airport." Charlie lightly tapped his shoulder, knowing not to startle him.

"How long was I out?" Mac questioned as he stood, shaking the cobwebs from his mind.

"About three hours." Charlie led Mac off the plane to the runway. "I've already secured you a car, and your bags are in it and ready to go."

Outside, Mac paused to take in the cool, pure air. "Thanks, Charlie. I really—"

"Don't worry about it," the pilot said, cutting Mac off. "I'll pick you up in a week. Wait till you see this car; it's unreal."

Mac and Charlie stepped out of the terminal building and into the street. Waiting there, to Mac's surprise, was a 1992 Ford Escort. What little silver was left untouched by rust gleamed in the midday sun. Both of his bags overfilled the backseat, with luck there was room in the tiny hatch for his personal suit case. "See? I told ya you'd love it."

"I can barely fit in this thing!" Mac exclaimed, as he squeezed his way into the driver's seat. The keys already inside, he started the engine. For being an older car, it sounded great. "Well, I better get moving," he grumbled. "I have to meet my partner."

"See ya in a week," Charlie stated, walking back inside the terminal.

Mac drove down NV 227 to reach the lodge. Even with the rolling hills and vast green forests to look at, nothing could take his mind from the mission. The closer he came to his destination, the more his heart sank. His mind tried to focus on his partner, on what he might be like.

Soon he was pulling into the parking lot. He was thankful the lodge looked to be in better shape than the car. Only Mac's weapons were important to him, so he left the science equipment behind for now. Before going in, he decided to ready one of the pistols; he could never be sure what would be waiting for him.

"Welcome to the Sky View Lodge. How may I help you, sir?" a young woman greeted him from behind the desk, her long, blonde hair accenting her pearl-white smile.

"My name is John Malcolm. I believe you have a room for me." Mac always remained calm and devoid of personality when dealing with civilians.

"Oh, yes sir. Room 246; your partner checked in last night. Thank you, and have good stay." Her smile covered half her face in a gesture of exaggerated politeness.

Mac walked toward the elevator, looking back at the girl as he entered. "If she only knew what I was carrying, her fake smile would become pure terror," he thought to himself. Reaching the second floor, he prepared his mind for what might come. He readied his pistol as he gave an ever-so-gentle knock on his room's door, set for anything.

"I'll be right there," a nervous man's voice called out. Mac assessed it as weak and frail. As the door opened swiftly, Mac drew his gun and pointed it in the man's face.

"Holy shit, put that thing away!" the man stated as he crumpled to the floor with his heart hammering in his chest.

As Mac stood there ready to shoot, the door across the hall began to open. An older woman emerged from the room as Mac lowered his gun, keeping it out of her sight. She glanced over the situation, her eyes showing confusion at the sight of a young, skinny, dark-haired man cowering on the floor while a bald behemoth stood over him. Giving them an odd look, she closed the door and walked down the hall.

Mac pulled the man from the floor, pushing him inside their room. "Are you trying to get yourself shot?" Mac asked in his deep, calm voice.

"They said you were jumpy, but I didn't—"

"Who are you, and what division are you from?" Mac demanded.

"M-my name is Simon Ferguson. I'm from the Omega division." The stutter in Simon's voice gave away his fear, though his eyes never blinked behind his glasses.

"Great, a tech," Mac put away his gun. "Can you handle a firearm?"

"Yeah, I was top of my class in marksmanship. I should have no problem if I need to," Simon explained.

"So, what do I need to know?" Mac's curiosity was driving him mad; with any luck, Simon held some answers.

Simon stood up and walked over to his laptop, open on the small desk by the shrouded window. After a few keystrokes he returned to show Mac the particulars. Without a care for computers, Mac was unimpressed by the detailed mapping system. Unpacking his personal belongings onto the twin bed near the window, Mac listened as Simon continued.

"The entrance to the facility is located here, just north of Mount Gilbert," Simon explained. "We'll be traveling up the mountain on this dirt road. From here we will have to walk. There's a cave right about here."

"A cave, how can that be secret? Anyone could find it," Mac expressed doubtfully.

"It's never been charted or mapped out. Not even the townsfolk know it's there. Besides, we won't be able to just walk in; there's a terminal hidden behind a rock formation that we'll have to access first."

"What should we expect inside?" Mac questioned.

Simon sat down on his own bed unsure of how to answer. "Well, there were several types of experiments going on simultaneously. I don't have any specific details yet. See, that's why they're sending me; I'm supposed to crack into the main database and copy everything. Why are *you* here?"

"To protect you, I guess. Just do me one favor—do not get in my way." Mac unpacked his guns on the bed. "When do we leave?"

"Not until tomorrow. I've already arranged it with the local rangers. Do you have the equipment?" Simon was a stickler for the details, all right. He wanted to be sure everything was in order.

"You mean the decoy?"

"Yeah," Simon replied.

"I left it in the car. Look, I just want to get this over with. Once we're inside, do you know exactly where we need to go?"

"I have a partial map in my computer. It's a direct route to their main system. Maybe five hours, tops. If the power's off, then we'll have to use the stairs, of course," Simon explained.

"What are we going to do in the meantime?"

"I'm going to go over the layout a few more times and—"

"How many times have you gone over it already, a couple of hundred? No, we need to get out and enjoy the night, see what kind of trouble we can get in," Mac insisted.

"But I don't think that's a good idea. We need to know every turn and corner without thinking. I mean—"

"I don't think a partial map is going to do us much good if we get turned around in there. Now, I don't know about you, but I'm going to go find a nice restaurant, the local bar, and maybe a strip club. You can stay here and spook yourself out all night if you want to."

As Mac walked toward the door, Simon jumped up to join him. "All right, I'll go. Just leave your toy here." Simon slowly walked over to the bigger man, and smiling, Mac put his arm around him.

He said, "No, that's my best friend. Have you ever been to a strip club, Simon?"

Simon just shook his head as they walked out the door. They went in silence, not breaking it going down the elevator. It was nothing personal, just procedure. Nothing could be known about their mission or themselves by others. As they reached the lobby, the girl behind the counter stopped them.

"Excuse me, Mr. Malcolm, Mr. Reynolds. A letter has just arrived marked for you both. It says urgent." Simon rushed up to the counter with obvious anticipation. "Is this something about the research you're doing?"

"No, I'm sure it's nothing." Simon looked back to see Mac approaching.

"It could be an earthquake." Mac snatched the letter from the girl's hand, all the while giving Simon a dirty glare. "Or worse, maybe a volcano." Mac walked outside, opening the letter.

"I'm sure it's nothing," Simon said, trying to reassure the girl, then he quickly ran after Mac. Outside, he found his partner standing next to the rusted Ford, the letter hanging from his back pocket.

"It isn't much. Then again, I get nothing but the best," Mac expressed tapping the roof with his hand.

"That's your car? I'm not getting in that." Simon turned around and pointed to a shiny black H3 that sat four spaces away. "I'd rather drive in this."

"They gave you that?" Mac stated with a jealous tone. "Now I really know where I stand."

"No, this is mine. I only live about three hundred miles from here," Simon explained, defusing his envy.

Simon and Mac climbed into the vehicle and drove to the nearest restaurant. After they filled up on finely grilled steak with savory garlic mashed potatoes, they went to a quiet local bar to down a few beers. After a couple of hours had passed, Simon's curiosity about the letter had burned him to the bone. Simon wasn't much of a drinker. With three beers down and working on the fourth, he finally built up the courage to ask Mac to see it.

"Look, you've been avoiding it all night. What does it say?"

"Shut up and drink your beer. The night's just started."

Mac, on the other hand, had lived his life trying to relax from all the work he had done over the years.

"Can I get ya guys a coupl'a more beers?" their waitress asked, coming up from behind and startling Simon.

"Yeah, I'll have another. How about you?" Simon held up his half nursed beer remains. "Maybe not for him," Mac added. The waitress walked away to get the order.

Mac continued, "Look, Simon, you can read this now if you like, but it doesn't matter."

Simon even used the manner of a five-year-old. "If it doesn't matter, you'd just show me." Mac just giggled as Simon's frustration grew. "Will you just *gimme* it?"

"Here ya go, fella." The waitress returned with Mac's drink. "That'll be a buck fifty. Is there anything else I can get ya?"

"Yeah, where's the nearest strip club?" Mac asked with a childlike smile.

"There's Mona's Ranch just thirty minutes north of here. It ain't a bad place, a lot of tourists flock there," she replied without hesitation.

"Thanks." Mac finished his old beer and started on his new one while Simon just stared at him. "Would you like to see the letter?"

"Yes, I would like to see the letter." Simon held out an open hand.

Mac reached into his pocket and slammed the letter into his palm. "Don't be too disappointed," he stated with a smirk.

Simon opened the letter with pure anticipation in his heart. Quickly he unfolded it and began to read. His eyes scrolled back and forth as his lips silently mouthed the words. After he finished, he just looked up at Mac and stared with his eyes wide open.

"I told you it was nothing. Investors, state, all things classified—do not go off track from the map we have provided. This is some kind of bullshit. They're not saying anything." Mac polished off his beer quickly and stood up. "You ready to go to Mona's Ranch?" Without waiting for the reply, he headed for the parking lot.

"What? I'm not goin' to—" Before Simon could finish, Mac quickly cut him off.

"I've got your keys, so it's either come with me or walk back to the hotel." Mac held up Simon's keys, jingling them. With no other alternative, the smaller man climbed into the car.

"All right, but I'm not goin' in. You can go do whatever it is you do."

As Mac drove, he unexpectedly turned south, heading back toward the hotel.

"I thought we were goin' to the—"

"No, we've got a long day ahead of us. We need to get some sleep," Mac said enigmatically.

Silent as before, they returned to their room. Once there, Simon set the alarm on the clock, 5:00 a.m. Both men lay in the silent darkness of the room until they drifted off to sleep.

Mac awoke hours before the alarm went off. Packing up his guns, he readied himself for attack first thing. His daily routine of exercise and stretching gave him all the strength of a survivor. He showered, dressed, then sat down on his bed facing Simon. Drawing one of his pistols, he waited for Simon to wake, his aim marked for Simon's head.

"Holy shit, what are you doing?" Simon rolled out of his bed to the floor. "Would you *please* put that thing away!"

"If you're so good with guns, then why are you so afraid of them?" Mac stood up and walked closer to Simon.

"I don't like them pointed in my face!" Simon jumped up swiftly, his eyes as wide as canyons. "Do it. Just do it!" Inching toward it, Simon approached until he felt cold steel barrel on his nose. Mac spun the gun around, facing it to himself.

"Actually, I thought you might like one. Just in case." Mac released the gun into Simon's hand then turned his back; it was the organization's gesture of recognizing their code of trust.

"Thanks, I only brought my computer equipment. Like you said, that's why you're here," Simon said, accepting the offer.

Simon stretched and began to dress as Mac loaded the decoy into the Hummer. Then Mac sat in the car, waiting for his partner, relaxing as he listened to some old country music.

Simon walked out and stood at the driver's door. "This is my car. I'm going to drive," he stated.

"They sent me to ensure your safety, right? Driving is one way I'm protecting you." Rolling his eyes, Simon accepted the situation and hopped in the passenger's seat. Mac threw it into gear and tore away from the hotel. "Which way, brain boy?"

"Turn left out of here and right on Ashburn Drive. I'll guide you the rest of the way; I know it by heart. Before we get to the ranger's station, we should change into our uniforms. I've got the permits in the glove box," he stated halfheartedly.

They continued driving toward Mount Gilbert, enjoying the scenic route of the mountainous terrain.

"So, how long have you been in the organization?" Mac asked, making small talk to help the long drive go by.

"It'll be four years in March. I was recruited right out of college. Top of my class," not being one for boasting, Simon tried to remain modest about himself. "By the age of twenty-three, I had single-handedly hacked into one of the largest banking networks in the world. I transferred over a hundred and seventy thousand before they caught me." Mac was stunned by the statement; seeing Simon as a nerd, he never expected that. "How long have you been ... doing what you do?"

"Since I was a kid, I guess. My father was a military man, mainly black ops. I grew up traveling from base to base. As I got older, it only seemed right that I follow in his footsteps, so I trained my ass off."

Looking at his laptop, Simon felt envious of Mac's adventurous life. "Most of my life has been spent behind that screen. I mean I've seen some serious stuff," Simon paused, seeing a smirk on Mac's face. "I have, just all the shoot'em up . . . kill ya type. It's more technical, like zero point energy theory, quantum—"

"Looks like we need gas," Mac stated, cutting him off in a hurry.

Stopping at a gas station, they used the opportunity to change into their science uniforms and ready the decoy.

"Why don't you drive from here?" Mac offered Simon.

"Oh, you mean I get to drive my own car?"

"Hey, you saw what I had to drive, besides, I don't know all that nerd mumbo jumbo like you," Mac smartly replied.

"Nice."

They both climbed in and headed for the ranger's station. Once they arrived, Simon took charge. "Let me do all the talking, okay, you Neanderthal." Simon slowed at the gate and grabbed the needed permit from the glove box.

"You boys the seismologists?" the ranger asked, acting as though he was a military drill instructor.

"Yes, sir. Here is our paperwork. Would you like to see our equipment?"

But Simon's excitement quickly drove the ranger away. "Everything seems in order," he stated bluntly, returning their papers. "You can go." Waving his hand, he allowed them through the gate. "Be careful up there!" The ranger shouted out, as they drove off up the dirt trail.

"That was pretty good, Simon. I'm impressed."

"Most people don't go for the whole technology thing. Try to draw them in and they'll run," Simon explained, clearly speaking from past experience.

They continued up the mountainside until they ran out of road. Mac jumped out and unpacked the decoy. Using his computer mapping system, Simon tried to locate the terminal.

"Would you come over here and help? I don't know how to set up this shit!" Mac called out.

"It doesn't matter. Do you really think the rangers know what it's supposed to do? Leave it. I think I may have found the terminal."

Simon rushed off up the rocky terrain with Mac following closely behind. Both stopped when Simon reached what appeared to be a large pile of rocks. "This is it, it has to be."

Feeling around on the back of the pile, Simon found the release trigger, a fingerprint scanner. With a slight hydraulic hum, a small door opened on the rock's face. "Now all I need is the code. It's a series of numbers: 8-6-7-5-3-0-9. Just kidding. It's 1-2-2-3-1-9-4-9. That should do it." Quakes rattled the loose rocks about as the wall shifted, revealing the massive entrance.

"I sure hope it's warmer in there than it is out here," the big man stated. Drawing his pistol, Mac slowly entered. Simon walked behind him, keeping close.

"You don't have to worry, there can't be anything yet. We still have two more security checks, due to probability of code breach," Simon quickly explained, trying not to be distracted.

"What's the next one, some kind of retina scanner?"

"Good guess. No, it's a coded program that I have to access through my computer. *Then* the retina scan," Simon stated, rolling his eyes.

As they continued through the tunnel toward the other security points, the main door closed. Darkness filled in the light, sending shivers through their bodies. Mac pulled out a flashlight just as the emergency lights kicked on. Simon had stopped in the center of a large, round steel platform. Right as Mac got onto it, the platform began to move down. Stumbling, he fell to the floor. Simon reached down to help him up.

"It would have been nice if you'd warned me," Mac stated, giving him a swift glare.

"Think of it as getting you back for the gun."

"That's fair." Mac brushed himself off as they continued downward.

"We have to go down two hundred feet before we reach the lab," Simon stated.

"How do you know so much about this place?" Mac questioned, growing suspicious.

"I spent four years in the biological research facility."

"Why didn't you tell me this? It might be just a little important!"

"I didn't want you to know," Simon explained, feeling embarrassed.

"Why not, what are you hiding?" Mac once again drew his pistol on Simon, who drew his gun right back.

"That's why not, because I knew you'd hound me for information I don't have. I was a tech for their research database. That's why I don't know anything other than what I have on my computer. I have no idea what kind of research they were doing, so if you would be so kind and put that damn gun away!"

"You better be telling me the truth this time, or I will kill you." Mac withdrew his pistol as his anger subsided.

"Now we have to go into the biology lab." Simon slowly lowered his gun as the elevator came to stop. "It's just up ahead, that way."

Suddenly the emergency lights went dark. "Shit. Hang on, I'll try to interface with the lab's system network. It should still be functioning." After a few keystrokes, Simon brought up the power grid and his basic map. He sighed. "We'll have to go around unless the doors were open when the power shut down."

"I knew this would happen. Nothing is ever simple." Mac drew his flashlight again and lit their way.

Both of them felt a dismal tingle run up their spines as they walked down the dark steel corridor. Water lines knocked against the network of piping that ran overhead. Working by the glow of his computer, Simon was tracing the pure signal of the mainframe.

"If we follow this signal by strength, we should be able to find the mainframe."

"Where is everyone? No bodies, no blood. What happened here?" Mac thought out loud as he scanned around the area with his light and gun ready.

"I don't know." Simon pushed a few keys on his computer, bringing up another screen. "There. I'll run a life scan, but it only covers a thirty-foot radius."

"It sounds like a submarine's sonar. Turn it down; we don't want to be heard," Mac ordered, giving him the evil eye.

They continued down the dark corridor, finally arriving at a partially open door. Mac stayed behind his pistol as he peeked around the door, scanning for threats. To his amazement, he found trees growing in the room. Letting his pistol be his guide, he stepped inside. On the other side of an apple orchard, he saw huge gardens bearing a large variety of fresh vegetables. This place was a perfect biosphere.

"It's clear, Simon, come in." Simon slowly followed him in, ready for anything. "Hungry?" Mac asked, as he picked up a large apple that had fallen from one of the trees. "No wonder no one knew this was here. They never had to leave."

"Yes. This place was designed as purely self-sustainable. I heard there were three of these biospheres within the whole facility. This was the only one I've seen, but they said it was the smallest. The next room should be the transmission room. I can get an outside link from there. Kira is waiting for us."

"Who the hell is Kira?" Mac demanded, livid.

"She's our contact within the organization. She was one of the lab's designers, though she had nothing to do with the experimentation. Help me push this door open."

Under both of their weight, the door shifted, then gave with a groan. This minuscule room, other than the two doorways, was lined with computers. Tiny yellow lights blinked all around them in random patterns.

"I'll patch in and see if I can get a signal." His laptop connected to the mainframe, Simon frantically hit the keys. "Kira, are you there? Kira?"

"Yes, hello, Simon. I take it you've reached the communication tower," came an intelligent, soft, female voice.

"Yeah, there's no power, and we haven't seen anyone," Simon revealed.

"Interesting, hold on while I run a diagnostic check on the facility." Kira cut off, leaving them in silence.

After a few seconds passed, Mac began to grow impatient. "Come on! I'm tired of sitting in this dark corner," Mac snapped at Simon.

"Calm down, Mac. This place is massive; it'll take some time."

"Right, I've got it," Kira returned. "The central system has been shut down. You have to reboot it in order to complete your mission. I've sent you a map of how to get there. Be careful, this map shows the rooms, but I don't know what is inside them. I will also send you the final transmission from before we lost contact."

The recording played from Simon's computer: "What have we done here?" A desperate man's voice asked. "He came through ... Now ... God, please forgive us, we ... and our sins. He's coming ..."

Several screams cried out in the background. The man continued. "It keeps passing in and out ... won't stop. We have to shut ... down. We have ... shut everything down!"

The tape ended in a moment of static. "This is all we have to go by," Kira explained. "Once you reach the central system, restore the power, and transmit back from there. We should be able to find out what happened."

"They're all dead or hiding. Either way, nothing good happened. Isn't that enough?" Mac said, hiding behind his pistol as he watched the open door.

"Simon, you have to hurry. Time is very relevant here." Kira ended her transmission and left Simon and Mac to carry out their mission.

"All right, Mac, I've got the route. Let's go get this over with. I should be able to open this door from here."

Seconds later, the door slid open as Mac stood ready for anything. His ears picked up on faint droplets as they fell in the distance. As Mac stepped into the hall, one of the drops landed on his head. Shining his light toward the ceiling, he saw that the whole hall was coated in blood. Several body parts lay scattered about, their clothing still attached. Mac continued forward very slowly, with Simon clinging to his heels.

"Holy shit, what the hell happened here?" Simon's mind became lost within the chaos he was facing. In all his time in the organization he had never seen any real action. This was far beyond his scope.

To regain his composure, Simon turned to do what he did best: analyze. Using his computer, he continued to scan for life. "There has to be someone still here. There's no way that all two thousand people are dead. No way. Mac, say something!"

Mac turned around and grabbed Simon by his shirt. "I don't want whatever did this to come back, so if you don't shut up I'll kill you myself."

They continued on through the blood rain in the hall, checking every door they found. Mac used his flashlight to look through one of the windows. Inside the adjoining room was the same scene of blood spatter, with several disassembled bodies. As he looked toward the end of the hall, he could see another door with something attached to the handle. Reaching it, Mac saw a lone hand, ripped off at the wrist, gripping the handle tightly. Simon's computer began reading several life forms on the other side. Mac turned off his flashlight and slowly pulled the door open. A shuddering sound rang out as it gave.

Sliding around the door frame, Mac lit up the room to find the source. One complete wall held homes for hundreds of rats. They were well-kept, being on an automated feeding system. Mac stepped back and pulled Simon into the room.

"This must be one of the experiment labs. We have to keep moving. The door on the left will take us straight there," Simon explained.

"Why are they still alive? Why did whatever did this leave them alone?" Mac questioned.

"I don't care; I just want to get out of here. Let's go!" Simon expressed, still spooked by what they'd seen in the hall.

Mac opened the door with caution, finding yet another hallway. The sound of raindrops echoed from within. Fearing the worst, he looked up to see that one of the overhead water pipes had ruptured and was dumping onto the floor. His nerves slightly eased, he walked with steps of relief.

Not a single door was closed in this hall. Mac scanned them with his light as they passed. There were no signs of a struggle here either, causing Mac to wonder even more. Even the elevator in the center of the hall was open and clean.

They had finally reached the central system at the end of the hall. Before them stood a massive room that was patched into every level of the facility. Several monitors lined the upper walls that covered the room's entire circumference. Simon stood in awe of the technology.

"All right, this is it. I can do this," Simon assured himself, as he plugged into the computer and patched back to Kira.

"Simon, you've reached the central system? I was beginning to think we lost you," Kira called back.

In a rage, Mac stormed over to the computer. "Look, lady, we just walked through a hallway that looked like someone had had a good time with a chipper shredder on your scientists. The lab rats, on the other hand, are fine, poor little things. Just do what you have to do so we can get out of here!" he insisted.

"I'm restoring power now."

Seconds passed, then with a click all of the lights came on. Suddenly a woman's voice could be heard coming from down the hallway. Her words were broken, repeating over and over.

Both men jumped with a start when Kira's voice came back over the computer. "This computer logs everything that happens within the facility. Now, I'm going to run a full analysis to find out exactly what happened and when. It will take several hours. Hold tight and you'll be out of there in no time. I will let you know when I'm done." With those words Kira ended her transmission.

Mac tapped Simon's shoulder. "Do you hear that? Let's go check it out."

Simon drew his pistol as the two walked down the hall. They drew closer, and the message became clear. "Wel … come to Miranda. With our new technology … Wel … come to Miranda. With our new technology …"

The repeating message echoed down the hall from another room. Upon stepping inside the room, Mac saw several seats that faced a massive flat-panel monitor, a beautiful, dark-haired woman's face fizzling in and out of view. It was shorting out as water ran down her broken face from the ceiling.

Simon stepped in behind him and noticed that the floor beneath their feet was vibrating.

Mac said, "We have to find out what happened here. That computer isn't going to tell her or you jack shit." Walking out of the room, Mac finally noticed the vibrations. "What's under here?"

"I don't know," Simon replied. "Let's just stay here until Kira's done."

"I'm not going to wait in that room to die. I want to know what these bastards did here. I'm going with or without you."

Mac walked off toward the elevator, leaving Simon in a panic. Fear filling him, he quickly joined back up with Mac.

Inside the elevator, Mac thought deeply as he looked over the buttons. Levels two, three, four, along with the standard open and close buttons, and a small panel that was secured with a lock underneath were his options. Mac took out his knife and started to work on the lock as Simon jumped in and closed the doors.

"What are you doing?" Simon frantically asked as he planted his body firmly against the back wall.

"I've been through enough of this shit to know that behind this is a button that'll take us where we need to go." After a few moments the lock popped, revealing a small, red button. "See? Now we can go." Mac pushed the button, and the elevator began its descent. "Just get ready to shoot anything that moves."

With guns in hand, they both readied themselves. When they reached the bottom, the doors opened onto a large stone hall. Dreadfully cold and dimly lit, it stretched on beyond sight's end. With full caution in their minds, they stepped out into the haunting hall and began to walk.

Soon the elevator became a distant blur, and then it vanished from view. Following the hall, they could feel the vibrations grow as they were led to a great chasm. In its center, resting on a structure of steel girders, sat a large steel ball with several tubes and wires running to it. Several computers and generators sat along the wall, creating enough power to cover the whole state. This was the source, the cause of the vibration.

"Oh ... my ... God! I didn't think it really existed," Simon spouted in awe. "I mean, I heard they did it, but quantum theory states—"

"What is it?" Mac broke in.

Simon wasn't distracted from his excitement. "A time machine. The sphere is a conductor that sucks in the energy and negates it back into itself, causing—"

"They built a time machine?" Mac asked doubtingly.

"Here, look." Simon walked over to the computer, bringing up the theory process on the screen. "See? It's simple—well, no, not simple, but ..."

As Simon went to explain, Mac made a discovery of his own. "There's some numbers counting down here!" Mac pointed out in a hurry.

Within three, two, one—all of the lights went out. An earsplitting amount of deep vibrations immediately filled the cavern. Suddenly, from out of nowhere, several small, glowing spheres began to appear throughout the room. Everything around the spheres became abstract, as though rippling in water. One on the far end of the room grew exceptionally bright then disappeared. Shortly all of the spheres vanished just as fast as they'd come.

When the lights in the room turned back on, there was a man in a lab coat lying unconscious on the floor. Both Mac and Simon were completely in awe and bewilderment. They put their guns away and rushed to his side.

The man in the lab coat opened his eyes to see Mac and Simon, sending him into a state of panic. "Who are you? Where's Professor Manglou? Did it work?" he asked, holding his head as he sat up.

"Relax. What is your name, wait, what day is it?" Simon asked, as he did his best to calm him.

"Tim Andrews and its Tuesday, February 12, 1963," he responded, trying to grasp what had happened.

"Shit, you came through a time portal. It's February 10, 2009," Simon replied, not holding back from the truth.

"How? We activated it?" The man asked, following Simon over to the computer. Looking at the screen, they found that the countdown had started over, presumably at thirty minutes.

"Can you stop it?" Simon asked the man. "You've created a continual vortex that'll continue to send things back and forth unless you shut it down!"

"We can't do it from here. There are two other control centers on the next floor up. We have to go to them both." All three ran back toward the elevator. "I hope they haven't changed things since I last saw them."

Reaching the elevator, the scientist pushed the button just above the now-broken panel. "Why are you guys here?" he asked.

"To investigate why we lost contact with the facility," Mac answered. "Now we know what happened. These assholes ripped a hole in time." Mac glared at the scientist, who only rolled his eyes.

The doors opened to the next floor. Electric sparks flashed in the hallway, creating a strobe effect as they walked. Every door lining the hall was broken into, and blood saturated the walls. Here there were no body parts, just whole bodies. Gashed open and torn, the remains of the scientists lay scattered about the room. Mac investigated one of the bodies, finding it was a female. She had been stabbed through her chest by something that left a hole the size of a Frisbee.

"I don't know what could have done this, and I don't want to see it. What other experiments were they working on here?" Mac questioned the scientist.

"I don't know. We all worked individually on certain aspects of one project. I was helping set up the electron transmitters for the subatomic particle transfer system. Let's go; the first control console is just up ahead."

Stepping over and around bodies, they reached the first control room. "All I have to do is type in this code, and … there. Now all we have to do is find the other computer, and we can shut this down."

As they turned to walk out of the room, one of the spheres of light from the lower floor appeared right in front of them. It brightened, blinding them, then leaving them unconscious.

They awoke to complete darkness. Mac sat up quickly, turning on his flashlight. He looked around and saw, to his pure amazement, that all of the bodies no longer held any flesh. "Guys, we're in the future," Mac determined.

"How can you tell?" Simon asked, rising to his feet. The scent of rotted flesh hit his nose.

"That girl had only been dead for about a week, tops. Now there's no flesh at all."

"The power is on; stand by, I can turn it back on," the scientist stated. Sparks once more shot through the hall as power was restored. "We have to go to the next control room, and fast."

"What does that matter now, even if we survive?" Mac sighed, feeling a small sense of defeat.

"Mac, we've still got a chance. With the process still running, more time shifts can still happen. If we shut it down, we can still escape. In a different time, yes, but alive." Simon glared hard into Mac's eyes.

"Fine, where is it?" Mac asked. Already fed up with all of this, he focused his attention on the scientist.

"Just past the second garden, Eden Two. It's near the demonstration room," the scientist added.

"What's that?" Simon inquired.

"It's a room with several cages of rats. They never do anything to them. It's just to demonstrate how this place is self-sustaining."

"My computer's right there by that room. We have to go check it out," Simon said with excitement in the hope that Kira had completed running her analysis on the central computer. He had strong hopes that she could shut it all down as well.

They stepped aboard the elevator without hesitating and rode to the next floor above. As soon as it stopped, Simon ran out to his computer. It was still operating off of the central computer's power. Mac and the scientist followed closely behind.

"Kira, are you there? Kira, this is Simon, do you hear me?" He knew it was a desperate attempt, but after moments of non-response, his faith began to fall. "Damn it! She's—"

"Simon, is that you?" Kira's voice came back over the computer. "Where have you been? Is the other one with you? What's happened?"

"Yeah, we're both here, and we've found a scientist," Simon replied with a smile and a huff of relief.

"Is he still alive? Did he tell you what happened?"

As Kira spoke, Mac became agitated. "He's from 1963," he stated, getting in front of the screen. "He doesn't know jack shit. Did your precious computer tell you anything?"

"Yes, it picked up several interval energy surges. We assumed the core had gone negative." Kira paused for a moment, clearly hesitant about telling them something. She continued, "You can't get out. In order to protect those involved, they've sealed the lab. We waited twenty-two days for you to report back. Simon, it's been ten years!"

"Great, just great. What now?" Mac snapped.

"I'm going to go shut this damn thing off!" the scientist stated, as he walked out of the room.

"You can't. If you do, we may never get back," Mac roared, chasing after him. "I'm not about to be stuck in the future!"

"Or we might randomly shift back to a time before this place was built and end up inside the mountain," the scientist sharply replied. "That sounds a little unpleasant. Besides, if all three Edens are functioning, we could live here forever."

Continuing past the demonstration room, they entered a new hall. Like the previous one, all of the doors were broken into, and bones lay everywhere. Eden Two awaited them at the hall's end. This garden was twice the size of the one Mac and Simon had previously seen. Fruit trees grew in rows of thirteen or more, with wild-growing vegetable gardens planted as far as the eye could see.

"We're almost there," the man assured Mac.

As they passed a small pond, they heard an immense thud come from behind, as if an elephant had fallen from a tree. Turning around, they both found a true meaning for fear. Before them stood a man-like creature that towered over them, rippling with muscle. Blackened eyes stared back at them from a distorted face, above two holes in place of a nose that had seemingly melted away. Large, jagged teeth protruded from its lipless mouth as it breathed in a heavy rasp. Its hairless body looked as though its skin was rotting.

As it reached out, stretching its muscles, they saw that this being's right hand had grown exceptionally long and thick like bone. Mac knew that this is what had gone through that girl's chest. This was the bringer of death for all of these people. With his weapon drawn, Mac froze in fright.

Howling in a high-pitched, gravelly tone, the creature charged at them. Using its claw hand, it fiercely knocked Mac to the ground as it passed. With the mutated hand, it ripped through the scientist's waist, severing him in two. Covered in blood, it turned to focus on Mac.

Walking toward him, the beast wiped its bloody claw on the soft, green grass below. Quickly Mac stood up and began to run back toward Simon. In a heavy-footed stride, the creature gave chase.

Mac ran at full speed, fortunately discovering that he was faster than the creature. He shut every door he passed through, calling out for Simon periodically. From behind he could hear one of the doors being ripped apart. With only two more doors standing between him and the monster, Mac knew he had to get out somehow.

"Simon, we have to move, now!" Mac grabbed him by the arm and pulled him back toward the entrance.

"Where's the scientist?" Simon asked.

"Dead—it killed him; it killed all of them," he replied with a full sense of terror in his eyes.

"What? *What* killed all of them?"

Suddenly a large crash and the sound of the creature screaming filled the halls.

"That did!" Mac stated. "We have to go."

Mac and Simon ran down the hall toward the round elevator. Fear being a common factor in their hearts, it took little time to reach their destination. When they arrived, there was no elevator to be seen, and the shaft was completely filled in with concrete and lead. Mac put his pistol away and brought out his 9-millimeter submachine gun.

"I hope this can stop it. Get ready."

Just then a sphere of light appeared four feet away from them. "We have to go now, Simon!" Mac dove into the light, taking Simon with him.

They awoke to the sound of construction being done. Mac stood up to a crew working on the beam structure of the hall. Simon rose to his feet as several people carried different small trees past them.

"Where the hell did you two come from?" a crew member asked, adjusting his hard hat. "Just what we need, more military guys sniffing around," he snidely stated.

"We were just leaving," Mac replied back.

As he began to walk to the elevator, Simon stopped him. "We have to report in. Let's go." Simon pulled Mac back toward Eden One.

"What are you doing? We can get out of here; we're alive," Mac pleaded.

"That's right, we are alive, out there. We can't go back. Not here." Frustrated to see the blank look on Mac's face, Simon broke it down. "Not *now*. Our existing selves here would cause a cataclysmic meltdown of the time fabric. We simply can't go back now!"

As they passed into what would be the demonstration room, they could hear heavy amounts of drilling going on. "We're lucky we didn't go back further," Simon noted.

"Yeah, we could have ended up in the mountain. That wouldn't have been pleasant." Simon gave him an odd look. "It was what the scientist said before he was killed."

They continued along toward the room of the central computer. Mac urged again, "If we go now, everything will change. We can stop this!"

"No," Simon insisted. "We need to blend in and wait for the next vortex."

"Are you two here for orientation?" A woman scientist asked, stopping. She was calm and friendly.

"Yes. Where do we report in?" Simon asked, playing his role.

"Right this way, gentlemen." The woman waved and began walking.

They were led to the room with the large screen from which the broken audiovisual recording had played. As they sat down, the dark-haired woman appeared on the screen. "Welcome to Miranda Laboratories. With our new technologies and research, we will help you create a new, brighter future. Miranda Laboratories will help you find tomorrow."

The demonstration continued on, showing the Edens while the voice-over of the woman explained all of Miranda's functions.

Suddenly the image began to distort as a sphere appeared in front of the screen.

"What the hell is this?" a voice called from just outside the room.

Mac and Simon darted to the sphere as fast as they could, vehemently hoping to land in their present day.

When they awoke from the transition, their ears were filled with the sound of screams—the screams of the mutated creature, and screams from people. All of the lights flashed throughout the hall outside. A man opened the door to the hall then ran past the room to the elevator. Mac pressed his body against the wall closest to the door, peeking around the corner. Simon followed his lead on the opposite side of the doorway.

All at once, the shuddering screams grew silent. In pure anticipation, Mac listened for a break in the stillness. With a heavy slam, the door at the end of the hall was bashed into the wall as the creature entered. Ducking down from the doorway, Simon caught a perfect view of the abomination for the first time. Fear ran up his spine as he shimmied his way out of sight.

Mac kept calm while the creature walked past the room. It was following the man's scent to the elevator. It roared out with screams as it tried to squeeze its way inside. Realizing it was no use, it turned back. Frustrated and angry, it reached up with its claw hand, cutting into one of the water pipes above. As water rained down around it, the creature walked past Mac and Simon's room, leaving the hall. More screams came from outside as it continued the bloodshed.

Mac made a dash for Simon, who was cowering in the corner, trying to gain his rational mind back. "Snap out of it, Simon; we have to move," he demanded, shaking him by the shoulders.

"Did you see it?" Simon asked, his voice trembling in terror. "What the hell was it?"

"Look, we're safe here. Otherwise we would have found our bodies when we were here before." Simon looked at him in awe, seeing that he had gained the idea of what was happening. "We need to go to Eden Two. We can go through the demonstration room and hide out there. It was clean."

Mac's logic seemed clear. "Okay, let's go. What happened to the man in the hall who came through with us?"

"Who, the construction guy, I don't know. Maybe each sphere leads to a different time."

Mac pulled Simon along as they ran through the hall that led to Eden Two. Several scientists hid in their rooms, locking the doors and screaming for help.

As more scientists flocked down the hall searching for a place to hide, Simon was forced into a room. He found himself trapped as the door sealed him inside with the other occupants.

Once he reached Eden Two, Mac saw several people running out the exit at the other end. With all that was happening, he had failed to notice that Simon was gone. "Simon! Where are you, damn it?" he yelled.

As Mac ran back to find his partner, the creature broke through the door on the opposite side of the hall. Coming to the first locked door, it began to smash it in. With pure terror in their hearts, the occupants screamed out. Mac ran back into Eden Two, heading toward the pond where, in Mac's present-day time frame, the scientist had been sliced in half by the monstrous creature. Just a little off shore, he spotted another sphere forming above the grass.

As the sounds of screams filled the air once more, he stepped toward it. "Good-bye, Simon. I'm sorry," he stated, disappearing from the danger.

He awoke, still lying in Eden Two, but in a dreadful darkness. Mac turned on his flashlight to see that it was longer flourishing. Now the trees lay dead along with the dried-up gardens. Even the pond had greatly receded, with what little remained covered in algae and bacteria. Rising to his feet, he shook off the dizziness that had begun to set in. His mind had taken so much that he was beginning to feel some effects of each displacement.

Stumbling and falling to the ground a couple of times, he made his way back to where Simon was lost. Upon reaching the door, he heard a faint growl coming from behind the dead trees. Cautiously he crept along, staying hidden behind the lifeless wood. There, in the thick of death, the creature sat slumped over. Its weak body leaned up against a tree as it sat, barely breathing. Mac knew it was dying. He walked up to the creature, realizing that he, too, had had enough.

"What are you? Where did you come from? ... Are you listening to me?" Frustrated and welcoming death himself, Mac stood inches away as he continued. "Is that why you killed them, for what they did to you?" Mac knelt down before the creature. "The systems must have shut down, and that's why the forest died. Does this mean it's finished?"

He looked at the creature and began to cry. "Answer me, damn it!" Mac stood up, stripping himself of his weapons and clothes, all except for his white, sweat-soaked boxer shorts. "I'm sick of this game; just kill me! Come on, kill me! You bastard, you killed Simon. Kill me, please."

A grunt came from the creature's mouth as if it were trying to speak. "What?" Mac asked, hoping it would repeat it.

With an unclear growl, it muttered the words, "Don't go."

In that moment, the creature fell over and gave its final breath. With the passing of the creature, Mac felt a hollow feeling of remorse. He crawled to its side, wanting to pay his respects. After a few moments of silence, he touched its forehead. Then he turned and slowly walked toward the hall.

Sifting through the remains of the dead, Mac found his pistol and what appeared to be Simon's hand. Accepting this closure, Mac headed for the elevator. He repeatedly pushed the button behind the panel, but nothing happened. He was at a loss; he no longer needed to fear the creature, but what remained for him now? Everything was over.

With nothing left, he walked back toward Eden One. When he reached the central computer, he found it, along with Simon's computer, completely destroyed. Their parts lay scattered about in rage's destruction. Continuing on his quest to Eden, he came to the demonstration room. All of the rats had died, shriveled up and withered from starvation. Without the automated system, they had been left to perish.

Stepping into Eden One, Mac saw that it looked the same as Eden Two, dry and dead. But then a bright glow appeared in the center of the trees, like a beacon. Dipping his head to the ground, Mac walked into the bright sphere.

When he awoke, he was surrounded by several scientists. They moved frantically around him, inspecting him to every detail. The sting of several needles pierced his arm as they shot him with several drugs.

"Where did he come from?" one of the scientists asked.

"I don't know, but by the looks of him we better isolate him now," another one cautioned.

"What's wrong with his skin?" a third one asked.

"It almost resembles leprosy," mumbled a fourth.

"Quarantine him to room nine, we'll monitor him from there," a man stated, approaching from one of the side rooms.

They placed Mac on a gurney and wheeled him down the hall. His skin burned from the inside, as did his bones. When he tried to get up, he found that he had no energy left to fight his restraints. He twitched in pain as they placed him in a small room, closing him in.

Soon Mac's muscles began to change, along with his skeletal structure. Slowly, over a forty-eight-month period of intense pain, Mac changed form. With melting skin and blackened eyes, Mac understood the pains of the butterfly's metamorphosis.

Cabin Escape

Never in all of their time together had Matt and Sandra fathomed that they would be running for their lives through the thick, lush forest, chased by an enraged moose. Moments ago, the Mustang Matt had received for his high-school graduation had been smashed into a tree by just such a moose. That same moose was now ripping through the woods behind them. The cracking of tree limbs and the sound of hooves pounding on the earth barely drowned out the sounds of other animals violently attacking each other throughout the woods.

"What the hell is happening?" Sandra shrieked.

"Just keep running!" Keys in hand, Matt searched for the one to the front door. "We're almost there; don't stop!"

With the full moon lighting their way, the cabin came into view through the tree branches. The moose's deep snorts seemed to be at their heels as it charged closer. Key in hand, Matt broke from the tree line straight for the door of the two-story log cabin. Sandra, gashed and bruised, followed closely behind.

In the slow motion feeling of the key turning, the moose crashed through the brambles and branches of the tree line with its enormous antlers flinging debris into the air. Grabbing Sandra by the arm, Matt pushed open the door and pulled her inside.

A shattering boom rocked the cabin right as the door slammed shut.

"Hide!" Matt demanded, rushing toward the steps to the upper level.

Sandra scurried to the den as another crashing boom erupted from the door. Covering her ears and crying, she curled up next to the couch under the end table. Over and over, the moose rammed its head into the door.

Then suddenly everything went quiet outside. Sandra crawled out from under the table and huddled in the center of the room. From a nearby window, the moose spotted her, its breath fogging the glass. Turning her head as she shook, Sandra saw the moose. Its face was deeply cut, and several small twigs were sticking from its neck. Even with blood flowing over its fur, it seemed unaffected by the wounds.

In one swift flick of its neck, its head crashed through the window. As Sandra screamed, a shotgun blast fired from next to the couch, then another. The moose's head fell onto a piece of the jagged glass as it dropped in death. Stuck inside the moose's neck, the glass shards broke as the creature slumped onto the ground outside. Matt instantly set the gun down and struggled to push a nearby cabinet in front of the breach.

"Would you help me, God damn it?" he shouted to Sandra.

"I'm sorry," Sandra stated as tears of fear ran down her cheek. Working together, they managed to push the furnishing into position, fortifying the cabin once again.

"That should hold," Matt expressed with a sigh.

"Hold what? What the fuck is going on?" Sandra asked, falling to the floor.

"I don't know. I've never seen anything like this. It's like the animals have gone nuts." Walking over to another window, he peeked out to see several of the forest creatures lurking outside of the cabin just staring back at him. "This is insane. What are they doing out there?"

"There's more?" In a panic, Sandra quickly grabbed onto Matt. "Oh shit ... shit, they're everywhere. What do they want, Matt? What do you want?" Screaming out, she hit the window frame with her hand. The animals were unmoved by her outburst.

"Calm down, they're just sitting there," Matt stated.

Suddenly several wolves rushed from the darkened forest and maliciously mutilated the other animals. Matt immediately covered Sandra's eyes, pulling her away from the window. Placing her shaking and whimpering form on the couch, Matt picked up the gun. Pulling shells from his pocket, he loaded two more rounds into the chamber. "Well, if anything else tries to get in, I'll smoke 'em fast," he assured her.

"We need to call for help! We have to get the hell out of here!" Sandra demanded.

"There's no phone here," he explained. Walking into the kitchen, he turned on a light and opened the refrigerator. After a few moments he returned to her side with a beer.

"You won't get a signal with your cell either." Reaching into his back pocket, he pulled out his cell phone, opened it, and tossed it next to her. The words *no signal* scrolled across the screen. "I told you we'd be all alone out here, no disturbances."

"This can't be happening," Sandra begged as she checked out her phone. It read the same. "How are we going to get out of here?"

"We'll have to wait until morning," Matt remarked as he cracked open his beer. As he took the first swig, he noticed Sandra's wounds. "Damn, you really got tore up out there." Moving her head by the chin, he saw several cuts on her neck and face.

"You don't look so good yourself." Placing her hand on Matt's face, she touched one of the deep cuts.

"Ouch, stop," he yelled out, pushing her hand off and leaning away. "What a mess. I guess we should have stayed to party with Bret and Melissa." Gun in hand, Matt went back over to the window. "They're gone!" he lied, looking over the mutilation that littered the yard.

"What?" Sandra asked, running to see. Before she could get a peek, Matt stopped her, pulling her to the couch.

"Every one of them has gone," he assured her. Lowering his gun, he sat down beside her. "Thank God that's over!"

"Thankfully they only destroyed a window and not your mother's plate collection," she stated with a slight laugh.

"No doubt. But my car! I just get the car I've always wanted, and a crazy moose smashes it to junk. I didn't even have it for a week. There's no way my dad is ever gonna believe that a moose wrecked my car, let alone the cabin."

"What do you mean? The evidence is right outside the window!"

"Yeah," he sighed, sipping from his beer. "I'm gonna start a fire. Why don't you go take a shower upstairs?" Rubbing her face, he gently kissed her forehead. "This whole night doesn't have to be a waste."

"All of our stuff is still in the car," Sandra noted, remembering she had no clothing to change into.

"That's all right," Matt stated, stacking logs into the fireplace. "My sisters have plenty of crap here for you to use. Just go pick something out of their room."

"Okay." Sandra walked up the stairs as Matt worked on the fire. "Wait for me," she uttered in a sexy voice. "I'll be right back for you."

Sandra made her way up the stairs and saw that the parents' bedroom light was on. As she walked down the hall, she passed the family portraits. Most of them were of Matt and his father fishing and hunting. Her heart clenched tightly at one in particular. It was a photo of Matt holding a shotgun, kneeling alongside of a dead moose as his father stood proudly beside him.

"There's irony on a grand scale," she muttered to herself.

At the end of the hall, she saw a closed door with a pink glittery sign that had "Princesses for life" etched into it. "This must be the place," Sandra expressed with a sigh.

She stopped at another photo and glared at it deeply. This one was of Matt's twin sisters. They were only a few years younger than Matt, and both constantly competed for head of the cheerleaders. Sandra, being a runner and a volleyball player, thought them both to be stuck-up, egotistical pigs. Matt, being a runner himself, had caught Sandra's eye instantly, though she'd never thought the friendly competition between them would save their lives as it likely had today.

Inside, the room was as she'd expected: everything was pink. From the walls to the bed sheets, pink. Stuffed animals of all sorts lined the tops of both beds. Resting on a small nightstand between the beds sat a small table lamp. She turned it on and went over to the dresser. Opening the top drawer on the soft-pink dresser, she was greeted by a mass of thong underwear.

"Gross, I'm not wearing this crap." Shutting the drawer, she moved on to the next. There she found the girls' pajamas. Though they were pink, she had no choice but to use them. She turned off the light and headed for the bathroom.

Matt, still trying to light the fire, was on his third beer. Grabbing a scrap of newspaper from alongside the stack of wood, he twisted it and shoved it under the logs. With the flick of his lighter, the paper ignited quickly, spreading to the logs.

"Finally!" he shouted as he leaned back onto his elbows. "Uh oh, need another beer." Standing up, he slightly stumbled toward the kitchen. He didn't hear the muffled shriek that echoed through the chimney as he walked away.

Upstairs, Sandra looked herself over in the bathroom mirror to see how bad the damage was. Seeing the deep gash across her cheek and under her left eye, she hoped they wouldn't scar, stripping her of her beauty. Several small, scattered tears lined both of her arms. In disappointment, she took off her sweaty, blood-covered clothes and stepped into the shower. With an eerie feeling, she glanced out of the small window in the shower. Her mind was eased by the sight of the lone tree. She proceeded to take her shower.

Angry at the marks and still a little confused from the situation, Sandra wrapped around in the flowing, hot water, every drop burning her wounds. Blood washed down her face and across her bruised breast to her arms, finally trickling off of her fingertips to the drain. Grabbing the shampoo, she cringed in pain as she washed the mats of blood from her torn scalp.

The slight ping of a rock came from the steam-covered window. Hesitant and fearful, she wiped away the condensation. Outside there was nothing except for the lone tree, a slight breeze caressing its branches.

Finishing her shower, she shut off the water and grabbed a towel from the rack. With her thoughts returning to Matt, she quickly dried off and put on his sister's pink pajamas.

Turning to walk out of the bathroom, she heard another ping come from the window. Looking past the shower and out the window, she spotted a raccoon perched on one of the tree's limbs. Confusion set in as the raccoon seemed to wave to her; then it threw a small rock at the window, causing her to flinch. Her fears suddenly rose when the next rock, in slow motion, smashed through the glass.

Sandra ran down the stairs in a panic, giving out a shattering scream that caused Matt to jump, spilling his beer. Leaping up to see what she had freaked out about, he grabbed the gun. He met Sandra at the bottom of the steps, she in full panic mode.

"What's wrong?" Matt asked, trying to get her to calm down.

"A raccoon just threw a rock at me in the shower," she frantically explained, shaking all over.

"Relax and tell me what happened, okay? Slowly." Rubbing the back of her head, Matt soothed her as he listened to her plight.

"I was taking a shower and I heard a noise, like someone hit the window with a rock. At first there was nothing there." Tears began to well in her eyes as she continued. "Then, when I was drying off, there was a raccoon in the tree. It threw a rock and broke the window." Looking into his eyes, she could perceive his doubt. "It's broken, go and look!"

"I didn't hear anything down here," he remarked, confused by her claim.

"Just go and look!" she demanded, stomping her foot.

"All right, wait here; I'll go check it out." Matt, gun in hand, left Sandra at the bottom of the stairs.

"The window's not broken," he yelled from the bathroom. Sandra quickly ran up to see. "Look, nothing happened," Matt said.

"No, I saw it sitting there in that tree!" Sandra pointed to the limb that reached toward the glass. "It was right there, I swear. It even waved at me."

"Waved at you? Sandra, you're just delirious from the attack." Putting his arm around her in comfort, Matt slowly walked her out of the bathroom. "Let's go downstairs and sit by the fire."

"You're right, I must have just imagined it. Damn it, this whole thing has got me seeing shit now."

Sandra made herself cozy in front of the fireplace as Matt strolled into the kitchen, humming. "How many have you had already?" Sandra asked, as she flicked an empty can.

"A few, but I saved the best for you." Sliding and gliding across the wooden floor, he continued his soft hum as he approached. He hid from her view a bottle of wine in one hand and two glasses in the other. "Close your eyes."

Opening the wine with a twist of its cork, he slowly poured them both a drink. "Here, smell," he requested, holding a glass just beneath her nose.

"Mmm, that's the stuff." Opening her eyes to see the glass, she gave Matt a long, sensual smile. "Mmm, oh, that's good."

"Save some of that for me—and I'm not talking about the wine," he playfully commented.

"Pig," she commented back as he leaned in for a kiss. Locking lips, they embraced in passion's grip. After a few moments, Sandra flinched and pushed him away. "Ouch, be careful, they still hurt."

"Sorry. You really got beat up out there."

"That's because every one of the branches you pushed back while running came back and hit me."

"Maybe if you were a little bit faster you could have taken the lead." Matt smirked as Sandra gave him a harsh look.

"Had we been on the track, I would have left you in my dust." Rubbing her own face, she was pulled out of the playful mood and back to reality. "They don't look too bad, do they?"

"No, there's nothing that could take away that beautiful face of yours," Matt replied with a twinkle in his eyes.

Sandra threw back her glass of wine then crawled over toward Matt. Pushing him onto his back, she climbed on top of him. Her lips locked onto his then she made her way down his neck. His fingers dug into her back and he ran them up her spine. She rose up so Matt could pull off her shirt, but he paused.

"What's wrong? It's my face, isn't it?" she asked, covering it with her arms.

"No, it's just … those are my sister's pajamas, and I've seen them wearing those a hundred times. It's weird." He chuckled.

"Knock it off," Sandra muttered, slapping him in his chest. Pulling off her shirt, she embraced him with pure sexual desire. Their passion rolled on into the night, until the fire flickered with its last flame and died.

Quivering in ecstasy, Sandra lay atop of Matt's sweaty body. Her smile quickly faded when Matt began to snore heavily. Rising up, she lost focus, almost falling to the floor. Trying to gather herself, she noticed that Matt wasn't wearing a condom.

"Great. Damn it, Matt. You better hope I don't get pregnant!"

With no response from him, she picked up her clothes and started walking toward the bathroom. As she approached the window next to the cabinet, she hesitated. Looking out, she sought reassurance of her safety. Outside, next to one of the trees, sat a solitary, average-sized red fox. Its eyes gleamed in the full moon's light. She felt them staring into her soul.

"It's only in your head, it's only in your head," she repeated to herself as she tightly closed her eyes. Opening them once more, she saw that the fox had vanished. Letting out a deep sigh of relief, she stumbled up the stairs to the bathroom. "Come on, girl, get it together. It was just a little wine." Once inside the bathroom, she glanced over her wounds. "You're looking good, girl, looking real good."

She hit the mirror with her hand, but her reflection remained motionless, staring coldly back at her. "This can't be happening." Closing her eyes, she began to shake her head back and forth. "This isn't real; it's just the wine ... just the wine."

Growing dizzy, she opened her eyes to see that her reflection was normal. "This is the best buzz I've ever had." She broke into laughter and put on her clothes. Still giggling in her slow, staggered way, she went back down to find Matt still snoring. "Sure, I'll have another glass." Spilling it over the edge and onto the floor, she filled the glass to the rim.

She sipped from her wine as she stumbled throughout the cabin, exploring her surroundings. Matt had always talked about the summers with his folks, but up until now Sandra had never been here. His father, being the head of the nation's largest pharmaceutical company, owned most of the property, including the nearby lake. Every year Matt and his father would spend two weeks together here. Those days were filled with nothing except for hunting and fishing. But for her, this was a special occasion that Matt had devised before they'd graduated.

As she walked down the long hall toward the library, the path slowly distorted, rolling around in a corkscrew fashion that extended on for what seemed forever. Dropping her glass to the floor, Sandra accepted the obscure vision. Hugging the wall for balance, she moved hand by hand down her spiral path. She tried to focus on the rug that lined the floor as it began to breathe and flex. Her mind spun, seeking for a grip on reality.

Finding a door, she turned the knob, discovering a small bathroom. She fell into it. Inside there was nothing more than a toilet and a small sink with a mirror above it. As she crawled toward the toilet, she felt a gurgling in her stomach. Just inches away from it, she started to vomit profusely. With her release, the dizziness leisurely faded. Leaning back against the wall to rest, Sandra managed to regain her sanity as she wiped the wine and chunks of dinner from her lips.

"This has to be a dream, all of it. Just one big, crazy dream," she whispered to herself. One hand gripped the sink as the other pushed off the floor. Hoisting herself back up to the mirror, she took another look. "You're going to get through this. Just remember, it's not real."

Leaving her reflection behind, she peered around the door frame, hoping the hall was normal. Grateful for the straight path ahead, she stepped out into the hall, though she was quickly overtaken by a harsh spinning in her head. Stumbling forward, she fell against the door to Matt's father's office, which gave way, dumping her flat to the floor. As the door rebounded back on a spring hinge, it swiftly slammed shut. Sandra lay in the light of the moon, brilliantly shining through the large window behind the desk. Rising up on her hands and knees, she scanned the room, desperately trying to figure out where she was.

"How the hell did I get here?" she asked herself. "Hello? Whose house is this? Ow, damn, my head."

Falling to the floor again, she stared off toward the wall across from her. All of Matt and his father's trophy catches were mounted all around the room. "What are you looking at? Stupid fish." Covering her eyes with her arm, she attempted to block out everything around her.

"Stupid? You're the one who's lost," Came a condescending, high-pitched, male voice from out of nowhere.

"What, who said that?" Sandra asked in a panic. Looking around, she became paralyzed by the sight of all the fish turning toward her.

"Do you have any idea what it's like to just sit here?" Amazed and frightened, Sandra realized the voice was coming from a mounted bass. "Every day it's the same shit. I sit here with my mouth open."

"I was just swimming there, and oh look, a free lunch. And now I'm here," a musky joined in with a deep voice.

"Oh look, guys, she's gonna cry," the swordfish added. Sandra began to deeply sob at her torn reality. "Aww, we gotta cheer her up, guys."

"I know," a much deeper voice rang out from behind her. As she turned, her heart filled with fear as she saw the head of a moose speak. "We can sing her a song."

"No ... no," Sandra begged. "Stop, just stop, please!"

"Okay, let me start," a deer chimed in. "One ... two ... three. Lolly pop, lolly pop ..."

"Lolly pop, badoom, boom, boom," all the fish joined in with laughter.

"No! Go away, all of you!" Sandra shouted.

"Oh, she doesn't like the song," the bass stated.

"What do you like?" asked the musky.

"You sure are a pretty thing," the moose pointed out.

"Shut up, just shut up!" she shouted as all of the creatures started talking at once. Their voices blended into one loud murmur. Sandra slammed her hand onto the floor, only to feel a thick, sticky goop beneath her palm. Her eyes fluttered about the room as she saw the walls and ceiling begin dripping with a dark-green sludge. "Oh shit!"

From behind her the door slowly creaked open. A creature made of the same sludge stood there, staring at her. Little by little, it stepped toward her, its right eye dripping down to its cheek and hanging there, periodically blinking as it drew closer.

Sandra jumped up and moved toward the desk. Green sludge coated everything her hand slid across. Never taking her eyes off of the hideous being, she reached back, grabbing a small lamp from the desk. She swung it at the sludge monster just as it reached out for her. One hit, then another, she vigorously beat it until it fell to her feet.

Leaving the lamp behind, she darted from the room. Once more the door slammed shut behind her. Inside the normal hall, she ran for the den. With Matt nowhere to be seen, fear pulsed through her veins. Next to the fireplace, Sandra spotted the shotgun sitting on the couch. Quickly retrieving it, she readied herself for a fight. She locked her sights on the office door and anxiously awaited the monster's coming after her.

"We did this to you," a strange, high-pitched voice spoke out from the kitchen. With the gun ready to fire, Sandra went to investigate. "It's a game," the voice continued, "to see how you'll take it." Trembling in fear, Sandra slowly stepped into the kitchen to find a short, light-blue-skinned alien standing on the counter. "Think of it as an experiment," it said.

Picking up a glass, the alien turned on the faucet. Spiders poured out by the hundreds. Letting it run, the little creature filled up its glass. The spiders scurried from the glass, over the alien's body, then down to the floor. Crunching them in its tiny mouth as it took a sip, it wiped the guts from its chin. "Ah, I love this planet." Jumping down off the counter, the alien became covered by a continuous flow of spiders.

Dropping the gun in absolute horror, Sandra watched as the wave of spiders covered the walls, floor, and ceiling. Reaching out like two gripping hands, the spiders scuttled straight for her. Sandra darted back toward the fireplace, screaming in terror.

As she stared back toward the wave of spiders, she failed to see Matt stumbling toward her. She ran into his chest with a hard slam and fell to the floor. Holding his head and bleeding, Matt looked down in a daze to see Sandra staring back at him. Her every breath was a gasp for life. Her eyes, cracked and red, never broke from their piercing stare.

"Sandra, what's wrong with you?" Matt asked, his form bouncing back and forth between his own and that of the creature.

"Who the fuck are you?" Sandra demanded loudly. Her cold eyes spoke of madness.

"It's me ... Matt. I'm the one who brought you here ..." His voice changed to a gurgle, along with his form. "Sandra ... I want to kill you."

Scooting back on her hands and feet, Sandra moved back toward the kitchen. With the spiders no longer blocking her path, she grabbed the shotgun from the floor. Matt made a desperate dash for the stairs as she stood to fire. Without a hesitant thought, she blasted a shot through the wooden rail of the steps, just nicking Matt's ankle.

Smiling deeply, she turned back to the kitchen to see the green sludge creature standing there. With pure acceptance, she was unmoved by the strange sight as she waded through the goop to the sink. Using the same glass as the alien had, she turned the faucet on. The glass filled with the thick, slimy substance. Leaning back, Sandra downed the whole glass in one motion.

"That's right, if any more of you fuckers comes near me, you're dead!" Sandra yelled out, scanning her surroundings.

"Is that any way to treat a friend?"

She turned to see the alien once more.

Taking aim, she shot it at point-blank range. As its body exploded, the remains transformed into hundreds of spiders. She paid no attention as they climbed all over her body then scurried away.

Moving slowly through the sludge, Sandra calmly walked back to the fireplace. Nothing except for the hot cinder ash remained. Tossing a few logs in created enough sparks to get the fire going again. The flames, like tentacles, extended out, wrapping around her body. Cocking her head toward the office, the flames instantly retreated back to the fireplace. Feeling vengeful, she stormed down the hall. Kicking the door open, she jumped inside with the full intent to destroy.

"I'm going to send all of you to hell!" She unloaded one shot after another, as the hunting and fishing trophies all screamed out in terror. With the final shell fired, she left the decimated room.

Leaning against the wall, Sandra closed her eyes with a smile, holding the smoking gun in a lover's embrace. Death's desire overtook her mind as she drooled over the thought of killing the melting sludge creature.

"Hmm, I love you," she whispered to the gun with a laugh. Slowly she opened her eyes, gazing at the ceiling above. "I'm gonna get ya, then I'm gonna kill ya," her melodious voice rang out through the quiet cabin.

Her eyes slowly shifted left as she heard the bathroom door creeping open. One hand on the trigger, she used the other to slam the bathroom door inward. Turning on the light, she tried to focus through the sporadic flickering of the bulb. Peeling paint and discolored walls gave her a haunting feeling as she stepped inside. A close search along the toilet revealed no threat to be seen.

At ease, she placed the gun across the sink and stared into the dust-clouded mirror. Her once-subtle wounds were now gaping and oozing with the sludge. Crystal-blue eyes had become swollen and filled with deep, red cracks in their whites. Reaching down to the cold water handle, she turned it with a squeak. Cold, crisp water poured into her cupped hands. Wiping her face to cool her burning skin, she again looked at her reflection. She smeared the glass with her wet hands, trying to get a better view. Through finger-lined smudges, she coldly gazed at herself.

Sandra reached up, and as she slowly peeled the flesh from her cheek, she could feel absolutely no pain. Sludge spewed out of her face, spraying the mirror. Dropping the skin into the sink, she turned off the water. She began to pick more away, but her playtime was cut short by the sound of soft, creeping footsteps in the hall. With her ear to the door, she listened as the steps trailed into the den. She slid the gun off of the sink quietly and snuck out of the bathroom without a sound.

Toe by toe, in a side step, she moved silently into the den. The creature looked off into the kitchen, unaware of Sandra's presence. Inches from its back, Sandra stopped, its head in her sights.

Suddenly sensing she was there, the creature turned to face her.

"Smile, fucker," she coldly stated, as she pulled the trigger.

To her surprise, nothing happened. Thinking on her feet, she gun-butted the monster in the face. Sludge spewed from its nose, spattering all over her. Stumbling back, it grabbed her by the arm.

Both plummeted to the floor with a heavy thud. Its grip was released as its head hit the floor. On hands and knees, Sandra scurried for the fireplace poker in the rack. The creature reached out again, grasping her by the ankle. In a dead stop, she was forced flat to the floor in front of the still burning fireplace. Arm over arm, the creature climbed up her leg, sludge covering her as the creature moved steadily up to her waist. It groaned deeply with every move it made.

Feeling no pain, Sandra reached into the fireplace and scooped up a handful of smoldering cinders and ash, heaving it into the face of the creature. It immediately let go and started rolling around on the floor, screeching horrendously. In one swift motion, Sandra slid across the floor and grabbed the poker tightly. With a quick leap, the poker was driven through the monster's chest. Sludge sprayed out as she pushed the poker deep into its body, pinning it to the floor.

Thrashing about, the sludge creature gripped the poker and tugged, sending Sandra to the floor on her butt. A deafening groan filled the house as the creature struggled to free itself.

Sandra screamed out in rage, trying to drown out its bellow. Emotionlessly, she stormed back over to the rack of fireplace tools and retrieved the small shovel. "Shut the hell up!" she yelled, hitting the creature with the shovel. "I killed you!"

Crouching down to its face with a smile, she felt victorious. "I killed you." Standing up again, she gave it one more whack with the shovel to the head. "Asshole," she stated, tossing the shovel on its chest. "Is there anything else that wants to play, huh? I didn't think so."

"You're not a very nice person, you know that?" The voice had come from the kitchen.

"How many times do I have to kill you?" she asked, stomping to the kitchen. There, leaning on the knife block, stood the alien. Striding up to the block and pulling out the butcher knife, Sandra showed no fear as she poked it into the alien's tiny, light-blue stomach. "You just keep coming back for more because I love this game."

"I know you do." It kept its calm demeanor, remaining fearless of her threats. "It's sad, really, to see you acting like this. I remember when you used to love to smile and be happy with your friends. Sandra, you are lost."

"Thanks for the flashback, but who the fuck is Sandra?" she coldly asked, piercing through the small body of the alien again. Flinging its impaled body over her shoulder, the alien slid off the blade, flying to the floor. Landing with perfect form, it turned to her with a smile, the wound no longer there.

"You will have to do far better than that to kill me, little girl," it remarked. In a blur it quickly ran up to the top of the stairs. "Come find me, little one; I will lead you to a place of rest."

Smiling and with eyes gleaming of evil, she gripped the knife and took up the chase upstairs. Standing at the top of the stairs, she looked down the long hall, the family pictures flexing in and out as the walls pulsed as though the house was breathing. At the end of the hall, the door to Matt's sisters' room was slightly open, slowly creaking closed from a soft wind behind it.

Teetering as she walked, Sandra glanced at the family photos. She watched as their faces melted and distorted. "I'll kill you all," she stated, punching the glass. Her knuckles tore open on the jagged shards, dumping sludge down her fingers to the floor. Leaving a trail alongside her, she continued down the hall.

Sandra used the edge of the blade to open the door and then dragged the knife across the door menacingly. As she crept into the bedroom, she closed the door to prevent the alien from escaping. Hundreds of faint, high-pitched giggles came from above the beds. Cocking her head swiftly, she went to investigate.

"There's more than one?" she asked, moving toward the sound. "It doesn't matter; I'll kill every one of you. Do you hear me? All of you!"

Lunging into a pile of the aliens, she hacked, ripped, and mutilated them. Pieces were torn off as heads rolled on the floor. With entrails and limbs scattered about, her frenzy continued into dawn.

With the sun rising on the horizon, Officer Marla Kingston started her morning rounds of the town. Heading out to Highway 9, she made her way into town. Just around the bend, the wreckage of a totaled Mustang came into view. Turning back, she stopped to run the plate. It came back Mathew J. Armstrong.

Fearing the worst, she quickly radioed for backup. "John, this is Marla," she called out over the radio.

"Whatcha need, Marla," came a raspy, older man's voice.

"I've got a situation at the Armstrong place; I found the son's car, and it's all smashed up," Marla calmly explained.

"I'll send out Paul," John replied.

"Better send an ambulance, too. There's no one visible in the car, but that doesn't mean no one's hurt."

"Gotcha. Be careful out there," John added.

Leaving her door ajar, she crept over to investigate the car.

Drawing her pistol from her hip, Marla used full precaution as she approached the wreckage. The hood was buckled and sprung from smashing into a large oak. The scent of antifreeze filled Marla's nose. Crumpled and pushed in, the driver's side door was jammed shut. Inside, the air bags were sprung, but there was no sign of blood. Putting her gun away she continued her search of the wreck. The smashed and folded rear quarter dripped heavily with blood. Smears and spatters lined the crumpled steel leading her along the destruction to the back of the car. Opening the caved-in trunk, Marla noticed both Sandra's and Matt's bags of clothing.

Paul pulled up behind in his squad car. Stepping out of his car, he joined Marla with the investigation. "What the hell happened here?" he asked, looking the car over.

"There are tracks all around at the back of the car. Look." She led him to the back of the car, where there were several deep prints dug into the ground. Judging the size of the tracks, Marla came up with a possibility. "I don't know; I think it was a moose. It looks like it stood up and smashed in the trunk," she observed, contriving a scenario. "There's blood on the outside of the driver's side."

"So you think the moose hit them?"

"Something like that. We need to go to the cabin, see if anybody's hurt," she stated, looking up the road.

They climbed back into their separate cars and continued down the road. Slowly making their way, Marla looked off into the woods, where she could see many broken tree limbs.

"Look to your right, Paul. See all the broken branches?" she asked across the radio.

"Yeah," he responded. "Do you think it ran through here?"

"Definitely, but I don't understand why it would run toward the cabin. Unless … it was chasing somebody there," Marla concluded.

They came to a small bend in the road, after which the cabin became visible, along with all the carcasses of the many mutilated small and even large animals surrounding it. Marla put her car in park as Paul pulled up behind her. Both stepped from their vehicles and surveyed the fly-covered mess.

"What the hell?" Paul bent down to look at the marks on the flesh and bones of what appeared to be a deer. "Is this some kind of sick joke … or maybe cult activity?"

"Can't be; a hundred men couldn't do this." Reaching over, Marla turned on her shoulder radio. "John?"

"Go ahead, Marla," John called back over the speaker.

"We need someone from fish and game up here, stat. We're going to need some blood samples taken," she explained.

"I'm on it," John replied.

"Let's check out the perimeter." Marla pulled out her pistol and started making her way to the side of the house.

Paul nodded and joined just behind her. Reaching the corner, Marla let her gun lead the way. "There's the moose," she pointed out, spotting its corpse lying outside of the broken window. "There's no glass on the outside. It must have broken in."

"Whoever shot it knew what they were doing," Paul stated, looking over the bullet wounds in its neck. "They even blocked the window." Using his boot, Paul pushed the moose's head. The gaping lesion in its neck opened wide, spilling blood all over the ground. "Damn it."

Both stopped and looked back from where they'd come as they heard the sound of a truck pulling up. Quickly they both ran back toward the front of the cabin, Paul leaving footprints of blood everywhere he stepped. Coming around the bend, the ambulance also pulled up, stopping behind the squad cars. Placing her gun back into its holster, Marla walked over as the two paramedics sprang out for action.

"Just wait here; we haven't secured the inside," she told them. "We don't know what's going on yet. We'll let you know if anyone inside needs help. Paul, I can't have you tracking blood in there, so I'll go in alone."

"Just stay in contact," Paul demanded, touching his radio.

As Marla walked up to the front door, a lump filled her throat. She knocked with her left hand while keeping her right on her gun. Pausing, she listened for any type of response. Not a sound came from inside the cabin. Trying the knob, to her surprise, she easily gained her entry into the cabin.

At a glance she could see the chaos that had taken place. She waved her gun around swiftly with a quivering hand. Walking blind into the situation, Marla expected the worst. Scanning the den from the doorway, she could see the empty beer cans and wine bottle lying on the floor. Moving toward the kitchen, she found the dishes on the floor and the fridge left open. Her instantly envisioning several horrible scenarios caused her heart rate to rise.

"I'm in the kitchen now. It looks like there was some kind of struggle here," Marla whispered into her radio. "I'm moving to the den now."

As she made it around the half-wall, she spotted Matt's leg sticking out from in front of the couch. Her gun steady in hand led her way. Stumbling back, she dropped to the floor at the sight of Matt nailed to the floor with the fireplace poker. Tears in her eyes, she crawled over to see if there was a pulse. A faint rhythm pumped through his veins.

"I found ... it's bad, real bad. Don't come in here!" Lying alongside of Matt was the empty shotgun. Marla, quick to hide it, slid it under the couch with her foot. If there were someone else in the house she didn't want it to be easily found.

Continuing to search the house, she slowly walked down the hall toward the bathroom. She cautiously opened the door and saw Sandra's blood smeared all over the counter and mirror. Gagging at the sight of the chunk of flesh in the sink, she stumbled back into the hall, closing the door. As she looked off to the library, every inch of her skin tingled in dread.

Marla slowly pushed the door open. It made a high-pitched creaking moan. Walking in, she discovered the small desk lamp covered in blood, sitting in the center of the room. All around her, the shotgun blasts with the destroyed trophies marked the walls. One shot was directly between the eyes of the mounted moose head.

"Marla, come in," Paul's voice called out over her radio.

"Damn it, Paul, I'm fine," she stated, taking several deep breaths. "I found a boy but he's ... I don't know ... barely alive. I still have to look upstairs. Just stay out there; I don't know what did this, but it might still be here."

Leaving the library, Marla used every precaution as she headed back to Matt. Checking him once more, he still pulsed with a little sign of life. Step by step, she silently headed for the stairs. She climbed to the top, lightly stepping, without producing sound. All of the doors were closed. Marla didn't know where to begin. Coming to the pictures, she instantly noticed the broken family portrait, along with a trail of blood leading to the room at the end of the hall.

"I'm upstairs. I think I found something," Marla silently said through her radio. "I'm going in."

Following the blood trail, she nervously stopped at the closed door at the end of the hall. A single, bloody hand print was smeared over the sign, "Princesses for life". She closed her eyes as she reached for the knob. Lightly pushing the door open with her gun, she opened her eyes to see the demolished room. Pillow stuffing, along with several pieces of fabric lay scattered around the room, blood spattered all over them. In the back corner sat a pile of several butchered stuffed animals. Spots of the cotton were colored deep red with soaked-in blood. Keeping her pistol drawn, Marla moved in closer to the disorder.

A slight movement came from within the mess, a short three feet from Marla, causing her to freeze, alert.

Sandra lunged out, screaming at the sight of the creature standing in the room. Her red eyes focused on its chest as her blade made its course. Then suddenly, all fell silent.

Marla, shaking and cold stood over Sandra's lifeless body. The smoking gun fell to the floor, smoke pouring from its barrel. Not a single noise graced Marla's ears as she existed in the moment. Not even the yelling of Paul over her radio could pull her from her mind, which was grasping for peace. It wasn't until Paul spun her around by the shoulder that her mind returned.

"Marla … Marla!" Paul shouted as he turned her around. "What happened?"

As he looked over at Sandra, Marla became coherent. "I ... had to. She—" Without being able to speak anymore, she broke down into tears.

"It's all right. Let's go down outside and get some air." Paul put his arm around Marla and walked her out of the room. "We've got one seriously injured in the downstairs den and another dead on the second floor," Paul stated over his radio. As they got to the top of the stairs, the paramedics entered and quickly moved to Matt's aid.

Outside, Paul took Marla to her car. "What happened up there? Damn it, you could have been killed!"

"I'm fine, Paul. I just ..., wasn't expecting to shoot anyone this morning." She opened her door and sat in the driver's seat, going over the situation over and over again in her mind. "There was something not right about that girl—her eyes, they were all bloodshot, and it looked like there was something else making her do it."

"What do you mean?"

"It was as if she was possessed or something. I don't know how to describe it, but she wasn't in her right mind," Marla explained, looking for an answer.

Both looked up at the cabin as the paramedics carted Matt out straight into the ambulance. Closing the doors, they fired up the sirens and drove off just as a vehicle from fish and game pulled up. A flat-bottom boat bounced in the bed of the large truck as it made its way down the road. Stopping just behind the squad cars, the driver got out to see the mess of animals scattered about.

"What the hell happened here?" he loudly asked. "Damn, that's one hell of a mess." Walking up to Marla he extended his hand to introduced himself. "Ethan Johnson, fish and game, who had the party?"

"It was no party," Marla angrily stressed, declining his hand. "People died in there, and we don't know what the hell did it. Take some blood samples; we need to figure it out."

251

"All right, calm down. I'll do it," he muttered, retrieving a small kit from the glove box. "How many do you want?"

"Get four if you can," Marla requested, walking up alongside of him.

Ethan set down the kit alongside one of the larger carcasses. Pulling out a small syringe he struggled to draw blood from the fragments. "Was gonna go fishin' over at White Tale Lake later. All right, I got 'em."

"Hey, Paul, you still got those road block signs in your trunk?" Marla had come up with an idea.

"Yeah, why?" Paul asked, confused by the request.

"Set them up at the end of the drive and get back here." Looking to Ethan as if to ask permission, Marla asked, "I'd like to take a ride up to the lake."

With no objections, Paul took his car to place the signs. Marla watched as he drove off around the bend, while Ethan put the filled kit back into the truck.

"So, what are you thinking?" Ethan inquired, slamming the truck door.

"I don't know, I just want to see if there's more of this mess up there," she replied, not taking her eyes off of Paul's direction. "I'm hoping whatever happened, happened here and only here."

With a small cloud of dust behind him, Paul returned down the dirt drive. Ethan, already inside of the truck, waited for them. Opening the passenger door, Marla rode alongside of Ethan as Paul climbed into the back. He sat on the wheel well resting his feet on the bottom of the boat. Checking to see if Paul was seated, Ethan fired up the truck. They slowly made their way up the dirt road to the lake.

Paul looked out into the woods as he held onto the truck bed's side. Several tools and a crowbar bounced around in the back under his legs.

The foul scent of rotting fish filled the air as they drew closer to the lake. Breaking from the surrounding tree line, they could finally see the water. The entire surface lay covered in dead fish.

Ethan pulled up to the Armstrong's boat launch. All three stepped out of the truck, not being able to remove their gaze from the horrible sight of lake.

"What could do this?" Marla asked Ethan.

"I don't know, I've never seen anything like this," he replied, crouching down by the water. "Two days ago I reeled in two big bass out in that very spot," he pointed out into the water.

Paul walked over to Ethan, holding a stick, "I hope you didn't eat'em," he stated, as he poked one of dead fish's bloated bellies with the stick.

"Nope, thank God," Ethan replied as he stood, "still got'em in the freezer."

"Would you two be careful over there," Marla ordered, "for all we know what ever caused this is in the water."

Ethan felt she might be on to something. "I'm going to get a few samples for the boys at the lab," he remarked, pulling out a couple of empty vials from the truck.

"Good idea, I'd take in those fish you caught too," she added. "If it's only been a couple of days they might give us a time line on this thing. Do you have any binoculars in that truck of yours?"

"Sure, there on the seat," Ethan answered, as he took samples of the water.

"What are you thinking now, Marla?" Paul asked, unsure of how to help.

Retrieving the binoculars, she began to scan the opposite shoreline. "I'm not sure Paul, this is just plain odd," she stated, trying to come up with an answer.

Ethan finished taking the water samples and returned them to the truck. "I think I'll get one of these fish too," he stated. Going to the back of the truck he grabbed the crowbar and a small cooler from underneath the overturned boat, "this should do it. Hey, Paul, you wanna give me a hand here?"

"Um, sure, what do want me to do?" Paul asked, excited about being able to help.

"Try and get that stick into one of their mouths and lift him into the cooler," Ethan explained.

Marla kept her eyes in the binoculars as the other two struggled to get the fish out of the water. "Hey, Ethan," she called out, focusing her vision on a small island, "how well do you know these waters?"

"Pretty good why?" he asked, helping Paul to guide the stick over to the cooler.

"There's something out there, over by that little island," she answered, "it looks like an old truck tire."

After several failed attempts, they finally managed to get the fish inside. Wiping his brow, Ethan walked up behind Marla, his curiosity began to grow. "Whatcha got?"

Marla handed the binoculars over to him, "There, just barely on shore," she pointed out.

Scanning the shoreline of the small grassy island, Ethan searched for anything out of place. On the corner of the island he spotted a tiny black metallic object that barely broke the water's surface.

"I see it," Ethan confirmed, "can't tell what it is though. Want to get a closer look?" he asked, hoping curiosity had gotten to her as well.

Marla glared at the unknown object as the water washed over it, then down again. "I think we're in over our heads here, boys," she stated, turning back towards the truck. "We have no idea of what could be causing this—"

"With all the dead fish floating around, I'm pretty sure it's in the water," Ethan demanded. Opening the tailgate on his truck he began to reach for the boat. "I'm going out there to see—"

"See what, huh?" Marla snapped back. "You're willing to risk your life to go see something that's probably a piece of garbage."

Ethan continued to pull the boat out of the truck, despite Marla's argument. "Look, if there is something in the water we need to know about it," the boat hit the ground with an echoing thud. "If that gets into the water supply the whole *damn* town will die!" A small trolling motor lay next to where the boat sat in the truck bed. Placing it inside the boat, he was determined to head out over the water.

Marla watched as Ethan pulled the boat to the waters edge. "If you go out into that water, Ethan, I swear I'll arrest you on the spot," she explained in a huff.

"You want to arrest me?" Ethan calmly asked, as he carefully stepped into the boat and pushed off the shore, "come arrest me."

"Get back here, *Ethan*," Marla shouted as he connected the motor and slowly cut through the water towards the island. "Where did he put those binoculars?"

Marla stormed over to the truck. The binoculars lay inside the cab on the seat. Snatching them up she turned to watch as Ethan made his way to the island. His boat slowly cut through the layer of dead fish as it lightly bobbed in the water. Within a few minutes Ethan had finally reached the island. Using the crowbar to hook the shore, he pulled the boat safely up. Marla, wishing she had gone, was forced to watch as he made the discovery. Once more, with the crowbar in hand, he reached out into the water trying to hook the object. Without success, he only managed to budge it. Giving up, he began his way back.

"Ethan Johnson," Marla stated as soon as his boat landed on shore, "you have the right to remain silent," pulling out her cuffs she managed to get his wrist. "Anything you say—"

"Anything?" he asked with a smart tone, "Well, then I guess I can't tell you what I found out there."

Marla, caught by curiosity, stopped cuffing him. "What *did* you find out there?" she asked, undoing the locked cuff.

With a deep smirk and a raised brow, he faced Marla to deliver his answer. "It's a barrel," he explained, pulling the boat onto land. "I couldn't budge it because it's buried in the mud."

"What do you think's in it?" Paul asked, as Marla was deep in thought.

"I have no idea what it is, but there was label under the paint. It must have fallen off due to the water. All it said was Armstrong Pharmaceuticals: Europhentron Deemed highly dangerous by the FDA. To be disposed of properly. We need to do something, *fast.*"

Mind Game

Awake, sitting in a bed I've never seen. The digital clock next to the bed shows midnight. A chilling breeze passes over my body. Did I leave the window open? Cold hardwood floors greet my feet as I fumble through the dark, searching for the light. With a flick of the switch, two fluorescent bulbs in the ceiling flicker on. This room is a dreary shithole. Torn, stripped wallpaper covers over gray paint in sporadic patches. Everything in the room shows signs of age, from the sweat-stained mattress to the worn, old dresser. Both look as though they've survived through two world wars.

The mirror above the dresser reveals a face and body I do not recognize. By my best guess I'm around twenty six, maybe thirty. Tattered dark hair with sleepless, baggy eyes make up my pale face, five o'clock shadow included. Though I appear to be in decent shape physically, I've gotten a few scars that mark my chest and shoulder. I just wish I knew me—or even knew this room. Yet there is comfort here, despite the fact that I can't remember.

I sit back down on the bed, trying to grab a thought. Like, do I always sleep naked? My clothes lay draped over the back of a red velvet chair. One pair of ratty jeans, two gray socks, a stained, white tee, one pair of white boxers, one wristwatch, and a pair of gym shoes that have seen better times. Putting on my pants, I scrounge through the pockets, looking for anything that might spark some memory. Only twenty-three dollars and fifteen cents, that's all there is. It's better than nothing, I guess. My stomach growls maliciously with hunger. There is no way of knowing when I ate last. I finish getting dressed and head out the door.

Beyond the front door is a hall; it must be an apartment complex. Number 342 is my place—at least, so it seems. An eerie silence drapes over me, as not so much as a footstep can be heard. Down two flights of stairs and around the corner and I'm out in the street. Dim streetlamps light my path, either left or right. Across from the apartment building stands an old cemetery; its rusty, wrought iron fence protects all of its many occupants. To the right feels like the correct way, but then again, I don't really know. After a few blocks' hike that way, an all-night diner comes into view. From outside I see several people dining; a few couples and some loners sit gabbing.

Right out front is a newspaper dispenser. Finally I can find some answers. Twenty-five cents … shit, I only have fifteen. I peer inside to see the date: July 17, 2007. How long have I been in this town? Where is this town, for that matter? The name Din-Gemma lines the top of paper. What kind of name is Din-Gemma for a town?

Walking into the diner, a man behind the counter greets me as though he knows me. His bald head gleams with sweat and grease as his eyes light up at my presence. "How ya been? I've got your seat right here," the man states with a big smile across his chubby cheeks.

"Do you know me?" I ask, slumping onto the bar stool.

"Know ya? Humph. Here, have some coffee; you look like you could use it," he remarks, filling a cup. "You want your usual?"

"What's that?"

"What you normally get. Man, you really are out of it, aren't you?" A smirk lines his face, but my cold expression warns him that I'm not in the mood. "I'm just kidding. You know, two eggs over easy with hash browns, sausage links, and wheat toast, no butter."

Finally something sounds right. "Sounds good."

"So, what's eaten ya, anyway?" He rests his elbows on the counter as he waits for my reply.

"Have you ever felt like you're having a lapsing moment, like déjà vu?"

"No, no I haven't," he says, holding back his laughter.

"Well, I'm living it right now."

"That's one of the things I always like about you. You always say the strangest shit." A gut laugh bursts out as he turns to slap my order ticket to the kitchen window.

I sit, sipping my coffee, looking around for anything that might spark a memory. Not a picture on the wall or any person sitting around me kindles any thought at all. Apart from my waiter, no one seems to know me either. Damn, could there be just one thing?

The front bell chimes as a girl steps into the diner. A light-skinned blonde, maybe nineteen or twenty, attracts me for some reason. She moves toward a booth with a nervous shuffle. Her eyes glance around vigorously, as though looking for someone. Not far behind her, the waitress came up. The girl sits as the waitress starts making small talk, as though she knows her.

"Here ya go," my server says with a smile while he places my meal down.

"Thanks."

"No problem," he states, as he pours me more coffee. "You know that girl?" he asks, nodding his head toward her.

"Should I?"

"I don't know, you just seemed to have your eye on her." His sheepish grin gives away his meaning.

"Do you have a pen I can borrow, and some paper?" Without reason, the need to sketch her pops into my mind.

"Sure." Reaching down into his apron, he retrieves a pen and an old receipt.

"Thanks."

"Anything else you need?" he asks, as two more people come in.

"Naw, I'm good."

The waiter walks away to greet the guests with some coffee. I sit, sketching the girl on the back of the receipt, as I enjoy my meal. Trying to be inconspicuous, I don't want her to notice. For some odd reason, I have no trouble doing this. After a few moments, my drawing amazingly becomes an exact copy. Wow, I've impressed even myself.

"Wow, that's pretty good," the waiter expresses, as he sets down my bill.

"Hmm, oh thanks." Folding the paper, I place it in my pocket as I retrieve my money. Slapping down a twenty should cover it. "You can keep it."

"Hey, thank you," he happily states, taking my empty plate.

"No problem." I wave as I walk out the door, just in case he's a friend.

Outside again, I'm in another position to make a decision, but I don't know where to go. One bad thing about a loss of memory—everything is new to you, leaving you lost. I begin to walk down a side street that leads into a neighborhood. Not much activity at this time of the night; not one car passes or is parked on the street, for that matter. No lights on in the homes; everyone must be asleep.

Pulling the sketch from my pocket, my thoughts drift to the girl. I know I've seen her before. Who is she? Is she as lost as I am, or is she just looking for someone? Better yet, where in the hell am I? Shit, I've lost my way in all of this, and I'm growing tired. A bench on the side of the road calls to me to rest. I place the paper back into my pocket as I lie down for a break.

***

Awake, in a room I do not recognize. The sun shines brightly through an open window. A digital clock next to the bed reads 10:30. I can't remember anything. I had a dream, though, about a girl. That's the only thing I remember. Damn, naked, I stand to get some clothes. A pair of jeans and white boxers lay draped over the arm of a red velvet chair. A stained white shirt sits folded on the seat. Gray, stained socks are stuffed into a pair of worn shoes; there's also a wristwatch inside. Getting dressed and reaching into my pants pockets, I find twenty-three dollars and fifteen cents. Where the hell am I? Peering from the window, I notice I'm on the third floor of an apartment building.

I go outside and find it is a glorious day. Clouds lay scattered about, just hanging in a crystal-blue sky. All the while a comforting breeze blows over me. Across the street stands a monumental cemetery. It covers four city blocks square. A place like this seems perfect for an undisturbed jog, a way to gather some quiet thoughts.

Headstones stand in rows, separated by hedges and trees, like a surreal maze of fallen mice. The outside stones hold dates that drift back in time the deeper I go. 1807 is the oldest entry I see. Beyond that, within the center of this place, rests a glorious marble fountain etched with angels along with other holy figures. The cemetery's perimeter holds benches intended for admiration and for weary people to rest. I sit.

"You come here to feed the pigeons?" a raspy old voice comes from behind me.

I turn to see a man looking to be in his late forties walk past me. An absurdly loud blue Hawaiian shirt peeks out from behind a thin, worn-out leather trench coat. A matching full-rimmed leather hat shades his unshaven face from the sun.

"Know what I realized today?" He sits down on the next bench, pulling out a small loaf of bread. "Nothin' really matters, nothin' at all." Opening the bread wrapper is a call to the pigeons that dinner had come. Tossing some pieces to the ground, he continues, "Your name holds no meaning, neither does any of this." Never once does his gaze leave the pigeons. "They know, the birds. They're free. Humph, to fly and eat, they know their purpose."

"You're searching for purpose?"

My question, triggering only laughter, must seem pointless to him. After a short silence, I feel it is best to move on. "It was nice talking to you."

"Yeah, you take it easy."

A surreal sense clouds over my mind, thoughts ripping through me in questions. This man—is he lost within himself as I am in myself? How long have we been in this town? How long without a memory? Why has nothing sparked anything? Dizzy, worn, and hungry, I search for a place to eat. Just across the street a small diner resides, quiet and quaint.

The door opens with a bell's chime. Four ratty booths line the windows, all of which were full. Out of the six bar stools in front of the kitchen, I have a choice of three. At least I get to see them prepare my food. A man behind the bar spots me. He is a lofty man, maybe in his mid-forties—his salt-and-pepper hair gives that away. Without a bit of hurry in his step, he moves toward the counter to greet me.

"Come on in, sit down; there's plenty a room." His voice is as casual as his pace.

"Thanks," I say. Being in no mood for small talk, I try to keep it simple.

"Ya know what ya want ... or?" he asks, handing me a menu.

"Two eggs over easy, with hash browns, sausage links, and wheat toast, no butter." For some odd reason, within my hunger, that's all that comes to mind.

"You're a man who knows what he wants, I like that." He continues as he turns around to prepare my order. "Coffee?" he asks.

"Sure," I say with a smile. "What do you know about the cemetery?"

"Ahhh ... it's full a dead people?" he states in confusion. "Why? Whatta ya mean?"

"There was this guy—"

"Feedin' the pigeons?" the waiter asks with a slight chuckle.

"Yeah, do you know him?"

"That's old Dave Forester. Every day he walks to the fountain and feeds those nasty birds. He's always talkin' crazy nonsense about life and purpose and how the birds know the truth." With a great scoop he piles my food from the grill to a plate. "Did ya run into him?"

"Uh huh, how long has he been doing that?"

"At least for the ten years I've been runnin' this place. He passes in front of here every day at about 10:40 or so." Leaning down, he puts his mouth near my ear and in a hushed tone tells me, "They say he watched as his parents burned alive in their house. Others say he started the fire."

Pulling back, he reaches to refill my coffee. "No one knows for sure except old Dave himself," he chuckles. "And he ain't sayin' shit." Busting out in gut laughter, a tear comes to his eye.

Shortly after, I begin to eat as a couple from one of the booths gets up and leaves. Wanting to look out at the strange world I've entered, I pick up my plate. Just as the waiter returns. "Is it all right if I move to a window seat?" I ask nonchalantly.

"Sure. One of the girls will get ya refills for your coffee," he answers with a nod and a smile.

I sit gazing out of the window and thinking of Dave. Am I like him, blocking out something I don't want to remember? Mother, Father, Brother, Sister, do any of you exist? I had to have had parents, but why can't I remember them? Does anyone else in this town have this problem? Why do I? All of these questions, all of which I have to keep inside.

"More coffee, sir?" an annoying female voice breaks in on my thoughts. A mouthful of rotting teeth and snapping gum greet me as I turn.

"Sure." Her sour expression never changes. Suddenly I think to ask, "Can I borrow a pen, please?" A bubble bursts from her mouth as she snatches a pen from her hair, slamming it on the table next to my paper place mat.

"Thank you," I state, but she only rolls her eyes and walks away.

I have to write things down; otherwise I won't remember. Time is an essential fact. Dave Forester, for ten years, has passed in front of the diner. What the hell's this place called? Above the stove I can see a broken neon sign; it reads Fortila's. Every day at 10:40 or so Dave comes by. Diner location is opposite side of cemetery. Holding concentrated thought on old Dave's face, I begin a rough sketch. I fold up the entire place mat, knowing I'll need the leftover space for later. Putting the mat in my pocket fills me with an odd sense of paranoia, like something is wrong with this action. The waitress finally returns with my bill, giving me the chance to get out and about.

"Anything else I can get for ya?"

"No, that'll be fine." My hand nervously rubs against the folded paper in my pocket as I pull out my money.

"Have a nice day," the unpleasant woman says, almost sarcastically, from her broken, condescending smile. She slams down the bill and heads back to the kitchen. Four seventy-five, that leaves me with eighteen forty. She is definitely *not* getting a tip.

As I step outside I begin to wonder how many times I have walked these very streets. If I fall asleep, will I remember today? Will all of what's been written on this paper be nonsense? Why does my mind itch for me to hide my note sheet? Where could I hide it that I'd remember and where it can't be lost or taken?

I try to close off my thoughts as I move down the sidewalk. At least one thing about this town, everyone I pass is smiling and friendly. A young couple heading toward me, holding hands, gaze off into the sky, not even aware of my presence. I move out of their way, catching my jean cuff on an outdoor display of twine.

Within that instant it comes to me. I have to sew the mat into the cuff of my jeans. Why? Why do I have this idea, why does it feel safe? Don't question, just do. I head into the store. Inside an older woman greets me with a smile.

"Can I help you, young man?" Her voice is soft and comforting behind her wrinkled face and silver hair.

"I'm just looking for a few needles and a spool of blue thread."

At my request, she begins fumbling through several shelves in a gigantic antique cabinet. "Whatcha need it for?" she asks, placing the thread on the counter.

"I need to fix a rip in my pants, near the cuff."

"Let me see." Her head bobs back and forth to get a better look. "I could probably fix it for ya."

"Oh, it's not this pair. Come to think of it, it's more like a hole."

"You're definitely gonna need a patch," she expresses with a toothy smile. "What size?"

"About the size of my palm," I reply showing her my hand.

"Here ya go. Anything else I can get for ya?"

"Nope, that's all I'll need."

The old register begins to clang as she rings up my bill. "Six fifty-two."

Digging deeper into my pocket, I give up a little more of my bank. "Good luck with your patch work," she states, as I pass through the door.

Now all I have left is eleven dollars and eighty-eight cents. I need to save that in case I get hungry later. I mosey back to the quiet, familiar grounds of the cemetery.

Dave is gone, as are the pigeons he was feeding. Not so much as a crumb remains. Sitting down on a bench with a plan in my head, I begin to work on creating a new pocket in the inside ankle of my jeans. I have to be steady for it to look natural. My leg crossed and pant leg rolled, the intricate work leads me into nightfall, I should have gone home for this. Grumbling sounds from my stomach remind me of how long I've been out here. Finished at last, I can leave this dreary place of the dead.

I reach the other side of the cemetery, near my apartment, to find another, larger diner. Bodino's, the red neon sign glows brightly in the night sky. Well, at least my stomach will get a chance to be content. As I step toward the door, it suddenly opens, and a girl about in her early twenties walks out, nervously chewing her fingernails. I see a glaze of distress in her eyes. She passes me as though I'm not even there. Without looking back, she continues down the sidewalk then disappears around the corner.

A spark flashes through my mind, telling me she's the one from my dream last night. Hunger pangs will have to wait; I give pursuit. In a full-out jog to reach the corner, I find that she's gone. Turning around, I see the sign flicker off. There is nothing left other than to just go back to my room.

Upstairs, I rummage around for the slightest clue of who I am. Everything is barren, from the dresser to the medicine cabinet—empty. Lying back in bed, I bash my mind for answers. Within a matter of minutes, my exhausted mind drifts off.

Visions flash through my dream-stricken mind. Great winds toss sand about, ripping past me, stinging my flesh. The strange girl, her gentle touch, people dying all around me.
***

Awake, I lie naked in a bed I don't recognize. Faint rays of dawn's early light shine through the open window. The digital clock next to the bed reads 7:14. Where the hell am I? Sitting up, I look around for familiarly. A pair of ratty old jeans, a pair of white boxers, and a faded, white T-shirt lay draped over a red velvet chair. There is only twenty three dollars and fifteen cents and a wristwatch in the pockets.

Putting on my pants, I notice a scratchy feeling at my right ankle. I search around to discover a folded piece of paper tucked inside of a hidden pocket. The words, *Personal notes, don't forget*, are boldly written in pen on the outside. Don't forget—like some kind of a sick joke in irony.

Unfolding the paper exposes a sketch of an older man with a hat. Apparently his name is Dave Forester. There's also a brief background on him and his past. Every day at 10:40 he passes the diner Fortila's on the other side of the cemetery. Is this my writing;

did I leave this for myself? Three hours remained before I could find Dave. I have to talk to him to see what he knows. Placing the paper back in the hidden pocket, I finish getting dressed.

Outside I can see the graveyard straight ahead. My stomach growls from hunger. I have time to kill, so I might as well get something to eat. Just down the road there's a large diner, Bodino's, that is thankfully open. Hmm, being the only patron, I have my choice of seats. Several stools line a bar in front of the kitchen. So as not to take away a table others might want, I sit at the bar. I turn over my coffee cup, desperately needing some java.

"What'll ya have?" The gravely voice fills the quiet air as a small, pudgy, bald man steps out from the kitchen. Grabbing a freshly brewed pot, he makes his way over.

"Can I see a menu?"

"Sure. Where are my manners?" A tone of sarcasm tinges his voice. Handing me a menu, he turns back toward the kitchen. "I'll be back in a minute."

At this point everything sounds good. A moment later, people begin to pour into the place. A few businessmen, a couple in their early twenties, and two older women probably near their late fifties come in, chatting away as they sit. A female server with a nasty look on her face dashes out from the kitchen with a pot of coffee to serve them.

"Know what ya want yet?" comes the harsh, gravely voice, startling me.

"Yeah, I'll have pancakes, with hash browns, and a side of sausage links."

"Good choice." I can sense a hint of confusion in his voice. "I'll get that right away for ya." After placing the order, he returns to refill my cup.

"Have you ever heard of a diner called Fortila's?" I question in mid-pour.

"Yeah, it's on the other side of the graveyard. Why, ya some kind of food critic?" he jokingly asks.

"No. A friend of mine named Dave Forester recommended it to me."

"Humph, never heard of him, but its there. I tell ya, it ain't as nice as this place," he chuckles, as he walks back to the kitchen to get my food. Glancing up, I see a clock that shows 7:30. I gulp down my food so I'll have some time to explore the city before my meeting. "More coffee?" the bald man asks, returning with the pot.

"No, thanks. I've got some errands to run." I pay the bill of six forty nine and leave.

Outside the weather has grown slightly cloudy, and the air maintains its morning coolness. Looking around my part of town, there isn't much to see. There are numerous older-looking apartment buildings, each one rattier than the last. Several larger buildings tower over everything on the horizon. To reach them would probably take at least a day's walk. One thing I've really come to notice is that there are no cars here, at least not here on the outskirts of the city.

Continuing my journey leads me to an old, abandoned church. Its crumbling walls reveal the interior plainly. Rotted pews lay tipped over, some of them turned completely into dusty remains. Light shines down through the remnants of a broken stained-glass window, creating an array of color on the dust-covered floor. This once-great temple now lies as a ruined waste. The only things left fully intact are the two marble pillars that stand on either side of the entranceway. Perhaps at one time they held up an overhang.

Moving on, I come to a clock tower. It's 10:10; shit, I have to move if I want to make it back to the cemetery.

Jogging in a heavy stride, I make my way through the cemetery to the fountain, but I keep my distance from it so as to not alert Dave to my presence whenever he shows up. A short time later, sure enough, a man of exact resemblance to my sketch arrives. A mass of pigeons fly down around him as he creeps toward a bench. He sits, pulling a loaf of bread out from under his coat. Crumbs fly but never reach the ground as the pigeons devour them.

"You gonna stand there all day gawking?"

Okay, so he is aware of my presence, as though he can see me through the thick brim of his hat. "Whatcha want?" he asks.

"Sorry." I step out from behind the stone monument. "I was just passing through, and you startled me."

"You know someone buried here?" He continues to feed the pigeons, not looking at me once. Not in the eyes, anyway.

"No, I was on my way to Fortila's. Why? Do you know someone here?"

"Nope, I just came here to feed the pigeons. It's almost as if they knew I was comin'." A smile emerges from under his hat.

There seems like no other way to proceed other than being blunt. "Is your name Dave Forester?"

"Hmm? Dave Forester? That name doesn't sound familiar. Is it me, I don't know. Do you know?"

"Well, every day for ten years you've been coming here to feed the pigeons—"

"How the hell do you know this? Who are you?" he says angrily. As his temper begins to rise, so does he. "Answer me!"

"Relax. I'm a writer, and this guy gave me some information."

"A writer, huh? The truth is," he sits back down, looking me directly in the eyes, "I woke up today not knowing anything, nothing at all. Hmm ... not even yesterday. After going outside, I saw a graveyard. It seemed like a quiet place to gather my thoughts, maybe put this puzzle back together." Looking back down at the birds, his eyes search for answers. "Have I really been comin' here for ten years? What life do I have?"

"I don't know if it's even true. Like I said, the information came to me secondhand." I hope my comments haven't confused him more, but then again, nothing seems to really fit. If he is as I, could there be more amnesiacs?

"If you're a writer, how come you ain't writin' anything down?" he asks.

The question catches me off guard, almost blowing my cover. Quickly I come up with, "I forgot my pen today."

"Well, I think I might have one; there was one there this morning." Reaching into an inside pocket in his trench coat, he rummages around. "Ahh, here we go. Well, you seem to know a lot about me, but I don't know you."

"Thanks, sorry. My name is Thomas Taylor." I do my best to wing it as I have a seat next to him on the bench. As I reach out to shake his hand, he just sits there, looking into my eyes.

Pulling out the paper from my pant leg boosts his suspicions. "Why the hell do you keep your paper there?" he asks.

"So it doesn't get all sweaty in my pockets and so there's no way I can drop it."

Not very satisfied with my answer, he watches as I write down his remarks. "What can you remember?" I query.

Seemingly at a standstill, his mind races for an answer even as I eagerly await it. "All I know is that someday it's all gonna end. So I'm not going to spend my days with worryin' about it."

He grows visibly upset as he speaks. I really can't tell if he is sad or angry, but there is definitely something there. "Can't remember, maybe I don't want to, or maybe I'm not supposed to ... I don't know. Time continues forward as we all drift within it."

Writing everything down as he spoke, I begin to get really confused. Where did this man really come from, and what does he really know?

"You can keep the pen; I don't see much need in it." He tosses the last crumbs of the bread down to the birds. With nothing left to eat, the pigeons just walk about, searching and cooing. "Look at 'em, wastin' their time." Standing up, he places his hands in his pockets. "Ya just gotta keep movin' and hope things will work themselves out." With that he walks away.

Sitting there, like the pigeons, I search—my search being for answers. Everything scribed, I put the paper back in its place. If anything, at least now I have a pen. I realize that he's right, though; there is no point in just sitting there. I need to look around this city, or town, or wherever the hell I am. Leaving the cemetery in the past, I walk to one of the nearby neighborhoods.

Several streets lined with two-story houses take up a three-block section of the town nearby. Each home is relatively similar to the next. All of them have curtains covering the windows. Trying to peek into a house at random, there is nothing to be seen through these damn thick curtains. There's not even a hint of furniture or that anyone lives here. Walking up to the front door, I wonder if I should just knock. One tap, then three. Nothing; screw it. Kicking the door in, I swiftly move inside.

There is nothing. Floors, walls, stairs leading up, and what seems like what a kitchen would be, except there is no stove or other appliances—no furniture to speak of. The next house is the same, as is the one next to it. Five, six, all empty. It's a lie. This place is a lie!

Going back to the first house, I get a feeling, a safe feeling. I'm going to stay here tonight, to see what the morning brings. If all goes well, I hope to wake up here and know why. At this point, I don't know exactly what to trust.

With nothing but time on my hands, I feel I might as well explore the house. Three more empty rooms reside upstairs. One would have been a bathroom. This all seems so pointless, yet I know there's something more. Back downstairs I ponder the thought of a basement. Searching around, the only oddity I notice is a creaky floorboard in the far corner of the kitchen. Pulling back the board and many surrounding it reveals an opening. Only a concrete hole with a ladder leading down stands before me. Not a speck of light can be seen, and there's a frigid wind blowing from within. Even though I can't see, my curiosity holds me fast. I descend. Ten or so feet down, the walls around me disappear.

Reaching the ground floor, I stumble in the dark, rummaging around for a wall. Looking back I can see a pin drop of light coming from the hole above the ladder. Tripping over myself, I accidentally stumble into a stone wall. It's ridged and cold. There are several symbols carved into the stone, like ancient hieroglyphs.

At least that's what they feel like. This is all too creepy—not to mention, I feel a presence, as though I'm being observed. I look up to see that the light from above the ladder has begun to fade, so I make my way back up into the house as night falls.

I have to quickly write this down—the symbols, the room, everything I've found. I have to remember. Scribing the symbols onto the paper, I can't help but wonder what it all means. I know this much, there's far more going on than I can possibly understand. Was this place, this city, built over an ancient civilization? Why are the homes empty, to protect the secret? Who is protecting what from whom? I have to stop or I'll go mad; just relax until the morning. Then I'll see, see if I remember anything about this.

Awake, still in the empty house. My memory is strong; there's no blank from yesterday's events. Shit 10:15, I've only got a few minutes; I need to see if Dave shows up at the cemetery. Peering from the window, I make sure my path is clear. At this point, I don't really trust anyone or anything. Moving back the curtains in the front window reveals an empty street. Quickly I head to the cemetery.

As I reach the cemetery, I can see Dave passing in front of the diner, right on schedule. He turns toward me and walks right past into the necropolis. I wait a short time and then follow him in. He's dressed as he was yesterday. Upon his arrival, the pigeons greet him and walk alongside him expectantly. Sitting down at the same bench as the day before, he pulls out a loaf of bread. As he starts to feed them, I make my approach.

"Nice day, isn't it?" I ask calmly.

"Huh? Oh, sure is," he responds with sorrow in his voice.

"Got family here?"

"No, not that I know of, I just come here to feed the pigeons. You?"

"Yeah, my parents, they died when I was young. I was adopted by a nice family, though, but I still miss my real parents. Ya know?" Even though this is a lie, I get a feeling of truth about it.

"Sorry to hear that," he sympathizes.

"It's all right. So you like feeding the birds?"

"Yeah, helps me take my mind off things."

"Like what?" I ask.

"Well, like what's going on."

"What is going on?"

"Hell, I don't know. I try not to think about it. I just know that I don't know, so there's no sense in worryin'. The pigeons, well, the pigeons are simple—they know the bread is food and that they get it for free. So they don't neglect or take anything for granted." Dipping his head, he falls silent.

"Are you okay?" My concern for him grows as I feel him becoming distant. "Hey."

"Look, just who the hell are you, anyways, to be botherin' me?" he says, his voice now heated.

All I could think of was yesterday's excuse. "I'm a writer."

"Well, shouldn't you be writin' stuff down?" he snidely asks.

"I forgot my pen."

"Here, you can have this; I don't have much use for it." He pulls a pen from his pocket. It is the same color, brand, and shape as the one he handed me yesterday. Now I'm really freaked out.

"Thanks, but I have to be going," I say hurriedly. I can't spend another minute here. Leaving the cemetery my stomach twists and knots. How long? How long have I been stumbling through this routine?

Back inside the house, I find nothing but a hollow frustration. Pacing, I fight off hunger. If I go out, they'll see me; they'll know where I am. Or maybe they haven't even noticed. Then again, who the hell *are* they? My mind paces faster than my physical shuffle, running through so many possibilities. Within that my curiosity … no, my determination to know who's running this maze evolves. I have to know.

Without pressing my luck, I pass calmly through the streets to the diner. Shit, I have to remember the time to see if the same people are in the same place, the time I went yesterday. It's

11:30 … should I go? I need to eat. Even with this critical motion I'm still losing out on gathering information. Damn it.

Those that pass look at me; they know. It's the paranoia in my eyes, followed by fear. Trying not to focus on it, I slide inside the diner. Just as before, there are several people scattered sporadically throughout. No one's sight is upon me as I move toward the farthest booth from the entrance. Out of all the faces, the working men are the only ones that seem familiar. I try to find solace in my booth in the corner.

Sounds of snapping gum come up from behind; I hate that sound. After pouring a few cups of coffee at one table, the waitress makes her way toward me, snapping with every step.

"Need some coffee?" she asks, finishing with a snap of her gum.

"Sure," I state, fumbling around with the table menu.

"Know what ya want or should I come back?"

"I'll just have the eggs and toast, over easy, thanks."

Her face never changes expression. There's just that snotty, better-than-thou look. She pours the coffee, snaps her gum a few times, and walks to another table.

Is she part of this? Does anybody know what's going on? How many people remember their everyday lives? There's no way of asking anyone the truth. Hundreds of other questions rise and fall in my mind, but the only thing I know is that I'm utterly alone in this.

This food will keep me going for a little while. It arrives quickly, and I down it even more quickly. I wish to leave immediately. Tossing my money with the bill on the counter, I walk out. I feel them staring, watching me as I stumble in a fit of paranoia. Within myself I feel as though I've seen this before.

Outside I see the girl. She acts skittish, as if in fear of her surroundings. She is heading toward me. My eyes drift away as she grows close. When she goes by, I give her a short moment and then follow.

Her head flutters around, glancing at everything she passes by. I know she's digging for answers as well. Her pace quickens; either she's on to me or she's beginning to lose it. Swiftly she turns the corner toward the homes I know are empty. As I peer around the corner, I see her walking toward one of the houses. Now's my chance; taking the back paths so she won't see me, I sneak around to my lawn to watch her.

She knocks on a door, waits, and then moves to the next house. Only one more door until mine. Waiting in the thick bushes between the yards, I decide to snatch her into my place. It is a bit malicious, but I know I can trust her.

As she draws near, my breath calms, my heart slows, and my thoughts clear. I know I can do this. Quietly I emerge from behind, creeping ever so slowly, ever so silent. Reaching out for the door, she goes unaware as my hand crosses over her mouth. With a twist I open the door and pull her close.

"It's all right, I won't hurt you," I explain as I shut the door behind us with a slam. "I know what you're going through." Her tears pour down my hand into a puddle below. "Let me explain, then you can go. Okay?" With a simple nod of her head, I release her.

"Who are you?"

Her first question is the fairest, but I hold no answer. I can only say, "I don't know ..."

"What the fuck is going on? What town is this? Why won't people talk to me? There's no furniture in this house! Oh God ... please." A breakdown brings her to her knees. Sobs are all that fill the air.

"Calm down, there's a lot to take in." At this point, she's as fragile as a child. I have to be careful. "I've only a memory of a day. Before that, I took notes. Dave Forester is man I had met in the cemetery. For some reason I wrote a note to myself about him. I found it in my pants, hidden. Down to the finest detail, it was right. There was also a part about you."

"What? What about me? Who am I?" Her mind seems lost. How long has she lived like this?

"Again, I don't know. I had a dream about you, but I didn't know you. After that, I saw you walking down the sidewalk and followed you, but you disappeared. That's all that was written. Hell, I was hoping you had some answers."

"Why are you telling me this?" Her head twitches as she looks around, searches for a way out of this reality. "How am I supposed to believe you, how?"

"I don't expect you to believe me, but try to remain calm. Please ... here, write this down and hide it on you somewhere in your clothes. Also write down how to get here and a time to come."

Although she's dumbfounded, she's doing what I ask. "What should I call you?"

Within all of the craziness that's going on, I can't think. "Gabriel ... I guess." So far none of the names I've come up with have felt right, but it gives me association. "What about you?"

"The name Sarah has always raced through my head, so," she states with a shrug of her shoulder.

"Okay, you can go ahead and go. If whoever is doing this doesn't find that note, I'll see you here tomorrow."

She opens the door wide but doesn't move. I'm surprised she's staying, but then again, she's as lost as I am.

"They who? What the fuck is going on?"

"Save it! Even if I told you what I thought, it wouldn't matter! You won't remember it. Just go; I need to think."

But with both of us feeling the insanity of the situation, we cannot seem to part. She says, "If this is true ... will you help me? I mean ... try to find a way out of here?"

"That's exactly what I'm working on."

As she walks away from me, I can't help but think of what's going to happen to her tonight and if she'll return. Calling most in my head are thoughts of the tunnel beneath this place. Two o'clock. I need to find something to use for a light.

Walking the streets gives me time to think. There seem to be more people walking around today. Moving past them, they barely notice me, or they don't care to. I don't know which. All of the shops, homes, businesses—everything here is across from or around the cemetery. This place is so odd, more so now that I'm partially aware.

Three forty-five, and there's no sign of anything I might use to produce light. Maybe from corner to corner through the cemetery I might find something.

Chills ripple up my spine as I glance over the names of the dead. There are so many, this one here is Jane Mayland. As her name passes my lips, I have a sense of knowing her. She died only last year. How? More names come to mind, others don't.

Now that I'm on the other side of the cemetery, it's four o'clock. Shit, what am I going to do? A costume shop; it's not Halloween, is it? I don't remember ever seeing a child in this place, anyway. But maybe they'll have something. And if not, it'll be amusing, anyway.

Inside the shop is an array of costumes, from dragons to witches and skeletons. The woman behind the counter is wearing a maid's outfit. A little excessive, but at least she wears it well.

"Is there anything I can help you with?" Her voice is as sexy as her appearance.

"I'm looking for flashlights or glow sticks."

Stepping out from behind the counter, she gestures for me to follow her.

"Here, behind the broomsticks." Bending down, she reaches in, pulling out a few glow sticks. "How many do you need?"

"How many do you got?" I hope she doesn't notice the nervousness in my voice.

"About thirteen. You want them all?"

"Sure." My eyes focus on her graceful sway as she returns to the register.

"That'll be fifteen twenty-one."

Reaching into my pocket, I've forgotten how much money I have. Sixteen forty-seven. I have just enough. I hand her the money, holding a half-ass attempt at a smile on my face. For some reason, this girl has penetrated into my every thought, making her the only one in the world.

"Is there anything else I ... can do for you?" Her smile pulls at my being, as do her crystal-blue eyes. Within that very moment, I am frozen, not knowing what to say or do.

"How long have you lived here?" I ask calmly.

"A few years, why?" she replies, her smile piercing into my soul.

"I was just curious. I've never seen you around. You would be someone I'd remember."

"Why do you say that?" She stares at me seductively with eyes full of innocence.

"I've never seen anyone as beautiful as you." What the hell am I saying? "Sorry ... I mean you really stand out." I think I'm blushing more than she is.

"Why don't you hang out? I'm closing for the night in a few minutes; we can go for coffee or something," she suggests.

"Sure." Even though there is no time for this, I just can't resist.

"I've got to go change," she states, locking the door. "I'll be right back." Once more I'm drawn into the precise pendulum sway of her hips.

After a short while, she returns. Her skintight jeans and black v-neck shirt ensure that no imagination is required. Lust and fear pierce my soul at the same time. How long has it been?

"Are you ready?" she asks, with bedroom eyes.

"Sure," is all that comes to mind, simple, one-word replies— those, and childlike fears.

We exit the store then walk down the street toward a diner. Thankfully it's not the same one I've been visiting. I couldn't handle the snapping-gum girl right now. Opening the door, I let her pass, then I follow. This is so not like me. Even though she's speaking, I hear only silence as I watch her sway while gliding toward a booth.

"Is this okay?" Her voice is a melody gripping at my soul.

"Sure, this is great."

She pulls out a cigarette as we sit down simultaneously. "You don't mind ... do you?"

"Not at all." Even if I did, I don't.

"Can I get you two anything?" I jump with a start as the waitress breaks the moment. "I can come back."

"It's okay, we'll just have coffee." Being quick on her feet to answer, she knows what she wants.

"Right away." The waitress gives my so-called date some sort of look then speeds off for the coffee. "Here you are," the waitress states, returning within an instant. "I'll keep it fresh for you." Once again, in a dash, she leaves.

"Do you know her?" It's a silly question, I know, but it's all I can come up with.

"No. This place is known for their fast service and good coffee. Do you like it?"

"I'll give it a whirl." Adding two teaspoons of sugar and giving it a slight stir, I'm ready to sip. "This ... is good."

I don't know if it's because I'm in the presence of this immense being or if the coffee really is this good, but it tastes better than any coffee I've ever had.

"So, this has been a good day?"

I don't quite understand her question. "Let's just say it's been very ... eye opening," I reply.

"Hmm. How so?" she asks, resting her head on her bridged hands.

"Have you ever felt like someone you're not?"

"Well ..." she laughs. "I do. That's why I work at the costume shop. I like being someone else from time to time. How about you? Who do you want to be?"

A scent comes from her cigarette that I don't recognize. It also seems as though everyone in the place is smoking.

"I don't know … who would I want to be?" It's a good question. I don't even know who I *am*.

The waitress returns with a smile. "More coffee?"

"Yes, please." My date smiles playfully at the waitress, like a child.

Again the waitress moves in high speed, as does everything around me, everything except for my date.

"I'd be a dancer, maybe, or a singer. Just for a little while though; then I'd go be someone else, maybe a …" Her words echo in my ear, but then everything stops when she mutters the words, "Want to go back to my place?"

Her lips don't actually pass those words, but they are there nonetheless. "Do you want to touch me, feel me, or become one with me?"

Lips deceive, as does sight, and understanding. *I have to have this girl!*

My psychedelic haze cracks away when I hear real words. "Are you ready?"

"For what?" I ask leisurely, as my nerves begin to rise.

"To go, silly." As she stands, I can feel a euphoric force caressing my mind, causing me to rise. Only a child's smile and a slight nod spark in my mind as my response. Leading me out of the diner, she reaches back to take my hand gently. It's so far away.

Outside, the sun has set, and the moon is nowhere to be seen. Starlight is the only thing lighting our way. Looking up in delight, she smiles as bright as the stars themselves. A warm, inviting glow surrounds her, pulling me in. Without reason, without doubt, I need her.

"Aren't the stars wonderful?" Her arms sticking out from her sides, she begins to slowly twirl. "Each one is its own, but yet they are all one, just like us."

"Yes, like us." Something has taken me over; the streets become a blur.

Like propelled by pure independent motion, we arrive outside of her home. Nothing else exists around us, just the ground beneath my feet and the door that lies ahead. With a slow creak, the door opens, her hands caressing my face as we drift within.

Inside, the room is dark, with a slight, dim glow of blue coming from behind another door. Floating free, we move toward it. Lips pressing and hands caressing, our clothes drop to the floor. Breasts press to my chest as she pushes me to the bed in her glowing chambers. Like an angel she falls before me, begging with her eyes for me to come. Within moments we wrap ourselves into each other, her gratification ripping through my soul as we intertwine.

"This is what it means to be one," she whispers. "To be a part of this ritual is purity."

She takes control as the blue light grows brighter with her every moan. My pleasure heightens slowly as she rises up giving me a full view of her body. My eyes roll in orgasmic pleasure, pleasure that goes beyond any other, pleasure that drains my being. I fight to not drift off.

"You were exactly what I expected." Those words echoing in my mind, her touch fades. "Now you have to be someone else."

Awake, lying on a park bench in the center of some park I've never seen. My head—how long have I been here? By my watch the time is 1:45 a.m. At least my light sticks are still here, along with my memory, wherever here might be.

From in the distance, I can hear something … a car? Shit! Grabbing my things, I make way for the nearest bushes. A slight, dim glow grows larger as whatever it is moves toward me.

Suddenly, with a squeak, a black van with no windows rolls to a stop nearby. After killing the lights, the driver emerges, dressed in all black, military-fashion, complete with night vision binoculars and a rifle unlike anything I've seen. Walking to the back of the van, he hits the doors. Without hesitation, the two doors fly open. Five more people dressed in the same fashion jump out. They separate into teams of two and start to scour the area.

Two of them head toward the bench where I was. Thankfully, now I'm a good sixty yards away. My luck swiftly changes as they move toward me.

"We found the girl; every night it's this shit. Any sign of the fox?" comes a voice over their radio.

"Negative, he wasn't there. Are we sure this is the right spot?" one of the men nearby answers back.

"This is the place. Just keep looking … even though we're late, he couldn't have gotten too far."

"Yes, sir."

I have to maintain my cool, wait it out. After a short time, another of the teams of two of the men returns carrying Sarah. They carefully place her in the back and get in with her.

At ten to three, they finally call it quits. I have to get back to the house. It doesn't matter how much time has passed; I still feel strange from that coffee. No idea which direction to head, I just stumble along randomly. At 4:24, things where I am look familiar. Is this it? My empty house—I'm so happy to see my empty house. I need to sleep. Once inside, there is nothing but a collapse.

Thoughts dance throughout my head, giving me a full display of my haze-filled night. In the dream, Sarah, laughing so intently, is happy and safe. Suddenly the happy rainbow shifts into nightmare. Beauty turns unspeakable. There is a creature I have never seen. Lights, motion—all is a blur within my vision. It leaves my mind in a cloud.

Awake, inside my empty house. Damn it, 2:40. Peering from behind the curtains, the way looks clear. Sliding down the wall in comfort, I can still feel paranoia's grip. Across from me lies the bag of glow sticks I bought. So whatever happened last night did happen. Who was she, why did she want me, and what was it that she'd said? I can't remember what she said to me.

Gazing off into the kitchen reminds me of my task at hand. I have to see what's down there. There is just one more hour before the appointed meet-up time with Sarah. I hope she's okay; I need her.

Beams of light from the kitchen window highlight the space like a beacon. Looking out, I can see a playground with a soccer field. It's surrounded by homes in a circular fashion, just like the cemetery. Why is everything like that, this whole town? Those men last night—who do they work for? Extreme frustration with a dash of defeat covers my being. My thoughts become broken. I am startled when a knock comes at the door.

I move in silence toward the door. No peephole, shit. Another knock comes. Pulling open the door, I grab the person outside. Swiftly, I fling them in, slamming the door behind. Sarah!

"What the fuck is going on?" she snaps out before I can speak.

"Sarah, I'm sorry. I didn't know it was—"

"Oh God … the note was right. Who are you?" Her words are muttered under the sounds of sobs. "Please tell me."

"My name is Gabriel. You need to relax." I move slowly toward her while she stares at me in confusion.

"Let me look at you. Did they hurt you?"

"Who … what's …?" As my hands reach out to gently inspect her neck, she closes her eyes and begins quivering softly.

"No marks anywhere. Did you notice any bruises on you today?" Frantically, I search her over.

"No, why? What happened?" she asks. It is clear she is more than a little freaked out.

"I don't know exactly, but I saw them carry you off into a van and drive away. They were looking for me too."

"Who? Who carried me off?" Her mind, still fragile, can only handle so much.

"They were dressed in all black, and their faces were covered. I don't even know if they were male or female." Silence fills the room as her mind tries to consume this. "So far it's safe here, and they don't come out during the day. At least not that I've seen. Look, there's more to this than I understand right now." I walk to the kitchen, and she follows. "I need your help."

Her eyes grow with fear as I uncover the ladder. "What's down there?"

"I don't know, but we're not going down there yet. First we need some supplies."

"We, I'm not going down there! I don't even know who the hell you are!"

"Sarah, listen to me. I really need your help. If I get out of here, so do you."

A war seems to rage inside her head, a debate of choice. Finally she states, "What do we need?"

"Paper, we have to write things down. There are these symbols …" I explain.

"You've been down there?"

"Once, but only for a short time, there's no light so I had to come back."

"How did you see the symbols if there's no light?" she asks fairly.

"I felt them with my hands. I'm not lying to you. Just help me."

"Okay," she agrees, with little choice. "Where do we need to go?" she must realize I'm her only lead.

"I don't know; we'll have to separate then meet back here. It's 5:30 now, so let's say, be back here by nine," I state.

"What if something happens?"

"Keep the note on you, and we'll have to try again tomorrow. Do you have any money on you?"

"Yeah, about two hundred and fifty, whatcha need?"

"I've only got a dollar and twenty-six cents." They gave her more. Why? "Is it all right if I take it?"

"Here, I don't even know how I got it," she replies, handing me a hundred.

"Okay, nine o'clock, here. Think you can remember that?" I ask.

"Is that a joke?"

"Yeah, a bad one."

Walking to the end of the street together, we part to find what we need.

Somewhere in this insane town there has to be a place. As I push on, the streets seem more crowded than before. I still don't recognize a single person here. Passing them quietly, my eyes search for the woman at the costume shop—her, and the diner.

Again I arrive outside the cemetery. No matter how many times I see it, it still gives me the chills. I wonder if Dave is okay. He must be a part of this too. He's lost and he knows it, yet he's content. Entering his domain, there is no sign that he was ever there. At least the dead have their stones; we only have our minds.

"Hey." Sarah pops in from behind me.

I jump and reflexively raise my fist. "Don't you ever do that again!" My stern tone and the fist should get my point across.

"Sorry. Look, I found some paper, pens, even paint." A gloating grin covers her face so proudly.

"Where the hell did you get all this?"

"My apartment, I don't know why it was there. Here, let's get this back to the house, because I'm not carrying this around until nine."

"Where's your apartment?"

"Right there," her finger points out her place. It's the same building I was in. "Come on. I don't want to be out here, okay?"

Grabbing some of the things from her hands, I walk beside her. She isn't talking; I guess she's trying to find answers too. Reaching for the door, she sighs. That's the first noise she's made since the cemetery. Once inside, she crawls into the corner on fallen knees and sits.

"Are you all right?"

"I'm fine. It's just been a long day, and I haven't eaten."

"What do you want? I'll go get it and bring it back," I offer, hoping she'll bite.

"Really, I just want something small, a hamburger or something."

"Okay, I'll be right back."

Figuring she could use some time alone, I walk off to one of the local diners, one I've never been to. The inside is packed. Moving my sight across the crowd, I wonder how many of them are like us. Or are we the only ones?

My appetite grows as the scent of the food fills my senses. After ordering our food, I stand and watch the people. The conversations are light and typical, talking about trips and sights. Suddenly my nose itches. Everyone in the place, one after the other, lights up a cigarette. The same strange smell as from the costume shop girl's cigarette now fills the air here. Paying for the food, I cannot wait to leave. Outside, the air is fresh and clean. A couple in their mid-thirties glares at me as they walk inside. Food in hand, I head back to the house.

I see that in her free time Sarah has lain out all of the supplies. Oil paints, markers, pens, pencils, pads of drawing paper, and brushes lie neatly on the living room floor, but there is no Sarah. Not in the kitchen, not in the bathroom. Then, from above my head, I hear a slight groan of wood.

Maybe it's a trick; maybe they got her and are waiting for me. Full caution at my heels, I make my way upstairs. Three rooms and a bath await my inspection. Where do I start? The first room ... empty, as is the bath. From behind the far door emanates a melodic, peaceful hum. Opening the door reveals a passage into the mountains.

"Holy shit."

Sarah drops her paintbrush with a start at the sound of my voice.

"Where did you learn to do that?" I ask. Before me stands the most realistic painting of a glorious mountain range, covering the entire wall, that I have ever seen—or at least think I've seen.

"I guess this is why I had the paint, huh?" Her smile is like the golden sun, beaming and brilliant.

All I can say is, "The food's downstairs, if you want to eat."

"Thanks." As she walks by, I can't help but feel a sense of satisfaction in her happiness. After a moment in awe, I join her for the meal.

"So, what have you figured out about yourself?" she asks, diving into her burger.

"Nothing, I try not to think about it. I can't even figure out what's going on now, let alone the past."

"I understand." Her demeanor is becoming so much calmer than before. "What do you think is down there?" She nods her head once toward the corner of the kitchen.

"We're going to see. I'll provide the light if you take one of your pads and draw what we find."

"All right," her nervous tone reveals her fear.

"What little bit I experienced down there didn't seem like it was threatening. Besides, no one knows we're here."

"Okay, just don't lose me." As soon as the last bite hits her mouth, she picks up a pad and some pencils. "Let's go."

Pushing down the last of my food, I grab the glow sticks and head for the kitchen.

After the exhaustion of day, we find the pitch of darkness. With a slight crack, my glow stick's light cuts through the shadows. Its dim, eerie green glow adds to the already disturbing ambience. Am I ready for this? Dropping down from the ladder, I land on the sandy floor. There is nothing here except the ladder and a seemingly endless hallway.

"It's all right, you can come down," I call. Dropping her sketch pad, she slowly climbs down to me. I say, "This tunnel was built by someone."

"It goes on forever," she states, her voice echoing through the passageway.

Immediately she picks up the pad and starts to draw the hieroglyphs. Stretching on down the entire passage, they cover both walls around us. Consisting of mainly figures and symbols, there doesn't seem to be any form of order or written word. It's more like cult or pagan art, with figures wearing the heads of animals. Her hand trembles as she works the pencil. I have to admit, there's a certain amount of dread spoken by what we're seeing.

"We better move on; there's no telling how long this will go on for," I say, indicating the light. As we disappear into the hall, I crack another stick, discarding the first, still glowing one as a marker, just in case Sarah has to return on her own.

Continuing down the path, we stop at one of the symbols I'd felt before, carved into the stone wall. It resembles a star that is broken. A full circle connects to one of the breaks, a half circle the other. Next to that, a figure of a man with the head of a bird stands etched in the wall; behind him is a sun.

"What is all this? Like a strange cult or something?" Her questions I cannot answer. All I know is that I have this feeling we are not alone. "Human sacrifices, rituals, and Gods of light. Who are these people?" she asks.

"I wonder how many know about this. The people in the town, are they all part of it?" A cold chill rushes down my spine, tingling through every hair.

As we proceed down the path, soon the walls become barren of the symbols. Only the cold, gray stone surrounds us.

"I'm starting to not like this." Every word escaping her mouth sounds of fear. "What the hell is that?" she cries.

Stepping toward a dim glow, we both walk in fear. Suddenly the hall opens up into a vast, perfectly round, stone room. As we step inside we are greeted by a glowing eye, gazing down from the center of the stone ceiling. It has the same glow as came from the costume-shop woman's room. "This is insane. We have to leave; they know we're down here," she says frantically.

"Who, who knows?" I try to calm her, but she must be feeling that the eye is upon her, as I do.

"Look, we just can't stay," she begs.

Her pleas tug at my fears, but we have to find out more. "Let's just go a little farther. I want to see what's on the other side," I explain.

"The other side of what?" her frantic voice echoes around us. "Oh my God."

As we reach the center of the eye's gaze, we stop at a large hole. The magnitude of its depth reaches beyond sight's scope. "This is huge." My voice echoes down into the abyss. Dropping my glow stick inside, we watch as it drifts out of view. "I guess we stop here."

Just as I go to break another stick, the dim light of the eye vanishes.

"Oh shit ... What are we?" Before she can finish her words, a piercing squelch comes from the depths of the hole, followed by a blinding blue light. Sarah leaves dust behind her as she runs toward the hall. As the blue light dissipates, I'm left once again in the hands of darkness.

"Sarah! Sarah, can you hear me?"

Waiting in the dead silence reminds me of the nothing I really am in this world.

My eyes play tricks, a dancing light show, as they search for a glimpse of something. A figure faintly appears in my vision. Standing three feet taller than I, it is bald and thin. Moving away from me, I blindly follow it. The image fades as I step on the stick I'd dropped in the hall who knows how long ago.

Climbing the ladder, I can feel the safety of the house again. Sarah is still nowhere to be seen. Rushing upstairs, I make for the back room. There, inside the closet, Sarah lies crying.

"It's all right, we're safe now." I don't even believe myself.

"I can still hear it ringing in my head. Make it stop." Her arms wrap around my legs for comfort. "I want to go back to the way it was. I don't want to know."

After a short time of rocking back and forth, she falls asleep. Carefully I carry her to one of the empty rooms.

My head spins in question, if the dome is right out there how come no one ever found it? With it falling on midnight, I can travel safely in the darkness. I walk out of the back of the house toward the playground. This must be directly over the round room. The center of the football field, by calculation, must be the center of the room, just above the eye.

What is the purpose of all of this? Curiosity eats at me, forcing me to dig into the earth. Even though the ground is soft, I quickly find I need a shovel. Glancing around, I spot a couple of sheds in the backyards of the homes. After ransacking a few, I find success.

Load after load, I slowly dig down into what feels like my own grave. Hours pass, but go unnoticed. Standing with my head beneath the earth, I still haven't hit rock. A little more and more still; I cannot stop.

"Gabriel, what are you doing?" Sarah's voice comes from outside of the hole. "What are you looking for?"

With those words, my shovel clangs against something solid, something metal. "Just stop," she urges.

"I found it. This is the top of the room we were in."

"So what, you want to go back?"

"Look, I just want to see …" Brushing away the dirt with my hand reveals steel. "This is solid steel. The room was rock. Why the hell would somebody cover it with steel?" Hitting it with the shovel casts off a massive vibration into the air.

"They're going to hear you! Let's go inside." Her arm stretches out to help me out of the hole.

Back on the surface, I brush what little dirt I can off of me. "You have to get some rest," she reasons. Within all of my desire to continue, she's right. I need to sleep.

Dreams don't bring much solace in these days of insanity. Images of the eye haunt my thoughts. It stares at me as I sit, lotus position, in the center of the football field. Blinding light blocks my vision of all things. Several beings like the ghost-like figure in the round room who led me to the ladder stand around me motionlessly. As they move toward me, the ground opens up, leaving me to plummet into the abyss below.

Awake, the sun shines on my face from the front windows. I quickly scurry to my feet when I see the door slowly opening.

Dashing toward it, I come to a halt when Sarah's face appears. Her hands are loaded with bags.

"Good, you're up." She seems happy about something. "I was hungry, so I went for breakfast. I got ya some too."

"What time is it?" My body still aches from last night's dig.

"It's 9:40. You've been out for about six hours. Come on, eat something." She takes me to the kitchen and indicates that I should look out the window.

"The hole is gone!"

"I know, it was already filled in by the time I woke up," she explains.

"Why didn't you wake me up?" Now my mind is racing even more. Who could have done this?

"It wouldn't have mattered if I woke you up; it was already done, and you needed to sleep." Placing the food on the floor, she begins to eat. "Just eat, we'll figure it out later."

"Did you have any problems getting through town?"

"No, no one was even out. The diner was empty." Evidently not wanting to face the truth, she tries changing the subject. "How are your eggs?"

"We have to leave, they know," I explain, hoping she'll figure it out.

"Stop!" she shouts as frustration fully takes over.

"Tonight we'll find a way out, after dark. We'll get out."

"Shut up! I just want to eat! I'm tired of all this running, hiding bullshit."

"That's why I want to leave!"

"We can't leave! We can't. There's no way out. Do you think whoever they are, are going to let us just walk out of here?" she yells.

"Okay, let's eat. We'll discuss it more later."

"Fine." Scooping up her food, she goes to eat in another room.

I leave her in silence as I try to contemplate our situation. We'll move through the streets, get some food, and make our way away from the city. If everything stays low-key, we should be out in a couple of days. Dave. What about Dave—we can't leave him behind. I've still got thirty minutes to get to his spot.

"I have to get Dave; I'll be right back. If I don't, get out of here at dark. Just run."

"Run, to where? You're the one with the plan here so you better come back." Seeking a sense of everything's going to be alright from me I smile, hiding my own fears from her.

She was right, the streets are bare. It doesn't matter though; I have to get to Dave whether the city's empty or mobbed. Clouds roll in, blocking out the sun, giving the cemetery an even eerier hue. Dave should already be here. As I reach the center, there— good old Dave sits feeding the pigeons. He still doesn't know the truth; then again, neither do I.

"Dave, you have to come with me!" I stride up and take his arm.

"What? Who are you? Get your hands off me!" Anger fills his voice.

"There're things going on here, strange things. You have to come with me!"

His harsh speech comes with no warning. "I'm not going anywhere! Strange things, there are strange things happening all over the world, but you're just worried about what's happening to you. People kill each other, rape, steal, destroy families, and you're worried about little ol' you. Look, the pigeons don't fight for food; they just grab enough and walk away, leaving plenty for the others. You just take—take people out of their homes and lie to them. You're the reason they're all here, all these stones!"

"Dave, listen. If you stay, I don't know what will happen."

"I'll keep feeding the pigeons, that's what will happen. Now go away, murderer!" Just as raindrops start to fall, Dave packs up his things and walks away. The pigeons huddle under the bench to keep dry. They just stare mindlessly at me as I get soaked in the rain.

Well, at least Sarah will help me; between the two of us we should be able to escape. Passing the diner at a jog on my way, I find that it's empty except for the man cleaning the countertop. He watches as I run by. Back at the house, Sarah is packing up her things.

"Did you find Dave?" she asks, running up to me.

"Yeah, he didn't want to come with me."

"Why not?"

"I don't know; he was acting very strange." I can't tell her what he'd said, I can't lose her trust. "He got infuriated and stormed off. It was weird, like he knew something." Shifting gears, I say, "If there's no one out tonight, like right now, we'll be out of here with no problem."

"That's reassuring, but how long do you think it will take to get out?"

"Maybe a few days. We'll find other places like this to stay along the way. I think it will be better if we travel at night."

"Okay. Should I bring any of this?" Pointing to the mess of supplies, I can see she has no intentions of bringing them.

"Just what you drew down there and a few pencils, markers, and some blank paper. I'd like to make a map as we go along."

"Are you serious? Why don't we just get out of here? We'll worry about other shit later." With her nerves rising, she is growing anxious.

"All right, calm down, we'll get out of here." Though I'm not really sure how. "Try to get some sleep. It'll be dark by the time we wake up."

"Will you come by me?"

Her soft spoken words come not just in her words, but in her eyes. That catches me completely off guard. "What?"

Her plea asks for comfort. "Come by me. I want to feel safe."

"Okay."

I lie beside her, wrapping my arms around her soft, warm body. My senses feel her thoughts of tonight's endeavor as she quivers with anxiety. Tears, rolling from her eyes, hit the floor one by one as her grip on my arm tightens. Like a child, she cries herself to sleep. Slowly I pull myself away. I need to form a plan.

Watching the storm grow outside helps ease my thoughts; there won't be many people out tonight. Once we cross the cemetery, we'll stop for food, and then we'll continue until sunrise. Finding a place to hide is going to prove difficult. How big is this place, anyway? How long will it take? Will we survive? Dave. My mind begins to flutter as the concepts and lack of sleep catch up with me.

All-seeing, all-knowing, all-controlling eye: it focuses upon me, pulsating with energy. This glow holds comfort, reassurance, and forgiveness. To do what I must, survive. Within the consumption of all of this, we must subsist.

"Gabriel, we are all waiting for you," rings a voice of splendor through my head, from the woman in the costume shop. "Your gift is a blessing of continuous subsistence." Her soft hands pat my soul as she speaks. "Soon you can rise; soon you will be free." A kiss forms as her face deforms.

I awaken in sweat and confusion. Sarah still lies in peace on the floor.

Outside, the storm has matured into an intense atmosphere. The rain has gone from drizzle to heavy downpour. Darkness covers the sky, giving us a good advantage. I hope Sarah is still up to this, though I'm worrying about myself as well.

"Sarah? Wake up, Sarah." My soft approach doesn't seem to be working. "Sarah … Sarah!"

"Holy shit, what?" Open-eyed and startled, she wakes. "I had this crazy nightmare. There were these creatures; they were doing horrible things to me. Poking in my brain, they were searching for something. I don't know." Dilated pupils, sweat pouring down her face, her dream was as real as life to her. "We have to go. I don't want to stay anymore."

"Get your things. I've got a plan."

We make our way outside, into the saturating rains. Cloud cover drowns out the moon's light. Glancing around I see a clear path for us to travel. Not a single person is here. I just hope one of those vans doesn't show up. It occurs to me that a weapon would help. We quickly make our way to the cemetery.

Passing one of the diners, I notice the empty booths. "Where is everyone?" I look to Sarah for an answer.

"I don't care as long as they're not here."

Once we reach the cemetery, a large overhang from the top of a massive monument brings us comfort from the rain. "Can we rest here? I'm a little tired," Sarah asks.

"Let's just go a bit a farther. There's a diner on the other side. We'll stop to eat then continue until sunup."

"Good idea. Hopefully the rain will quit."

Walking toward the cemetery's center, I notice something sitting on the bench Dave usually occupies. Pausing, I pick it up.

"Whose hat is that?"

"Dave's. That's strange. Why the hell is his hat here? Let's just keep going." I have no idea what to think. Did they get to him, or is he like the pen, an easily replaced object? None of this shit makes any sense.

We continue walking. Sarah stops suddenly, pointing at the empty diner. "I don't want to go in there. Let's go into that house over there. Just get carryout, okay?" Panic echoes in her trembling voice. "I'd feel trapped."

"I agree. All right, go back to the monument. I'll go get us some food. Here, take Dave's hat."

"Get me something light," she instructs, placing the hat on her head as she heads back.

From outside I can see no one except for the man behind the counter. He stands, leaning on the counter, reading the paper. He doesn't even bat an eye as I walk through the door. Without even looking up, he finally acknowledges my being there.

"Whatta ya need?" His voice is cracked and gravely.

"I want to order carryout."

"Okay, what'll ya have?" His eyes never once lift from his paper.

"I'll take a turkey club, a BLT, and two small fries."

"Okay ..." He pauses as he finally lays eyes on my face. "I'll get it right away."

The patterns in his voice change and his mannerisms alter; he knows something. "Have a seat; it'll be a minute." Pouring me a cup of coffee, he smiles.

As I watch him disappear into the kitchen, I get a really uncomfortable feeling. Paranoia lifts me from my chair. Peeking into the kitchen confirms it; there is nothing on the grill, and he is nowhere to be seen. From behind the office door, I can hear him. "Yeah, it's him. The girl's not with him ... I don't know where the hell she is ... Okay, I'll delay him as long as I can."

As the phone hits the receiver, I bust in. A short struggle is all it'll take to bring this bastard down. Blows exchange. The phone is a fantastic weapon—a blunt, hard, and durable tool to kill with. A few blows to the head and a cord around the neck and he drops to the floor. His legs quiver in a final attempt for life—something I deny him. Red face becomes blue as his life slowly stifles. Soon a corpse lies at my feet. I know I have to leave, so I grab a few small boxes of cereal, an apple, and a couple of single-serving milks. Swiftly I head for the door.

The rain has gone, but it's still cloudy. There's no sign of a van, or anything else for that matter. I hope they didn't find her. Or if they did, that she was smart enough to hide.

In the darkest shadows, I find her wearing Dave's hat. "Oh, thank God you're back. What did you get?"

"Here." I drop the food everywhere as I slump to the ground.

"What happened? Tell me, damn it!" she demands.

"They're looking for us."

"What?" Her furious tone reveals her fear.

"They're looking for us. The man at the diner pretended to take the order. Then he called someone. I had to kill him. I didn't see anyone on my way back, but we can't stay here anymore."

"Where the hell are we going to go?"

"We'll head east from here. Hopefully we'll find another house."

"Okay," she states, taking a huge bite of the apple.

Running through the cemetery, we reach its edge quickly. Sarah, still eating at the apple, spots a church spire deep within a neighborhood. "Let's go there."

"Seems distant, but it'll do."

Luckily there is still no one present. Walking into the neighborhood is simple enough. But once we reach the inner layer of homes, we hear a vehicle. "Quickly, into the backyards," I state.

Dashing around, we come to a privacy fence. I hoist Sarah over then follow behind. The yard is desolate, though the grass is perfectly trimmed.

"Now what?" Her voice is full of panic. I know I can't rely on her to kill if it comes to that.

"Stay out of the view of the windows, and move to the other side of the yard."

The cloud cover makes the feat simple, but the sound of the van is on the street right in front of this house. It stops, the doors opening, and several footsteps can be heard. Sarah's heart rate begins to rise.

"Stay calm," I reassure her. "I'm going to see where they are."

Peeking over the fence, I can see four people. They are suited all in black as before, and the driver waits inside the van. They break into two groups, then go separate ways. "They're searching around for us. Just stay here, silent as a statue. I'll take care of this."

Watching, waiting for the right moment to pounce, I feel different. There is something driving me, a force I do not recognize.

There is a proper way to do this, a specific sequence to follow to get it right. Though I don't understand, I will do it.

As the teams get farther from the van, I make my first move, staying low to the ground and shadowed by the night. All of the elements are on my side. Pulling the driver out of the van with my hand strongly clasping his mouth, I search for a way to end him. Force becomes my only means. A foot to the chin, pulling his arm toward me, and a snap is all it takes.

Inside the van lie a small handgun and a radio. Not much, but now I have a stronger advantage. Placing the body back in the van, I go to hunt the hunters.

Light flashing around in one of the homes is a dead giveaway. One man is upstairs, the other on the ground floor, this should be simple enough. Placing the gun in my back pocket, I needn't use it here; the sound would be a bigger giveaway. Around the back side of the house is a sliding glass door, an easy access point. The door opens to a dining room off the side of the kitchen.

Inside, I wait. Walking toward my position, the one on the ground floor is oblivious to my presence. As he steps into the kitchen, I grab him swiftly, snapping his neck with silent precision. Then up the stairs I creep, one soft step after the other. The wall and I are one. From within the shadows, the man walks right past. There is a deafening awe of stillness looming.

Now that the hunter is the prey, the guard fearing his life, reaches for his radio. Before the receiver can reach his lips, I grab him by the chest and leg and make a simple crashing toss down to the first floor. I quickly follow with a knee to the sternum. His ribs crack. I drive my hand into his throat at the same time, finishing him.

Rummaging around their bodies offers new supplies. A shiny blade, night vision binoculars, some kind of futuristic rifle, and a couple of flashlights add to the means with which I can become free.

Outside once more, I have to locate the other two. Down the street, scanning the area, they walk toward another house. With stealth, I quickly follow. An unlocked door allows them in with no resistance.

Before the door can shut, I rush in for the kill. Spinning the closest around, his eyes widen as I bury the knife deep into his throat. One firm push and draw back sprays his life's blood. As the second turns to see his falling friend, he is met with a rifle's butt to his face. Drawing the pistol from my back, I know this shot must be precise. His mind's center is found by the ripping of my bullet.

All objectives encountered and eliminated, I must find Sarah. Without haste, I head back to where I'd left her. She sits, curled up in a ball, in the shadows of the fenced-in yard.

"All right, it's done." I stand over her, not realizing how much blood is covering my clothes and face.

"Oh, my God, what did you do?" Terror fills her eyes as she buckles tighter into a ball.

"I did what I needed to for us to survive. Now we have to move quickly." I've become cold to this act though it's unknown to me why. Who did I used to be?

Trembling, she rises to her feet. As I reach toward her, she pulls away. She must not understand; her mind is too fragile. I say, "The church, remember? We're going to the church."

"Yeah, all right." Passing through the house, she begins to cry. "Why does this have be happening? I just want it to be normal. You killed all of them."

"They were going to kill us."

"You don't know that. Maybe they were going to put us back asleep. Make us not remember. I'd rather not remember than go through this."

Passing the van in the street, I can hear the radio calling out. "Omega team, have you found the subjects? I repeat, have you found the subjects? Be cautious; the man at the diner is dead. Do you copy?"

"Shit, we better move. They'll be here soon."

We run as fast as we can to the church, where we gain easy entry. Inside is dark and still.

"Help me move this." Grabbing one of the long, heavy pews, we barricade the entrance. There's a creepy silence here, and I have a sense that I've seen this before. "Search for another way out. I'm going up to the tower to look around. Only use the flashlight if there are no windows around."

"I'll come up when I find something," she states, her eyes wide with fear.

A long, spiral staircase leads me to the top of the tower. I hope she finds something fast; I don't think we have much time here. Hitting my head on the ceiling, I find the trapdoor to the top.

The tower peak is completely enclosed. Other than four slatted vents, there's no place to see from. The large, brass bell makes movement hard and tight.

Peering from one of the vents, I can see the van. All is still. Suddenly I see more headlights coming. Two more vans pull up behind the other. Stopping, the doors fling open, and eight more soldiers come out of each. We're hopelessly outnumbered.

One walks up to the van; upon finding the driver dead, he points to the others to spread out. They quickly disappear into the neighborhood. Hopefully they won't think to look here.

From beneath me I can hear footsteps—Sarah.

"Ouch." A loud thump comes from the closed trapdoor.

"Shhh!"

"What? Is someone out there?" Crouching down beside me, she sees as well. "What are we going to do?"

"Did you find another way out?"

"Yeah, there's a back door and a basement."

"Did you go down there?"

"No way, I'm not going down there alone!" Her eyes tell me how crazy she thinks I am for suggesting this.

"I want to stay up here and watch. Why don't you lie down and try to get some sleep? If they don't come here, we'll have to leave in the morning."

"I can't sleep now," with panic in her voice I know she's afraid.

"Then go see what's down there in the basement," I order, simultaneously realizing that sometimes I demand far harder than I need to.

"What, I'm not going anywhere without you," she barks back, angered by my orders.

"If they come in here we're going to need another way out. So I'm giving you a choice, sit up here and watch them while I go look around in the dark or you go find a way out. Either way we are going to be apart." I hope that by explaining the situation at its fullest will help calm her fears.

Accepting my offer she gives in. "Fine, I'll go look around," her face shows the displeasure in her decision, "but if anything happens, I'll scream so loud the whole world will hear me."

"You'll be okay," I state, handing her the knife. "We're the only ones in here. You can use this if you get into trouble."

"You better be right about this."

"Trust me, nothing is going to happen to you. We're both getting out of here." My insistence is for my own reassurance as much as for hers.

Sarah heads back down as I continue to watch. A short time later, three of the men return to the van, dragging the bodies of two of my victims. Opening the back doors of the first van, they place the corpses inside.

Moments later, the other two bodies emerge. They are also placed in the back of the van. One of the soldiers hops in the driver's seat then pulls away. Those that remain continue their search for us. Time passes slowly as I anticipate all possible scenarios. Fifteen soldiers are still out there, looking, watching, waiting for a signal or sign. I know they cannot hear me, but still my breath is stifled and my body shudders.

Shortly, the van comes back, and only the driver gets out. Two more hours pass, and then eight men pile into a van and leave. At the church, there has been no sign of Sarah, not even the slight creaking of a footstep. I have to go find her, but what if there are bad guys inside?

Startling me, the trapdoor opens slowly at just that moment. Sarah steps up silently, her face a canvas of fear, pale and lost in confusion.

"Sarah! What happened? Sarah?"

"It's not, not …" Slumping in the corner, her eyes still search for an answer. "Not."

"What did you see? Are you hurt?" Finally her eyes come back into focus. "What?"

"Great blue light, beams onto me. The eye saw, it came, great and blue. It's narrow … tall. I can't move … want to run." Tears rain from her eyes as in a downpour, streaming down her face. "It won't go away. It just stands there. It moves so fast, behind me … touching me. Dinner-plate eyes, hollow, vacant. It's not …"

Within that breath, she fades into slumber. Placing her on the ground, I hear the second van start up and drive away. Sunlight begins to glow through the vents. At this moment, I too need to sleep. It's too much, it's all too much to think about.

Sleep is the thing that matters most. It's a time of healing, a release from life. You dream, though; you always dream. Thankfully there are times you don't see, you don't remember. This is the time your mind truly sleeps, gives you peace. The mind is kind.

Awake. Three o'clock has come fast, and I wake up calm, though not free from last night's events. Outside it is quiet and serene. Birds sing their chatter songs through the calm, cooling breeze. Sarah, still sleeping in the corner of the bell tower, seems at peace. I still wonder what she saw. Could it be the same thing I saw in the basement of the house? Grabbing a flashlight, I head to the basement.

Cold, musty walls greet me as I slowly walk down the rickety wooden steps. As in the basement in the empty house, there are no furnishings. But there is an opening leading to a long hall. No symbols or signs are visible on the walls. Far off in the distance, I can see a slight beam of sunlight coming down from the ceiling. Could this be the light she was talking about? Nothing blue, nothing tall, and nothing is moving.

As my feet move, I kick the knife I had given her. She must have dropped it. Cracks within two wooden doors above leading out allow the light to trickle in. Opening the doors brings me to the outside—not of just the church, but outside of the neighborhood. Standing up from the storm door, I am surrounded by rows and rows of corn. Behind me I can see the church steeple barely sticking out above the corn. I don't know why a church would lead to the middle of a cornfield, but we can use this to get out. Leaving the doors open, I head back for Sarah.

The ground floor of the church is radiant. Gorgeous, bright sunlight flowing through the stained-glass windows colors the floor. Greens, blues, all colors shimmer around me, a true beauty to behold. The windows are etched with some of the same symbols from the house. Here there are also twelve different figures of man, each with a different head. Owls, cats, dogs—what does this mean? They worship animals? From the ceiling above, a great sun peers down. Who are these people?

"It's so beautiful," Sarah's voice comes from behind me. "Where did you go?" She seems particularly calm after last night.

"I went down to the basement. There's a way out that leads to a cornfield. Are you all right?"

"Yeah, why shouldn't I be?" she questions lightly.

"Do you remember last night?"

"A little, I remember coming here and hiding, waiting for the soldiers to leave. That's it. I don't remember falling asleep," she explains.

"Do you remember going down into the basement at all?"

"No." Her eyes seek mine for an answer.

"You came back up pale and rambling incoherently."

"No, I don't remember," she says, mildly laughing.

"Well, let's get going." I don't want to dig too deep, in case I would trigger something unpleasant. I wonder if she can't remember because she doesn't want to or because of whatever she saw doesn't want her to. Either way, I believe she saw something.

Outside in the cornfield the sun beams down upon us. Warmth followed by a cool breeze makes this day seem so perfect. Walking between the rows makes our travel simple, though the corn seems to go on forever. Sarah remains quiet; perhaps she's just taking in the weather as I am.

At long last, and an hour and a half later, we reach the end of the corn. We've come to a barn. Several cows graze behind a wooden post fence. There are also several sheep, goats, and chickens.

"Stay here, I'll have a look around," I command.

Sarah remains in the field as I make my way toward the barn. No one is present. On the other side, there are dirt tire tracks. The dirt road seems well taken care of and seems to be traveled often. Beyond that, a huge stretch of forest spans the horizon. All of this seems way out in the middle of nothing, and there are no houses to be seen.

A rope hanging from above an opening in the loft allows me access inside the barn. There is nothing up there but three bales of hay. Below, several pieces of what I assume is farming equipment sit dormant. They are clean and well-kept. Since no one is around, I decide I better get Sarah.

"It's safe, there's no one here," I say, as I rejoin her in the field.

"Where are we going?"

"There's a large span of woods. We can hide out there, depending on how far we get tonight."

"What about food?" she asks, holding her stomach.

"We've got chickens. Maybe some eggs, too; we'll have to look." Though I'm not into poaching, some food sounds great.

"Sounds good, I'm starving."

Walking toward the chicken's yard, Sarah has a smile on her face. Once we reach the fence, she jumps over and starts chasing the chickens around. I head over to the coop in search of eggs. With no luck, I return out to see Sarah diving on one of the chickens. Snapping its neck, she holds it up, showing me her prize.

I can't help but encourage her since she's having so much fun. "Get another one."

"It's not easy," she states, dashing around for another. "They're so damn quick." Pouncing again, she lands another. Again she snaps its neck and holds it up. I wonder if, in the past, she might've come from a farm. "That should do it, don't ya think?"

"Yeah," I can't stop from smiling, "you did good."

"When do we eat?"

"Later. Right now we need to get deep into those woods."

Each with a chicken in hand, we head off. For the first few hours, the woods are thick and intricate. Vines hanging down around us and heavy foliage block out the sun. This seems like more trouble than it's worth. Time passes, and the sun begins to set. Another hour's walk and the woods begin to thin. Finally the trees give way to a grassy field. It's as though a small patch, maybe half of a football field, was cut out of the forest. A thin shallow freshwater stream cuts through its center, flowing with crystal clear water. Finally we've found something to drink.

"Let's rest here, okay?"

Sarah's plea is exactly what I have in mind as well. "Okay. I'll go get some firewood if you clean the chickens."

"Sounds good and maybe afterward you can wash some of the blood off of you," she points out, reminding me what's been done.

"What?" Through everything I have forgotten my appearance. My hands and clothing are stained by the blood of my victims. "Oh yeah," I still do not understand what was driving me back there.

Sarah plucks away as I walk back into the woods, gathering sticks and logs for our feast of chicken. Two piles later, and Sarah is done plucking. I build the fire as she rummages around for branches to make a spit.

"Shit!" The sticks are placed and ready to go, but I've forgotten something else. I have no lighter.

"What?" she asks laughingly.

"How in the hell am I going to light this? Damn it!" A moment's thought brings me an idea. "I'll have to do it the old-fashioned way, two sticks and a bow."

"You go, nature boy," she mocks, with gentle laughter.

Storming off to find appropriate materials, I find a piece of small vine hanging down. Tying it around two ends of a stick, I make a small bow. That, a log, some brush, and few more small sticks will work just fine. Walking back, I hold my nose in the air. I'll prove to her what I can and can't do. Back and forth with the bow, I grind the stick into the log. Faster and faster I go. Sweat pours down my forehead. Soon there is enough heat that the bark on the log lights. I let it grow, and then place it in the pile to burn.

"Impressive." All sarcasm in her voice is left behind. "Now wash up while I cook dinner."

I thought she was beginning to act like we were married. "Okay, dear," I play along, trying to bury the last two days in history. "Make sure they cook all the way through."

"I will."

I strip down to my underwear and step into the cold stream. It's only knee-deep, but every inch is like ice. My scrubbing of my clothes and every inch of my body goes quickly; I hate cold water. The sun fades into night as I lay my clothes next to the fire.

"They should be done." Sarah's words are just what my stomach needed to hear.

In a flash, the chickens' bone remains litter the ground. There is a passive calm in the air tonight that brings us relief. Our stomachs full, we take time to relax. My eyes drift over to the full moon.

"Look at that. It's huge. Ouch, what the—"

Sarah had pelted me in the head with a chicken bone. "You little shit." I throw one back, to see her smiling.

She pelts me again, a deeper smile across her face. "All right, stop. What is wrong with you?" Though I am not used to this, her playfulness has sure lightened the mood.

With laughter in the air, I go to retaliate once more. Suddenly something appears out of the full moon's light, a brilliant object. It wisps down with speed I've never seen, crossing the sky. "What the hell? Run!"

Gathering my clothes, I quickly dress. Sarah runs across the stream heading toward the woods on the opposite side of the field. I chase shortly after, though pausing to kick the fire down.

As we reach the tree line, the object passes overhead without a sound and with not so much as a gust of wind. It hovers above the field, searching about with several spotlights. All the lights fade except for one—the one that shines directly on the smoldering remains of the fire.

"Let's go!" Sarah whispers, tugging at my wet shirt. "Are you just going to stand here?" My mind lies fully embraced by the moment. "Damn it, Gabriel, let's go!"

In the clouds behind the object, there is the shape of an eye. The flying object is its cornea. "Look at me, damn it. Snap out of it!" Slowly Sarah's words begin to fade. "Come … on … we … have … to …"

Silence—her lips move in hysteria, yet there is no sound. She hits me, yet there is no pain. There is nothing. Falling to my knees, I watch as she runs away in a blur. Darkness becomes my eyes as I drift away into the nothingness.

Flashing light dances around my head. The eye visits my sleep once more. Gazing through me, it knows all of me. Even the parts I do not know. It reveals nothing, only its looming presence. How long has it been watching? What does it see?

Awake, the morning sun greets me coldly. Sarah is nowhere to be seen. How long have I been out? Looking back to the field, there is nothing out of place. What happened? Why did she run? The only answers I can find are with her. I have to find her. I remember which way she went. Heavy brush lies broken and trampled. She had to have gone this way.

Stopping at a fallen tree, I can barely bear to look on the other side of the drop-off. Sarah, mangled and broken, lies thirty feet below on the rocky floor. Scurrying along the cliff's edge, I have to find a way down. A large vine drapes down the wall. My eyes welling with tears, I scramble down it and rush to Sarah's side.

"I'm sorry, Sarah. I tried to help you. I'm sorry." No matter how I plea, I know she is gone. It's my fault. I promised. The only person who knew is gone. Now I'm truly alone.

She deserves a proper burial. Gathering stones, I completely cover her body. She can finally be at peace, finally sleep. Within my sorrow, I swear that I will have revenge.

This massive wall stretches out in both directions endlessly, as does the rocky floor beneath my feet. I guess I'll stay down here; I'm not climbing back up there. Continuing away from the cliff seems like the only answer.

Hours pass, and the sun's rays beat down relentlessly upon me. If it weren't for the continued cool wind, I'd cook. With the cliff far from my view now, I have no idea of which way I'm going. Sweat dumps from my pores, soaking my clothes. Occasional clouds drift by, blocking the sun; they are a blessing no matter how long they last. My mind is going now. One mirage after the other, some as great as lakes, fills my vision. I'd kill for a drink right now. Out here there is nothing. No life, except for my own.

Wait, I hear water! About twenty feet off to my left I discover a calm river cutting through the stone. At last, something to drink. Crystal clear and cold, it's so inviting. I reach into the water, and several fish dart past my hand. I drink and drink until I can drink no more. Even though I hate fish I have to eat before moving on. After a few moments struggle I manage to trap one in a shallow spot. Its spines extend out from its fins, pricking my hand across the palm. Choking down the raw meat I force it down for hungers sake. Resting by the waterway's side, I wonder where it leads. It has to go somewhere.

Day quickly becomes night as I travel the river's edge. Still there is no sign of life anywhere, and the river has whittled down to a very small, shallow stream. There haven't even been any fish for a couple of hours now. Collapsing with exhaustion, I can move no more this night.

As the moon shines down upon me, I can't help but be in awe of its enormity, so close it seems I can leap to it. Even the stars are glowing radiantly. Within this solace, I try drifting into myself, searching for what is me. Nothing of my past is clear—my parents, and my childhood? And why would whoever is doing this, do it to me? The girl from the costume shop, Sarah, and Dave … are we all pawns here? First, I have to get out … then … then what? Who would believe this?

Well, there's no sense in staying here. I might as well keep moving. Night brings the cold winds. Shivering, I move on downstream. Like my mind, the stream slowly drifts on. Only slight ripples form on the surface, nothing big enough to create a disturbance.

Time passes slowly as the moon follows its path across the sky. It reflects off of the shrinking stream. Suddenly the water vanishes, as does the rock floor below it. As sand replaces the stone, the stream's water disappears right into the ground.

I've been surrounded by a city, farmland and forest, rock, and now sand; where the hell am I? I can truly continue no more. The soft sand offers comfort over the cold rock. Removing my shoes brings great relief. Resting my head on my arms, I am asleep within seconds.

Light disturbance, flash, seeking me out. Soldiers with men in black suits, they can see me. I have to run, but where? I can't run, people are shooting at me. Hundreds of them in the church perform rituals of blood and power. Dancing in the night, their minds have control over all beings.

Awake, the sun greets me on the horizon. A few hours' sleep is better than none. Looking around, I realize there is nowhere for me to go now. I'm a failure! I couldn't save Sarah, and now I've led myself to nowhere. Damn it, damn it, damn it! I didn't know it would be like this. There's nothing for me to do now. I can't go back.

Time passes as time always does, and I'm still sitting here by the stream. I'm tired of waiting, tired of just sitting. The desert that lies before me can't go on forever. Besides, I might find some food, a snake or cactus fruit. First I'll fill up on water, as much as I can drink. I have no means of carrying any.

Putting my shoes back on, I head into the desert. After only a few moments, the winds begin to rise. I continue despite the sting of blowing sand. Out here, everything looks the same, and so far I haven't even seen a cactus. Luckily though there are lots of clouds today; otherwise I'd bake. A light rain would be nice too. Looking back, I find that I can no longer see my footprints. I don't even know if I'm traveling in a straight line anymore.

Hours pass, and the winds have finally called it quits. Flatlands of sand have become rolling dunes—small, yet very tedious. Tired of all the climbing, I stop to rest atop the tallest one I've encountered yet. Using the binoculars seems like it would be moot. Even from on top of this behemoth, I see nothing but sand. It stretches on and on. At least the dunes appear to level off and vanish before the horizon. With everything else, there is also no sign of water anywhere. Shit. I feel the defeat as I fall to my knees. I'd cry if I weren't so dry.

Cold winds mix in with the already cool breeze, bringing me relief. Back on my feet, I attempt to walk down the dune. Five steps in, my legs quiver then buckle. I find myself now rolling down this massive slope of sand. Flopping in the air, I meet the ground with several hard punches. Legs and arms flailing, I land at the inevitable bottom. Pain shears through my arms and ribs as I lie there, still. Then suddenly the skies grow dark, and I feel the most refreshing thing I can. Rain! Cold, wet, succulent rain dumps down from above. Rolling to my back, I open my mouth wide. I hope this lasts for hours.

I don't know how long I've been standing here, but my thirst is at least slightly quenched. I continue on over the dunes all the while rain continues to grace me with a light shower. I am saturated. I check my belongings and notice that somewhere along the way I've lost my rifle and pistol. All I have left are a few glow sticks and my knife. And I must have lost the binoculars when I rolled down the dune. I have to keep going, can't stop. With the dune fading in the distance, I continue on for an hours hike. The dune becomes a distant memory.

Suddenly I come to a complete stopping point—a wall made of solid stone. Its color's the same as the sand. No wonder I hadn't seen it. It towers above me as far as my eyes can see.

This must be a border of some kind, the final barrier that is keeping me from freedom. Can I dig under it? There's only one way to find out. Digging into wet sand is not an easy task. It moves like concrete. Heavy sludge piles up fast and runs back into the hole. Feet down, still there is nothing but the wall. Forget it. Maybe there's a door; I'll follow the barrier and see.

Walking within the wall's shadow keeps me dry until the storm passes. As the sun reappears in the sky and the rain fades, the heat rises intensely. Clumped sand becomes grain once more, and I start to shiver in the shade.

Night comes with the setting of the sun. No door, no change at all. It's the same wall now as it was when I found it. What the hell am I going to do? There's no way over it, around it, or through it. Not even under it. What is this, damn it?

The bright moonbeams are my only form of solace. I sit with my back to the wall, looking for comfort. My mind is as empty as my blank stare. Open-eyed, my mind begins to fall away completely. It doesn't matter that I'm not me. I am irrelevant—a single, minute part of an intricate design that is … is …? Damn these hunger pains, I can't think anymore.

Awake. Sunshine graces my face. Off in the distance, dust devils form. Within seconds they whip through the sand violently then quickly disappear. Even my legs have a light dusting of sand over them. What seems like a full night's sleep has left me still exhausted. Brushing off, I think I should continue down the wall.

As the winds begin to pick up, the sky becomes one giant cloud of sand. It stings like hell. Even with the wall as a backstop there's no protection. I can't even tell if the wall is there anymore. Shit, I can't see.

"Oh shit!" I say aloud as the ground beneath my feet gives way without warning. I'm sinking, faster and faster, being consumed down into the sand. This is no way to die, buried alive. After moments, I can't tell if I've stopped. I've got to get out of here. Even as pure grain, sand is heavy in compilation.

I feel as though I'm passing through a tube, like a drain in the sandy floor. Giving way, I am spit out into darkness, evidently below the desert. Now where am I?

With the quick snap of a glow stick, my tomb is revealed. It must have been a sinkhole, because now I'm in some kind of cavern. The light radiating from the glow stick is nothing compared to the darkness of this chasm.

Standing, I move on. The walls and ceiling narrow, leading to a single opening. I've never seen this place before, yet there is a sense of comfort here.

Walking into the opening, I see that there is something written on the wall: "There is no eye here." Someone has been here before?

Down the passageway a little ways, the path opens to a cavern as wide as the eyes can see. A single path cuts through hundreds of thousands of stalagmites and stalactites, each one varying in shape and size. At least I know there's water down here somewhere.

After a few winding bends, I come to another room. Water, I hear water! Off in the distance, a pool's ripples glisten off the walls, so there's light coming from within as well. Written on the wall above the pool, in the same fashion as the message before, is, "Eat, they will give you sustenance."

Swimming in the water are several small, glowing fish. Their bright-blue illumination drowns out my glow stick. They seem docile, just drifting slowly by, not worried by my presence. Dipping my hands in, I find the water frigid and crisp. I needed that.

After quenching my thirst, I decide to search around a bit. There have to be other traces of whoever was here before me. Looking back the way I came, I can see a fire pit. The ceiling is definitely high enough to support the smoke; it's completely out of view. Within my quest for water, I must have stepped right through it, not even noticing. This room alone is as large as the empty house I'd lived in.

Strange words are everywhere on the walls. "Central Intelligence" is written in the form of a cross. "Watchers in the maze." What does it mean? "Hands around us within the darkness"; "Sleep"; "Three rule all"; "Concepts are illusion." This person was completely insane.

There are also drawings of pyramids and suns, symbols like those inside the basement of the house. One symbol in particular stands out from the rest. It is a double-sided pyramid with an eye—*the* eye—in the center. Several markings I've never seen surround it, like some kind of cult badge.

"Hello … hello … hello are you still here? Who are you?" With no answer coming, I continue to look around.

Beyond the pool is another opening to this room, and there's another to the right of it. Did my predecessor wander off and die down here? Approaching one of the paths on the other side of the pool, I see a large *X* drawn on the wall. Maybe this is a bad sign. Next to the other path is an arrow. This makes it obvious.

My chosen path is no more than a crack, a long, narrow path as though the rock was pulled apart. I'm glad I'm not claustrophobic. Traveling slowly along, walking sideways, I feel the temperature drop. My breath is nearly visible; it can't be more than thirty degrees. The walls become still closer together. I suck in my stomach and push my way through, rubbing my skin raw. But finally the crack opens up.

I find myself facing a large, multiple-tiered hollow. From here there are five different paths to take. It's warmer too. Hopefully whoever came before me has marked these paths as well.

One of the paths is actually just a small nook. Inside there are several used glow sticks just like mine. I wonder how long the person before me had to stay here, or if he had a choice.

The second path smells as though it has been used for a restroom. Another holds an obvious description: "Dead End." The next path is labeled with the word "Unknown," which has been scratched out and replaced with "B1." Finally is a path that seems interesting, it's called "War Room." Now, that one is worth checking out.

I head up a slight incline through a small tunnel, which leads me to a large, round room. It is cut to a perfection that is unnatural. Straight across from me is another tunnel leading out of the room. There's a large *X* written above it, followed by names. "Nicole White, Daniel Stevens, Bethany Dodson, Thomas E., Philip A. Marcus, Sarah Whitmore, Stephanie Camp ..." The list goes on for a hundred names. Who are these people? Are they all inside?

Lost within my pondering, as I scan around at all of the names, I don't see the small pit in the center of the room. I lose my footing and fall backward into it, landing on a large piece of wood. I stand, brushing myself off, and see that my head just pokes above the pit's edge.

As I turn around, my glow stick fades to darkness. With a now-familiar crack, my way is lit once more. To my surprise, at my feet stands a large wooden crate. The words "We Are All Slaves" are written on its lid between two heavy rope handles. I grab the handles and try to pull the crate out of the pit, but it's a real struggle.

Not budging it in the slightest fashion, I surrender to the crate's massive weight. Finding a seam in the lid I pry it from the crate. I drop the lid to the floor with a smack, creating a massive echo. If there was anyone here, they definitely heard that.

The crate is crammed full of all kinds of belongings. Chalk, paper, pencils, glow sticks, and blankets fill it to its rim. This guy was prepared. Flashlights! Come on … damn it, just what I figured, dead! What else? Black pants, boots, a shirt, and a solid leather coat with a Kevlar insert. I know this will come in handy. Oh, a knife, just like the one I lost. And finally, resting ever so silently underneath a couple of pistols at the bottom of the crate, is a thick black binder. My anticipation rises as I pull it from the crate and open its cover.

The opening page is covered with more names. Females, males, there are so many. Page two falls to the floor. Picking it up, my eyes light up to see a detailed map of the cave system.

The caves lead back into the town at several points. There is also a huge question mark at the end of a certain passageway in the caves; it leads away from the town, towards the outskirts. Whoever made this either never got that far or did and never made it back to update this.

On the third page, a journal begins:

"I've spent four days escaping the nightmare of that town. Once I searched the caves long enough, I found my way back. It was difficult, but I managed to get some supplies, including this book. I know it will come in handy. Time has escaped me down here, since I never see the sun or moon anymore. Thankfully there is enough freshwater here to drink, and even though I hate fish, the ones that glow taste more like chicken. They also must be a form of good nurturance, because my wounds are healing faster than before.

"One thing I've noticed is that down here nothing electronic will work. Even my watch just keeps spinning. I guess the flashlights I stole are useless. Thankfully I still have some glow sticks left. I just wish I knew what day it was. Well anyway, there is only one thing left to do now: map this place out completely.

"I heard voices coming from behind a pile of large boulders at the dead end. They might be still looking for me. Not a single word was clear, but I know they were voices. I won't let them find me. There are so many places to hide."

I wonder, did this guy go mad, how long was he down here? Skipping on through the pages, I come across a major discovery. More than one person wrote in this book:

"I don't know who was here before me, but thankfully all the difficult work is done; I'll update the map as needed. Who he was is unclear, but he was running too. Maybe I can find him. Together we'll be free.

"There is no one here other than myself. I've been everywhere I can go, and I haven't seen any sign of him anywhere—not even remains, which means maybe he escaped. I'll keep searching. I've also gone into town and stolen more supplies. These glow sticks go faster than you think."

Skipping on again, I find another entry from another person. A few pages more, another person. By count, it would seem I'm the sixth person to come here. The last entry reads as follows:

"It's been three weeks to the day. I think I have figured out what's going on here. The question mark holds the key. This path hadn't been found by them. It has to lead to an answer or a way out or something. I'm packing up three days' worth of water and food. It takes two days to get there. Who knows what lies on the other side?"

Not a single answer is given. No reason for the names written on the walls. Only the word "players" gives the people writing in this book any form of definition. Whatever is happening here, I know one thing. I want out! Thankfully, whoever was here left me all the supplies I'll need.

Inspecting the guns reveals I only have twenty-six rounds total. I guess I'll have to be choosy when I fire. With these clothes I could blend in nicely with the soldiers. If five made it here before me, then I have to be able to make it out.

Using the blank paper and a few pencils, I'll copy the map in order to leave the original behind for the next person that comes along. Some chalk will be useful for marking the walls, just in case I get turned around in these dark passages. I'm guessing I'll need as many glow sticks as possible. Taking the supplies I need, I place the rest back into the crate and drop it back down into the hole.

Walking back to where one of them, or maybe all of them, had slept, I know I have a lot of work ahead of me. It's a comfortable spot, and with the tight walls the light from my sticks will illuminate it nicely. Though with just the three I have left and the seven in the crate, I must use them sparingly.

This map will be useful; without it there's no way I could ever find my way out, so my copy has to be perfect. Whoever made this was very precise about their markings. B1 is a long path that leads to what appears to be a giant sinkhole; the words "Great Wind" are written there.

From that room there are several paths to be taken. One is the path to the boulders. "Voices" is written several times here. Maybe he wasn't crazy; maybe more than one of them heard the speaking. Either way, I think I should investigate, maybe to find something none of the others have. Next is a tunnel that is marked "Path to the Clouds." This doesn't make sense; what do they mean? Three of the other paths lead to separate sinkholes, each of which has several dead ends. A couple even have water, those spots being marked by pictograms of fish.

Finally, the longest route from "Great Wind" leads back into the town. It's a set of narrow, winding paths that has several spots marked clearly, indicating where they slept. With all of the little veins trailing off of each path and their destinations marked, this had to have been mapped out over several years.

Now I have to decide. Do I truly trust this, or did each one meet their ends somewhere inside these catacombs? Though, under the given circumstances, what choice do I really have? It's either die down here, or avenge Sarah, Dave, and every one of the names written on the walls. I will shut this place down and end this!

With the map copied, I have to leave the original behind, in case I fail—in case there are others. Opening the chest once more, I feel as those others before me must have felt—rage. And as they did, I too shall leave something behind, my contribution to the book:

"By the count of the book, I am the sixth person to find this dungeon. I have done nothing to the map. I am going straight for the question mark with one other stop to check out the boulders. I've added the names of Sarah and Dave Forester to the walls; I pray no one adds more. And may my entry in this book be the last, in that I hope I can stop this."

Placing the book back inside the crate sends lightning through my body that tingles inside my brain. With all that has happened, I unquestionably need to sleep. Luckily here is warmer than the rest of the cave, though my newfound clothes also keep me much warmer. My old clothes still serve a purpose, acting as a very lumpy pillow. By the fading light of my glow stick, I drift away, not knowing if it's day or night.

Dreams come in vivid form. A massive lake, clear and bottomless, illuminates the surroundings with radiant light. Purple-blue light forms a creature, a man with the head of a dog.

Awake, be it morning or night, I am ready to begin my journey to whatever lies before me. With the soldier's uniform I can easily strap on my guns, the knife, and the extra glow sticks without them getting in my way. By looking at the map, I determine that if I make a few stops in certain caves, food and water shouldn't be a problem. Right now I am starving; I can't leave on an empty stomach.

Using the *X* path in the war room leads me back to the small water flow from when I first arrived here. Drinking from the crisp waters is as refreshing as it was before. Only one thing left to see … do they really taste like chicken? Reaching down, I find the fish are not afraid of my hand, even as I lightly grip one. Pulling it out of the water is no struggle at all, as though it has no regard for its own life.

Turning up my nose, I take a bite … it does, it tastes like chicken, almost the same texture, too. Muscle, meat, no flakes, no fishy taste, it makes me wish I had dined last night as well. Eating some more of the raw food source, my hunger is soon satisfied, and I start on my path toward the question mark passageway. I can only hope I can find something of relevance with this guess.

This path is simpler than I expected. Early in the journey there has only been the fantastic sight of rock formations with shiny crystals sparking as the light from my stick reflects off. Distant trickles echo faintly around me as I step along the cold stone tunnel. By the map I should be arriving at the "Great Wind."

But after a while, it feels like I've been walking for days and I still haven't reached the "Great Wind." My first stick fades to nothing. They were right; it is a long way. With only nine sticks left, I hope I can make it without running out.

Before long, a freezing chill rips through the tunnel from ahead of me. Finally I've reached something. Every step brings on a heavier air stream. My breath becomes visible, but it is swiftly swept away. Continuing down the path, soon it opens up to a great sinkhole that would cover a football field. I am left with only a small ledge to walk on, with no choice in direction. To my left, the path is broken and crumbled away; one slip would send me deep into the bottomless abyss. Across from me lies the path to the boulders. It's a long way around to it, but if they made it, so can I.

Keeping my back to the wall and my hands planted against it, I shuffle along carefully. As the wind picks up, I can feel it separating me from the wall as it forces its way behind me. All of my muscles tense to their limit. I hold on with all my passion. Not only is the path long, but it has become far more tedious. Minus the wind, this would go so much faster. Passing the first tunnel to a dead end, I have four more to go until I reach the path to the boulders. I still want to see what they were hearing. Twenty minutes pass and I finally reach it. I wait silently, patiently for anything to be heard. Thankfully this cubbyhole at least gives me a place to regain my strength. With too much time spent, I leave the boulders with nothing more than disappointment.

Panting with frozen breath, I can't waste time. I continue moving against the wind as it whizzes around me. Keeping my balance, I reach the "Path to the Clouds." As I come to the mouth of the path, harsh, cold winds nearly push me from the ledge. This must lead out to something. Why didn't the others mark down what they'd found here? Now that I'm here, I have to investigate.

Using all of my strength, I move at a staggering pace, forward then back from the force of the severe wind. My face burns from the harsh cold as it blasts my skin. I bury it deep into my jacket, doing all I can to avoid the sting. Suddenly the light from the glow stick becomes minute as pure, golden sunlight graces me for the first time in days. Walking around a bend, I am fully consumed by sunshine. Squinting to see, I have no choice but to feel along the wall for my path.

Within a few steps, the tunnel ends. Before me, as it was so described, lies nothing except for an endless layer of clouds, hanging just beneath the sun. My feet are no longer visible as the clouds have consumed my path. If only it were so easy as to just walk across them to escape from this maddening maze! I wonder if any of the others had tried.

Feeling around, I discover a ledge leading off to the left. I don't remember this being on the map; then again, maybe the others never got to add it. My heart sinks with my fear of falling as I decide to see where it leads.

My heart pounds with every passing wind gust, as my path is far narrower than the last. Small stones fall into the clouds as I push them along in my shuffle. With absolutely no vision, I have to just hope that my path does not suddenly end. My hands feel along the stone wall behind me as my feet judge the ledge.

I come to another opening, a pocket in the stone wall. I hope it's a way out of these caves; then again, to be off of this ledge will make me happy enough. Thankfully there is plenty of room for me to get inside; I just hope I don't have to go back out. This tunnel not being on the map may be a great discovery.

Forced to use another glow stick, I travel down the passageway. Damn it! Pulling my map out, I know where I have been led, as my path ends at a pile of boulders. At least I'm off of that ledge and can take a small break.

Slumping with my back against the blockage, I can see something shiny in the corner. Suddenly, several muted whispers can be heard. The closer I get to the shiny object, the louder they become. On hands and knees, I crawl over to find a large steel vent cover. Its thick bars make it absolutely impenetrable.

Now the voices are loud enough to hear—two men, no three, though I can't understand what is being said; it's in some odd language I've never heard. By the tone it seems to be of an intellectual manner. So, the others weren't crazy. If there was only a way to get inside, to see where the vent leads, then maybe I could understand all of this. But now, with another glow stick wasted, I am left to go back across the hellish ledge.

Outside the sun is slowly fading into the western horizon. Reaching the main chamber, the sun is completely gone, not that it matters inside this dark, desolate tomb. The good news is that the winds have fallen to a minimum velocity, meaning much easier traveling to the tunnel marked as B1's connecting path—the stretch that is supposed to lead me to a way out of the caves and into town.

According to the map, the distance down this tunnel is three times that of reaching the "Great Wind." Several trails lead off in various directions. Luckily there is a place marked with water; I just hope I can last long enough to make it there.

This tunnel is warmer than the others; my fingers are finally gaining their feeling back, as is my face. Here I am surrounded by stone, but it is nowhere near as tight as the crack I had to squeeze through a couple days ago. By its shape, I would almost guess this passage was cut out by a flow of water. Perhaps at one time this whole place was filled, that great sinkhole being a lake. Everything is so smooth and symmetrical, perfect in every way.

There's a scent in the air now, a sweet aroma that replaces the musty, stale stone. In a slow ascension, I come to the bend that is the first vein in this system. My lungs are soaked in the scent as I stand at its entrance.

Curious to what is giving off that succulent odor, I have to explore deeper. With every step I can feel the temperature drop and the moisture rise. Something plantlike grows on the walls, covering them, as they lead me to the small pocket at the trail's end. A mushroom of some sort covers the floor. Hundreds of tiny, red, glowing tops fill the room with a dim, eerie ambiance. Nothing on the map spoke of this. Their sweet scent fills my nose as one of them spray out dust, launching millions of spores into the air. Strawberries, fresh-cut and perfectly ripe, call to me.

Though my stomach is growling and my mouth is salivating profusely, my mind quickly catches back up to my senses. Nothing about this room seems right. I need to get back to the task at hand.

Back in the main tunnel, I can't help but feel as though I'm in some other world. Glowing fish and mushrooms that smell like strawberries, all inside of a perfectly cut cave system that is high above the clouds. And the voices … who are they, and where did that vent lead to? There is no reasoning here, nothing adds up. And never during this wonderful trip did I pass through the distant city I saw from the cemetery. Damn it, I want answers!

With all of my pondering, I've lost track of time, and I arrive at the path with the water before I know it. The familiar glow of the fish is a comforting sight. As before, they show no resistance to being caught and eaten. One just isn't enough for the appetite that has grown within me. I think of the strawberry scent as I sink my teeth into the soft, tasty flesh. With my glow stick fizzling out, I lie back and watch as the fish slowly move about in their tiny nook. With their calming glow, I feel myself dropping into a long-awaited sleep.

Awake—opening my eyes swiftly, I sit up to see nothing. The purest, pitch-black darkness is all there is. I reach toward the water for a drink; it's a refreshing way to start up again. But where have the fish gone? There must be tunnels that connect the ponds to each other, or maybe it is just one giant lake branching off throughout this maze. Either way, there is no chance of me getting breakfast.

Cracking my fifth stick leaves me at my halfway point. If there is a decision of going back to be made, this is the time to make it, but that thought is left in the wind as I quickly move toward my final destination within this madness. I just wish there was a way I could carry water.

Finally, after hours of just walking, I arrive at the illustrious question mark. Crumbles of stone now crunch beneath my feet. Several large stones are piled along the wall. A small hole just large enough to crawl through lies exposed. From here my map is useless; now I travel into an unknown territory.

Shimmying through the tight fit makes me wonder if I will find the remains of my predecessors stuck inside. As I proceed, it would seem that I'm climbing, though it's slow and gradual. My glow stick fades, and with no room to crack the next one, I must continue blindly. Reaching ahead, I try to feel my way the best I can.

My knees are sore, and my hands have grown numb. I swear I can feel the grip of this tunnel tightening, compressing my chest as I gasp for a breath. I have to get out of here, I have to get out! In a panic, I can't help but scurry along as fast as my surroundings will allow.

Without warning, my outstretched hand finds an end to this path—the soft, flaky dirt of the earth. Pushing through, I have finally found the outside world once again. I crawl through the mud, and it saturates my body. Night greets me as I lie on my back, encircled by trees, just happy to be out of that nightmare.

Though I am free from the caves, I am faced with the same dilemma as ever. Where the hell am I, and which way should I go now? I really didn't expect to end up in the middle of the woods, but then again, I'm sure the others didn't either.

Heading off into the forest, a thick fog rolls in like a heavy shag carpet, surrounding me in the night. With only three feet of visibility, I travel on, not knowing what lies only steps ahead of me.

A slight rustling noise comes from in front of me. I draw a pistol defensively; I haven't come this far for nothing. Closer and closer it comes, only one step away from where I am ready to kill. A large, black nose leads soft, brown eyes into my clouded vision. Whew, it's only a deer. It picks up on my scent instantly snapping its head up to see me. Without hesitation, it scampers off.

Placing my gun back into its holster, I continue. Walking into the wind, I pick up the faint scent of a fire. It can't be the woods burning; I'd see the glow of the flames in the fog, like a sunset. Moving through the dense, lush wilderness, I find my way to the canopy's edge.

Like the forest, the soupy fog is also left behind me. Now I face more corn, just like outside of the church tunnel. I fear what might lay ahead, the beginning of this whole damn thing. Did those before me end up where I started, or has my destination been right under my nose?

As I pass through the rows, the sweet scent of burning wood grows stronger. Spying through the edge of the cornfield in front of me, I try to anticipate what is on the other side. Peeking out from the rows' end reveals a two-story farmhouse. From here, I cannot see any activity inside. Staying within the first row of the border, I try to get a little closer. With the fields on three sides of the house, I can easily move around it.

My nose begins to burn from the smoke. Before long I find its source; a raging fire stretching high into the moonless night appears on the other side of the house. A single giant stake of wood protrudes from the bonfire's center. Charred remains hang from the burning stake. Several people dance around the fire, their white pants drifting in the wind as they sway about, topless. Each one is wearing some kind of dark mask that covers their head. As one passes the fire, I can see she is wearing the mask of a cat, as is the next person—all of them, six by my total. What kind of cult ritual is this?

Moving to get a better view, I see a large man standing outside of the dance circle; he, too, is wearing a cat mask. Unlike the others, he just stands there motionless, with his arms folded across his chest. Three, seemingly normal, people are on their knees at his feet.

Suddenly one of the three captives gets up and makes a furious dash toward the house. Once the door slams shut, three of the dancers stop in motion, each retrieving a burning timber from the fire. Running up to the house, they whip the timbers through the fragile windows. Flames quickly engulf the house, fire spewing out from the broken windows. Crying out, the other two on their knees pound their fists to the ground.

I can't stop this; as much as this sickens me, I can't do anything! Unfolding his arms, the large man reaches behind him. Pulling out a knife, he spills the blood of another's throat. Meanwhile, the remaining three dancers move their spinning circle to be positioned around the last. With every rotation they creep closer to her. In one swift motion they reach out, grabbing her by the wrists and ankles. Continuing the hypnotic routine, they lift her high into the air, spinning and twirling her about as they spin back closer to the fire. Bloodcurdling screams fill the air as the victim whirls in the air. Two twists and a heave send her into the wicked blaze. Her screams rapidly cease as she is consumed in flames.

All of the dancers return to retrieve the body of the other. Tossing it on the fire, they gather as the flames grow higher into the night. With the house in full blaze, the darkness of night recedes.

Without warning or me making a single sound, all of them stop what they're doing and turn, staring directly at me.

I freeze, then creep deeper into the corn. They do nothing as I slowly backpedal. Stumbling, I fall to the ground. I look up to see one of the dancers standing above me. The head of a black panther peers down, as though looking into my soul. My hands rip into the earth as I pull myself along the ground, trying to get back to my feet.

He's gone; the man with the mask just disappeared. Looking back toward the fire, I see the others are coming my way. There is no way they could have seen me. I have to get out of here, and fast! Quickening my pace, I continue along the first three rows of corn; if I need to escape, I'd rather not get twisted around. A rustling comes from behind, telling me they are getting closer. Then unexpectedly the corn ends at another patch of forest. I dash through the brush, hoping my thin, light frame will let me gain ground. Smoke tickles my nostrils once more as I glance back to see that flames now engulf the corn—an attempt to burn me out.

Continuing into the woods, I move as silently as I can. The forest's span is a short-lived ten feet. As before, the trees open up to a large clearing, a perfect forty-foot sprint could get me across to the next set of woods. As I make my way athwart, I stumble over the foundation remains of another home. By the looks of the soot that covers the cinder blocks, I'd say this place has suffered the same fate as the farmhouse.

Light shines from my pursuers' burning sticks as they follow my trail. With the clearing's end in my sights, I move like the wind for its cover. But my sprint is cut short when I fall into a deep, empty well. Crashing hard onto several wooden planks, I lie silently, holding back my pain in hope that they won't find me here. My bruised muscles twitch in pain as I feel around the walls. They are constructed of cold, clammy stone that extend high above me. From beneath the planks I can hear the sounds of dripping water. This well must be fed by a deeper source. With the slippery walls above, below may be my only way out.

Faint footsteps come from above, and I can see the orange glow of the cultists' burning timbers. I rise to my feet and look up. Damn, they know I'm in here; I see them looking down at me. One of them drops their torch down next to me, then another. If I stay, I will burn; there has to be a way out. All of my might focuses on my feet as I begin kicking at the floor below. As one of the planks cracks, another torch falls, hitting me on the back. Pushing it off frantically, I pound at the floorboards. Another torch comes directly toward my head. Finally the planks give way, causing me to fall deeper into the well.

I reach the bottom with a hard thud and a splash. Rolling to avoid the burning timbers that are seconds behind me I narrowly escape their falling. The flaming torches hiss as the few inches of water douse them, leaving me in complete darkness. I have no choice but to continue on in darkness, seeking a way out down here.

My bones aching and muscles tender, I rise up in ankle-deep water. Feeling around, I discover I'm inside a massive cavern. The walls are cut to perfection, silky smooth, making the bowels of this well resemble a massive stomach. At a time this must have been full of water, but now there are only the faint sounds of dripping from down a tunnel I can only feel.

Thankfully this place is warmer than the rest of the caves I've been in. I just wish I had more glow sticks; I must have dropped the last few I had and I have no faith in walking blind, but I have no choice. Feeling around me, I make my through a small stone tunnel. Its walls are slimy from the moisture in the air.

The trickling of water grows louder as I walk in what I think is the direction of the sound's origin. I must be getting closer. My dark tomb brightens as a soft, dim glow illuminates from around the corner in front of me. The tunnel opens up, allowing me to stand. Now I find myself in large dome-shaped room. By the looks of it, I've come to a dead end. There's nothing here but a small, deep pond with hundreds of tiny glowing fish swimming about.

Kneeling down at the water's edge, I am drawn to drink. As the cool water trickles down my throat, I get a burning urge to eat. As I reach down into the water, these fish, like the others, don't seem to care. After satisfying my hunger with several of the undersized creatures, I notice more coming into the puddle. Where are they coming from?

Searching through the crystal waters with my arms, I find a medium-sized opening at the back side, just below the surface. I have no other option but to investigate the insane idea of going in there.

Shivers run through me as I jump into the frigid water, my clothing not much of a barrier from the bitter chill. I move toward the hole sluggishly, the fish only moving from the current I create. Chin deep, I reach the passage. With one deep breath I duck down to see if there's a chance I'll even fit.

Inside there is the same glow as on the walls of the tunnel; there must be thousands of the guppy-sized fish here. Losing breath, I return to the surface. It's a tight fit down there, with no room to move my arms. Maybe if I scurry along the bottom I can make it somewhere. That or I'll drown trying. Multiple deep breaths prepare my lungs to hold a little more oxygen. I'll only go as far as I can for now and hopefully come back; all of this just feels so crazy. One final breath and I'm off.

With no current, I move along amazingly quickly, darting through the water like a dolphin. I pass several tiny passages; they must be what feed this vein. My lungs begin to burn, but with the tightness of the tunnel, there is no turning back. My heartbeat pounds and panic consumes me as I struggle to find a way out, a way to breathe once more.

Off in the distance I see a dark patch above. Racing toward it, I pray it is a pocket with air. If not, this is where I will rest, food for what has been feeding me. Reaching the dark beacon, I emerge.

Gasping for breath, I lean against the smooth stone walls that tower high above me into black nothingness. I am lucky to find that this is more than just a pocket. My guess is that I've found another well, but this one is deeper then the last. Being soaked would make these steep walls impossible to climb. Damn, every blessing comes with an equal curse! I'm growing tired of all of this.

As I wallow in defeat, suddenly the surroundings begin to tremble. A cave-in, shit! I have to get out before I'm trapped in here! The trembling intensifies, the world around me violently quaking. The once serene water below rages with a massive current. It pulls me down by my feet and wrenches me further down the passage. The flow becomes faster and faster, taking me along for the ride. I am thrown into a hole in the side of the waterway, spit out to fall feet-first through a cavern into what appears, by the light of a dim glow, to be a massive lake.

Plunging deep into the immense body, I sink from my weighty clothing. I fight to discard my boots and jacket. Successful, I make a slow ascension. Breaking the surface, I get a good view of all that's around me.

This hollow is larger than any cave I have ever seen, expanding to the horizon of my view. In the distance a tower spire reaches up from beneath the water like a needle. Several girders follow alongside, supporting a giant bubble at its peak.

My surroundings are being lit by the enormous fish below— giant versions of the bioluminescent fish that have shown up at many stages of my journey. Like buses and planes passing each other, these prehistoric monsters cover the length of football fields with a few whips of their tails. I don't like this; I can't be here! Fear rushes through me as I watch them move about below, hoping they don't notice my presence. In a mad dash, I swim for the closest girder structure, though it seems miles away.

Never moving my eye from what lies below, I stop to rest halfway. Neither the fish nor any people who might be within the tower seem to notice or care that I am here. Still, I'm not taking any chances with the monsters underneath. Reaching the structure many agonizing strokes later, I am beaten, tired, and sore. I have nearly drowned, and I've feared for my life for far too long now. I labor to pull myself up the steel beams and wire. Closing my eyes, hoping to wake from this nightmare, I grip tightly around the supports.

Time passes, and I am still here, wherever here is. I open my eyes to get a grasp of where my path goes. Next to me, the tower makes me feel small, expanding beyond two skyscrapers wide and reaches up further then I can see. It must go to the very depths of this great lake.

I cannot spot a single window in the structure. How do they get in? There has to be a point of entry somewhere. Having rested, I climb higher on the girders for a better view. As I climb, the air becomes warmer and sweet smelling, almost like those strange mushrooms from the cave. The ceiling comes into full view as I reach tremendous heights. Wind flows freely here from a large, gaping hole directly above the tower, the breeze caressing my body. Up here I can see where the water meets the walls. The beasts below now look minute, each no larger than a pencil.

Islands in this lake are scarce in that there are none that I can see. Of course, there is no way of knowing what's on the other side of the tower from here. This cannot be the end of this. What's over there, beyond the tower?

With only a ten-foot drop, I dive from the beam that holds me; it is far quicker to fall than to climb back down. With little splash, I delve deep into the water. After resurfacing, I make my way around the tower, a tiring feat. Relief comes when another set of beams appears around the bend.

Climbing up for a little rest, I spot a small section of land off to the right. All three buildings reach three stories high. Their corners touch, creating a center court with the tower before them. They look ancient and unused; I don't know if they hold purpose. If nothing else, they are something less imposing to investigate than the tower. I can go there to figure out what I'm going to do next.

I dive back into the water to head for the shore. Just as I start to resurface from the splashdown, one of the massive eel creatures below rises toward me. Its long, snakelike body surrounds me. With no escape, I am forced from the water onto its back. Warm, soft, slimy skin makes it hard to keep from rolling off as it sways through the water, taking me closer to my destination. Upon reaching the shallows, it turns back and makes its descent back into the depths, leaving me to continue my journey. In minutes, I am sitting on the shore.

Wet and covered in sand, I walk to investigate the smooth sand construction. Intricate artwork, perhaps made by some ancient tribe, lines the bottom of each cracked and weathered block. Several of the carvings are of a cat-human hybrid creature that seems to be a representation of a god to whom sacrifices of flesh are offered. It would seem this whole civilization was centered around cats, strange.

Each pyramid has a large stone door facing the courtyard. They are marked by a single, different symbol. One has a large crescent moon with a star above it, another has the sun, and the last, the door of which faces the tower, has the "all-seeing eye" that I've encountered all too often. I wonder what these structures mean. Are they temples of worship, or tombs for fallen kings, portraying themselves as gods?

Dust begins to fall from the sun symbol as that door begins to sink into the ground. Hiding behind the adjacent pyramid, I watch as two dozen soldiers step out into the yard. They gather, talking among themselves, as they seem to be waiting for something. A man dressed in a blue uniform steps out. His stern eyes and bald head give him a look that demands respect. All of the soldiers fall in line with each other as he paces before them.

"All right, men, you are in the final moments of becoming one of the nation's greatest teams of elite soldiers." His voice is stern and powerful. He continues to pace, staring them down as he passes. "Remember, what you see here is strictly classified. If anyone breaks their silence, they will not only be eliminated from the team, but they will be removed from their life as well. Do all of you understand?"

"Sir, yes, sir!" the soldiers cry out.

"Good. Now you have a few moments before they take you inside. Have a good look around, take it all in, and then forget you ever saw it." He stops and salutes the men then walks back into the sun pyramid.

As the door closes, the soldiers begin to wander around the area, looking at the amazing sights before them. I move along the wall of the eye pyramid so as to keep my presence a secret. One of the soldiers walks along the edge of the water, staring into it. He moves along as if following one of the fish below.

Making sure he's alone, I silently move in. One hand over the mouth and the other around his neck, I pull him behind the stone monument. With a quick twist, I end his life, slowly lowering him to the ground. Quickly I replace my wet clothes and take the identity of Marcus Lamburg—according to his identification tags. I should fit in fine; thankfully with these outfits, we all look the same.

"Somebody's coming!" one of the soldiers yells out, as the rumbling sound of stone comes from the yard.

I quickly move to join the others. Coming around the pyramid, I see that the door with the eye is halfway down. As before, the soldiers all stand in line; I take my place among them. With a boom the door stops, fully open. Standing on the other side is a thin, nerdy-looking man wearing a lab coat. Clipboard in hand, he adjusts his glasses as he walks out before us.

"Okay, gentlemen, I will be taking you inside the control facility for the prison." His words are as harsh as the commander's, though his voice is softer. "We at Din-Gemma run a tight operation; you will stay together and in line. The rundown of our operation will be brief, so keep up, and everyone will be fine."

Raising his clipboard into the air, he waves for us to step inside the temple. "Let's be on our way."

We walk in two rows into the temple, lining up in front of a large set of elevator doors. Being the last one in, the door begins to close as my feet touch the inside floor. We all stand silently while the man in the lab coat looks at his clipboard, counting the men.

"Good, it looks like you have all made it this far. Hopefully we won't lose anyone along the way," he says as the elevator doors open. "This way, gentlemen."

We all step inside the large, round elevator with plenty of room to spare. Without a sound, the doors quickly close, and we start our descent into the ground below. We stop sinking and begin to move sideways; the unexpected motion causes most of us to stumble. The man in the lab coat chuckles, clears his throat, and regains his composure. Stopping once more, we ready ourselves for the next change of direction, but the doors simply open. Once again the man chuckles under his breath.

"This is it, men. Remember, all that you see and hear here is strictly classified!" he reminds us, as we step out into a long, white hall that seemingly has no end. Bright bulbs from the ceiling create a blinding atmosphere. Though in our black uniforms we stand out greatly, the man in the lab coat almost disappears.

"Let your eyes get used to the lights. Everywhere you go, every room in this facility is lit the same. If you start to get nauseous, just stop and focus on the person in front of you; it should pass in a few minutes."

We follow his floating head and clipboard to the end of the hall. There he raises his hand next to the wall, and white light turns to red flashing light as purple smoke pours out of the ceiling. "First, we have to be sterilized before we step inside," he explains.

The red quickly turns back into white, and a door opens silently, leading to another hall. Here there are several floating heads about as everyone is dressed in white. "We are on the lowest level of the tower. This is where we study the more hostile inmates. We try to figure out why they cannot function in society."

Could all of this be true? Am I a criminal? I don't trust their information. What are they covering up? Take me further conductor, open the door for me.

"Our next stop is the orientation room." Pausing along one of the side walls, he adds, "Please step this way." With another wave of his hand, a door opens.

Behind us, all of the other white-coated people have gone to their respective destinations. As the others in the group follow the guide into the next room, I fall back and wait, biding my time. The door closes, finally I am free to infiltrate. Alone in the bright hall, I start to feel the effects of the distorted vision, as my surroundings ostensibly go on forever. Falling to my knees, I close my eyes to get a grip.

"Are you lost?" asks a deep, annoyed voice from behind me.

"Sorry, just feeling sick," I reply calmly.

"Great, another new guy, I'm so tired of … never mind, come with me."

Pulling me up by the arm, he leads me to one of the walls. He too uses his hand to open a passage. He takes me into a room with a large steel table. "Have a seat and I'll check you out. Have you felt any problems with your equilibrium in the past?" he asks, walking over to the far wall. With a wave of his hand, a shelf containing several medical instruments extends from the wall.

"No, not that I ever remember," I answer, extending the lie.

"Okay, let's have a look."

When he turns back toward me, I quickly snatch his wrist and snap it then grab him by the throat. "What is going on here?" I demand.

"You're a soldier," his eyes grow in fear of what I might do. "You're here to keep track of the inmates. Didn't they tell you in—"

Cutting him off, I squeeze his throat tightly. "All they told me were lies. Now tell me the truth! What is this place?"

"You're him, aren't you? The one they've been looking for?" His voice barely escapes his lips. "If they find you down here they'll kill you," he explains with a hateful smirk.

"Who? Who is going to kill me?"

"So you really don't know? They're strong, and they will find you."

"No they won't."

I grip him as tight as I can. Struggling to live, he swings about, kicking his feet and trying to claw at my face. After a few moments, he goes limp.

I strip him of his clothes and place him on the table. Then I go to inspect the tools that are at my disposal. Finding a scalpel, I dig it into his right hand to pry out whatever it is that gives him room access. Blood slowly pours from his dead hand as I uncover a microchip. Being no bigger than a dime, I have to be careful not to lose it. I also have to just hope that this body isn't discovered until long after I leave.

Replacing my soldier's uniform, I now take another identity. Using the chip, I scan the walls in this room more or less at random looking for another door. Suddenly part of the wall disappears, revealing a large window. On the other side is a scrawny man curled up on a small cot in the corner of the room. Only a faded pair of white boxers covers his body. Next to him is a toilet and small sink. Like every room I have encountered so far, there are no doors.

"Hey!" I shout, banging on the glass. "Wake up!"

"What the hell do you want now?" he blurts out as he moves to face me. "Another new guy." Sitting up, he runs his hand through his tattered, greasy hair. "Why do they always send them to me? Why can't they just leave me alone? I've already told them everything, nothing's changed."

As he stands to stretch, every bone in his body is visible, like a skeleton that walks and talks. With a loud pop in his back, he reaches around to rub it as he sits. "Where's your clipboard?" he asks in a smart tone.

"I'm not one of them; I'm from outside, from the town," I explain. "Do you know what's going on here?"

"Sure you are," he states sarcastically. "Those mindless bastards would never find this place."

"You mean the prisoners?"

"Prisoners, they're not prisoners. Look, don't believe what they tell you." Holding his head, he lies down on his back and continues. "You are right, though, this place is a prison. But none of those people have done anything. They're mice. Some get part of their minds, others don't get any. Those unfortunate bastards just walk around in a lost daze, repeating their days." He starts to laugh. "Others just get enough information to work so it all seems real. Slavery has been accomplished."

I am lost by his words. Incredulous, I ask, "What are you in all of this? How did you end up here?"

"Well, I wasn't one of you pieces of shit. I was a soldier, yeah, one of the elite." Sarcasm fills his voice. "I was keeping the inmates in line, making sure they were doing what they were supposed to." His gaze points straight at the ceiling. As he continues, his voice grows soft and fills with regret. "I even killed a few of them, ones who'd gone out of control. It wasn't their fault; they just couldn't take it anymore."

Tears fall from the sides of his eyes to the floor. Even if what he is saying isn't true, he sure believes it is. Suddenly he stands, approaching the glass that separates us. "Look, I told you I don't want to talk about it! Get out of here and leave me alone! I said get out of here, piece of shit!"

His voice is so loud that he gains the attention of others. From across his room along the bed, the wall disappears. Another scientist is standing on the other side. "Number 47, quiet down immediately," he demands.

The skinny man in the room stomps over to the other side. "If I ever get out of here, I'm going to kill all of you. You hear me, huh? Do you?" he shouts out.

Raising his hand up to the wall, the scientist activates something that causes a thick, green smoke to pour into the skinny man's room. His frail body falls to the floor instantly.

"Don't worry about him; he has been like that since they brought him here. What have you got there?" the scientist asks me.

"What?" With all that the man was saying, I completely forgot about the guy I had just killed. "Oh, he's a soldier. He fell from a building while chasing after one of the prisoners." I pray with all my life that he buys that excuse.

"Really, why did they bring him here? Normally they just throw them in the water outside. Hmm, let me have a look."

With those words, his transparent window closes. Waving my hand around on the wall, I get it to return to normal. Suddenly a doorway opens to my left, and the scientist from the other room walks in, straight to the body. "Looks fresh, how long has it been?"

"An hour maybe," I reply. I know if he sees through my bullshit this is all over. "I was told he was chasing the one they've been looking for."

"What happened to his hand? Did you do this?" the other man asks, his voice suspicious.

"I cut out his chip to see if it had been tampered with. It was intact, so I doubt the person they're looking for knows about it."

"Good, he can't be allowed to get inside. Though if he did gain entry, there is no way he'd be able to move around, not without a chip. Have you put your report into the central computer?" he asks, looking over the man's neck injury.

"No, I had just started my investigation and couldn't find the computer. When I was looking—"

"You accidentally opened number 47 cell?"

"Yeah."

"That's all right; it took me a year to get used to this place. It's worth it, though." He walks over to the wall where the medical tools are and places his hand on the wall. He continues as a holographic computer screen appears. "Have you ever used one of these systems before?"

"No," I state walking up to his side. As I get a closer look, I notice a map of the facility in the background.

"It's simple really. Here, watch." With a fast hand, he starts moving things around on the screen, opening a notepad. That brings up a holographic keypad. "What was his name?"

"Marcus Lamburg, I believe." I have to hope that this man is registered, being a new recruit and all.

"Hmm, there's nothing here. I'll check the archives; he might have been pulled from the prisoners." He plugs in the man's name and we wait. It comes back unknown. "Are sure that was his name? Where is his chart?"

"It's right—"

Instead of finishing my sentence, I surprise him with a left hook to his head. Crumpling to the floor, he curls up in pain. Rolling him over, I sit on his chest then strangle his life away.

Now I have some free time to work. With the computer screen already displaying the archives, I can search for some answers. Typing into the search field "list of prisoners" brings up a long list of names with photos. There have to be thousands here.

Scrolling through, I come to a man who looks just like Dave. I open his file, revealing his true identity. His name is Kyle Morgan Brown, age thirty-eight. From Pie Town, New Mexico. It seems Kyle ran a small convenience store that was passed down to him from his family. No wife or children, Kyle was brought here four years ago for murder. Knowing him as I did, I just can't picture him as a killer. At the bottom of his file reads the word *deceased*, but there is no cause of death listed.

Moving on, I search for anything I can find on Sarah. After a few key strokes I come to a photo that looks just like the man I killed in the diner. Marvin Anthony Jones, age forty-nine. Fitting his position here, he comes from Joliet, Illinois, where he was a short-order cook at an all-night truck stop. He was simply charged with theft and has been here for five years. He is also listed as deceased. I know that I am the cause.

With all this information, I just wish for something that can bring this all to light. What about me; what am I doing here?

Searching on, finally I find her, Sarah Marie Wise, age nineteen. From Norfolk, Iowa, she was an art student in Chicago; this explains the beautiful painting she did in the house. She was brought here a year ago for forgery and theft. None of this can be true; I don't believe she had the heart for it.

Now on to me, searching and searching, I finally uncover myself. William Donald Hess, age twenty-nine. I'm from Ontario, Canada? A gas station clerk, I was brought here seven years ago. My crime, it seems, is that I blew up the gas station where I worked, killing fifteen people, including three children.

This doesn't make sense. How could I not remember any of this? Though I don't know the definite truth, I know this is not it.

One more thing still plagues me; I need to find the woman from the costume shop. My search leads me nowhere as I run through every name in the list, all 150 females. Scrolling through them all reminds me of the walls inside the cave. There are a few faces I remember seeing during my journey that are not listed here. Waitresses, people on the streets—not one of them are here. Oddly, some faces of scientists I recognize are registered with the prisoners and the same with some of the soldiers.

With all of the time I've spent here, I am not surprised when the door I originally came through opens. "What the hell happened in here?" A frantic female scientist asks, running up to the corpse of the scientist I killed. "Who did this?"

"Number 47 has gotten out; I've been trying to report it to the top level, but I don't have access." I kneel down beside her. "Do you?"

"Of course I do, but you should have sounded the alarms!" Darting for the computer, she looks over what I was doing. "How do you not have access if you can get into the archives?"

"It was already on when I came into the room," I explain, trying to cover my ass. "I couldn't figure out how to get—"

"It doesn't matter, I'll sound the alarm."

Just as she goes to hit the button, a voice comes from the other side of the wall. "Are you still there?" number 47's voice calls out. "I'm ready to talk. Hello?"

Walking over to the wall, the female scientist opens the panel to his cell. Number 47 stands on the other side of the glass. "Oh, I didn't know you were here, Alice. Are you training the new guy?"

"I thought you said …" Turning toward me, her face turns to horror as she comes to the realization. "You did this!"

She rushes for the door next to the adjacent cell, where the first scientist had entered from across the way. As the door opens, I grab her by her lab coat and pull her back, flinging her into the wall. Her nose breaks upon impact, splattering her life's liquid into her long, blonde hair. Bloody and scared, she faces me knowing that her last moments are near. I move toward her, while number 47 watches as I grip her throat.

"Kill her. Kill the piece of shit!" he shouts even as I squeeze, sending Alice's vision to fade into darkness. "You really are from up top, aren't you?" he asks with excitement. "If you're going to shut them down, you have to get to the central control center at the top."

"Do you know how I can get there?" I ask. My lips moisten in anticipation.

"There is an elevator that will take you straight there. Control is far above us. You will have to pass through the hall out there and go to the center of the room at its end. From there, turn left, then go into the next hall. There is an elevator on the right side of that hall. You will need to find someone else with access beyond the fortieth floor. Find a top-level scientist; they are the only ones who are allowed to talk to them."

"Them?"

"The ones who run this lie. I've never seen them, and neither has anyone else I know of, but there are those who take direct orders and are responsible for the Zinat Nine Serum. You have to shut them down!" he explains.

"What is the Zinat Nine Serum?" Finally getting some answers, I am eager to learn more.

"There's no time; it won't be long before more of them show up and find you. I will distract them as long as I can, but you have to hurry."

"Thanks."

"Destroy this place, friend. Make us all free again," come his encouraging words as I run out of the room.

Back in the hall, I am lucky to find that it's empty. Using the chip I pulled from Alice's hand, I gain access to the next room. With the lighting and color, the room seems to go on forever. I feel my way along the wall toward the left side. More scientists enter the room, coming out of the walls. They, too, follow the walls, not stepping out into the room.

"Man, this place is disorienting isn't it?" one states, passing me.

Continuing on, I open a door, which exposes a room where a scientist is watching a half-naked woman in a cell similar to number 47's. Waving his hand on the wall causes a panel inside of her room to open. A small amount of purple smoke pours out into the room. Her eyes seem to focus on unseen objects floating around. She swats with her hands, screaming. Then she gives up and huddles in the farthest corner, arms covering her head as she tries to hide from her visions.

The scientist turns toward me as though to see what I need. "Sorry, wrong room," I state moving back into the main chamber.

As quickly as it opened, the door shuts, leaving me in the big, disorienting room. This place must lead to several points of importance, because as I wander, several scientists come and go from the rooms and halls of this twisted maze.

Feeling along the walls and opening a few different rooms, I eventually come to the hall I need. With Alice's chip in my hand, I move along the wall. To my surprise, I quickly find the elevator. Just as I have one foot inside, another scientist comes toward me. My nerves rise in the fear that I've been caught.

"Hold the elevator, please," he calls out, running toward me. "Thanks. When there's a door open, I grab it. It's too easy to get turned around in here."

"I can understand that," I reply trying to make conversation. As the door closes, he reaches out, placing his hand on the wall. A small panel appears with the numbers. Pressing the number forty, we start on our way.

"Are you on your way to get more Zinat Nine? My test subject went into mass hysteria. Only four more tests and I can wipe her mind," he explains.

"What exactly are you looking for?" I ask, seeking information.

"Her psychological breaking point, of course. This girl is strong, though; it took over thirty tests before she finally lost her sense of reality. Luckily for them, they get to forget it all with one injection. That's one of our benefits, too, of course. We can do whatever we want to them. She's so beautiful." A smile cuts across his face. "So, what are you working on?"

"My test subject was moved topside. He seemed to handle the serum well. Right now I'm working with Alice on number 47." It's all I can think of at the moment; I just hope he buys it.

"You must be moving up; before you know it you'll be up with the top dogs. I've been trying for years to get up there, but they keep me on doing these mundane experiments. At least this subject is a girl, and subjective implanting is so easy that she'll do whatever I want."

Thankfully our conversation ends as the doors open to the fortieth floor. Without another word, the man steps out into the large laboratory.

Stepping out after him, I take in my surroundings at their fullest. Three massive chemical mixing stations line the walls. Burning glass feeds mists of chemicals down long tubes as scientists stand nearby with notepads, documenting everything. This must be how they process the serum.

Most of the lab workers here are female, none of which notice me as I walk about in awe. One of the women walks over to a blank wall and holds up her hand, opening two large panels of glass. From the other side, all that can be seen is the dim glow of tiny red lights, like stars in a moonless sky. Getting close, I can see they are the mushrooms like the ones I saw in the cave.

"Beautiful, aren't they?" she says to me in a soft, friendly voice. "I'm still amazed at how well they grow in this environment."

"Yeah," I state simply, not knowing what else to say to her.

"I'm Lisa. Is there something you needed?"

"Alice sent me to get some more Zinat Nine."

"Are they still doing experiments on number 47? I don't know why they waste the serum on him; it doesn't even affect him. The person you're looking for is Dr. Mary Hahn." To our left a door opens to let in two soldiers and a female scientist. "Here she is now."

Mary is carrying a large metal case with both hands, a few documents lying on top. The soldiers escort her as she walks into the room. Moving past Lisa and me, they head across the lab. As they reach the center of the room, some of the papers fall from atop of the case to the floor. Mary stops, bending down to retrieve them. The soldiers just stand there watching her struggle. Walking over, I stoop and pick up the papers. Our eyes meet as we both stand.

"Thank you. At least someone around here is courteous. Come with us; I don't have time to juggle." Moving on, she opens a door to another room. Placing the case on a table, the door closes with her, me, and the two soldiers inside.

"My papers, please," she requests, reaching out. As I hand her the documents, all of the white light becomes replaced by red. "The alarm?"

"You stay here and protect them. I'll go check it out," one soldier tells the other. Both draw weapons as the first walks out of the room.

Mary quickly snatches up the case and walks over to one of the walls. She activates a pull-out drawer, where she hides her case and papers, all the while not knowing that I'm the one they're looking for. Her hand waves on a different spot, opening a computer terminal.

"This isn't a drill. We've been infiltrated!" she states excitedly.

"You got another piece?" I ask the soldier. "I'll look after her while you secure the others."

He tosses me a gun, in confidence at my words.

As quickly as I catch it, I send a bullet into the soldier's brain. Turning toward Mary, I silence her screams before they can be heard. I first take her life, then her chip, in order to gain access to my destination.

Once I open the door, I make the couple soldiers patrolling this floor my first targets. Dropping them with ease, I cover the white walls in the blood of the scientists until my slide clicks. I discard the empty gun onto the floor and gain another from the convenient corpse of a soldier.

Steadily I make for the elevator; as the door opens, so does a door from another room. My final target in the room falls as the elevator door shuts. Without my having to touch anything, the elevator begins to ascend; I ready myself for any unexpected stops.

Shortly I feel my ascension leisurely come to an end. My sights lock straight ahead as the door opens into darkness. Not even the elevator light can crack through the pitch darkness as I step out into the unknown.

The door closes silently, and I am left to find my way. Feeling for a wall around me, I find nothing except for the round elevator shaft. I move through the dark, searching for anything that could bring me light. Without warning, an orange, flashing glow in the shape of a box appears before me. It expands in all directions as the flashing solidifies into steady color. Suddenly like on a movie screen, an image starts to form. It's me! When is this?

I watch myself walking through the cemetery looking at the names. Is that Dave? My image stops to talk to someone who's feeding the pigeons, but he's not dressed like Dave, not like I remember. Now I'm inside the diner. Without sound I can't tell what I am saying as I converse with the man behind the counter.

All of the images disappear, as does the screen. The choking grip of darkness slowly loosens as the room brightens. At least now I can see around me, though I see that this space is nothing more than an empty bubble. Also, I'm sure beyond a doubt that they know I'm here.

Another small screen appears, followed by two more. Side by side in front of me, I watch as all three play images of Sarah's death, each from a different angle. All three stop and zoom in on her twitching body as she lies at the bottom of the cliff. Who the hell could have seen that?

"Congratulations, number 342. You never seem to disappoint us," states a deep, calm voice from behind me. "It's good to see you again."

Turning around, I point my gun toward the sound. My sights lock onto a man dressed in a suit, his eyes hidden behind a pair of dark sunglasses. Before I kill him, I need to get some information.

"Who are you?" I ask harshly.

"You don't remember? I understand. You can shoot me if you'd like," he states, spreading his arms out, leaving his chest open.

"If that is what you want, then fine, I'll get my answers elsewhere."

I pull the trigger and can see the bullet travel right for him. Stopping halfway, the bullet hangs in space, just floating. Suddenly I feel a loss of control over my body. Trying to, I find I can no longer move.

"You see, it is pointless for you to try to destroy us." With his hands behind his back, the man walks over to the floating bullet. "This is such a primitive way of life. Here is an example for you."

Touching the bullet with his finger causes it to break apart into several pieces. All of the pieces then become more pieces until there is nothing left except for a thin layer of dust.

"Nothing is solid; within every space is more space, and between those spaces are more." With one swift breath, he causes the dust to swirl about like a small tornado. "Within all of this is a vibration that courses throughout everything, bringing forth substance. Do you understand?"

"No," I reply truthfully. With all that has happened, I am lost. "Why can't I move?"

"I'm getting to that. Your kind is an intelligent one, though your primary interests are baffling. It would seem that you thrive on self-satisfaction, no matter the cost; understanding, though you don't even know what it is you are trying to understand; and freedom, a term for something that doesn't really exist. We provide you with everything—from money to your favorite foods, even the sexual pleasures you so long for."

A chair rises out of the floor behind the man. Sitting, he continues. "Even with everything given to you, it is never enough. Please, sit."

Stepping backward against my will, I fall back into a chair. Five small monitors appear next to us, each displaying a different person in the town. "Take this soldier, for example. He is following what he believes is a rogue prisoner. Within your species' complexity, suggestion—what you believe in—is your weakness. This soldier desires nothing more than to kill his mark. His reasoning is for personal gratification that he will have somehow saved the day."

The monitor shows the soldier shoot a woman in the back, killing her as he celebrates with a smile.

The scene shifts. "This man here seeks only to fill his sexual desires with control." I can see the scientist that rode in the elevator with me. He has his female patient dancing and touching herself at his command. "It doesn't take long for him to get bored with a subject, so he empties his cell." Now I see the woman gasping as a thick smoke fills her room.

Another scene comes. "Here is number 426. She is a drone, believing whatever is fed to her through the media. Whatever we print is what gives her faith." A woman paces back and forth in a tiny apartment; biting her nails as she reads the newspaper. "There are weeks where she won't leave her home."

Next I see those cultists wearing the cat masks. "Even within the path to a so-called god, your kind murders in the name of the righteous." The video shows the incident I witnessed at the farm.

The next monitor shows me walking into the empty house, where Sarah is waiting inside. "How did you see this?" I demand. "And why didn't you stop me then?"

"Stop you? Oh no, number 342; you are the most important one of all." I am completely at a loss to see myself going along on my path. "The first time you came to us here was a complete surprise; never before had your kind ever found their way here, but you figured it out."

"First time?" How many times have I sat in this chair?

"Yes, this is your seventh time, and every time you arrive faster and with far fewer casualties created. Do you remember this?" Drawing out a piece of folded paper from his pocket he unfolds it revealing a picture of Sarah. "You drew this," he continues, "though you don't remember. We took it from you, along with all these others." Reaching into his pocket, over and over, he pulls out one paper after another. Seven total.

"Though we have no true data from the first incident, we believe that it took you several years to get here," he adds. "Since that time you have raised much interest in our people; your intelligence and drive exceed that of all of those before you."

Despite knowing I've lost this game, I still want my answers. "Your people ... how many are there of you?"

"Thousands, and that is just here at Din-Gemma; our home world holds many more. I believe you met one of us at a costume shop." All of the monitors begin to display the same thing, various points of my entire encounter with the woman. "She took a great interest in you after watching your third and bloodiest run. Begging her father, one of our highest investors, she was allowed to breed with you. The vibration you give off made it easy for her to assimilate exactly what you wanted her to be. You believe your eyes, what you see beyond that of what you don't. Haven't you pondered how we can see your every move?"

My actions with the woman disappear and are replaced by images of me sitting here, now. As I watch my image spin and rotate, the lights fade to darkness. Four small, purple orbs float around my head, stopping and moving as the footage does. They disappear as the lights come back.

"Even the image of the vast city is an influenced vision fed by vibration, for the sake of giving your people comfort that there are things to achieve and places to go. In reality, number 342, all you and your kind have to do is live."

"How can we live when you feed us these lies?" I counter forcefully.

"They are only suggestion; it is up to you to determine what is real—something you have gone to great lengths to discover. Influence can only go as far as ones determination for truth allows. As I said before, you have been an exception to the rule. We have and will take the truth away from you, though as I have told you in the past, I know we shall meet again. But I do hope that you can learn to just live."

"You will see me again, but next time I will destroy this place and all of you within it!" I yell out defiantly as my hatred grows.

"Repeating words to my ears—you cannot destroy us, just as we cannot destroy you. Your perception of our being the law keepers is an abstract one. In truth, we all have rules to follow."

With those as his final words, the lights and monitors vanish. Stuck in the chair, I watch as a serpent of mist forms out of nothing. Its blue, translucent body sways about as it moves toward me. Wrapping around me, it faces me directly as it readies to strike.

Awake, in a room I've never seen. Naked, I sit up in what I believe is my bed, the sun pecking through my window. Looking at the digital clock next to my bed, I see that it is 9:00 a.m. My clothes lie draped over the back of a red velvet chair, one pair of jeans, white boxers, one stained, white shirt, a pair of socks and ratty pair of shoes. Getting dressed, I leave the run-down room to see where the hell I am. Closing the door, I see that my room is number 342. How long have I lived here?

Going down the stairs and out through the door leads me to an empty street. A few people walk down the sidewalk, but there are no cars to be seen. Across from my building stands a large, round cemetery with a massive wrought iron fence protecting it.

Stepping through the open gate, I walk among the stones. Reading their names, I get a cold chill as I stand on the loose soil of a woman who's been recently buried. Her name is Sarah Marie Wise.

Justifiable Torment

"Is that when you saw her, Mr. Mar?" the man in white asked.

"Yes, my daughter," replied the filthy, naked man from the dark leather sofa. "She ran down the alley."

"And you followed her?" Doctor Donabba asked. His voice was cold and emotionless.

"Of course—I had to see where she was going. The alley was long and narrow, more like a gripping hallway. Steam was pouring out from several vents and pipes in the walls. One of them had to be ventilation for a kitchen. I could smell roast beef and hamburgers looming in the air. I made my pursuit after her, but I was a good distance behind. Only a hazy figure was visible. I reached what was a dead end to see a large steel door closing slowly. Jenny must have gone that way.

Without a second thought, I rushed through the doorway. It led to what seemed like a janitor's closet. Several plastic spray bottles lined a couple of shelves on the back wall; a rusted mop bucket sat below. Against one of the walls stood an old metal wash basin that probably hadn't been used in years. Everything was covered in a thick layer of dust. No one had used this place in years.

After that short moment of glancing around, the door shut behind me. Darkness took over, making be blind. Except for a slight beam of sunlight from the top of the door, that cut through the dark like a razor, there was nothing. Reaching out, I searched for the knob, but there wasn't one. Feeling around for any way out, my fingertips only grazed along the seam of the door. I tried to remain calm, to think it through, but this place started to close in on me. The shelves, the bucket, and the tub were all there was. Time seemed to stand still, long minutes with grueling seconds. I broke down, hitting the door and yelling, hoping someone would hear me.

Disappointment was all that came … that and a tiny loss of hope. Sweat dumped down my face as the temperature rose, along with the humidity. A sickening, musty stench filled the room. Choking back my stomach's contents, I knew I'd have to get used to the conditions. The oven-like heat must have taken its toll, because about then I blacked out for a while. It must have been night when I awoke, because I sat in complete darkness.

At least now it was cooler. Dizziness came over me as I stood, and I really had to piss. Using the wash tub seemed like a good idea, right down the drain; unfortunately, there was no drain pipe, and my piss just ran down out the hole and onto my shoes. The scent of that didn't help the odor, which was already burning through my sinuses. Then my hunger came. Gurgling and growling, my stomach made it clear how long it had been since I'd eaten. Just then the wind must have shifted, because I swear I could smell the roast beef again.

Trying not to think about it, I concentrated on the thought of being rescued. I even tried pushing on the door again in the vain hope that it might give, nothing happened. Feeling around on the walls, I came upon a slight crack in the plaster. Frantically I searched for something to help me break through.

I felt around on the lower shelves, the ones I could reach, but there was nothing. Using the mop bucket as a step stool, I reached for the top shelf, where I found a large pipe wrench. While pulling it down, I fell back, hitting the door with all of my weight. It didn't even buckle slightly. The wrench fell, clanging off the floor next to me. Picking it up was easy; it was swinging the damn thing that was impossible. I hadn't eaten or had anything to drink for at least twenty-four hours. I was weak, and this tiny space held no room for an outright swing.

Using what little energy I had, I began to slowly chip away at the crack. Every hit shot out small pieces of plaster against my face. My slow pace quickened with the thought of escaping. I attacked the wall until I created a small opening. Then hundreds of cockroaches and other bugs poured out onto the floor, scurrying about and crunching beneath my feet as I shuffled around.

Leaning in, I reached into the hole. It was only slightly larger than my hand, so it was a tight fit inside. Bugs crawled all over my forearm, as I was in up to my elbow. I could feel some pipes and brick. I knew any chance of escape wouldn't come here. Everywhere I felt had something to block my path.

The sharp edge of the plaster dug into my arm as I tried to pull back. Twisting to free it only caused the edge to dig deeper into my flesh. With no choice, I worked out my arm, tearing a gash several inches long. Falling against the door, I felt the warm blood dripping off my hand. My heart and wounds pulsed to the sound of each drop as it pooled on the floor.

Suddenly a beeping noise came from the other side of the door; it must have been a garbage truck. In an insane fury, I stood up and began beating on the door, yelling out over and over until I was hoarse. Blinded by my own tears, I listened as the truck released its hydraulics then drove away. I couldn't stop crying. Like a child, I curled into a ball, and my tears lulled me to sleep.

A dream came that night; it was so real. My cell door had opened, releasing me. On the other side there was nothing but darkness and a plank that led on into infinity. There was nothing beneath, just a straight drop to nowhere. As I stepped onto the plank, it bowed under my weight. With an extreme fear of falling, I moved forward slowly. Looking back after a time, I saw that the door was now far from my view, and yet there was still nothing ahead either.

Then I heard her laughter—not laughing at me, but a joyful and content laughter echoing all around me. I cried out for her to answer me, but there was no reply. From in front of me, off in the distance, I heard footsteps approaching. The plank bowed further and creaked with every step. It was her coming to save me. It was her, but only her *presence* could be felt.

She passed through me as she had so many times before. I could smell her and feel her inside of me. Closing my eyes, I wanted to take all of her in, to remember. As my eyes stayed shut, my mind began to lose place of where I was. My balance began to falter, and dizziness set in. One step forward and I lost it all, falling into the abyss. I watched above as the plank receded from my sight. After a long descent, I hit a concrete slab.

I awoke—that's what it felt like, anyway—dealing with the agony from the fall. I stood up painfully, wiping away the bugs from my wound, finding myself back in the room. Morning had come, along with the faint light above the door. A slight scent of breakfast teased my senses and caused my stomach to knot. Aromas of pancakes, eggs, sausage, bacon, hash browns, bitter coffee, and ever-so-sweet syrup danced through my nose. I could almost taste them. My wrenching stomach ended the fantasy as I threw up. First there were dry heaves, and then came the bile. All of the pleasant scents of breakfast were replaced by the odor of the musty room combined with stale piss and now vomit.

My throat burned from the acid; it had been so long since I'd had a drink. I tried the wash basin only to find that the handles turned, but that was all they did. Following the pipes, I frantically searched for a shutoff switch. I found a junction in the pipe where two pieces had been screwed together. Using the wrench, I loosened the fitting. Breaking one of the pipes free sent a splash of water down. I only caught a little bit in my mouth. It was foul and smelled of rot. I only tried to swallow a tiny portion, spitting the rest out.

As the day grew on, so did the heat. Removing my shirt, I covered the pile of puke and piss. The bugs were now starting to feed off of it. All because of this goddamned door! Pacing back and forth, my anger began to grow. I stepped toward the door to hit it when I slipped on my shirt and fell into the mess beneath it.

I stood, covered in my own waste, to fly into a violent fit of rage. My arms swung about, knocking the shelves and sending the bottles skittering to the floor. The dry, weathered plastic cracked and shattered as I stomped the containers. Even the mop bucket crumpled and gave with a few swift kicks. This hellish room now lay in ruins.

I sat again, rocking with my knees pressed against my chest. Soon the bugs moved their feast to me. Climbing up my body, they clung to the spots where the vomit was. Bastards, I'd show them. Reaching down, I pulled one of the roaches off my pants. I could see in the dim light its legs thrashing about as it tried to free itself from my grasp. Biting it directly in half, I could feel its legs moving inside my mouth, grasping my tongue as its bitter insides ran down my throat. Gagging, I tossed the rest of the bug into my mouth. As I munched away on its crunchy shell, I took off my socks to clog the drain of the basin in case I had to throw up again. My body began to heave as I tried to block out my reality, instead thinking of things like caramel corn with nuts. It didn't matter though; I still threw up. Chunks of shell lodged themselves between my teeth and ripped my throat as I tossed my meek meal into the basin. Cursed room and those wretched bugs!

Wiping them off me, I stomped and stomped and stomped. I killed as many of them as I could. My body pleaded for some food or a drink, any drink. Dry and starving, I wanted *out*!

Suddenly what little light came from above the door faded into dark. Ripping, rolling thunder roared throughout the air as bright, blinding light periodically flashed into the room. A torturous, beating rain dropped heavily outside. I envisioned myself dancing in it, drinking and saturating my body in it.

Smiling, I could feel a few drops hit my face. From above the door, the winds were pushing in the rain. There wasn't much that flew past, but there was enough that water started running down the steel door. Pressing my face against the door, I tried to pool the water in my cheek. Then I began to lick it. Like sandpaper my tongue slowly slid over the dusty surface. It tasted like a bland, moldy cheese.

More drops of water came from the ceiling. Slowly, it began to rain inside the room. Sticking my head up, I gathered a mouthful. It tasted as though someone had taken a rotting carcass and let it sit in warm, stagnant water. Quickly I spit the rainwater out on the floor. I had to lick the door to get that taste out of my mouth.

Pushing the mess I had created into one corner of the room, I sat to think. All I could do was wonder how long the rain would last. At least the vomit and piss were being washed away as they drained under the door. The heavy downpour outside eventually turned into a light drizzle, slowing down the drops from above, but it still rained inside the room.

Having drowned out the day, the storm passed completely, leaving the night. Crickets chirped outside as trickles of water dropped without timing or tune. Covered in sour water, I could smell the stench of my body. My head began to pound right in the center. Each drop of water hitting the floor was like a shattering blast as it echoed throughout my ears. Make it stop, make it all go away, please make it stop! It was a plea that would go unheard.

Sleep never came that night; I just sank into a delusional sense of displacement. I was neither here nor there, not really anywhere. A pale shade of gray, an outline of a figure is all that remained. Each plunk of the drops took me farther away until nothing more remained.

The park—I remember the park, seeing my daughter play. It was as real as the room, but different. She was there just as before. We were there after school that Wednesday. Chills filled me as I felt her pull me toward the swings. Talking back and forth, I was there, but I wasn't in control. A sort of autopilot for the soul while reliving moments that have long drifted away.

It rained that day. Heavy, warm drops fell, soaking us before we reached the car. Her smile was so genuine, so pure, as she shut the door. All we could do was laugh. I went to start the car, but she wouldn't have it. "Let's just sit here and listen," she said, then with a click she reclined her seat and closed her eyes. Closing my eyes, I followed right along, to feel her happiness. "Isn't it pretty?" she asked. I could feel the room, my cell, my hell, calling me back. "I could stay here forever." With her final words, I opened my eyes to the sun peeking in above me.

For a moment, just a minute second, I thought I might be free. Surely this flashback hallucination couldn't have taken me through the night, for what had lasted seemingly minutes would have wiped out hours. Not that I felt a loss for that time, but to be lost for that time was a blessing. Inside the room, the rain had stopped. Still everything inside, myself included, was saturated. My knees met the concrete floor with force as I slipped on the surface, trying to stand. Rolling to my back, I stared into the beam of sunlight, questioning why I had to come back at all. Within surrender's grip, I lay there as the day slowly dawdled on.

Slowly the temperature rose. All of the moisture from the rain gathered like a fog. Aromas of mildew and mold filled my lungs, choking my airways. Every breath was a gasp for life. My eyes, trying to focus, could only grasp clouds and a blurred haze. My mind swirled about, spinning, lost, and out of control. My skin itched and crawled with life as the bugs returned to the room. My face became home to some, my chest and legs to others. I couldn't stop them. I felt sharp pinching and pulling of my skin sporadically over all parts of my body. How long till they'd reach the bone? They'll find me as a skeleton, I thought—that would be funny—with a bony grin. These are the only coherent thoughts I can remember having; after that there wasn't much I could lock onto. I just sort of lay there, subsisting.

I could hear cars rushing by in the distance, or at least I thought I could hear them. Moving, honking, the squealing of tires—they were all so close to me, just beyond the door. Now standing on the corner of the street, I could see all I was hearing. I gazed in amazement as they passed by. There are people too, lots of people. The hustle and bustle kept them moving without giving me a single glance. From across the street, kitty-corner from me, I could see Jenny standing there. I made my way against the flow of people, being pushed and bounced like an unwanted stone in a smooth, graceful river.

Poking out between the bodies of the crowd, I could see she was wearing her blue dress, the one with the white ruffles and the giant blue bow in the back. Her eyes spoke of glee when they met randomly with mine. Once I reached her, I tried to speak, but nothing would come as I melted into her smile. I kneeled down in front of her, and she took my hands in hers. Pondering eyes that spoke of peace softly gazed over my face. Leaning down, she kissed me on the forehead. A pure state of bliss came over me; there was only her and me.

Out of nowhere a large bus passed by. Its exhaust choked my lungs, making me cough. I hunched over with a whooping, dry cough I couldn't control. On hands and knees I crawled toward Jenny as she became more and more distant. Her once-loving face had turned cold as she pointed away from herself toward the street. Looking over, I saw that it wasn't the street she was pointing to, it was the alley. The alley that ends with my cell. Crying, I didn't want to go back there. Her face grew stern, as though demanding I go back. My coughing returned as a cab passed by. I shut my eyes, which burned from the fumes. For moments I sat there with my eyes shut and fearful. I knew what awaited me when I would open them. I knew I was back there. I hate this cursed, hellish hole.

Upon my peeking, my expectations were fulfilled. At least it had cooled down drastically and the mold had gone idle. Breathing was still a little difficult, but I felt better than I had before. Standing up, I felt around my body for all the sores the bugs had caused. My skin felt pitted and tender. Several large marks and hundreds of small ones littered my body. Even my face had suffered several small but significant marks. Bastards, I'd pay them back.

Reaching into the hole I'd created, I pulled out several smaller bugs. A tiny roach would be the first I'd dine on, then several others of variety. Within the darkness I couldn't see what I was eating, but it didn't really matter. Reaching in again and again, I gorged myself on their crunchy, gooey bodies. Sitting down, I finally had some satisfaction. Not only had I gotten to eat, I'd also been able to get back at some of those bastards for eating me. For the first time in days, my hunger was satisfied. Belching up my stomach's contents, the throatful tasted just as it had when it went down, mostly slimy.

From outside the room, I could hear some garbage cans rustling around. Someone or something was out there. Pressing my ear hard against the door, I listened closely because I didn't want to waste my breath if there was no one there. More clangs, then a great big bang; the cans must have been knocked over. That still didn't mean there was a person outside. Maybe whatever it was would come to the door, be curious as to what was inside. From out of a cat's mouth came a loud hiss, then a growl. More noise came from the garbage cans as another cat came, ready for a brawl. An ungodly ruckus broke out as the cats fought over the rights.

I sat back just thinking about the past, the summer cabin we had stayed in. Many summers were spent in that little cottage. There was only an outhouse, the tiniest of kitchens, two very small bedrooms, a single-couch front room with a fireplace, and a shed where we stored all of our boating equipment. Jenny loved to fish, even if there was no catch. Sometimes I think she preferred it that way.

Martha would stick around the cabin gathering wood for the fireplace or cleaning that night's dinner. She never really cared much for going, but she knew how important it was to Jenny and me. The last year we went there this cat showed up. Black, mangy fur barely covered its bony body. It looked as though it hadn't eaten in weeks. Running up to Jenny, it pushed its body between and around her legs. She fell in love immediately. Martha gave in right away; seeing Jenny's bright smile, she couldn't disagree. I thought it looked sickly and rough. I hated that cat, but I let her keep it. Besides, Martha said it could keep her company while Jenny and I were out fishing.

After a week of dealing with the cat, everything seemed okay, other than it jumping onto my lap every time I tried to read something. Knocking the book to the floor, it would just sit there staring at me, knowing I hated it. Those deep, green eyes would just stare, telling me it got the best of me. "Leave Dad alone, Mitten," she'd say. Jenny called him that for his left paw was the only spot of white on his body. Even the claws were white. No matter how much I wanted to get rid of him, Jenny managed to keep the peace.

On the last night we were there, it began to storm violently. Swaying back and forth, the cabin moaned from the great winds that battered it. Trees creaked and snapped down around us. We huddled around a lantern, our only source of light, dressed in our pajamas. At first light we'd be on our way home; the storm would be gone by then. I kept telling them that, trying to keep them calm. Jenny held on to that cat for her life and his.

From out of nowhere, with malicious force, the wind blew the door down. Dropping Mitten, Jenny stood up with a start. The cat swiftly scampered for the door. Within a lightning's flash, Jenny went out after him into the hellish storm.

Nothing but blinding darkness waited outside as Martha and I went after her. We screamed out, but it was pointless. The heavy drops of rain beating down on the leaves washed out our cries. Only when the lightning flashed was there even a hint of light. Blind and deaf, we searched through the woods. I made my way down to the lake as Martha, in a panic, whimpered and paced about. Hundreds of heart-wrenching scenarios flashed through my mind as I raced down to the water's edge. None of them held a bit of comfort.

Part of the dock was still visible. It poked out from under the water's surface as small waves washed over it. The shoreline had risen two feet within four hours. Even the boat had been ripped off of its line and had drifted away. Looking over the wavy surface, I saw no sign of Jenny.

I joined back up with Martha in the woods, her face showing terror as I walked up alone. All of the hope in her eyes had fled. We searched on through the storm, weakening with every step. After a while it stopped raining; at least now our shouts could be heard. Dropping to her knees, Martha crashed in a sense of hopelessness. I pressed on, walking along the water's edge.

As the sun slowly rose, I could see something floating off in the distance. My heart stopped, then fell into my stomach. I knew long before I got there what it was. Silence filled my ears as I tore down the shore to get to her. Martha saw me dart off and slowly began to follow.

When I got there, I found Jenny lying face down in the water, her arm draped over a log. Both just floated there, bobbing with the waves. All of my emotions collapsed on top of me as they screamed for an answer. Why my ten-year-old daughter, why? Martha ran up beside me as I fell to my knees. Her mouth was open wide as though screaming, but I heard nothing. Tears clouded my vision as a true storm let loose. Martha covered her eyes then ran back toward the cabin.

Wading over to Jenny, I pulled her body from the water. Her white skin was now a translucent blue, as all of her frozen veins were visible. Crystal-blue eyes that were now glazed over stared out at me, saying nothing. Lips that were once full of life now stood purple and cold. Rocking her back and forth, my hands caressed her matted, wet hair. I just kept yelling out. This single moment that had occurred so fast seemed to drag on through lifetimes.

She lay limp in my arms as I carried her back to the cabin. From outside I could see Martha through the doorway. Her legs dangled high above the floor. She must have taken some rope out of the shed while I was walking back. Slowly her body swayed, as I walked in and gently put Jenny down on the floor.

That damn cat sat there beneath Martha's feet, cleaning its one white paw, so smug. That cat had to pay—that's all that would pass through my mind. One swift and precise boot caused its ribs to give. It shrieked as it flew through the air. Mitten's spine snapped as his body hit the stone mantle of the fireplace. He lay there moaning in agony as I carried Jenny to the car. When I returned for Martha, the moans had grown louder. As I stepped out of the cabin the final time, its whimpers quieted.

My thoughts were ripped away from this memory as more noise came from outside my cell. It was much colder now, almost like a meat locker. If it hadn't been so dark I would have sworn I could have seen my breath. Shivering, I concentrated on trying to hear the disturbance. Muffled noises came that sounded like jumbled words running together as vibrations. I could have yelled out; maybe they'd have heard me, but the question remained. Do I deserve to be saved?

All I could do was cry quiet, shallow tears. Over time, the muffles drifted away as the people passed on by. It didn't matter, though; I accepted this place to be my end. Once I was gone, they'd find me from the smell.

A grumbling came from inside me. It was painful and twisting my stomach. My body heaved, though I had no desire to move. Slumped over, I crawled my way to the basin. With barely any strength left, I pulled my head up to it. I fell to the floor as I threw up; that was my reward for effort. Convulsions caused me to defecate on myself, too. The warm, gooey liquid ran down my pant legs to the floor. After a few more times throwing up, I started to feel better. Standing up, I peeled my pants off my body and tossed them into the basin. I had to get those disgusting things off of me.

Once more pain rushed through my body. One of the bugs I had eaten must have been carrying something, some kind of bacteria. I curled into a ball. Assuming my time had come, I awaited death.

Suddenly all of it stopped. All of the pain, all of the fear—everything just faded away.

Jenny stood before me, her hand reaching out to mine. I reached back as she pulled me up from the floor. I tried to speak, but she placed her finger over my mouth and just smiled. A loud clank filled the air as the door shifted. It let out a horrible moan as it crept open. My vision went from darkness to whiteness in a blinding light I couldn't see through. Slowly my eyes began to focus. I came to see that we were headed down the street away from the alley. People who passed by stared blatantly, watching as a little girl led a half-naked man along his way.

After a few turns we came to a white, four-story building. I could see several people moving about in the large windows. They were dressed in gowns and scrubs; it had to be a hospital. My hand in hers, Jenny walked me into the building. The automatic doors opened as to greet us, but I didn't understand why we had come here. A chill came over me as my bare feet hit the cold, tile floor.

No one seemed to notice as we walked down the hall to an open elevator. All of this seemed so real, like a creepy disjointed fantasy. I knew in the back of my mind I was still there in that room. Stepping inside the elevator, the door shut with only us inside. Jenny pushed button number three as though she knew where we were heading. She never spoke, though she swayed about to the music playing over the speakers.

We slowly stopped, and the doors opened once again. In the hall, the same music played. It was a calming tune meant, if nothing else, to keep the patients relaxed in a tense place such as this. Striding down the hall, we passed several people who sat in wheelchairs. Their mouths open, they drooled down their shirts as they stared off in a daze.

Jenny stopped in front of a door and looked at me as though to tell me something. The plaque next to the door read: Room 313; Dr. Ben Donabba. As I finished reading the door, it inched open, as if to invite me in. Not yet fully used to the luxury of bright lights, I walked in, squinting as the rays beamed off the white walls. Only the dark-stained furniture offset the light enough for me to make my way to the couch. Even the doctor himself was hard to see, as his white uniform blended right into the light.

I lay down on the couch to gather all of what remained of my mind. I closed my eyes tightly and begged for this to be real. I want it so bad to be real—this man, the couch—anything to be out of that hell, anything to end my suffering."

* * *

Mr. Mar concluded, "So tell me, Doctor Donabba, what is real?"

Not once did Doctor Donabba lift his gaze from Mr. Mar's eyes, as he activated his intercom with the push of a small, red button on his desk. Two large orderlies stepped into the room. With caution in their eyes, they slowly approached Mr. Mar.

"Raise Mr. Mar's medication to 150 milligrams and return him to his room," Doctor Donabba demanded.

Both large orderlies picked up Mr. Mar from under his arms. His feet dangled along the ground as they carried him down the hall. They stopped at his room and paused to open the door. Mr. Mar's eyes squinted at the painful sight. As the door slowly opened, he found himself back in hell.

Unravel

They're here again, those chirping cicadas, a sign of change once more. Summer, though they always remind me of how desolate the world is. Piercing my ears sharply, their song drowns out all things around me. Sounds of swinging children, cars, and life are simply smothered. Is there any true release? Only in my destination, that place where most no longer go. There a freedom of mind can be found, and no one else. Bright, streaming light peers down onto darkness. I stand covered in rage for loss, injustice, and lack of dignity.

"What's right? No answer. How typical. Just when we're alone you clam up. All day, 'ieeeee a ieeeee e eee eee,' now nothing." Silence is so embraced by the rejected. Ripples form as frogs chirp. This marsh stands where an overgrown forest once resided.

"So what now? Something, anything!"

I'm a walking disappointment surrounded in death. That's all I can do, walk. Releasing myself from self, of self, by self, for self, is exactly what I need. Evil steps lightly today, for nothing seems disrupted. All things are stone-set and in motion for time's ticking hand. The mind's eye vibration sees through the lie. A door?

"A door, is this a joke?"

Standing alone in space is a door. Just hanging there, a door? This door is of old, a door that breathes with a soul's haunting whisper. Reaching out to me, it moans with sensual delight.

"H-h-how?" With disbelief, I fumble my words.

Deep crackles mixed with wise, agonizing groans shudder as the door's depths are revealed. Behind lies a stone hall, endless and hollow. Cold winds pour past me as they spill out from it. The hands of the damned caress me, pleading for me to step inside.

"What the hell is this?"

There is not one witness to this. Even the frogs have fled, along with the birds, the bugs … where has everything, within everything, vanished to? Gone, lies fade, I gladly give them. The door goes as it came. The hall remains with me inside. Forward, back, left, right? Direction is a lost sense of nonsense. I'm to walk either way.

"Hello?"

No echo, even from the tight, stone walls. Though the ceiling is an endless abyss, there is nothing to cast vibration. There is nothing but these unforgiving stone walls. I am to walk an endless path.

"Do you ever end?"

Hours pass in seconds; perhaps there is a way to keep track. Still, I'm not winded. How long has it been? It's a pointless effort to stop. At least here silence is spoken well.

"What the—" I experience an instant chill as I feel a watchful eye. "Hello? I know you're there. You're always there."

Winter wispy winds gallop around my soul, payment for the break of silence, a harsh reminder of control. Falling temperatures follow my outlook about this uninvited escapade. My breath, a mist, still there is no rest. Hell, I don't even know how I got here.

"Why are you wasting our time? There are far more important thi—"

SIN, the word written at my feet is an etching of close relations. This word, this meaning, this desire—it has plagued me as of existence dawning, a debate of my standing.

"This is all you have for me, a word? This simple solution?"

I feel the embrace of old, a wise ruling for chaos to sleep. Tales of burning torment never felt, chaos's fear of order. Friends are they of sin, chaos. I step beyond this point of existence. Leaving it as I once had. Perhaps I've come to the place of resting.

"Death, this is death? Ha!" There is comfort in a simple answer to a frightful question. A streaming, frozen desolation of nothingness; it's a lie. "On forever then?"

A forceful slam of steel and stone ripples the skyway. To my left, a door, cut freshly into the stone. Thick chains embrace its contents, hidden behind experienced wood. Suffering reaches out for me to come in. My senses haunted, I reach out blindly. A tattered mess, this stone chasm is. The broken television facing a ragged couch is a familiar place, though alien. If nothing else, at least it's a place to rest, to lay myself down. Hours pass, though unknown. Sleep, awake, it's all the same. With a familiar click, the television comes to life. Black and white shows of a childhood past.

"Who is this child? Me?"

Flashing like lightning, the television depicts an unknown, forgotten life form. Times of impossible sights of denial come across the screen. To watch as this child is spit upon and beaten. I understand weakness felt.

"You have to be strong, coward!" Droplets of blood trickle down from the cracked screen like tears. "Don't cry! You're a loser because you're weak."

This couch becomes a vessel, floating free. A simple trickle becomes a river's flow. I am not alone. Two others ... no, three. They wish to kill me. Have to flee. No door!

"*Damn it!*"

Waist-deep now, it won't stop flowing; movement is agony. No escape from inevitable demise. Reaching out, they're so close.

Startled, I'm awake. On the tattered couch I lie, as the television sits, cold and dead. Was it a dream? The bloodstained ring around the walls is a giveaway. As is reality is a dream, that child who was treated so harshly.

"Why show me this, why?" This room holds no comfort now.

"You have to abandon. You have to desert. You have to leave," whispers in wind tones echo softly then die. An unfamiliar, genderless tongue speaks.

The frozen hall is home once more. A twisted nightmare of my reality, unknown reasons, visions, demons, this place. I must take up again; there is no choice.

"Okay then."

My continuation does not go without thought. They want to kill me. Why? I have felt many before, but not for my demise. Are they here now, watching, waiting, in hopes of striking? There is no image to see them. Only slight vibrations, concepts of what they could be.

"What time is it?"

Within my wandering mind, the surroundings go unnoticed. Cold winds are replaced by fogged vision. Damp moss patches the floor. Scents of sweet nectar and fruit become the air's fragrance. Could there be something so pleasant, here in hell?

"Is this a joke?"

No laughter is heard, but stronger is the scent. So inviting, like the wrought iron gate that stands before me. Through it a distant tree stands alone, within a fog-filled hollow.

"One has come; our time is near. Salvation in the mind's eye, a time of peace shall rise," more whispers say.

Understanding is no longer a belief. The voices that come and go haunt me, forever etched in the child's mind. A friend for when no one notices. Nothing is ever considered of the fragility. So willing am I to enter. With no delay, the gate fades into the fog. Growing close to strawberry fields, I'm led by a stone walkway.

"Eat of the fruit. Eat of my life. Bleed from me of the cycle's strife."

They've stepped into light, the whisper walkers. On the wings of the fog, they blend so absolutely. Shapes take form in their free-flight dance as they revolve around. Beautiful angels that embrace your soul, flying, dancing, taunt my being.

"Have you brought me to Eden?"

I stand in awe of its ancient birthplace; this colossal tree towers over me, showing me my significance. Its branches reach beyond the horizon and could shelter worlds, bearing every fruit that can be imagined. Every berry, melon, passion, vine, apple, guava, grapefruit, banana, lemon, limes—all are within my grasp.

"Are they all for me?"

Whisper walkers travel through us, never around us. Within their passing, visions are held. A truth is revealed. No love from anyone. It's such a disgrace to be an unnecessary factor. Participating parents strengthen the disappointment. Times of denial can't hold back the breakdown. I sit at the tree's base, crying over life's burden.

"Get out of my mind! It wasn't my fault; they did this."

Sinking into self is never a pleasant ride, for there is only you, an inescapable you. As my tears saturate the ground below, the tree is nourished. Its scent satisfies my senses as it seeps into me.

"Eat and all shall be forgotten. All will be forgiven. So you can finally rest."

They speak of rest. A dream so inviting it cannot be real; the mind will not allow that. This they know is a temptation so great. Lies and blinding betrayal are their ways. A siren's song is their tune.

"Eat, child, eat. Eat. Eat. Eat. Eat!"

I reach for the fruit of choice. "Shut up! Shut up! Shut up! Leave me alone. I can't handle … My mind's …"

Their mockery comes like needles in my ears. I cast my pickings into the fog, hoping to make a mark. They screech silently in agony as the tree withers then dies. The sweet scent that once filled the heavens now reeks of rot.

"Ha! Screw you!"

My glory is cut short by the shearing sound of steel through wood. It is a crushing resonance to hear treetops fall. The presence of one of three, ripping the very breath from my essence is an aura so great. This virtuous beast, this keeper of wise, I've desecrated you.

"Stay back! *Stay back*!"

This being understands no fear. Stumbling over stone and foot, I never turn my back. A massive blade of black-laced gold plunges into the ground before me, tearing the earth to its heart. Blazing fire swallows up the tree's remains. Smoke and flame etch out the demon's flashing form. It has immensity beyond that of mountaintops. I'd be no more than a spatter on its boot.

"What are you waiting for?" This female's voice is soothing. "*Run*!"

No second thoughts or arguments to be made, I must return to the hall. Winds carry swiftly the coward's tail. Safety, but no loneliness is felt. She is of no one I have heard, an unfamiliar manifestation with unknown desires. Breathing: a necessary means of catching one's breath.

"Who are you?"

"Names hold no meaning." Her speech is an angel's song of knowledge and peace.

"What are you?"

"A perception." Her answer is more complex than the question itself.

"A perception of what?"

"Of a tomb for damned eyes. Like the rest, lives of servitude."

My mind races for thought like a squirrel scampering for nuts, rummaging around for the next words to come. Alas, there is nothing, nothing but this damn hall. No answers, no questions, just to walk. The fog has lifted, giving a new air to the hall. Solid stone walls are now replaced with a castle's quality, a touch of humanity.

"Do you like this game?" she asks, though she already knows.

"Game?"

"Yes, the one you've created."

"I created! I *created*? Who do you think I am?" My tone grows harsh, incredulous.

"Still hateful? Humph."

Falling into a deliberate silence, she abandons me at a split off, a fork in the path of monotony. Finally, a choice! A choice … To choose … which path … left or right … left … or … right?

"Damn."

Sitting in silence, I glare at such a simple decision. There's not even a coin to flip. Bursting laughter comes with a shower of tears. I fear the fall of wrong.

"Which way?"

A face emerges from the wall before me. Open eyes reveal only sockets. Its cracked smile grows disdainful as it seems to focus upon me.

"Isn't it time you got off your ass and did something?" This deep, mocking man's voice demands respect. "I said—"

"I heard you." Here I am, in all of the world's insanity, talking to a rock.

"Well …?"

"Give me time … I have to think!"

"Think about what? Direction, time, or fear?"

His questions create a burning within my mind, as they pass from his stone lips. They are questions I have always asked myself. I stand and eagerly charge, stopping at his stone nose. "Fear, why don't you tell me about fear?"

Within a blinking moment, two hands grasp my head. Memories flash like a summer night's lightning show in my mind. Failure after failure is felt, along with a dissatisfaction of all that has been, all within the nothing that is my accomplishment.

Untaken risks without a consequential fall, never even saying hello.

"A path is a path that leads to a path. Are you stupid?"

This mocking stone dizzies my mind. "Whaaa?"

In a state of bemusement, stumbling is all I can do. No path is chosen, but given. To even remember which way is an impossible feat. More faces have come to watch the freak show dipshit hypocrite roll off the walls and down the hall. Smiles and laughter bounce me around like a pinball fantasy.

Voices of all pitch and gender shatter into me.

"Loser," "Wimp," "Freak," "Waste," "I hate you," "Wicked," "Coward," "Leech," "Letch," "You're scum," "Lazy," "Fat," "Worthless," "Insipid," "Ugly," "Piece of garbage," "Idiot," "Dork," "Liar."

They intensify, merging. "*Loser, weak, ugly, fat, worthless, stupid, piece of filth.*"

"*Enough!*"

So many times heard, one begins to believe. Even with my pleas, they banter me. All because of what I followed, someone who wasn't *I*. The prime example of what I would be in their minds. Call it a truth of creation by unknown hands. Running and screaming can't obscure the words. There is no hiding the truth from self.

"Stop, stop, *stop!*" Silence, in the dead of all, silence. This place to gather my thoughts is a round room with eight paths. "Which way did I come in?" An unknown point of origin with no true destination is life's trial.

"This is bullshit!"

One finds solace in dysfunctional bliss. A barrage of fist to stone, stirring of dirt under foot, screaming in full pitch—all are meaningless.

"I hate you! I hate you. I hate you. I hate you. I hate you. I hate you."

From out of nowhere comes a continuous roll of thunder. Pulsing throughout my body, it passes on waves of life's energy.

There is nothing and elation all at once. Blue-green light flickers before me, visions of a serpent. There is no true substance beyond that of mist. It twists around me, staring at me in bewilderment.

"Yes. I see you."

Rearing to strike, it focuses on my chest. My reaching out has never been slower, to grasp it within its attempt. Forceless and weak is my grip, though it holds no bearing. Questions of how roll across its eyes. A massive shock wave, like no other, screams through me. Morphine to the soul, I stand drooling and unmoving. Sight and sound aware, I watch as it ties up loose ends. Its achievement drops me to bent knees, a place of forgiveness. A cracked-face smile is a replacement for fear. Quivering legs of elation's touch carry me along down my path. As I travel along it, this path eludes me. Feeling the walls, my hands brush along for support in this LSD state of being. Brick turns back to stone.

"The hall is home and shall always be."

"How long do you plan on spending here?" She has returned— the angel of comfort or a demon of truth?

"As long as it takes."

"As long as it takes to do what?"

Her questions are my own. "To reach the end, if this damn thing does end."

"All thi—"

"All things end, I know." Perhaps I cut her too short.

"You sound exhausted." Her sympathy is a complement.

"It's been a day or days, whatever."

"There's plenty more to see, child."

"Child, you sound as though you're eight and you call me a child."

"Yes, a child. You are so naïve, yet far from innocent."

"What do you know of me?"

"I know you as you know you. Better than you know you."

My eyes cast to the floor, I continue. This haunting nightmare, this dysfunctional perception, has become my existence's purpose.

The loss of self and all that is self overtakes me. These hands are not mine, nor are these feet or face. No me, no her, no other, just this hall. There is only the hall. The hall is all. A convincing of self that cannot be had. My mind drifts in and out of a delusion that is what a life was once. Tears shower and pain's reminder of a past I deny.

"You don't have to cry, but it's all right if you want to. I understand pain ... lies, murder, deceit ... Should I continue?" Words of truth she speaks so freely. To shed this life would be heavenly, murder that is surely justifiable.

"I get it."

Within my ignorance, she grows impatient. "Do you? Did you really think it through?"

"I thought I did."

"You sleep while you walk. Closed eyes blinded by a façade. You need to wake up." Her demand is made of a lost soul.

"So this is a dream."

"It is what you bring."

"And what is that?"

"*Death!*"

Within that moment I stand trapped. The path behind is engulfed, as the walls merge into one. Faster and faster the merge point seeks me out. Another door stands in the distance, calling to me as a safe haven. A lightning's beat carries me swiftly. Understanding my plight, it willingly opens its vault. Blurred vision, and a word I cannot read. I stop to hear a great crash of implosion. Behind me, once again, there is no door.

"Another room, this grows tiresome."

This room, this twisted atrium of death, is far more wicked than the previous. Vile smell and tastes of death saturate my tongue as I view the spectacle before me. A fat, bloated man sits in a chair, his neck cocked with a cold-eye stare frozen in slit-wrist suicide. Trickles of black blood create a dance display below, with every falling drop. Another sits along the wall, this one a woman with splatter-brain art on the canvas wall behind her. Many hang from the endless dark above, a festive display of hell's piñatas. All littering ground since man's dawn.

"You're one of us, ya know," a gravely voice of dimness says, spoken from the slit-wrist man. "That's why ya here." The dead man stands, as a moving marionette guide of strife. "To feel it, this place, it gets to ya. Pills, guns, choking life—we've got 'em all. What's you're choice, pal? Impalement? Tetsuo will gladly give ya his sword. There's supposed to be some kinda honor or shit in it."

"Why did you do it?" At this point, only whispers can pass from me.

"Oh, I knew what lay ahead, didn't want it. The wife and kid did better. That doesn't matter, it doesn't matter why. Soon, though, ya have to take your place here."

"I'm not one of you. I—"

"Then why are ya here? Is it because ya sold your soul?"

Self-inflicted scars of old reopen for another release. Warm, red liquid of life flows freely to the ground. Am I to take my place here in this time?

"See, I can always tell. But for a woman, a soul is worth far more than love." He smiles at my downfall.

Fear, confusion, anger—all things except for acceptance swallow up my essence. Others take on life to entice my crossing. They seek comfort with like cells. Surrounded, helpless, and alone—all things I've grown accustomed to. This joining would be divine.

"To be as you are? No."

Snap, hatred's blast for times gone need to stay gone. Pushing, shoving, and trying to squeeze my way past the horde, they paw at me for my weaknesses. For true life still flows here. It's fundamental to the dead.

"Hello, Tetsuo," I yell out, pulling the sword from his chest. Tetsuo falls lifeless once more. "I shall bring death to the dead." Slaughter-book dreams of gore spew oceans of blood and a joy felt like no other. "This is *freedom*! More … more… *more*!"

Escape becomes meaningless as I enjoy the massacre at hand. I cut my way, as waves of sin wash over me. With each of their passing, I take on their burden. Souls of the damned pour onto me. A shock-wave disturbance of intent evil soars from the other side of the room, making its presence known. One of whom I felt from before. I know it seeks me, to kill me, to kill all, to spoil my newfound fun. This repulsive being of darkness has come.

"You think I'm afraid of *you*?"

Covered in blood with gathering desire, I seek death. Sinister, glowing red eyes behind a mask of steel focus on me intently. Steam pouring out as it breathes, I feel its cold desires. Great black raven's wings protrude through bloodstained plate armor, dripping with all that's been spilled.

"I want those."

Standing in utter defiance, it is unmoved by my wish. I make haste to embrace its call for war. Weak are the dead who seek to live; they want no part of power. They are an audience to watch as I devour their master. I circle then strike. The sword is nothing but a mere toy to it. Stab after stab, there is no reasoning with it. A quick, hand slap leaves me on the floor four feet away.

"More!"

A gleam of silver blinds my eyes as it draws a weapon. Purity in all its glory is this sword of demons. To slay the beast of light is its design. That is another want of my selfishness. Traveling motionlessly, it makes a strike. My toy sword defends, shatters to dust. Being an animal, keen am I to ravage in rage's magnificence.

"I will kill you!"

Lunging with the utmost purpose to taste death, my newfound talent for destroying heightens. I escape every strike. The crowd is awed, as tearing flesh flies. More souls rain onto me, more guilt, more denial, with more loss of sense. Bloodcurdling screams of torture pierce above, my mouth the orator.

"Die, you bastard demon. I'm taking over!"

Its mighty blade slashes once more with a vicious squelch of steel on stone. My ears bleed as the blade becomes one with the wall. Moments pass without a thought, only task.

Wings give an armored being weakness. Hatred is strong, as is chaos—forces that can massacre worlds. Pulling back the plates, I reach in for spinal fragility. Quick snap followed by shrieks of a sickened end. All it possesses becomes mine. Evolution is painful, to become what you shouldn't be.

"So ya come to set us free."

Those were the last words from the slit-wrist man as I divided his body. Like a savage, I rip and devour till there is nothing more. With all souls taken, I long for the hall.

"All right, I'm done here. I did what you wanted!"

"Did you find comfort here? Or do you seek more death?" my unseen companion angel says upon her return.

Cooling my anger, I am taken back to the hall. The urge to press on now fills me more than ever. Her presence is known. To ignore her is denial of self. Ringing within me, her voice comes with no origin. "Scales cannot balance for chaos with such one-sided abhorrence."

"To kill is divine, those who deserve. This world is sick and needs to be cleansed."

"What bestows to you that honor?"

"No right, just want of more than self-satisfaction."

For once no reply, have I made her stumble?

"The rock was right; you are stupid." Her voice is a reminder of truth.

As my fury grows as does the ambiance around me. Peeling off clothes, I seek to lighten the load. Bloodstained and covered in sweat, they are left to fester in my past.

"I'm in control now! I get it more than ever." Naked and oblivious, I rush on, my body fueled by blinding hatred. Hatred for self's existing form covers me, hatred for the girl who haunts me, and hatred for those who created all. "All shall die at my hand, even you."

"To die, I wished myself that lullaby in the warmth of the womb," she replies in a smart tone.

"Is that why you're damned here?"

"I'm not damned. I am as you are."

"Like I said, damned."

"Keep closed eye blind. To see in absolute will devour you."

She speaks of sight in a blinding nightmare.

Another blast of thunder rolls from the abyss above, like great beams of steel flexing in heat. Dizziness followed by distorted sight, I stumble to the ground below. Cold rock is replaced by soft grass that dies with my touch. Reaching to gain my balance, the walls become dry and crack at my hand.

"What is this?" I seek any form of reasoning.

"It is what you wanted."

Everything twists and bends within light. On knees I crawl, I deserve. Beaten like a rabid dog. Drums pulse within a native dance of ritual divinity, chants of chaos's desire for balance.

"More." My eyes drip of blackened blood, purity in sin. Everything is justified and absolute, a struggle of defiance. "You won't stop me."

Frailty sets into my tattered soul as I am worn to my fullest. Silence, then darkness comes. Unconscious, or am I conscious now? Nothing is certain other than the fact that I'm standing above myself. Just short of hitting the ground, my body stands frozen in space. Before me lies a vast garden of purity; joy is all that is felt here.

"This place?"

"Come, let's play." An unfamiliar hand comes with a known voice.

With a slight touch of the delicate hand to mine, I see her beside me. Dark hair on milk-white skin; wise eyes gleam happily back at me from the glory of her presence. This asylum conductor is a child. An instant flash reveals truths unknown. This child is my own?

"Why did you choose to die?"

"You needed me in this time, in this way," she explains with a smile.

Abandoning my body, she leads me into the garden. Miles of scattered forest with gentle, breezy plains stand before me. Flowers reaching high toward a sun's glow grow sporadically from the earth. Oh, to see the sun. Its rays' gracing my face is received as a gift.

"Thank you."

A smile of pity crosses her face, but it's no matter; I'm home. Hundreds of different humans run out of the woods in some sort of game, each and every one naked. Women and men of all nations dance together in rhythmic harmony. This must be a dream; that is the only answer to an impossibility such as this.

"These people, don't they know who I am?" I question at seeing their ignorance.

"They do not care."

Circling us in a handheld, spiraling chant, they greet us as their own. They move along with us toward a magnificent pond that is fed by a flowing, crystalline, blue-green waterfall. Unknown to them am I, for a demon has never passed their eyes before.

"Soon all things to sand." She vanishes once more into nothingness as darkness befalls the land.

Loud chants become whispers as the humans wait back in the distance. I slowly continue toward the lake to wash the sins of the damned from my skin, to drink of its purity. Leaning down, I cast the reflection of someone I no longer recognize. This distorted face of evil, these claw-like hands. Turning back, I see they're still smiling. Sick am I to think of those who remain in unexpected peril.

"Run," my voice is breathless and meek.

Crying, I'm crying? Droplets of black blood dump out from within me in a river's flow. My eyes become bursting dams, my nose an overflowing well of darkness. The clear water becomes tainted and dead. Within a heart-pounding rush, there is nothingness.

"A dream … where are you? I need you!"

I remain alone at the water's edge, sitting in lotus position, staring over the stillness of it all. The blue mist returns, but in a form unlike any I've seen, humanlike, but not. Its head an elongated pill with eyes twice the size of mine, offset only slightly. Its mouth is hinged farther back toward the neck. I study it deeply, for I know no understanding. From behind, two hands of the same mist press lightly against my forehead. Frozen, I am helpless to their deed. The hands pull back my skin, tightening it. A finger extends out from in front of me, touching me in the center. A rush beyond that of any imaginable force rushes through me. All my emotions crash into each other at once, truly a breakdown of my psyche. Visions pass swiftly, but I cannot see; too much, too fast. Now it's time for the inevitable crash.

"What are you?"

Words are spoken as I am sent back to my falling form. My body collides in the entrance of the garden. The grass beneath me dies. Death branches out from me, streaming along the ground. Everything in its path dies. Cheering people now scream as death rushes toward them. An instant touch turns their bodies to sand, leaving them in piles for the wind to carry off. In all its former grace, this garden now lies dead. I walk back to the pond, feeling no remorse. My senses still aware, I pick up on the keeper's coming. The one from the tree has come. The blessed one of all that is pure is a woman.

"You're still a demon."

She appears not as before. Now she stands as I do. White wings extend out to the heavens from her bare back. Forest-green eyes stare at me from behind a gold mask. Her dark-brown hair blows in the wind as though being caressed. This body of perfection, a tool of seduction, pulls me in as she slowly makes her way to me. Her sway is the wind.

Decimation of my being is her only desire. I have no escape. The garden that now stands in ruin starts ablaze. An open-arm embrace is her offering. Wrapping around me tightly, I feel her olive skin is so soft. I'm pulled onto her as fingers dance about my body. We both melt into one. Love's passion, an evil curse, is bestowed upon us. Enfolded within, we become all there is. Fires roar as passion's vibration is felt emanating within us. A gust of wings' impulse sends us high to free-float in this space. This moment is ours. Shedding her mask reveals an unmentionable beauty that only gods have the allowance of.

"I love you." These whispers pour out from our lips.

Those words bring a climax of emotion. The tips of her toes curl, following a rush into extension. Heightened within our pleasure, she is cast into sand, starting at her toes. The sand whirls around me as she slowly dissolves. I retch in pain as her remains tear through me, a cleansing of true necessity. Darkness, light—it's all within perception, coursing with chaos's question.

"Why?"

My entire being is left in wreckage as I plummet toward the pond. This instant free-fall is a breathless blur of excessive velocity. As a stone, my body cuts through the water. There's no energy to resist my descent, acceptance of my resting place. I close my eyes to join with the nothingness.

The radiance of a small ring appears in the distance. It is minute and undisruptive. Reaching out, something pulls me out of my body and toward it at a million miles per second. One ring after another flashes by, becoming a true light show to behold. The ride becomes faster and faster. There are spaces between the spaces where history is told. Visions of the past appear, like film, flickering all that's been, showing times of being when all things were different.

Looking onward as I stream, a great pyramid stands as a miniature. This hollow being pulling me looks back at me then forward again towards the growing structure. Streaming faster than light itself, there is no stopping, nor time to stop. Two microseconds from sudden impact I am released to bungee back into my body.

With a water drop's vibration disturbance, I am awake—if that's what you want to call it—back in the hall. A stream of water no wider than my hand runs beneath me. Coming to what little sense I have left, my eyes open to a great hall of solid gold brick. The center is shaped in a *V* for the water's flow. Behind me, carved out of the wall, stands a lion's head of enormous size. The crystalline, blue-green water runs from its mouth, pouring out of a hole no larger than seven inches in diameter.

"Is this how I—?"

Questions come and questions go, but only one truth remains. This is paradise. Emotions begin to race through me, like children warring for control over a toy. Joy is a feeling loathed by chaos, something I haven't felt since the delusion of life's drama. Love for all and seeing all things in their place. Time ticking that has become so precise.

"The clock strikes two—"

"Hickory dickory doc, it's good to see you happy." Her voice speaks of sorrow. "Do you love them? All you are one with now?"

"Yes and no; there's too much to think about. Those who deserve, and what do they deserve? Points of death that are etched in time, elements that are the foundation—"

"Relax. All things will come in time."

"Are you a product of her and me?" Time is so lost within the elements.

"No, I am a product of what was to be, before the interruption, at the start of the downfall."

She's the one, the one who forced me back. Made me breathe outside of the nothingness as my body lay lifeless, telling me I had to wake up. As if there's any importance to my being here. She made me come back. *Why* is the question I fear the answer to.

"This place?"

"Here you are free."

An archway stands before me, leading into another room. Another stands open on the opposite side. This room is a library that soars to heaven's height in spiral form. Books float about freely, as do quills, the tomes opening and closing as they're updated and information is crossed over. Every creature—man, woman, tree, bush, and blade of grass, from microbes to universes—and every subject is covered.

The cool floor calls to me as I lie to watch the information pass. Great beasts change with time, dying to make room for new ones. Energies divide and collide in concepts to form everything we know. Spaces of nothing hold together everything. Minds are conditioned to live within the lie. Now I see past all of what once was perception's clarity. Foundations of truth are becoming one with all. Understanding becomes a simple task. Life comes and goes on the wings of a butterfly, birthing here and there, everywhere in every moment.

"Where have I been?"

Looking with intention, I cannot find myself. With newfound wings of black and white, I ascend the heights of the archives. One book after another, there is no me. Rustling with fury, I rip through one level after another. Where am I?

"There has to be something!"

"Only concerned with self? There's so much here."

Her disappointment goes unheard by me. "I know. So there has to be something." A hummingbird's envy am I, buzzing from pile to pile. "Come on—"

"First of all, who are you?"

"I'm ... my name's ... I know who I am. I'm just having trouble." Being lost within the all that is, I have forgotten myself.

"It's all right. Here, read this."

A book floats down from above. Its red cover is worn and dusty. It is a thin read of only a few pages titled *A Simple Vision*.

"What is this?"

"One of my favorites; I think you'll enjoy it."

A Simple Vision

There isn't much I remember before my time of being. Just sort of floating there, swimming within the nothingness. They decided it was time for me to be, so I was thrown into the storm that is conception. A lightning blast of fury is life's beginning. Time becomes a factor of change.

At first there were only waves of vibration. Rumblings of speech, music, and of things of the outer world that could be felt. Soon it came to me as something indescribable, feelings. These were the thing that tugged at me. Slowly, it wiped away the previous times. Anger, fear, rage, sorrow, and self-pity were what made up Mommy.

Time ticked continuously as more changes took form. A vibration of another source came in. This one was different, deeper and more aggressive than the other. Its anger was immeasurable, as was its love for the one who held me. This one was Daddy.

All I felt was hate. Hate from the one that held me and hate from the one that loved her. I tried my best to hold on to what once was. Interruptions of hurt-filled regret pumped through me from her. Caught within a drama I didn't understand, I lost all sagacity of my beginnings.

A month and a half had gone by, or at least that's what they said. I saw things then, light and darkness. Though there was something there in the dark with me, a cloudy light that sparkled. It told me things and showed me things, horrible things.

Mommy only wanted me as a weapon, a tool to use against Daddy. She didn't love Daddy; she only loved herself. Drugs, alcohol, smoke, and sex—are those what self-love is—or a love for the daughter inside you?

Daddy's a coward and a drunk who lived in front of the TV. He hid from the truth of life. He's afraid of me, of what I'll be, of what he'd have to become, and of the past that haunted him. All of what he'd done and what had been done to him.

Visions flew into what would be. They are going to split up. He'd fight for me, but she would hold on strong, at least until I weighed her down. Then she'd resent me. Yelling and screaming at me. "How I wish you'd never been born." She didn't see that I'm just like her.

The man she lived with I won't call Daddy. I hate him; he beat Mommy and yelled at me, "If you were my kid—." But I wasn't. With white powder games on the support check, soon there would be another where I sleep now.

Dad has moved, staying at his brother's house to help take care of my cousins. "He's on a business trip," they said. I knew the truth; the sparkle showed me. He touched girls he shouldn't, in ways he shouldn't. I hate him.

My brother was born. Happiness was felt, but not for long. His dad won't stop the white powder and anger. Mom did it too, to block out all of her regret. She said we stop her, hold her back. We were abandoned at our aunt's house, but Dad came to get me after a couple of days.

His brother came back from his trip. "My, how you've grown," he said. Sickening words. I'm not supposed to be around him, at least not alone, but there was a time. My mother taught me well, as I watched her use her body to know his intentions. I didn't want this. Trying to scream out, he covered my mouth and nose. Forcing his way into me, pain scared me, oh such pain. Crying, please stop, let go, please stop. Clawing at him, I became breathless. Dying, I want to die. I want to die. I want to die. I want to die.

Dad's pace was only a footstep away, though it was one footstep too late. My life gone, stripped of innocence and destroyed before I'd even be ten. Dad beat him until there was no breath left, revenge for my sake. After years of psychiatric care, he was released, only to take his own life.

I didn't want this life I was forced to have. The mist, a comforting glow, calmed me. Another path was shown, one of greater importance. I would become a light for his way. I had to die much sooner, and to be that for him I did! With their help, it happened.

Two disruptions, and I became released from the wall that fed me to die. I was there when they took me out. Dad was eager to see, as Mom lay there disappointed. A tear fell from his eye that passed through me. It glistened of purity. My death was justified, just as it said.

END

"Why did you show me this? How does it pertain to anything?" I feel hollow as the book closes its cover.

All senses begin to stem at once, every emotion pulsing in and out as human lives unfold. I see and feel them all. Connections of every gear turning in perfect order. Passing from one to the next, I am all within understanding in chaos's order. Still there is no self inside of myself. With no answers for anything, I'm lost in the ponderings of this hellish nightmare.

"Make it stop. Please!" I beg for a resting in mercy

"This is what you wanted."

"Just tell me something, anything."

"You don't know who you are, where you are, or what you are."

She's right; I don't know who I am. "I'm what I'm supposed to be."

"Yes, you are that!"

Out of nowhere a force of extreme energy slams me into a wall of books. There is no other presence to be sensed. Before I can move, it slams me again and again. Unseen hands toss me against one wall, then another. Finally the energy flings me high into the air, only to be forced back down with a crash that crumples the floor beneath me as I land. I'm helpless, broken, and unable to move. Somehow I manage to get to my feet. There is nothing—no sound, no pain. I turn to see the lion's head grin as I'm pushed out the other side of the room. Gold bricks fly through the air to seal off the library. I'm back in the hall. Shit, where the fuck am I?

"Hello! Anyone? Please! Help me. Help me. Help me."

My new understanding of the crash of ego goes far beyond words. It's a cracking in the foundation of belief and the lie that holds us tight. Fuck, I can't feel anymore, but I haven't the choice. To feel would create my end.

"I'm sorry! For whatever I did! I'm sorry … just don't make me go on. My mind's too weak; I can't! *I can't!*" My only wish is a simple release from all that is.

"It's not over. It's far from over. You don't see the blessing in it. You never did, so you left to hide from the responsibility of what you created." Her knowledge is great in understanding.

"I didn't create anything!" I refute forcefully.

The walls shift and moan for me to go on. I look ahead to see only darkness, a void in the mind's eye. Fear, there is no fear. That is also a lie. Moving with ripples of pain, I continue down this path.

"Look around you. Do you see the nothing that chaos creates? Zero, the absolute." Then, with her disappearance, I'm left to the void.

Within the pitch darkness of all nothingness, there is only nothingness. Light shows dance for eyes that struggle to hold on. Hands, feet, and the sense of awareness trickle away, leaving the lie behind. After time, even the soul begins to question its existence. Floating, falling, which one is it? Am I feeling the original state? Trying to hold on to form within the features I know, a race of the mind to grasp the lie. I know I'm real because others see me, because I can touch what's in front of me. Lies, all are deep-seated lies.

The mist returns, like the mist figure from the lake, but now it stands in full form. It towers over me, standing nine feet tall. Two others come into view, one on either side of the original. The one on the left walks into my soul, then we become one. The one to the right follows next; we become one. The original reaches out to me in sympathy because it knows what will come of me. It fades, leaving me once again in darkness's embrace. Wondering and wandering, I finally see light. It's the only comforting thing of substance here for me to hold. Folding into itself, the darkness leaves me back into the golden hall.

"Who are they?"

"They are unknown by any truths," her voice mutters with fear.

"I can't feel them."

"They hide within vibrations," she explains.

"Are they of—"

"I don't know!" she yells.

"They scare you?"

"They have a greater hold on all of this than you realize. An ability to hold you in your place as they search for something within that you cannot stop." Falling silent within her trembling soul, she lingers.

"For holding no truths, you seem to know a lot."

"They are strong, maintaining the lie all for the sake of understanding."

"Understanding of what?" My mind races for an answer.

"Of what will blossom from zero's birth, to behold the benevolent son."

My head grows dizzy as pressure builds between my eyes. A pulsing spikes from the center of my forehead, the intrusion of a prying eye. It allows me to see the truth of the lie. Within a blinking second, I know. Then, like in a faded dream's memory, it's gone.

"I don't understand," I cry out.

"You're not meant to. Nor were you meant to see it."

"They came onto me."

"There was no intention of what you saw. You just saw."

"Saw what, the door, them?"

"You're becoming full." She laughs at all my irrelevant questions. "Do you still feel them, those inside?"

"Yes."

My every sense is a sense of all. Pulling from each one is a small portion of them, seeing myself through them. It falls apart again, drifting onto concepts of action. Those who victimize and those who are victims are all the same. Without one, there is no other. Hate, so much hate. A scale's balance there is not. Only a sort of tipsy wave that holds pure repetition is present. What have we done to ourselves throughout our passing?

"They love you. Did you know that?"

Her assurance brings me no comfort. "For what, what have I done that's so important?"

"You're silly. They said you would be. So, you've truly forgotten?"

"Forgotten what?"

"All of those things that hold you here."

My mind grows numb as all mankind's minds compress upon me. The hall's golden glow tarnishes beneath one step, then glows with the other. One hand is death, the other life. This is me? Golden brick ends where mirrors begin. Floor and walls cast back what I've become. My wings of white, mighty in their way, stretch out toward the heavens. Tips of cold, dark wings of death brush at my ankle. Is this what I've always been, or is it something I've just become? Do these questions even matter? Images wash over the walls containing all of the what-ifs and could-have-beens. The faces are all the same, as are the lives. Point to point then back again. All is done in sequential order to match the inevitable outcome. Here and now.

"This isn't fair. I didn't ask for this."

"Ask for this? You pleaded to the heavens for it. To know."

"The door, where's the door?"

Searching for an escape leads me nowhere but to an infinite reflection of self staring back at self. I hate you more now than ever. Any attempt to break the mirrors proves worthless. "Well? *Say something!*"

Her presence fades from mine, leaving me to uncertainty. Which one am I? This place is as discombobulating as the darkness. A sort of faint touch of reality with a side of nausea takes over. Up, down, left, right—which one am I, going in this spiral maze of self-delusion?

"I'm sorry I can't let go."

I continue my journey down the hall of lies, glancing at the reflection I do not understand. A twisted form of all's creation, an ever-so-slightly out-of-balance scale teetering toward the brink of extinction. I'm stopped suddenly. With a pain-stricken forehead, I look up to see myself—a wall? There is no corner to turn or any other path; I'm trapped.

My reflection holds its pose as I shuffle about. Looking at it questioningly, it pulls me through itself. I'm cast to the floor of a hexagonal room of mirrors. I turn about to see myself in several states. Happy, angry, loving, hating—all things and the opposing come to be known. One holds no expression at all. Its three gray eyes speak of cold, but calm intentions.

"You're pathetic. All of you."

I sit, lotus position, in the center of the room. I need to find myself in all of this. Where exactly do I fit in? Closing my eyes is no form of release. How could it be allowed here? Myself, whatever that may be, stares back at me.

"Look at you. You're a weak nothing," they begin to speak, passing straight into my mind with my own voice. "How many times did she say I love you? Do you honestly think she meant it?" Each one awaits its turn to sweep over me. "If you had only thought about it, just taken one second to look," the gray-eyed one says as he stands before me, just staring. "She loves you, that one over there. Think she could? You know you could." Songs of the ancients echo from above. "You're a loser! How you could kill an innocent? Liar, defiler, murderer."

Faster they come unto me, the vessels of judgment. "Those girls asking strangers for money, you set them straight with a fear of God. They soon understood death. You stole their innocence." Tears ready themselves on the rims of my eyes, smearing my crystal-cut vision. "Do you know how screwed you really are? It's a dream, that's all it'll ever be. It's all you'll ever be. A sweet, loving, spiteful, awing, grotesque, beautiful, ugly as hell, angel of darkness's descent, water-walking screw-up, this is you, your life. Your *wasted* life! Meaningless, no good, waste of spa—"

"Enough."

I stand with calm eyes as a burst of pure energy erupts from my center then outward. The shattering of glass is music to my ears, to end this bashing. All that remains is the floor at my feet. It stands alone within the mirror-less hall, surrounded by void but still casting my reflection.

My burden now lightened, I travel swiftly. Within the serenity there are blip disturbances. A new mirror rises up from the empty spaces. Its words go unheard as I use my newfound gift to destroy it. Soon another comes, then another. One great way to harness a skill is by playing the game of self-destruction.

"Will they ever stop coming?"

This comical game of target practice comes to an abrupt close. A reflection of her—the one I love, the one who set me free from sin. My heart sinks in remembrance of our embrace. I long for her touch. Within a trance of desire, I remain held to this vision. Watching me as though she were here in front of me now, so exquisite, so divine, so—

"I still love you. I feel you inside. Thank you for the wings."

"Who are you talking to?" The little girl returns to me.

Within a millisecond's interruption, the image is gone. An image of myself now stands in her place, laughing at my loss. A wrist's flick decimates the mockery.

"What? Why did you interrupt me?"

"You were just standing there. At first it was a day, then a week. Decades passed and still you stood. Finally you spoke."

"How long have I been here?"

"Since the beginning or do you mean at the moment you stopped?" her question is more confusing than my own.

"What does that mean?"

"They are the questions about the inaccuracies of your question." Why bother? She won't tell me anything. "To bother is not a question of want."

"So even my thoughts aren't safe? Here, listen." I flood my mind with all parts of my being. A flickering nightmare of conflicts I give to her.

"Why are you doing this?" Her pleas come as pleasure to me.

"So you know how I feel."

"I know how you feel. I've always known." Her struggling speech speaks of truth. I release her from my mind, not even she deserves this pain. "Thank you. I needed to feel something."

Continuing down the mirrored path, my sense of disappointment sets in deeper. Remembrances of her soft, delicate lips and euphoric touch that cut through my soul make me yearn for an embrace of purest love. Two bodies entwined as one pure soul. It was so divine it was sinful. I still seek it. "At least you truly loved her."

"So it wasn't a waste?"

"No, it held purity. You didn't have to be pushed. It was just there."

"She's within, I still feel her."

"As do I."

My lonesome road leads to the cave again. It's cut like paper into the void, a flat panel dropping. I loathe these cold walls. The distance is a short shot around the bend to another door. A massive door of steel, iron, and brass stands blocking my path. It has a glimmering cross center with seven faces circling, each one holding a different expression. Greed, envy, lust, sloth, gluttony, wrath, and pride mark their faces. An invitation to a crypt is spoken through the metal's cold, hard stare. There is no knob, handle, hinge, window, or method of opening the door. Cocking my head in wonder, I reach toward it. My hand passes through as though it were an illusion. Pulling my hand back, I'm intimidated by the lie. Striking out only leaves my hand sore. Not even a wave of energy can mark this beast.

"How the hell do I open—"

"Only divinity may pass."

"But my hand—"

"Pacify, center the being, then hold it for just that tiny moment."

A blanket shrouds my mind. All is quiet, all is still, there is no chaos, there is no orchestrated plan, there just *is*. A universal moment squeezed into a blink of an eye. Blissful and free of judgment, I flow through the lie. Thoughts come, thoughts of some sort cling me to me once more. The seconds of harmony are worth lifetimes of misery. I'm released through my passing.

"If that could last forever."

Now I stand in a field of flowing grass, comfort for worn feet. Slight winds caress the field within, a creation of oceanic waves. Beams of a brilliant full moon give life to an ancient cemetery. It stands alone, a great mountain of death surrounded by a field that forever rolls. Lonely and chilled with death, a tree stands at its peak. Though there's greatness for this landmark, it emerges as a tear in the eye of the moon. My spread wings make a short time of distance. I glide on the hands of the wind, drifting toward the mountainous mausoleum.

Landing at its base, I seek to scale this on my own, to take it all in. A great wrought iron fence lines the bottom. Old and rusty, fully covered in vines, this place seems forgotten. Even the grass between the stones is overgrown and filled with weeds. The gate lies open; this must be an invitation. I make my ascension toward the tree.

Grinding stone vibrations dance quietly in the air. Looking at a grave reveals not a name, but a purpose. This one is labeled "Hunter." There's a list of names, male and female alike. Times of birth and death span thousands of years. Another reads "Victim." Like the other, there are multiple names of both genders and spanning time, each one bearing common names with the others. The more graves I pass, the more purpose I see. Repeating names are seen of victim also being the victimizer. Were they victims of self, or at one time did the victim become the victimizer, creating more victims?

My thoughts are broken by sounds of clashing steel. In a rush, I make for the tree. From this point I can see all. In a distant region of the field, a battle ensues. Men and women fight for all things of belief—power, land, respect, and acknowledgment. All are nothing more than human addictions. I sit to enjoy the display of their games. Limbs are severed and fall, while heads roll and bodies burn. This is pure comedy!

"Have they nothing more to do? There's enough for all, you crazy bastards!"

I grow bored with their futile struggle. I could help them, help them reach their goal. Spreading my wings, I swoop down upon them, grabbing a man. This one seeks to rule with a power to make others suffer. Is this any true goal of use? With the hand of death, I spread his remains over the others. It goes unnoticed by those with blood in their eyes.

"There's sickness within you, within you all!"

Passing again, I retrieve the corpse of a woman. She had struggled at the hands of rape. With the healing hand, she returns to the struggle, strong and full of power. Another woman here, of greed; a wave of energy leaves her halved. As they fall, more rise. A busy bee I am, to enjoy death and casting life. The scribing sound of stone grows fast, as do I.

Out of nowhere, a blasting force, like from the library, hurls me into the tree, which is unmoved as I smash into it. Turning in pain, I now see what I had neglected to before. On one side of the tree there stands an open grave, above it an unmarked stone. How could I have missed this? Hugging the tree, I use it for balance. Within its branches dangles a skeleton key of ancient design. Shiny and radiant, it gleams in the moonlight. Pulling off a piece of vine, I fashion a necklace then quickly turn to face what struck me.

"What the hell was that?"

There is movement in the crowd, something pressing forward. It is truly in its own realm, for no one will provoke it. What could it be? Flying down, I seek a closer view, quickening to sound-breaking speeds. Within twenty feet of its reach, I am sent tumbling back.

"It's some kind of energy barrier."

He picks up on the envy in my voice. Lunging into the sky, he reveals vast, gray wings that stretch out over the center of the battle. Naked as I, he stands with eyes shut and head down in defiance. His hands across his chest like a coffin's occupant. A slow motion of stretching out his arms casts the battlers into sand. Passing bit by bit, they dissipate in a gusting wave.

What power, what grace, what desire. Instantaneously he grabs me by the throat, streaming toward the tree. Once more my back is slammed against its unforgiving lumber. He squeezes tightly as he raises his face to mine. He is I, the one with three eyes. Open eyes are gray and unfeeling, though his face bares hatred.

"Why, why are you doing this?"

He tosses me high into the moon's light. I try to focus on direction as I roll out of control. He flies up, tearing off my lower left wing, a mark of my darkness. Within another pass, I'm relieved of my upper right one, a mark of my purity.

"Help me!"

Once more I'm sent hurtling to the earth. Movement is forceful pain; no balance, I remain in my place. He paces around me, hiding nothing; I know what he seeks. Lifting me by a palmed head, he smirks at my limp body. I want to kill you; I have to kill you to kill myself. There is no strength left to kill with. With me still in his palm's grasp, he takes me to the open, unmarked grave. I'm cast inside to an endless descent. Pain, all I feel is pain.

"Help me, please. Where are you? I need you!"

Roars of great winds strengthen from above—a sound I fear because I know. I've always known more pain is on the way. Breezing by me, he drops to come from beneath. Clasping onto my healing hand, he whirls me around. Faster and faster he spins until my arm is separated from my body. A fountain of blood surges from my socket.

"No more ... please."

Speeding up my downward spiral, he pushes me to the hall. Radiant in its way is this hall's make of marble statues and pillars. Figures of gods and goddesses tower high into the void. I become familiar with each as I am smashed into them. Thrown, kicked, punched, elbowed, kneed—how much more can I take?

Vibrations, followed by a deafening gong, ripple through the hall. He stops, dropping me to the ground. Falling to one knee, he bows in respect. As a second gong tolls, he flaps his wings and flies off into the void. I am left here to die by the hands of what I do not understand. My eyes flutter as I blink in and out of existence. Vibration is felt, but no gong is heard. Temporary deafness: a temporary loss in order to maintain other senses. Floating with shifts of footsteps, I travel. Who? Darkness: a lack of sight for sound.

Hushed tones of children's chatter echo through my head. "Do you think he'll make it?" The conversation of a boy and a girl is muffled.

"He has to," he harshly insists.

"If he doesn't?" she doubtingly asks.

"Don't you trust me? Hasn't everything gone as they said?" he tries to assure her.

"I guess so, but—" Her voice weak and frail.

"But what?" he asks in anger.

"I don't want to, you know." Within her fear, her voice drops quietly.

"I know. It'll be okay." Sympathy comes, for he knows her fate.

"I'm glad you're here."

"You'll be okay." His assurance is taken well, as I'm released to the floor.

A warming ease passes unto me; slight strength begins to return. Rolling onto my back, my eyes open to a glorious crystal door etched with two magnificent angels that hover around a fruitful tree. Above one angel rises the sun, the other a crescent moon. My remaining hand, the hand of death, rests ever so slightly against the door. Dim, blue light emanates from my fingertips. Pulling myself up, I kneel before its glory. Pain rips through my chest and down my back then pulses with agony. My arm and wings are gone.

In crippling pain, I double over, opening the door from its center. Wind-chime tones ripple through the air as I fall into the room. Ankle-deep water lines the floor. Landing face first into the bowl-shaped pool, I roll myself over. Looking higher, I see a magnificent sun glaring down. This room is a healing fountain. Stone, glass, crystal chimes, every element and awe of life's beauty. Birds chirp above as fire dances about upon the water. A rush of light hits me as I feel the water change around me. Within their prayer, such might.

"Thank you."

With those words I melt onto the floor. Pain fades to nothingness. They're here dancing around me, loving me, wanting me to play with them, wanting me to be with them. Becoming birds, fish, walking as man, studying as the others, lifetimes of crossing back and forth through the spectral plane.

"It's wonderful!"

There's more, so much more—more to see, to hear, and to feel. Water structures change form, an embrace of love's crystalline state. Water heals the wounds of a shattered soul, makes you young. My back burns from the loss that has begun to reform. Pain-stricken delight to become whole in body and mind. A fiery will to be. Chaos survives in the fear of crossing. Even with a known ending, there's struggle, holding onto the lie and the creation of its purpose. Rebirth, to live once again, to be, I see.

"I see. I know."

"You must." The girl returns to me with a greeting in a field of sunflowers. She graces me with a solid form of flesh.

"And you."

"I know," she quietly mutters.

"Are you afraid?"

"Should I be, to become one?"

"There are many here. They will love you." Trying to calm her, I approach.

"As you love me."

"Yes," my hands tightly around her throat, "as I love you." She is cast to sand by my will.

Her passing into me is a blissful vision of a dancing angel who has once more returned home. It is done. I feel her inside. An overdue rest for a pure being, she once more drifts within the nothingness. My eyes flutter open, placing me back into the room. Pushing myself up, I look down to the washed stone floor to see two hands. My wings also have been returned to me.

"How?"

The statues hold no expression as they rain their healing liquid down. I wash my body and soul free of filth. Within purity there is understanding—a way to know, to see, to grasp what lies in wait. Find death and its true meaning. Oneness is all within this state of being touched by a god. A breath is taken in a blinking second that is one's lifetime. Each gear in this clock which spans throughout infinite time is placed with precision. Each layer overlaps the others, existing simultaneously. Yesterday and tomorrow will forever be etched within spectral time, a constant cycle of repetition.

"All things shall always remain." They are her words pronounced in my voice.

Even though I could stay here forever just gathering knowledge, I know I have to move on. The meadow awaits me. Moving to the center of the pool, I gaze into the crystal wall. Melting away, it becomes one with the waterways. A towering, rectangular hall beckons from the other side. Cold, dry walls of sand line my path. Hatred grows as I make my way, knowing what lies ahead, to die by his hands. Does he really believe he can? I'll show him a strength that goes beyond measure. This bastard abomination by-product will die as so many have before him. Seeking death, chaos takes flight. Another door, another greeting card from the puppeteers appears before me.

"It's the same as everything else. Pointless!"

Scriptures of an ancient race cover an immense sand wall. Large figures of their God of Death and God of Life are intricately carved within, details that hold no meaning. Waves of thought change structural form, washing away the door. Soon after, the hall follows. I'm left in a great field. A darkened, cloud-filled sky reaches farther than the eye. He stands in the distance, his back to me. There is no essence of any form, no fear, no calm, nothing.

"Don't you know who I am?" I bellow. Lightning crashes throughout the sky as the winds forcibly change. Eyes closed and wings shut, he slowly turns to face me. "You won the last one, but now you die!"

I rush in, only to be repelled as before. Like a moth bashing its head into a light, I swarm in from every direction. "Let me in, you coward!"

He opens his third eye alone. It sees my unbalance. Pausing, I stand just outside of the barrier. Following me as I pace, he's trying to anticipate my thoughts. "I know why you're here," I say.

"Then you know what has to be?" The voice of a child comes from not his lips, but his mind. Its calm nature of naïveté speaks of innocence.

"I won't let that happen!"

His guard drops, leaving me to my desire to kill him. I rush in for a strike, but to no avail. Delicate in his way, he stays just out of my reach. Force energy divides, rippling the land around him with scars as he cuts through it.

"You should be calm, acceptant." He takes flight, swooping around me. Reaching out, he cuts open my chest with his hand. "Father, what is the truth?"

"What?" Images flash through my mind. This child … my child … to kill. He passes again, throwing me to the ground.

"Is this what my hands are for? To kill, to maim?"

"No, they're to embrace." I launch up, nicking one of his wings. The winds shift again as tornados reach down to kiss the earth, surrounding and passing us in waves.

"Then why did you show me that?"

"I had to." Still lost in a daze, I try to reason with him. He flies toward me, dashing around a massive funnel. A thumb's gouge removes part of my sight; my left eye is gone, leaving only a hole.

"They lie to you, your eyes, as does your heart. What's the point of feeling?" he taunts from an unseen point. I spin aimlessly, casting hundreds of small energy blasts around me. Several cut through his wings, forcing him to the ground, leaving a cloud of dust.

"To love ... is divine, being loved, more." Landing, I stumble, trying to regain balance and clarity. He steps from the cloud, holding the remains of his left arm. A shot guided by angels.

"*Liar*, it's about control and being controlled. You have no control." He lifts his hand with an open palm straight toward me. Plasma energy blasts my wings of purity into dust. Their feathers, bloodied, dance throughout the wind. Hatred comes in unbalanced chaos.

"Abomination!"

He takes flight, passing through a tornado. I quickly give chase. Weaving in and out of the winds, he makes his way to a vast forest. A path cuts directly through its center. Inches from the ground, he glides to the path. As I follow him in, the trees grow beyond sight. They reach unimaginable heights, creating ... the hall? I'm stopped suddenly by smashing into him. He grabs me tightly by the throat.

"I told you they lie." He folds in a wounded wing, removing my other eye with its tip.

Blinded, I surround myself with energy. "What do you want?"

"The truth."

Hearing him, I throw energy toward the sound. I hope to hit him to avoid the known outcome. "I am what you are. You just can't see it," he claims.

Dizziness and nausea fill the center of my forehead. I blink once, then again. My eye is fully open from the center of my mind; now I can see through the lie. The passing is nothing more than transcendence.

"Son, there are so many things within this vision. Understanding is one."

"An end of all things, this is what you want, if we are so great then why? To share, hold, give!"

My guard down in awe of new sight, he grabs my arm, pulling me close. Eye to eye, we meet.

"Balance, it's tipping out of control." Ripping his arm from mine, I fling him down our wooded path. As I race toward him, a pyramid comes into view. Is this my final destination?

"I can't let you in," he barks out. Landing on his feet, he rises up, with wings spread. This is order's fear of chaos's rule.

"You have no choice!" Rushing forward, I make for the structure.

Bolting past my adversary, I gain significant ground. An amazing sight stands before me, a temple of all. Built of gold with a door of black onyx, it reaches the heavens. Carvings of all kinds mark the entryway, none of which I can understand. Searching frantically, I must get inside. The figures of the blue mist return, surrounding the temple. They have come to watch. Above the door stares an all-knowing eye; it gazes upon my single eye. Unraveling all of history's past into me, it shows me a god.

"You can't open it. Nothing evil can."

Looking up to the top of the temple, I see my rival perched. Jumping down, he lands, crashing down before me.

"I'm not evil. I'm just doing what I'm supposed to."

"Isn't murder an act of evil?"

"Murder?" Reaching out, I slam him by the throat against the door. "Death is not murder. Death is absolute."

Squeezing him tightly, I strip him of breath. With a final effort, he grasps the key from around my neck, driving it into my throat. It unlocks my airway for drowning blood.

"Now I see, you and I. Father, son ... I love you."

With our dying breaths, we both turn to sand. Whipping around and within each other, we become one. Reforming as self with everything inside, his voice now shadows mine.

"We have become one, purity within chaos and order."

With a great rumble, the door to the temple opens, sinking into the ground. Blinding light pours out from behind, dissolving everything. I spread my six wings to hover as I feel the ground beneath me fade. Darkness fills my eyes as the lie of nothing being nonexistence, fades. Time withers away. There is truly nothing.

"Within the all of everything there are spaces in between, a place of solace, a dynasty to behold absolute."

A snowflake's glimmer shines alone in the center of darkness, light years from my reach. My wings open, I glide toward its soothing glow. Those swimming within me are at ease. Their beings drift as I move through the nothingness. Each one begins contemplating life, a chance to be again. They seek strife, drama, love, happiness ... all things within the great desire to be. Creation comes through their conception, equally of mind and body, a lugubrious fact of purity. Here is where it lies, inside. At last all three eyes are open to see all as I stand before them. All of the misery of an unbalanced humanity fades. The distant grain of sand grows closer.

"I pity them. Within all of their greatness they are so blind."

The grain stands before me, floating in freedom, containing all that is. Reaching out, my hands engulf it, drowning out the remaining light. Hundreds of billions of souls cry out as all of life dies. Unto me they pour, their souls filling me. Each one forms their own salvation. Within a concept, heaven and hell are born, resting spots for the dead to gather. One's purity is another's misery.

"I am all that is."

From my center, a sun is born, followed by planets. A galaxy is molded, then another—thousands of galaxies all connecting and intertwined with revolutions and axis given. All create a mass cell structure for life to begin again. The start of the clock, existence in flesh forms once more. Eden's fabrication giving man a point of origin only to be followed by woman, purity unfolds its wings. Forever is a way that cannot be. The lie begins again. Dark wings spread as the tree of wisdom grows. No choice is given with the creation of evil. Gray wings of unbiased judgment open the way for birth and death. Life pours out of me into the spectrum. Existence in all things divides me, spreading me throughout infinite space, zero to zero.

"One day I will return to you, to be one again, Annihilation and Creation."

Christopher M. Hull has won several awards for his poetry, including being named Outstanding Poet by the International Society of Poets. Hull lives in Coal City, Illinois, with his family. His inspiration comes from watching the world pass.